The Weight of Stars and Suns

The Weight of Stars and Suns

Dawn Christine Jonckowski

ISBN: 9781653803217

Copyright © 2020 by Dawn Christine Jonckowski

All rights reserved. No part of this publication may be reproduced, distributed, or transmitted in any form or by any means, including photocopying, recording, or other electronic or mechanical methods, without the prior written permission of the author, except in the case of brief quotations embodied in critical reviews and certain other noncommercial uses permitted by copyright law.

For Mom, the first one to believe in my stories.

ACT I
DARK

1

There was a shadow on her book.

It was spiced tea hour. There were never shadows at spiced tea hour.

In fact, there were rarely shadows at all. Call it an occupational hazard of living on a planet ringed with thirty-six suns.

Dameia sat up from her lounger, pushing a fistful of dark strands off her forehead. "Hannah, do you see this?" she asked her human companion. The smaller, pale woman paused her teapot mid-pour to aim her glance where her mistress pointed.

"I do," she acknowledged. Dameia sighed.

"And what do you make of it?"

It was Hannah's turn to sigh. She had been trained out of all her opinions. Or, if not to be devoid of them, at least to never offer them to the race the humans called "master." Even if asked. *Especially* if asked.

"I don't rightly know, *neqeba*." It was the best response she could give. Never mind that Hannah *didn't* actually know. Nor that Dameia should have actually listened to any opinion that Hannah had deigned to give. Humans clamored to serve in the palace simply for the hope of working for—or at least marginally interacting with—the Chieftain's daughter. Just unpredictable enough to defy the kindly princess stereotype, Dameia nonetheless had a compassionate streak that meant she was prone to treating humans like, well, people, rather than the chattel the Tavarians tended to view most humans as.

Hannah had been born into captivity, knowing only this multi-sunned planet and a life of being *slightly less than*. Any memories of Earth were seeded only by stories passed down from the Origin Generation, tales of a green and blue planet with fantastic natural phenomena, like oceans, tides, and something called "the moon." Earth also only had one sun—think of it, one sun!—which meant shadows. Natural shadows, at any rate. Tavarians knew how to create shadows better than anyone. The main source of traditional Tavarian entertainment was the most elaborate shadow puppet shows one could dream up, with each theater spending piles of scores to outdo the next. A great while back, Hannah had accompanied Dameia to a shadow show one evening in her first few years of companionship to the princess. Though already much older, Hannah's excitement built at the same rate as the young pre-teen princess beside her, and when she returned to the colony midway through the second cycle to share her wonder, one of the last remaining Origin Generation had scoffed. "On Earth, you step outside the door at any given hour aside from noon, and you see shadows. Shadows should be natural, not fantastical."

And that was that about shadows.

But here it was, spiced tea hour, and there was a shadow. A natural shadow.

The Weight of Stars and Suns
Dawn Christine Jonckowski

Tucking a finger in her book, Dameia reached for the cup of spiced tea. Despite the heat of the hour, Tavarians relished these cups of tea that curled hot steam over the rims and warmed already heated fingers and palms.

But this cup wasn't destined to be sipped and savored, wasn't destined either to have its contents slowly rolled over a tongue and swallowed down a royal throat.

Instead, the teacup suddenly dropped to the bricked veranda floor, its death-shatter startling servant but not mistress. For Dameia wasn't looking at the broken teacup or the stain of spiced tea slowly creeping toward her bare toe. She didn't stop to look where she might be stepping to avoid the shards, but rose straight to her feet despite Hannah's clucking.

"Hannah," Dameia breathed, "where is my father at this hour?"

"In with the Council, as usual, *neqeba*," Hannah replied steadily, blinking at the princess' sudden discomfort.

"Send a messenger to precede me; I must see him. Now."

"Of course, *neqeba*. But the Chieftain may not favor the interruption, even from you. Must it be immediate and urgent?"

Dameia turned a sharp gaze on her human companion. "Yes, Hannah. It is urgent. One of our suns has gone dark."

As her mistress pivoted to rush inside, Hannah shaded her eyes and counted.

Indeed, horizon to horizon, there were eighteen suns.

And one was dark.

The Weight of Stars and Suns
Dawn Christine Jonckowski

✧ ✧ ✧ ✧ ✧

The Chieftain loved his daughter. No one could say otherwise. If he didn't necessarily show it with traditional parental gestures of hugs or seating her on his knee in her younger years, it was abundantly obvious in her quarters, her education, and the quality and breeding of her humans. And not least of all visible in his gaze when she filled it, which was often. Now that she was of age—a bit past, truth be told—his expressions of love may have become more gruff in the form of combat training and relentless grilling on military history and less of the already scarce physical affection. But buried beneath the rough shell of his tutelage was a tender royal heart. (Or as tender as his royal heart could get. Which according to some, wasn't much. Although that depended entirely upon who was being asked.) He prided himself in his singular offspring, pouring hours into the young princess to ensure that when she was called on to become Chieftain, she would be ready.

But when she burst unannounced into his Council Room in the midst of a tightly-wound discussion over rumors of a human rebellion, it wasn't love that shone from his narrowed eyes, or even begrudging respect. The Council felt the room dropping by rapid degrees. The Chieftain was downright perturbed.

"Dameia." His address was short and without a shred of its usual warmth. Perhaps he felt guilt; he should have made sure she was already in the room, not bursting on an intrusion. After all, her future depended on her ability to handle human uprisings, a regular occurrence in recent history, but generally weak, disorganized, and easily put to bed if a Chieftain knew the proper promises to make and the right words with which to make them. Even with full intention of never keeping said promises. Truly, it was an art form, and one that Dameia should learn sooner than later. Especially considering she had already come of age.

And especially if she was going to be the Tavarian's first female Chieftain.

Progress came slowly, what else could he say.

More of the Council surmised that he was just that, though: perturbed. This was the thirteenth human disruption of the Chieftain's headship. Traditionally, there were two—in leaner times, maybe three—every so many seasons. And this one had undercurrents of organization, of the potential to not be placated merely with unfulfilled promises and pretty words. The Chieftain didn't have time to be interrupted by what the Council perceived to be a silly girl.

And how could they see her as anything but? This old Council who still believed in keeping wives at home, who occasionally regretted the hundred-year-old abolishment of leaving female infants out to the elements on hillsides when one had a few too many. Here stood Dameia, not only the Chieftain's sole legitimate heir, but his sole heir by any count, being the first Chieftain to also abolish harems. (The Head Councilman regretted this most, as under the Chieftain's father, he had enjoyed exclusive access to the harem and any *neqeba*—willing or not—who was not currently serving her duty in the Chieftain's chambers or carrying one of his children.)

Dameia was certainly a force to behold. While not considered beautiful by conventional Tavarian standards, she carried herself with the same long-limbed, broad-shouldered confidence that her late mother had, bore the same thick ebony tresses and wide-set eyes as her father, though her irises tended more toward indigo from her grandmother. She had the traditional Tavarian facial structure with a wide forehead and semi-pointed chin. As with most of the royal bloodline, her face was paler than most, with the lavender spanning to the edges of her cheekbones and her skin fading into the Tavarian race's deep purple shading at her jawline, flooding the rest of her body with the rich royal hue accented with lightly freckled arms and back, and a curious white stripe along her spine. (More than one temple priestess had mused upon that stripe when the tiny princess was born, marking it a portent of things to come.) Of the daily, she often favored short military tunics that highlighted the definition of her rounded muscles. In public, she dressed in the latest fashions as befit her station, causing such sighs and flutters and eventual imitation among the other wealthy Tavarian ladies. Quick, dusky laughter and a reputation for kindness toward humans made her out to the Council to be a flighty female more interested in the latest adornment than anything of true consequence.

So when they saw her standing there, chest heaving and eyes lit with fervor, the Council assumed it to be nothing more than a tirade over a dress or a party or some other inconsequential essentially female ridiculousness.

Imagine their shock.

"Father," Dameia responded, forgoing the traditional bow and acknowledgement to plunge ahead. "I saw a shadow—"

"Truly, you would burst into a Council meeting unannounced to declare you saw a shadow?" This interruption from

The Weight of Stars and Suns
Dawn Christine Jonckowski

the Head Councilman, who was still regretting the lack of a harem, for surely she would be in it and not disrupting with her feminine foolishness.

Dameia shot him a glare that would have withered his lined face farther if indeed that was possible. "I ordered my human to send a messenger to announce me, but clearly my legs outdistanced his. That unimportant detail aside, it is not the shadow itself that is remarkable," she continued icily, "but the cause of it." Warming her glare by only a few degrees, she turned eyes back to her father.

"One of our suns has gone dark."

She expected pandemonium, indignation, or at worst, a single raised eyebrow.

Thus, the distinct lack of response was disappointing, to say the least.

"Did no one hear me? One of our suns. Is dark. Dark! As in not burning. As in, we have seventeen suns left to light this cycle, and thirty-five to warm a planet used to thirty-six. And if one sun is dark, what's to say another couldn't follow? We can sustain the loss of one, perhaps, with the help of our Agricultural Council to adapt farming practices for its particular swath. But two? Or more?"

Her outburst was met with continued silence, disdainful from a few Councilmen who still assumed that nothing but fizzed bloodwine and party moths filled Dameia's head, disbelief from a few others who couldn't decide if their reaction was to the act of her outburst or its contents, and finally, considerate calm from the Chieftain. Behind his eyes, gears churned as he slowly moved his focus from the uprising they had been discussing rather heatedly before his daughter pounded through the doors to this admittedly surprising—and disconcerting—news that the planet Tav of the thirty-six suns was currently less one.

"This is . . . surprising news," the Chieftain finally allowed. He barely suppressed the urge to smile at the satisfaction of a challenge that curled around his daughter's expression. He knew she had a long road toward gaining any shadow of acceptance from this Council, knew it was his job to help pave the way yet not show obvious favor so as to make her journey too easy or her respect undeserved.

"'Surprising' is certainly one descriptor," Dameia shot back coolly with just enough deference as to not be disrespectful. The Chieftain felt the smirk pulling at his lips. She was unquestionably his daughter.

"Please," scoffed the Head Councilman, straightening his long blue Council robes with a decisive shake as if he could brush the princess off just as easily. "This is impossible news. Our suns could never go dark."

Dameia raised one regal brow and turned to the Head Councilman. "I assure you, sir, it must be possible, for it is currently fact. Perhaps my father and his esteemed advisors would care to step outside the Council Room to observe the dark sun for themselves and see that I speak truly."

The Chieftain raised a single hand before his Head Councilman could speak again. "Let us recess briefly, *zakar*. We could all gain greater perspective on this uprising after a few steps away from this table. I myself would like a bit of fresh air; I will walk a pace with my daughter and return with my assessment of the situation at hand." The wave of assent that rippled through the

| | The Weight of Stars and Suns | |
Dawn Christine Jonckowski

Council was peppered with more than a few grumbles, but all pushed chairs back, stood to stretch stiff muscles and hail their Chieftain briefly before separating into smaller pockets to discuss the uprising, the darkened sun, or in one case, the continued and disappointing lack of a royal harem.

The Chieftain proffered his arm to his daughter, and together they left the Council Room. As soon as the large doors shut behind their departure, formality fell away. "Show me the sun, Dameia." Nodding, his daughter beckoned him through the open-air walkway and out into the West Garden. There, she simply pointed.

No words were needed. It was clear: A few suns off-center of the middle, a single sun hung a dark round pit made ever more obvious by its brilliantly-lit companions.

Could it be called a "sun" if it no longer shone?

The Chieftain sighed. "So it's true." His words fell flat, not a surprised admission to Dameia's truth, but rather a resigned statement crawling with why-nows and what-nexts. He stood, arms crossed over an aging but still strong chest. Ceremonial tattoos ringed his dark forearms, spiraled across his shoulders, and ran down his thighs. Ink that documented bloodline, station, marriage, coronation, and even diplomatic success in supplanting the past twelve human rebellions. He was a military mind, not a scientist.

Give him unhappy humans any day over a planet that was in the space of an afternoon, losing one of its primary sources of light, heat, and life.

And yet, inspiration struck.

It struck in the tall, lithe form of his daughter. Or more, in the form of the shadow she now cast from the missing light. Her shadow lacked visible tattoos, though Dameia had her fair share bearing witness to her lineage. The dark silhouette did not exhibit royalty, or even beauty. But its composition did prove determination, hands fisted on hips, feet planted as if daring the snuffed sun to shine again and make her a liar.

Dameia—it pained the Chieftain only a little to admit to himself—was smarter than he was in the ways of science and planetary lifecycle. While bringing her into the negotiations around the uprising would prove her mettle to some of the council, what better way to evidence her sufficiency for Chieftainship than to let her single-handedly manage this new and potentially deadly natural disaster?

"Can you handle this?"

Dameia heard not only the question on the surface, but everything that lay underneath. Her father was going to trust her with something big, something that had the potential to shut more than a few doubtful mouths about her suitability for leadership. Not only *could* she handle it, but she *would*. And she would prove that she was worthy not only of being called "princess," but of bearing the title "Chieftain."

She wanted to throw her arms around her father and shower him with promises to fix everything, to make him proud, to prove to the Council that she deserved more than the harem roles of princesses past.

What she said instead was simply a short and unequivocal "yes."

It was a promise that—unlike those the Council would return to planning for the humans—Dameia fully intended to keep.

The Weight of Stars and Suns
Dawn Christine Jonckowski

☼ ☼ ☼ ☼ ☼

The one thing Hyam hated most about Tav was that it was never dark.

Evening on Tav—the start of the second cycle of the day—meant only "slightly less bright than midday or any other hour." Earth, on the other hand, Earth had *true* dark. Hyam dreamed of skies full of stars, lit only by a single moon, if by anything at all. Just like their shadows, Tavarians created dark. To them, the artificial dark and shadows *were* real.

Then again, technically, they were the most real dark and shadows Hyam had seen, either.

It was not like he'd ever known Earth at all to miss it as intensely as he did.

Perhaps it wouldn't have bothered him so much if he was a native Tavarian. They could afford houses big enough to have center rooms for sleeping, rooms with no windows and therefore, no light from the constant revolution of thirty-six suns. Just as one set of eighteen suns plunged below the horizon, the other eighteen were rising on the opposite side. It was never, ever truly dark.

Hyam also liked to imagine that center rooms also weren't so blessedly hot as every single enclosure in the human colony. Each nuclear family in the colony had their own dwelling; it was a stretch for any of the older generations to call any of these dwellings a "home." Though the youngest humans had more easily adapted to the reality of growing up on Tav, as the generations spaced further and further from the Origin Generation, anything more of Earth beyond stories began to seem too fantastic to be true.

The close of this cycle found Hyam folded up into a cave with representatives of the other eleven main families in the colony. The cave was cooler than a standard enclosure, but with this many men inside, only just.

Calling the area a "cave" would be just as kind a term as calling this hour "night." Caves were another unnatural phenomenon on Tav, and creating caves like this one was technically a forbidden practice, just like pretty much everything else the humans had ever wanted to do. But weeks and months of subtle chipping away had resulted in enough of an insulated space that the Twelve could generously label it their cave. It wasn't named such for its geographical structure, man-made though it was, so much as its ability to let the Twelve feel as if they were underground, hidden from the Tavarian patrol or any prying purple ears that would report their goings-on to that nefarious group of Tav cronies dubbed the Council.

Ithai, Hyam's childhood friend and now compatriot in planning this latest uprising, had stumbled in late to the meeting, his apology followed closely on the heels by a pronouncement that brought the conversations to a dead halt.

"Say that one more time, Ithai," Oren advised. "Slowly and with less tangle."

Ithai closed his eyes and drew a deep breath.

"One of the suns is dark." He opened his eyes to find eleven sets staring back with full attention. Encouraged by Oren's nod, Ithai continued, "I was out in the fields at spiced tea hour, and when I reached for a stalk to harvest, I noticed that my hand cast a shadow. You know as well as I that shadows don't occur here naturally. When the overseer saw that I'd stopped, he obviously came to investigate. I pointed out the dark sun. He acted as if it was nothing, but behind his eyes I could read worry. And of course, I was lashed for then missing the daily quota." Ithai tried to shrug nonchalantly, though his wince told a different story. "But that has to mean something, doesn't it? That one of the suns is dark? Maybe this planet isn't as sustainable as the Tavarians believe." Here, Ithai paused. Hyam had known the other man for a lifetime; whatever was damming up and ready to spill over his tongue would be truth.

Wildly unpopular truth.

But truth nonetheless.

Hyam broke the pregnant pause. "Finish it, Ithai."

"I think we should change our tactics with this rebellion. Instead of fighting for our freedom to live here as equals, we should negotiate to leave Tav altogether."

Whatever response Ithai was expecting, laughter was not on the short list.

It was certainly a day for unexpected responses to great pronouncements.

Another of the Twelve, Yair, who had more grey hair than sense, guffawed. "You are proposing that we waltz into the Chieftain's Council Room, demand the skeletal ship be returned, and hope against hope that someone among us can manage through ancient texts from the Origin Generation to fix it well enough to ferry every single human back across countless galaxies in hopes of landing on Earth."

Red crept up Ithai's neck, yet the younger man stood his ground.

"Yes."

"You're mad."

And then all hell broke loose.

2

"Congratulations, Father: I hear you have extinguished the most recent human uprising."

The Chieftain uttered a single grunt as he speared the first bite of dinner. He contemplated the rough cut of mountain rabbit. He'd have to have a talk with the kitchens. They had to know by now that the gristly game was not his favorite. "Not exactly extinguished so much as punctured to let some air out. I don't qualify twelve young rebels pulled from a covert meeting and thrown in a prison block as much success." He shook his head as he chewed. He knew the capture would put a significant kink in the rebels' plans—hence why all twelve were also in individual cells at the moment so they couldn't continue to plot—but it was by no means a truly measureable success. Rumors would fly as rumors were wont to do, and if it meant the public adored their Chieftain for his prowess, well, he wasn't about to tarnish that sparkle. Though with Dameia, he would be honest. Unfailingly so.

"But I'm curious, where did you hear this celebratory news?"

Bent to be honest in return, Dameia turned a flat gaze to her father. "It wasn't so celebratory when I overheard it, to speak true. It should turn out that my companion's nephew was one of the twelve captured and jailed. She is in no way connected with his scheming," Dameia was quick to amend. "She is, however, concerned for his wellbeing and naturally, that she should come under suspicion because she works at the palace and they are blood."

"Technically, aren't they all blood?" mused the Chieftain offhandedly as he contemplated the thickly fizzing contents of his goblet.

"Well, yes," Dameia allowed, "some just . . . more so than others." Her father chuckled, a rare and soft sound, quickly replaced by a more somber air.

"We didn't just capture the twelve; we ran a complete comb of the colony. Your companion can rest assured that she is under no suspicion, else she would have found herself down in the prison block quite some time ago. These twelve minds are decidedly darker than hers, I can assure you. Though to further your own education, I suggest that at some point before their trials—which I shall delay until the close of the Secondary Council—you visit the prison and see what you can do to understand the minds of our rebel guests. It will go a long way toward enabling you as a future Chieftain to predict and prevent uprisings."

"It is settled, then. As soon as I finish dessert, I will pay these humans an educational visit."

The Chieftain nodded his approval. The silver shots in his dark hair caught the low torchlight before melding into the thick bound tail at his nape. "And Dameia, you will be well protected by the wardens, but I nonetheless recommend you be seen largely alone. Some may open up to you if they do not see an accompanying battalion, and therefore decide for themselves that you pose no threat. To others, presenting with a guard shows weakness. And that is a perception that you especially can ill afford."

"It shall be done as you suggest."

✧ ✧ ✧ ✧ ✧

Perhaps it was the shadow from that afternoon. The knowledge that the heavens were not as infallible as they seemed, that something so constant despite change and chaos below was suddenly not. That shortly, the other side of the planet would see the rising of seventeen suns as the other eighteen sank below the horizon. While their greatest scientific minds would be packing to head to the Capitol at Dameia's request, what would the remaining citizens think? Would they even take note?

At any rate, Dameia felt a shift in everything, not just the light. As if the dark sun was a harbinger somehow of *more*.

Silliness.

Most likely.

Alone, she entered the prison corridor.

✧ ✧ ✧ ✧ ✧

Not even the prisons were dark. Hyam pondered that as he sat alone in the corner of his cell. Surrounded by hot brick on three sides, a grate of metal bars separated him from the small visitor's area that created a gulf between his enclosure and the heavy soundproof door set in the brick wall that led to the corridor.

As if he would have visitors.

The bench alone was a mockery.

Of the other eleven, Hyam could hear nothing. He didn't even know if they were still alive, though a meeting where the colony patrol had burst in too quickly to hear much of anything was hardly grounds for execution. At worst, they might get extra labor for their cave. Likely the job of filling it back in permanently.

But really. They could have at least made the prisons dark. Unless that would be considered a kindness.

Then the door opened.

And there stood the princess.

☼ ☼ ☼ ☼ ☼

She was clearly the last one the prisoner expected to walk into his solitary cell, but she gave him mental points for folding his surprise away quickly. Did he even know she was the princess, or did he simply assume she was just another one of his captors?

Perhaps all Tavarians looked the same to humans.

Which, clearly, they didn't all look the same. But she doubted he'd had either education or care to learn the subtleties of Tavarian skin tones and markings or know how to read the ink that ringed their violet limbs.

The Weight of Stars and Suns
Dawn Christine Jonckowski

He himself had a curious shade of skin the humans called "olive," though his skin was a burnished bronze, nothing like the sickly green fruit that Hannah said was native to the humans' home planet. That olive skin stretched taut and shined with sweat across muscles broken and rebuilt by labor. Browned hair fell lank across a bruised and scabbed face that once given time to heal and a good long washing could show some measure of attractiveness.

There, Dameia mentally shook her head. Humans were not attractive. They arrived to serve. To breed, to serve, to die. That was the extent of their usefulness.

She should do well to remember that.

What precisely was the protocol here? She hardly had anyone preceding her to formally announce her. Her intrusion could scarcely have been an inconvenience to the solitary prisoner. It wasn't like he currently had a full schedule, unless he was trying to figure out how to fell her and escape with only a small wooden spoon for his defense.

He'd have to try awfully hard to beat her with a wood spoon.

Or anything else, for that matter.

Lucky for her, the prisoner solved her dilemma by inclining his head ever so slightly and drawling, "Princess."

He didn't even bother scrambling to his feet. She wasn't sure why that irked her, since everyone else's groveling often did to no end.

Blasted human.

She would not be made to look a fool, or worse, an empty-headed girl.

"And this is the mighty face of the rebellion, is it?" She sent a single eyebrow winging upward. "I expected you to be . . . taller."

"Ah," the prisoner allowed, dropping his head back to leisurely study the ceiling of his confines. "That is simply because you have not met me standing at my full glory." And yet he lounged, not a singular muscle twitching to betray any thoughts of rising.

"Most humans would be scrabbling to stand and offer their respect."

"So you can next command me to prostrate myself before you in deference? No thank you, I'll spare myself the effort and energy, especially since it appears I won't be much fed here." He straightened a leg to poke at the empty bowl with one foot striped with dirt. The fresh streaks clearly outlined the ghost of sandals that were the most difficult of a prisoner's meager possessions to give up when imprisoned. "I don't suppose you know—or have any control over—when dinner is in this place? You seem like the sort who would have some influence."

The normally even-burn of Dameia's temper notched up. "No, I surely am not in the know with regards to prisoners and their treatment."

"Well," here the prisoner finally looked squarely at her. "Then you are shaping up to be a very poor future ruler indeed, aren't you?"

✧ ✧ ✧ ✧ ✧

Hyam usually knew when to quit.

The Weight of Stars and Suns
Dawn Christine Jonckowski

This was clearly not one of those times.

Where in the human colony his angled comments and frank observations were laughed at (at best), shrugged off (at worst), or pointed to as reason why he should help lead the rebellion (for better or worse, which depended entirely on who you were talking to), here on decidedly Tavarian turf, he might have pushed just a step too far.

The Warden would give him refuse pail duty for sure.

For heaven's sake, he'd just flat-out told the future Chieftain that she was bad at her job.

Potentially not the smartest thing he'd ever done. And there was already a long list of not-smart things in his past.

It was too late to backtrack. He was solidly travelling this road. Might as well keep going.

After he gave her a moment to stew and reply.

Assuming she replied and didn't just have him thrown into whatever next level of hell dreamed up for humans. Really, when one's whole life was a strict structure of servitude, labor, and rules, when one already didn't have freedom, what additional hell could there be, what was there left to take? Other than his sandals. He'd just finally gotten them to that sweet comfort spot. Nothing irked Hyam more than breaking in new sandals.

"And you know so much about ruling." Her response was just timely enough to persuade Hyam out of believing that she was truly concerned by any truth that could be in his statement.

"Not from personal experience, no."

"So who are you to tell me what makes a good ruler?"

Hyam engrossed himself deeply in studying the varying layers of dirt that had embedded under his fingernails. He wondered how long it had been since his hands had been truly clean. "I may not have experience as a ruler, but I have a lifetime's knowledge of being ruled. It seems to me that a ruler should have a vested interest in every subject under his or her rule, regardless of race or status. I wonder how many rebellions could have been minor commas in history rather than the devastation they were if a Chieftain had managed to be bothered by the state of humanity."

He felt the heat of temper begin to roll off the princess' violet skin, though he gave her immense credit for not letting it show. He thought that was awfully big of him, all things considered.

"Oh, we are certainly bothered by the state of humanity."

"Mmm, yes, bothered that we are here, that we won't simply do as we are told without question or thought."

The princess leaned casually against one bricked wall, crossing one elegant ankle over the other as if her biggest concern was the line of her posture. "If you simply did as you were told without question, it would make a great number of things easier."

"For you, perhaps."

"And for you." Her easy stance belied the fire glowing behind her eyes.

"Oh yes," Hyam grinned easily. Too easily. "Spend your lives groveling before us, devoid of opinion, without quarrel, told when to reproduce and with whom so that we may have more humans to serve our every whim and work our fields, and never, ever think of what life could have been for you if some ship had not crashed on our planet and your ancestors bargained away your futures for their immediate safety. Do all this, and it will be well with you. Sounds peachy." Hyam's grin dissolved. "No thank you."

The Weight of Stars and Suns
Dawn Christine Jonckowski

To her credit, the princess' demeanor didn't falter. Hyam would have joked to himself that clearly she wasn't human, but since she, well, *wasn't*, the punchline fell flat even to him. "Well it's hardly my fault that your predecessors were so careless with the future of their offspring, is it? This is what the world is now, for both of us. I suggest you learn your place in it."

✧   ✧   ✧   ✧   ✧

Here's what the history books taught:

Tavarian education brought purple-hued students up to believe that while humans were by and large an intelligent race in the beginning, it was clear after their arrival on Tav that they lacked the capacity to understand Tavarian life, and as such, needed to be shepherded. In exchange for safety, the humans promised—rather gratefully and with much relief, or so the textbook read—to serve the native race so long as humans remained on Tav. A colony was rapidly constructed to protect the frail human race from the Tavarian elements, including all thirty-six suns. The humans flourished in their new habitat, joyfully taking up odd jobs in Tavarian houses and fields, learning to harvest new plants in peculiar growing cycles and cook them into ever-more exotic dishes, performing household chores and minding Tavarian children, steeping and pouring spiced tea.

As years passed, the human population began to expand. A few became more, more became a generation, and the humans grew content on their new home planet, resulting in a perfect balance of servant and master between human and Tavarian that built upon the strength of Tav and made it the most perfect social system in documented history.

But here's what really happened:

On the day the sixth Hubble telescope was replaced by an even younger and less myopic model, scientists of Earth could finally see to the end of space.

Or at least that's how they described what they saw. The stars seemed to run out and all that was left was one final planet beyond which was only darkness. A planet just large enough to be called so (thanks to poor Pluto's plight) all by its lonesome, without solar system, moons, or any visible neighbors, and with perhaps the most startling peculiarity: a ring of thirty-six miniature suns.

Having successfully colonized Mars, the moon, and, through consistently improving space-jump travel via strategically-paced hubs, at least twenty-six mostly inhabitable planets in neighboring galaxies across the cosmos, man was beginning to thoroughly enjoy playing the role of God. Over the past three decades, space colonization had solved the issue of an overcrowded Earth whose population far exceeded its ability to sustain all that life. Colonization was now driven largely by "because we can."

So at the next Global Alliance Summit, presidents and diplomats from around the world agreed that the next frontier—perhaps the greatest frontier—was this little planet at the seemed edge of existence.

The Weight of Stars and Suns
Dawn Christine Jonckowski

They dubbed it "Tav," for the final letter of the Hebrew alphabet. They built a ship they wittingly called *Genesis*. Selected forty of the most brilliant minds in science, engineering, linguistics, botany, medicine, and politics. Trained them for seven years. And finally, *finally*, put them on a ship and waved goodbye from afar as the entire planet (and several others, thanks to a rather impressive intergalactic satellite system) watched the broadcasted blastoff.

Somewhere around thirty-seven days after *Genesis'* final space jump, which took them within six weeks of landing on Tav, the space jump hub's satellite lost contact with *Genesis*.

That was the last that the people of Earth heard of *Genesis*.

But it wasn't the last of *Genesis*.

Technically.

Suffering from a faulty grav stabilizer due to some miscommunication and a too-short screw (the European Union was still salty that the United States belligerently refused to switch to the metric system), *Genesis* bucked and sputtered as she attempted to enter Tav's orbit.

She plummeted.

And then she crashed.

(Little did the engineers realize that Tav's gravitational pull and orbit were vastly different than any other planet due to its general lack of a solar system and overabundance of suns. So the calculations and blueprints were wrong anyway, and crashing inevitable even without the wobbling grav stabilizer. Mission failure was certain. But due to the communication loss, they never learned this. Everyone retained their jobs and still got a holiday bonus. After, of course, a moment of silence for the lost *Genesis*.)

It was a minor miracle of engineering science that kept all forty souls aboard alive and well, if not more than a little shaken by the surprise landing, even while the ship was half disintegrated. But once the crew discovered they were all breathing and more or less in one piece, there came the slowly dawning realization that the ship was beyond repair, they had no contact with Earth—or any other somewhat neighboring planet, for that matter—they were marooned, and . . .

. . . they were alone.

Or at least they were until the first search party reached them.

They were tall. They were graceful.

They spoke a language similar enough to make communication manageable.

And they were purple.

Once the shock of color wore off—on the part of both parties—it became clear that the humans likely wouldn't be leaving anytime in the too near future, and they needed the protection of the natives in order to survive until rescue arrived. Little did they know that aside from an annual day of remembrance for the lost *Genesis* that would fade out of style after a few years flipped over, Earth had long since given up on ship and crew. Deemed the most costly space mission failure since long before the formation of the Global Alliance, the *Genesis* project was shelved and resources that could have gone to a second mission were eventually redirected elsewhere.

But humanity on Tav was blessedly unaware of this, and in quiet desperation to survive, agreed to a rather imbalanced treaty with the natives. Since the foreigners lacked local currency or anything the natives deemed valuable enough to trade, they bargained instead with their lives. They agreed to work for the natives in exchange for the most basic provisions of shelter, food, and clothing. Foolishly, they bargained too the lives of any children they might beget, assuming that none of them would be there long enough to follow through on the urge that could create offspring, much less give birth on Tav. Rescue had to be coming soon. It wouldn't matter to what they agreed, so long as they could stand the terms for just a few years until help arrived. Surely the Global Alliance would know what had happened; surely they would not leave the forty humans stranded alone on the last planet in space.

Surely.

✧ ✧ ✧ ✧ ✧

And time passed.

And passed.

And passed.

Until this moment, where a rebel and a princess stared each other down through a gridwork of prison bars.

"Let's say, for amusement's sake, that while I have been forced to learn my place in this society, I refuse to accept it." The prisoner was the first to break the silence, turning his gaze to the short wooden spoon he was twirling across his knuckles.

"Oh, let's." Dameia's sarcasm was not lost.

"Hear me out," the prisoner invited.

To Dameia's surprise, she did.

"My ancestors were quick to agree to Tavarian terms because they never believed they'd be here long enough to reap any consequences. And yet here we are," he mused, gesturing to the prison, the planet, either/or, it was anyone's guess really.

"Don't you dream of more?"

His question was so quiet, so wistful and seemingly out of character that at first Dameia wasn't sure if she'd heard correctly. More? She was the Chieftain's daughter, lacking nothing, poised to lead a planet, her future before her every time she opened her eyes and looked out at her beloved world.

She had Tav.

What more could she possibly want?

✧ ✧ ✧ ✧ ✧

It was a foolish question. What more indeed? Hours after the princess left his solitary cell, Hyam still couldn't believe he had asked that question. The princess could hardly want more. She had a life mapped out for her, a purpose. She didn't have to earn respect; she commanded it simply by existing. For certain, she hadn't chosen her birth status any more than he had. He could have been born to parents who lived happily on Earth, or any of the other multitude of planets humanity had colonized. She could have been born just another common purple person (or whatever the proper term was for a Tavarian native, he still wasn't sure if there was one) without status or claim.

And yet . . .

The Weight of Stars and Suns
Dawn Christine Jonckowski

And yet, if he hadn't been mistaken—or it wasn't a trick of too-dry eyes from imprisonment and too little fluid—he'd seen a tick in her gaze. Something that told him she wondered about the question and didn't simply brush it off as the crazed talk of an imprisoned rebel.

Still. Whether he'd caused her to think or not, the bigger question weighing on Hyam's shoulders was why the blazes he even cared. He had a rebellion to plan. Why was he worrying about the emotional state of a violet princess?

What he *really* should be worrying about is how to rebuild a half-disintegrated space ship on a planet that had no technology to speak of using the severely limited knowledge base of rebellion leaders who had only ever known life on Tav and whose "memories" of Earth and all her tech savvy were planted and imagined based on scribbled texts handed down from the Origin Generation.

Definitely bigger things.

✧ ✧ ✧ ✧ ✧

She told herself that it was because her father had suggested she get to know the minds of the rebels while they were imprisoned awaiting trial. She told herself it was for educational purposes, to make her a better Chieftain. She told herself that she would talk to *all* of the rebels this time.

She told herself, she told herself, she told herself.

But in the end, the only cell Dameia walked into that next morning was the same one she had walked out of the second cycle before.

The prisoner sat in approximately the same spot, one leg stretched out before him, the other bent so he could rest arm on knee. His head tilted back against the warm stone wall, eyes closed to the plethora of sunslight streaming through the lattice-work of the barred ceiling. Stone was small comfort as a bed; she knew he couldn't have slept well and must be exhausted.

She wondered why she cared.

"I can hear you breathing, Princess." The prisoner lifted a brow and pried open one sleep-crusted eye. "If you're going to stand there and gawk at me like I'm in a zoo, you could at least throw some food in my cage."

Dameia wanted to ask about the rebellion, wanted to demand information about what the twelve men had been planning in that hollowed-out cave. Instead what she asked was, "What's a zoo?"

This opened both the prisoner's eyes.

"What's a zoo?" he repeated with incredulity.

Dameia's face heated, the blush of her race causing her purpled pigmentation to simply intensify. But she stood her ground, unwilling to let this prisoner know that her question was a slip of the tongue.

"Yes," came her reply. "What is a zoo."

"Oh, well," the prisoner shifted. "On Earth, animals from all over the world used to be gathered into a single place, usually one per major metropolitan area, and placed in cages on display for humans to see." He turned a lazy grin toward Dameia. "And depending on the type and ferocity of the creature, visitors were able to pay a small fee for food to give the animals."

"That seems rather barbaric."

"I suppose that depends on whether you're the animal or the observer."

His response stopped her short, not because of its delivery—which, by the way, was casual and lacking all trace of malice—but because of its simple truth. Dameia had come to this cell specifically to look at this prisoner. As much as it pained her to admit, she was drawn to his dry wit, his fearlessly honest responses. No one, Tavarian or otherwise, spoke to her like that: without fear of her station or deference to her race. So she supposed she *was* gawking.

Only a bit, though.

"Tell me your plans for the rebellion."

The prisoner looked up at her, amused. "No."

Dameia arched one fine brow. "I could have you beheaded, you know. No trial, no chance, just straight to the block to lose yours." The prisoner chuckled softly.

"If anyone was going to behead me, it would have been done at the moment of my capture. I'm not going anywhere for lack of supplying information. Not yet, at least." He rested his head back on the wall as his eyes slid shut. "Ask me something else."

Surprising herself, Dameia sat down on the splintery visitor's bench along the same wall that the prisoner reclined.

"Tell me something about Earth."

The Weight of Stars and Suns
Dawn Christine Jonckowski

☼ ☼ ☼ ☼ ☼

Now there was a question Hyam did not expect. Continued demands about the rebellion, sure. Perhaps some questions about the state of life in the human colony (which he would be expected to answer with a glowingly positive review). But not about Earth. Never once—that he knew of, at least—had any Tavarian deigned to ask a human anything about Earth.

Where did he even begin?

"Earth. Well, for starters, Earth only has one sun."

"Everyone knows that," the princess scoffed. "Everyone knows that Tav is the only multi-sunned planet in the universe."

"The humans certainly didn't."

"Which explains a lot." Hyam could hear the smile sneaking through her response and allowed his lips to curl into a small one in return.

"Okay, well, Earth has a moon, too. The Moon orbits Earth much the way Tav's suns do, while the Earth orbits our single sun. This moon gives off no light of its own, but reflects the light of the sun at night. When the sun sets on one side of the planet, that's when you can see the Moon. Based on its orbit around Earth, we can't always see the full reflection from the sun. Sometimes it's only a sliver, other times it's completely dark. And once a month, you can see what they call the full moon, when the entire reflecting side of the Moon lights up the night sky."

He sat in silence, unsure of how the princess would respond. It was basic knowledge for humans, the Moon. Would she find it at all fantastic? There was more he could tell her, about tides and how the moon pulled the oceans along their shores, about the Man in the Moon and how his face had changed as humans colonized along the craters and lakes. Did she care?

More importantly, why did he?

Solitary confinement must be getting to him more quickly than he wanted to admit. Take him to trial, give him extra work to punish his impudence, do anything but let him languish in this cell talking to—of all people—the Tavarian princess.

Hyam waited for her response.

"It sounds . . ." the princess began, her voice halting. In that split second of hesitation, Hyam imagined a dozen different endings to her statement, each progressively more dismissive than the last.

". . . romantic," she finished.

Which was the absolute last word Hyam ever anticipated she would say. Constant and continual surprises, this one. He didn't know if that was a good thing or a very, very bad thing.

✧ ✧ ✧ ✧ ✧

Romantic. She had a thousand other words she could have used to describe the prisoner's tale of the mystical Earth moon, and the word that had slipped out was "romantic."

Dameia's small sleep chamber—one of many rooms in her wing of the Chieftain's complex—was a windowless room at the center of the hub. When the humans had landed on Tav and struggled to sleep in the constant sunlight, they spoke of this mystery of "night" and "moon." So much so that the Tavarians soon adopted the practice of sleeping in the dark. Not as much because they needed, but because the humans wanted. The wealthiest Tavarians had the darkest rooms, sealed in the centers of their houses. Windowless. Lightless. Soulless. Even the highest ranking human slave—such as any human ranked above another—at best could only hope for a dim room pierced with shafts of rogue sunlight that needled through the cracks and breaks of the colony's shoddy construction.

    Dameia slept easily in the dark now. As a child, though, she had been afraid of the black. More often than not, her mother or a nursemaid would find her curled under a table in a sitting room or playroom, sleeping in the shadows of the well-lit space. Even a candle flickering in her sleep chamber couldn't calm her young nerves.

    But what if she'd had a moon? If a lesser light than the suns could filter through her windows and cast gentle shadows across her floors. If she'd had the phases of the light to mark the passing weeks. If even the time the humans claimed as night on Tav lacked the harsh light and instead had a kinder resonance.

    The moon would be a sympathetic mistress, allowing those under it to enjoy its semi-darkness. She could picture lovers meeting beneath a moon's light, reveling in the secrecy that the night and its solitary reflector provided. She imagined soft breaths and even softer kisses in that dimly-lit darkness, and for *goodness* sake, what was she doing imagining all this in a prison cell when she was supposed to be interrogating this slave about rebellions instead of his planet of origin?

The Weight of Stars and Suns
Dawn Christine Jonckowski

Dameia stiffened her spine, sat up tall on the hard bench. The prisoner felt the shift, and she saw his eyes hood.

"Well, if that wasn't quite the fantastic tale." Dameia forced a chill in her tone. And hated it. And wondered why. "But as you are not the only thing on my agenda today, prisoner, I must go and deal with bigger problems, speak with bigger minds." She rose to her full height, shoulders squared, chin high to disguise the storm in her chest that she could neither understand nor explain. "Farewell, prisoner, until we meet again. *If* we meet again." Dameia strode to the door in three brisk paces.

"Hyam."

The word stopped her in her tracks and she turned back. "What?"

The human cocked his head. "My name. Is not 'prisoner.' It's Hyam." His head dropped back against the stone, eyes slid casually shut once again. "In case you cared."

"I don't."

She did.

She let the door slam behind her.

3

Scientists and scholars from across the planet had converged in the Secondary Council Room, and it was utter mayhem. Dameia's head was in her hands, fingers rubbing temples in attempts to stave off what promised to develop into a wicked headache. These were a cross-section of some of the most brilliant minds on Tav. One would think they could act more like adults than petulant children arguing over a favored toy. Her first report to her father and the Council could very well be a disaster.

A few of the more piercing voices broke through the din of general argument.

"The darkened sun is nothing to be concerned about. It is only a large sunspot, and will reignite within a week's time."

"Nothing to be concerned about? Outrageous! The sun has burned out, and others will soon follow. Life on Tav will be unsustainable. We are doomed!"

"Doomed? Hardly. You're overreacting. Our suns have shone for millennia. If another is to burn out, it will take several thousand years. We can easily adapt to thirty-five suns and begin planning protocols for the unlikely event that another sun burns out. It's a simple matter of adjusting some crop rotations, perhaps an eventual climate change. But that will take generations. We have nothing to fear. Not now, not for a great while in the future."

More conversations of similar vein flowed around Dameia, some catching her ears, some passing swiftly by with no notice. They fell into one of two camps: those who blithely remarked that nothing was wrong, and those who were convinced the end was coming, even if the due date of said end varied from tomorrow afternoon to sometime thirty thousand seasons from now. This had been going on for the better part of the day.

All the ruckus and only one thing was clear: No one had a clue about what was really going on.

The Chieftain had put his trust in Dameia. He was counting on her to handle this, to arrive at a correct and actionable conclusion. She was not keen on failing, either her father or her subjects. That would be a decidedly out of tune note on which to start her future Chieftainship. With a deep breath, she rose to her feet.

"*Zakar.*" The single word that named them all, delivered with respect but also with flavors of authority and a dash of annoyance, managed to silence the entire room. Since shock was a reaction she could ill afford, the princess instead masked it with what she hoped was an accurate replication of the stern look she had seen the Chieftain employ on many such occasions.

"I think we can all agree that no matter the cause, the fact that one of our suns has gone dark is troubling. We in this room have been tasked by our Chieftain to discover the cause of the darkness,

The Weight of Stars and Suns
Dawn Christine Jonckowski

the probability of further darkenings, and how to adapt our lives—from farming to climate control—to this current and future darkness." She paused to fix a steeled gaze on each scholar individually. They would know by the end of her speech that she was more than just the Chieftain's daughter. She was their future ruler. They may as well get used to taking orders from her.

"Now is not the time for squabbling. This unprecedented occurrence must lead to a time of action, a time of discovery, a time of planning for sustainability. What is at stake is bigger than you, bigger than me. Bigger than your reputations, bigger even than who among you is right and who is not. *Zakar*," she intoned, her gaze sweeping the lot of them, "this is about the future of Tav and all her inhabitants. They look to us for answers. They look to us for safety. They look to us for reassurance. And we will *not* let them down."

The room was enveloped in silence. Either the Councilmen were heeding her words, or they thought she was off her head (more than one attendee was likely still wishing there was a royal harem with her in it instead of in front of them) and were only quiet out of respect for her father's station and fear of what he might do if he heard they disrespected his only child. She hoped it was the former, committed herself to accepting nothing less than their absolute respect for *her*, regardless of lineage.

"As such," Dameia continued past an increasingly dry throat, "you will all take the rest of the evening to plan for how best to observe the darkened sun tomorrow when it again rises on this side of our planet. You will work together to determine the cause and postulate the three most likely outcomes. And we *will* have a plan by the end of this Secondary Council session next week that is ready for presentation to the Chieftain and his Council, or you will answer to me. And I can guarantee, you will not like it."

One scholar rolled his eyes.

That was all it took: One single Tavarian's audacity to belittle her, to outwardly express his disdain. Between the rebel prisoner and these scholars, Dameia was at her limit.

"Saronis, you seem to lack solemnity. If you think this a trivial matter, I dare you to try my patience and authority and discover precisely how serious I am." Dameia could feel every soul between her and her dissenter shrink back from her icy words.

At least a few someones were taking her seriously.

It was a start.

"*Neqeba*," the scholar offered a mocking bow accompanied by a sardonic twist of his mouth that one could call a smile of sorts. "I find myself unable to continue on this Secondary Council, as a matter of principle over the leadership."

The room contracted with the collective intake of breath. He had dared. They could hardly believe it. Penalty for blatant disrespect of the Chieftain often included death. Would the princess proclaim the same consequences? Could she? All eyes swung from his pronouncement over to the Chieftain's daughter in eager anticipation of her reaction.

Dameia refused to disappoint.

"Is that so?"

"It is. I hereby resign and take my leave." Without hesitation, Saronis gathered his books and notes and swept out of the room.

Silence reigned for a split second.

The Weight of Stars and Suns
Dawn Christine Jonckowski

Then Dameia turned a regal head to the guard on her right. "Find him. And then execute him."

✦ ✦ ✦ ✦ ✦

"Today I ordered a Tavarian's death."

It was the second time she'd uttered the phrase, yet she felt no diminished shock for her action.

The first time she said it was to her father. Surely the Chieftain would understand the trauma it was to call for someone's execution. And yet he had accepted her pronouncement calmly, seemed rather matter-of-fact about it when she explained why. The scholar had disrespected her to a degree that warranted death; the Chieftain shrugged and said he would have done the same. He didn't seem to notice the tear on his daughter's heart, the ragged edges of her emotion that barely held together through dinner. She managed through just enough of the meal so as not to seem impolite and then rapidly excused herself.

Dameia had never known her father to be an unfeeling *zakar*. When her mother, his wife, had died trying to bring a second heir into their family, forfeiting both her life and the life of the tiny prince, the Chieftain wept harder than the young Dameia had. For the entire year of mourning, she scarcely saw him without a tear threatening to spill. Negative emotions weren't the only ones he had seemed unafraid to display with abandon. His laughter was quick and hearty, whether with his daughter or between friends and advisors. He maintained a steadfast loyalty to his late wife, never once seeking companionship (that Dameia knew of, anyway) or a new queen.

Surely he must have felt the weight of cutting off another's life, no matter how deserved the sentence may have seemed.

Surely he couldn't have become so calloused to the value of a life.

This hardened side took Damiea by surprise.

Finding no solace in her chambers, she wandered aimlessly around the complex's grounds and should have been unsurprised where her feet took her.

Should have been, but wasn't.

She found herself standing at the door to the rebel prisoner's cell, fingers wrapped around the latch handle, poised to open the heavy portal and cross the threshold. Why here? What comfort could a jailed human slave offer that her beloved father could not? (Would not?) What possible absolution could a rebel prisoner bestow?

Hyam. His name was Hyam.

She entered the cell.

Dameia sat down on the bench without a single word. Hyam raised one eyebrow at her long silence, but waited.

And waited.

And waited.

Until she spoke, and for the second time that day said, "Today I ordered a Tavarian's death."

Hyam echoed her silence for the space of several moments. She wondered what he must be thinking: *Poor purple princess, so burdened with privilege and prosperity*. Why was she even here? Telling him this?

As if he cared. As if he wasn't at that precise moment judging her a monster.

Disgusted by her weakness, Dameia was near to rising for a hurried escape when the man's voice came through the bars that separated them.

"I'm sorry." It was a simple statement, without malice or verdict. Straightforward, not a hint of irony.

For all that, it angered Dameia.

"You're sorry," she parroted bitterly. "I'm certain you are. One less Tavarian to order you around, one less sentry to regard you with constant suspicion, one less purple brute lording superiority over you. Yes, oh yes, I'm sure you're 'sorry.'"

Hyam gave a soft dismissive snort. "That isn't the case at all. But I suppose the Tavarians tell me everything else to do, so it stands to reason that you should think to dictate then how I do and do not feel." He leaned his head back against the warm stone wall. She wondered if he had yet moved from that spot on the floor. She wondered who in the colony might be missing him, might be worried for the state of his life and whether or not it hung in any sort of balance. She wondered if he had been assigned a mate, and if he loved her. If that mate would mourn him if in the end his life was forfeit.

She wondered.

She wondered why she felt this way. Why she cared.

(And perhaps she knew in that moment, but would not—could not—admit it to herself.)

It all made her angry. *Angrier.*

"I don't even know why I'm telling you this."

Hyam didn't turn his head, didn't even open his eyes, but pronounced simply, "Yes, you do."

She *did* know. He was the only one who would give her an honest response. While most humans were trained to defer in all things to the Tavarian race, rebels were obviously of a different ilk. And this one was clearly a rebel. He already knew his life was signed away to a rebellion, already knew that he might not live to see middle age, much less old age. He was imprisoned; at the moment, he had nothing left to lose, so why should he feign deference to a Tavarian he clearly had no respect for? This human, this rebel slave, this Hyam was the only individual in the Capitol—perhaps even the whole of the planet—who would talk to her as an equal. For that was how he saw himself. That was what he was fighting for: the chance for humans to be seen as the equals they believed themselves to be.

And in this moment, she did not need placating by Tavarians who only stood by her for the proximity to the Chieftain. She did not need to fight the battle to hide her feelings from her human companion Hannah, who surely would not do more than offer her spiced tea while harboring some exultation deep within her heart. She clearly was not to find solace with her father, whom she had thought to be the one who would understand what she was going through and could offer coping strategies, if not at least a little sympathy.

What Dameia needed was someone who was not afraid of her, someone who would speak to her as an equal.

Pity that the only one to fit that bill was an imprisoned human slave.

"Do you want to talk about it?" Hyam's soft question surprised her.

The Weight of Stars and Suns
Dawn Christine Jonckowski

"Not really," Dameia admitted. "It was protocol, and had I not done it, the fallout would have been worse than it already is. It's just . . . he was alive this morning, and now he's not. He may have a family who cared about him, may have had children or even grandchildren who were eagerly awaiting his return after this Secondary Council. He will not return, and while one can argue that it was due to his own actions and choosing, ultimately it is because of me. Because I chose to follow the law as it currently stands." She paused, the next spill of words caught in the knot of her throat. Then softly, "There is weight to realizing that you are responsible for the outcome of someone's life, that because of your station, you are in control of everyone around you, and with the slightest whim can change everything."

Hyam sat in prolonged silence. As the quiet stretched out, Dameia inwardly cursed herself. She had just described the ongoing struggle between humans and Tavarians. He must think her so unfeeling.

"I was wrong." His soft graveled voice cut into her self-flagellation.

"What?"

"I was wrong," Hyam repeated, opening his eyes. With some effort, he rose to his feet. Startled, Dameia stood too, surprised to see that this human stood tall and straight, so tall that her eyes leveled with his chin.

"About what?" Dameia queried, suddenly short of breath.

Hyam smiled, and his faced transformed. "You are shaping up to be an excellent future leader after all."

Dameia couldn't help herself: She smiled back.

The Weight of Stars and Suns
Dawn Christine Jonckowski

✧ ✧ ✧ ✧ ✧

If the princess had been shocked to find her feet leading her to Hyam's cell the second cycle before, then the prisoner was downright dumbfounded. Multiple visits to a prisoner who had more dirt on his left elbow than she'd likely ever sported in the entirety of her life. Was she visiting all the prisoners, or just him? And if she was visiting every single one in turn—all twelve of them—how could she possibly have time left in a cycle to do whatever princess-y duties she had to attend to? (Though he imagined that princesses didn't do much with their days aside from flit around a palace wearing sparkling gowns and drinking an excess of bloodwine; to see her at his door in a serviceable military-esque dress and decidedly sober forced him to tweak his mental picture by quite a bit.)

Then after their encounter that morning and her subsequent stormy exit, Hyam figured he'd never see her cross his cell threshold again.

Which was likely for the best.

He seemed to have an inability to control himself where she was concerned. It was likely to get him into significant trouble.

At some point.

It was her continued and ready acceptance of his consistent addressment of her as if she were not a princess. As if, in fact, she weren't even Tavarian. It was too tempting an invitation to ignore, and so he continued to banter, to offer frank replies, to outright challenge her in a way no ordinary human would ever dare.

He was a rebel. Bucking tradition was what he was about, wasn't it?

It was her *tolerance* of it that left him rather gobsmacked. Not just tolerance, but an inclination to volley straight back with no consequence.

For heaven's sake, she'd had a Tavarian executed for *his* impudence.

What made Hyam so special that his life—his *human* life—was still more or less intact?

He didn't have an answer. But he knew he was in trouble that next morning when the door to his cell opened on a protesting squeal of a rusted hinge, and he greeted the prison's Warden with a much larger smile than the thin gruel the Warden carried—or the Warden himself—truly warranted.

"If this gruel makes you that jolly, you should see how happy starvation makes you," the Warden growled, tossing the bowl into the cell such that the majority of the contents slopped onto the dirty floor. Hyam swore he could hear the spilled liquid sizzle as it rapidly evaporated off the hot stone in the already roasting sunslight. Though, if he wasn't mistaken, the light seemed oddly shifted from the days prior.

"And a good morning to you as well, Warden," Hyam replied cheerfully, reaching for the bowl. Quicker than thought could process, the Warden's hand flashed through the bars and Hyam felt the hot purple hand closing around his wrist.

"What are you about, prisoner?" the Tavarian snarled, spittle flying. "Do you think you can make nice with me and earn some sort of pass, some sort of way out of the mess you've so finely dumped yourself into? Well let me tell you this," he yanked Hyam's arm, pulling him so close that his face waffled on the bars, cracking open the skin on the bridge of his nose and sending blood dripping down while the sweet decayed scent of the Warden's breath filled his senses. Hyam fought the urge to gag. Or wince. Or both.

"No prisoner under my watch ever escapes, ever misses out on what he's got coming. And you won't be the first one to break that."

"No, sir," Hyam choked on his response, knowing full well he'd choke on the gruel later too. It was going to be that kind of a day.

The Warden wrenched at Hyam's arm once more, making sure the bars grooved an indelible mark on his nose, if not slightly less permanent ones latticed across his face. Then with a satisfied grunt, he released his human prey and slammed his way back out of the cell.

Hyam was once again alone, only this time, also oh-so-very aware of his humanity.

But he was more than just any human. He was a rebel.

Reaching for the few spoonfuls of gruel that were left to him, Hyam began to plot.

He had a rebellion to organize, and—so it appeared—all the time in the world in which to do it.

✧ ✧ ✧ ✧ ✧

The Weight of Stars and Suns
Dawn Christine Jonckowski

Dameia's day wasn't off to a much better beginning. The morning of the sophomore session of the Secondary Council began in absolute pandemonium. As the seventeen-sun day began to set and the Tavarians breathed a sigh of relief that they wouldn't have to stare at the mocking blank space in their sky for another day, they were greeted with a nasty surprise.

The new cycle that should have dawned with eighteen brilliant and fully-fired suns broke with only sixteen.

Over the course of the second cycle, two more suns had gone dark. At the same time.

Tav's citizens knew that the Chieftain had assembled a group to investigate the darkenings, but that did little to quell the panic, and the early hours found the complex gates teeming with the terrified public. Dameia could scarcely hear herself think over the din. She poured blackflower juice down her throat with abandon, only just registering it on her taste buds. Anything to quickly sharpen her sleep-fogged mind and keep another raging headache at bay.

"*Neqeba,*" Hannah's soft voice broke through Dameia's brain acrobatics. "The Chieftain—"

"—can announce himself." Her father's no-nonsense interruption propelled Dameia to her feet, had her hurriedly setting down the half-drunk carafe of blackflower juice. "You are dismissed," the Chieftain said over his shoulder, directed somewhere in the vicinity of where Hannah crouched frozen in a half curtsey. The human scurried away, a tiny bog mouse in the presence of a ferocious predator.

"Father," Damiea inclined her head with respect that she did not altogether feel after their previous encounter. The Chieftain grunted, strode to the small table strewn with Dameia's abandoned breakfast, swilled down the remainder of her precious blackflower juice. Sluggish synapses whimpered in protest. She had wanted those last dregs, needed them to function of a morning. A flick of the Chieftain's wrist and the carafe sailed in a wobbling arc across the veranda.

"Do you hear your subjects panicking, Dameia?"

She swallowed past the hive of frustration buzzing in her throat. "Yes. But I am just as recently aware of this change as they are, and as the Secondary Council is. They will simply have to trust that we are working as quickly as possible to discover the cause and formulate a solution and do their best to go about their days as normally as possible."

Her father arched a brow. (What was it with individuals arching singular brows at her as of late?) "Then I suggest you get out there and tell them that."

And out he strode.

With a long-suffering sigh, Dameia knelt to retrieve the carafe. Churl. Drank every drop and left none for her. If this was how the rest of her day was going to progress, then it had the makings of a very long one indeed.

✧ ✧ ✧ ✧ ✧

Hyam jolted awake to the princess' cry, pried a heavy eyelid open to find her on the other side of the bars, kneeling before him, hand to mouth with face arranged in horror.

| | The Weight of Stars and Suns | |
Dawn Christine Jonckowski

All his excellent intentions for rebellion planning had fallen quickly to the wayside earlier that day as his nose rapidly enlarged and a bass drum beat a deep rhythm just at the base of his skull. In the absence of anything resembling sustenance, he opted for sleep. It seemed the smarter option than being awake for any repeat performance with the Warden, lovely obliging individual that he was.

Somehow he mustered the energy to try a chuckle, a dry barking sound that couldn't quite convey amusement.

"You should see the other guy," he croaked.

"What happened?" she demanded.

Hyam readjusted slowly, swearing he could hear his joints creaking from disuse. How long did it take muscles to atrophy?

"Ah, just a guard who was a tad jealous of my overlarge bowl of gruel and dashing smile. I think he wanted to help make me a little prettier." Here, Hyam offered a lopsided approximation of a smile. It was difficult to tell past the swelling. "What do you think? Mission accomplished?"

The princess' lips worked to form a reply; Hyam could almost see the volley of commentary scrolling across the backs of her eyes. Her surprising and violent concern warmed his core. Not that he needed any additional warming in this cell, despite waking in the middle of the cycle to look up through his barred ceiling and discover that two more suns had since extinguished.

Intriguing.

As if she suddenly remembered her place, the princess settled her crouch back on her heels. Fingertips twitched with the internal war between how she had been raised to regard humans—especially considering her station—and this new and genuine concern for the man before her. Hyam wondered if her hands itched to reach out a cool palm to his face, or if she fought the urge to demand the name of the guard (well, Warden) so she could pummel him herself.

Or perhaps it was neither and Hyam had been languishing in prison entirely far too long. As much as two days and an evening could be considered "too long."

Also, he really wouldn't have minded if she'd pushed a hand through the bars to touch him.

Hyam cleared his gritty throat. "So," he began, a heroic attempt to distract his mind from wandering where it shouldn't. "Any brilliant thoughts on why the suns keep going out?"

The princess blinked rapidly, as if rearranging her own thoughts and corralling them to a safer topic. "Many thoughts, few that are brilliant," she admitted. Mimicking his feigned casual air, she settled onto the floor, leaning her long back against the visitor's bench and arranging her legs into the same stretch and bend that he had maintained for all moments of their visits save the brief instant the second cycle prior.

"At my father's order, I've assembled a Secondary Council consisting of what are deemed many of the greatest minds on Tav. Although the way some of them act when confronted with similar intelligence in the same room would belie that they are the greatest *anything*." The princess shook her head as her eyes wandered away from Hyam's to stare aimlessly through the grated ceiling and over to where he imagined the blank suns may currently be hanging in the sky.

"A little healthy competition going on, is there?" Hyam smiled.

The Weight of Stars and Suns
Dawn Christine Jonckowski

The princess lips curled into a matching grin. "Hmmm. I don't know if I'd call it 'healthy.' Would you believe that one of them actually threw a chair today? It was mayhem! They'll be lucky if they all make it out of this alive." She began to chuckle, then choked halfway through, sobered at the recollection of the previous day's goings on.

"I didn't mean it that way." Her words came out soft and broken, pieces that Hyam reassembled to clearly read her pain.

"I know."

And he did.

Hyam was long and well-acquainted with grief. He was a slave: Grief was practically a way of life. Though he knew hers was a different breed, colored straight through the middle with the dark shades of guilt. How to assuage that, he could not say. But it gave him hope to hear her wounds, to have evidence right before his eyes that not all Tavarians were ferocious, unfeeling beings who spent human lives like ready currency.

"I should go." But she made no move. Her face read such naked loneliness that the blade of it cut through the bars and into Hyam's own chest. The loneliness didn't surprise him, entirely. After all, here she was keeping repeated company with a jailed rebel slave. Those with overlarge circles of friends had no need of caged confidantes.

"I should go," she repeated, this time folding her long legs beneath her and rising gracefully to her feet. "Beware, friend," she cautioned with a sad and surprising tenderness. "Watch that the guards do not make further meat of that face. I'd hate it if you could no longer smile."

Before he could respond, she took her leave, the door whining shut behind her, the sturdy latch snicking into place.

Friend.

She had called him friend.

It was enough.

4

The third day of the Secondary Council fared somewhat better than both the second and the first.

To start, the day had crowned itself with the seventeen suns everyone was beginning to expect. More than a few realized the absurdity of their relief, since one sun of that cycle was still dark, but after the prior day's revelation of only sixteen suns, seventeen felt like quite the odd blessing.

But more than that, Dameia sat at the head of the Council Room and thus far not one piece of furniture had become airborne, and not one voice had been raised beyond the volume of a jovial day's greeting. For the fact that the day was nearly two-thirds complete, this was quite the enormous feat.

More than a few had picked splintered chair out of their notes from the day before, and that seemed to encourage a dash more maturity in most that led to a considerably more courteous conversation in this session. After all, as Dameia had reminded them the day before at a near shout, they were many of the most brilliant minds on Tav, and it was high time they start acting as such. It was that coupled with the icy way she had flicked the clawed pieces of chair foot off her lap and rose to her feet in such a deadly silence so as to make the Chieftain proud that had finally shaped up the lot of them and earned her their begrudging respect.

Perhaps she was good for something other than just a harem after all.

Perhaps she might just lead this Secondary Council to some success.

Perhaps.

They would let time be the judge.

Meanwhile, time also served as a harsh mistress, as the week was progressing and they were just now settling down to discuss the darkening suns like the educated thinkers they were.

"I think this Council can all agree that several of our suns have simply burnt out and will not reignite," began Arganon, methodically pacing to the front of the room. He had been proclaimed the head of the Secondary Council a bit by default for his calm demeanor—he was one of only a few who had not resorted to name-calling, doomsdaying, chauvinism, or furniture chucking—and ability to corral the others into more or less of an organized and respectful group.

"What we must next decipher is the possibility of predicting the expiration of the remaining suns," Arganon continued. "If there is indeed an expiration," he added swiftly as the din of panic began to build. His pacing had finally brought him to the head of the room, just below where Dameia sat poised to quell any rising panic and resulting aerial objects. Arganon raised hands in supplication, and the congregate immediately—and surprisingly—ground to a halt.

"Who among you has his observation equipment at the ready?"

Several hands slid silently up.

Arganon smiled. Progress. He turned toward Dameia.

"With your permission, Princess, I propose we recess early for the cycle to allow this smaller contingency observation hours of both today's darkened sun as well as the two pits that will rise with the morrow. It is my firm belief that if we can find any such anomaly on these dark stars, we may be able to discover the cause and predict if and when subsequent lights may extinguish. I furthermore humbly propose that these witnesses assemble and present their completed findings in two days' time for this Council's consideration."

Dameia feigned consideration, knowing full well that while she fooled most, Arganon understood that her ponderous look was merely for show. She was exquisitely grateful for him to have taken the lead and made headway toward some form of solution. He would be one to keep in mind for her own main Council when the day came that she assumed the title of Chieftain.

"I concur. Let it be done as you have suggested, Arganon." The older *zakar* bowed his head at her acknowledgement while she turned to the balance of the Secondary Council. "Heed what has been told you by Councilman Arganon, and prepare to reassemble two days hence. Those of you who are not directly involved with observation equipment will make yourselves available to those who are, to assist in whatever way they deem necessary."

Grizzled heads bobbed their assent as a bubble of sweet relief filled and popped in Dameia's chest, chasing out some of the panic that had set up camp when first she saw the shadow from the darkened sun.

Perhaps it was all going to work out after all.

Perhaps.

That cycle, she fell into the first semi-peaceful sleep she'd had in the space of several days. It wasn't until she awoke the next morning with a curious pit in her stomach that she realized that she had not been at all to see Hyam.

☼ ☼ ☼ ☼ ☼

She hadn't been to see him.

An entire day had passed—two entire cycles—and she hadn't been to see him.

Hyam told himself it didn't matter. He told himself that he was better off without her friendship. He told himself that *she* was better off without his as well. He was a human, and she wasn't just any Tavarian, she was the princess.

He told himself.

But each time he told himself, the stone sitting in his own heart grew a little heavier.

He really needed to be planning the next phase of the rebellion. Assuming, of course, he ever got out of this blasted prison to put any plans into action. Hyam didn't know much of what went on in rebel trials. Most rebels who had been tried and returned to the colony at least alive could hardly have been considered returned in one piece. Often they were missing vital pieces that inhibited their communication, and whether those pieces were fragments of fingers, tongue, or mind depended entirely on the severity of the rebel's infraction.

Other times, they just didn't return at all.

Hyam was personally hoping for life, even if it meant at the expense of a working appendage.

In the middle of his mental roulette of which body part he could best function without, the door to his cell block cracked open and the princess slipped in, a smooth purple shadow against a rough bricked wall.

"Hi." Her greeting was guilty and breathless all at once but overshadowed by her smile.

He was not going to let on his levels of relief at the sound of her voice. She had called him friend; of course she should return to him.

Of course.

Hyam smiled back.

✧ ✧ ✧ ✧ ✧

The sweet relief Dameia felt when the smile split Hyam's face made her stomach jump.

He still didn't look like he'd moved but once from his seat on the cell floor. Though over the past day of her absence, his nose had reduced down to more or less normal size (or at least what she imagined its regular size to be, since she didn't think she'd ever seen him not at least partially beaten to a pulp) and many of the abrasions had crusted over with scabs. His smile may have cost him to display, but she was glad for it nonetheless.

"So tell me what news?" Hyam greeted her. "Have you been cowering from flying furniture again? Ducking a table? Dodging a desk? Perhaps the occasional throw rug?"

Dameia crossed her arms tightly and feigned derision. "First of all, a princess never cowers. Secondly, I'll thank you to know that all furnishings stayed exactly as they were intended to yesterday, and we even—" here she broke to put hands to mouth in mock surprise, "—made something resembling progress by the end of the session."

Hyam affected a gasp. "No!"

Dameia was too happy to stop the giggle that bubbled from her throat. "Yes!" She paused to arrange herself on the visiting area floor. "By tomorrow I hope to have the beginnings of a solution that we can present to the Chieftain and his Council at their next session. I will be glad to have this uncertainty behind us and be able to move forward."

"Until, of course, the next catastrophe," Hyam offered helpfully. She eyed him not altogether kindly.

"Let's just take it one big planet-shattering crisis at a time, eh? Speaking of which, I've heard no comment on when the Courts will try the rebels. Have they made mention?"

"What, to me?" He feigned indignation. "I can't believe that my good friend the Warden has said nothing. After all, we're so close." Dameia saw his hand sneak up to rub the bridge of his nose before he thought better of it and his fingers twitched back down to rest on his up-drawn knee. His head rolled against the stone as he fixed his gaze on her. "Though if anyone would know, Princess, it would likely be you."

She would give him that.

She should know.

In fact, she was now determined to know. After all, she was the upcoming Chieftain. It was crucial that she be privy to the goings-on of her kingdom, from the science of darkening suns to any lives—both Tavarian and human—that hung in the balance. A man's life could no longer be left to chance.

Especially not this man's life.

She didn't want to stop long enough to dwell on that thought and the implications it dragged along with it like a favorite toy.

"You're absolutely right." Dameia jumped to her feet. "There are those in the know, and I should be one of them. I will go make some inquiries and return with a conclusion." Her resolve propelled her swiftly to the door.

"Princess?" His voice cut through and stilled her hand before it could crack the latch. She turned, saw the perplexity run across his face.

"Do you do this for every rebel?"

The question stopped her heart; his eyes drove her to honesty.

"No," she replied softly, pulling the door open and nearly drowning her final words in the creak of hinges.

"Only you."

The Weight of Stars and Suns
Dawn Christine Jonckowski

✧ ✧ ✧ ✧ ✧

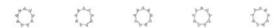

If the planet Tav of the thirty-six—now thirty-three—suns could have ecologically sustained a winter, snowflakes would have fallen in the dining room during the mid-day meal. Slaves whispered behind flattened hands, guilty pleasures passed lip to ear on a long chain from the Chieftain's complex all the way back to the colony.

There was a decided layer of frost between the Chieftain, whose adoration of his singular offspring was the stuff of stories and legends, and his daughter.

Some said it began when the fizzed bloodwine was spilled across the late Queen's favored tablecloth, spreading an unquenchable stain across the delicate embroidery that had been wrought by her own hands shortly after she wed the Chieftain.

Several claimed it was because it had taken too long for the Secondary Council to make progress, and the Chieftain was rebuking his daughter lest the Secondary Council not bring a report to bear the following week.

Still others suggested that it had something—though they couldn't quite puzzle it—to do with the twelve rebels languishing in prison.

Maybe they were all a percentage correct.

Dameia was surprised to see her father present at the mid-day meal. After coming of age only a few seasons ago, she had been invited to the royal table for any meal she chose. Mid-day was a particular favorite, which may or may not have had something to do with a peculiar dessert that the kitchen had crafted from a modified

The Weight of Stars and Suns
Dawn Christine Jonckowski

human recipe of something mysteriously—and likely mistranslated and mistakenly—called a riced and crispy treat that for some wildly unknown reason, was only served at mid-day meals. But while her father was regularly present at the evening meal when they would discuss the politics, the monarchy, and the occasional party dress (which discussion the Chieftain would never let on to actually enjoying), he was just as regularly absent from the mid-day meal for his many duties and responsibilities.

No matter, that simply meant more dessert for Dameia. The slaves had never once heard her complain about repeatedly dining alone, and continued to delightedly serve the riced and crispy treat dessert as if for two.

So when she loped into the Dining Room and saw her father seated at the royal table and already eating, she skidded to a quick halt and did her best to scrub the surprise off her face and replace it with a ready smile. Bygones could be bygones; perhaps the Chieftain had dismissed her guilty conscience over Saronis' execution, but Hyam had offered solace for her grief, so she held no lingering grudge over her father's cold dismissal of the death. What good would that do anyway, other than give her indigestion during a meal that would surely conclude with her favorite dessert?

Even if she would have to share today.

"Father!" Dameia greeted brightly, bobbing her head in a quick show of respect before adding a brief kiss to his weathered cheek and dropping into a seat.

"I hear you've spent considerable time at the prison."

Dameia's hand froze halfway to the meat platter. Quickly regaining herself and hoping it only looked like a stutter in her movement, she forced down the surprising panic and began filling her plate.

"Per your orders, I've been trying to learn the rebel mind and further my understanding in order to circumvent or even outright prevent future uprisings when I am Chieftain." She prayed that her voice sounded as steady as she hoped. He was addressing her as if she were one of his Councilmen, and those she knew he rarely addressed straightforwardly. Every question had an angle, every sentence was finely crafted to get what he needed from the other party. Royalty though he was, the Chieftain was still above all a politician.

The Chieftain wasn't asking his daughter anything.

He was baiting her.

"And what have you learned?" His tone was nonchalant, his eyes deceptively casual as he studied the leg of roasted sand hen dripping grease down his fingers.

Dameia swallowed hard, chasing her own mouthful with a sip of fizzed bloodwine, both to push the lump down and buy time. What did the Chieftain already know about her visits? She'd just admitted to Hyam that he was the only one she was talking to, the only one she had concern for.

She had called him—a human—"friend."

And she'd *meant* it.

"Nothing much yet. But it is early still. With a little more time, I should know their minds further and be able to provide intelligence before the trials."

Her father's gaze did not waver from his food, which was not an altogether positive sign.

The Weight of Stars and Suns
Dawn Christine Jonckowski

"I trust this reconnaissance is not taking undue time from the Secondary Council you pledged to lead to conclusion over our troublesome skies." He paused to rip a shank of meat from the bone. "I do hope we will not need to experience additional darkening and further panic from our citizens to incite you into promised action. After all," his eyes slid finally to hers. "I noticed that this morning the Secondary Council room was suspiciously empty, and you seem to have a bit of prison filth just there on your knees. An odd location for dirt on a princess who should lower herself to no one save for her Chieftain."

Damiea's mind circled. "I dropped an earring and was forced to search for it quickly before the prisoner found it and could use it to pick his lock."

"Don't lie to me."

His voice was quiet. Calm.

Deadly.

"When have I ever?" She prayed her voice held the same balanced tone, perhaps even with a timbre of indignation. "The Secondary Council has set up observation equipment and is to spend the next days in study and solution. Those who are not directly observing are taking part in disseminating and compiling results to present when we reconvene. Meanwhile, for my part, I have continued to study the rebel so that I can become a better ruler and deserve the respect I command."

"Rebel?" The Chieftain fixed her with a pointed glance. "Singular?"

"Rebels. A mere slip of the tongue."

He knew. He had to know. A roiling grew in her chest. Though what crime had she committed? Was sharing a laugh or a smile with a slave an offense? Every human slave serving in the palace knew everything that Hyam did about Saronis' execution, the Secondary Council, the delayed rebel trials. Which meant that gossip trails had carried those precious stones of information back to the colony, and by a day's end, everyone would know everything.

Although.

Although these humans knew from observation, from personal witness.

Whereas Hyam? Hyam knew from the very heart of the princess herself.

And that was a much different testimony.

"You forget, Damiea, that you are a princess. You have no secrets. Not from me, not from your subjects, not from the Council—either one—not even from the slaves here in the palace. Slaves of any station. If you think you can hide something, you are gravely mistaken."

"I hide nothing from you, Father." She locked her gaze on his.

Faster than she could think, the Chieftain shot to his feet, chair crashing behind him, hands planting squarely in front of his daughter and sending her goblet spinning. Bloodwine fizzed a dark spiral across the table covering stitched with her own late mother's design. His eyes even with hers, the Chieftain drew his lips in a half snarl.

"You'd best not. You will not like the consequences."

The Weight of Stars and Suns
Dawn Christine Jonckowski

Damiea's heart thudded hard against hollow ribs as her father's eyes bored hard into the depths of hers. Finally, on a growl, he righted himself and threw a hand out at the table cloth.

"Look what has become of your mother's favorite piece. Ruined." He turned sharp pupils back to her. "Let us hope that is the only casualty of this interaction."

Directing a blank stare at the spreading stain, Dameia sat silent even as her mind whirled. This interaction? This interaction with her father? Or—she hardly dared to think it—every interaction she'd had with Hyam? Those prison cells were supposed to be sound-resistant to prevent prisoners from collaborating with each other or sending messages to other slaves on the outside. Hyam's cell should have protected him, should have protected *her*, from anyone knowing what was transpiring inside.

She was learning about the rebels. Perhaps not in the way her father intended, but in a better way. Hyam let her see beyond the lower-class label the Tavarians had slapped on his race. His refusal to show a deference he did not feel was teaching her how to earn respect. And she *was* earning his respect: She'd begun earning it when she paused to see, to interact with, to value his humanity and the beauty it contained.

What they were building was a friendship.

Only a friendship.

How could that be criminal?

When she finally looked back to her father, the Chieftain was wiping wine and grease from his fingers with the hem of the wrecked table cloth. Satisfied that he'd cleaned all evidence of the disastrous meal from his hands, he took one final swill from his upright goblet.

"I have trusted you, Damiea. Do not let me learn that that trust has been misplaced."

"I won't," she replied, her voice far smaller.

For the first time she could remember, the Chieftain did not smile at his daughter as he made his way toward the door.

"Oh," he added, an afterthought as his grip tightened to pull the large door. "And I like those earrings. Lucky for you that you saved the one from the prison floor. Which did you drop?"

"The right one," Dameia replied without hesitation.

"Hmmm." The Chieftain lifted his chin a tick and left the Dining Room.

Dameia waited for the whoosh of air as the door closed behind her father, and only then allowed herself to deflate against the back of her chair. She rested there for only half a breath before her hands reached up to finger the earrings her father had so openly admired.

Then her eyes flew open, her stomach pitched, and she ran for a different door to be quickly and violently ill.

Her earlobes were completely bare.

5

In prison, it was hard to tell where the first cycle of a day ended and the second—the ones humans considered the equivalent of night—began.

To be fair, anywhere on Tav it could be difficult to discern where one cycle ended and the next began. It was just far easier to decipher when one wasn't locked in a cell.

So Hyam wasn't sure what surprised him more: that he knew it was somewhere around the middle of the second cycle or that the princess was sneaking into his cell at such a late hour. Whichever it was, he couldn't stop the smile when he caught the scent of her as the closing door blew a weak draft across the solitary cell. She was fresh air and sunshine, flowers and spice.

He was, well, dirt. And layers of it.

He was in prison. There wasn't much he could do about the dirt.

"He knows."

The princess' only two words snapped Hyam from his olfactory reverie, plunging him back to a reality where the young royal poised flattened against a wall, chest heaving and eyes panicked. She finally lifted herself away from the ragged brick. "I don't know who has been telling him. The Warden? Or has he forced the other prisoners through inquisitions? Or perhaps the guards have been speculating. These cells are soundproof, so they can't know, can they? But he *knows*. Gods, how does he know?" Words poured from her lips as she paced a frantic path to and fro and back again. For the second time in her presence, Hyam lifted himself to his feet.

"Hey, hey," he soothed, reaching a calming hand through the bars. It didn't reach, not even close.

If only he could touch her.

"Take a deep breath and slow down."

She looked up, an animal hunted, predator surprised to be found as prey. But her feet stilled and the pacing ceased.

"Let's start from the beginning. Who is 'he' and what does he know?"

Her eyelids slid shut. He saw her ribcage rise and fall as she drew a forced slow breath.

"'He' is my father. And I think," her eyes opened even as her voice caught on the words. "I think he knows about us."

"Oh." Hyam could think of no better response, aside from voicing pleasure that there was an "us," which he didn't think would be entirely appropriate in the moment. Especially because he wasn't even certain what that "us" entailed. Sunshine and flowers versus dirt, and all that. He wadded up those feelings and stuffed them into

The Weight of Stars and Suns
Dawn Christine Jonckowski

a dark and decidedly dusty corner of his mind. Pulled his hand back through the bars to hang at his side.

"Yes, 'oh,'" the princess echoed softly.

"Which explains your secretive second-cycle visit."

She nodded. "Which explains my secretive second-cycle visit." Her head shook, tumbling dark curls across bare shoulders, and the pacing resumed. "I don't know what I was thinking. I'm the princess, I'm not allowed to have secrets. Everyone in the palace knows everything about me, even the slaves. They know when I go out and when I come in, what time I sleep, when I awake, what I like to eat and the horrid state of my closet. Why shouldn't someone take notice that when I visit the prison, I only ever go to one cell? That I go there almost daily and linger far longer than a fact-finding interrogation should warrant. That I return with dirt on my knees from sitting on the floor." Anguish dripped from every word. She stopped right in front of him, just on the other side of the bars, close enough to reach out and touch, dropped her forehead onto the iron grate. "He knows I've lied to him. He knows. What am I going to do?" she finished on a whisper as a single tear tracked down her face.

Propriety be damned, Hyam thought, and reached back through the bars to brush the tear away with the rough pad of his thumb. Her skin was hot purple velvet and he found he didn't want to stop touching her. Hyam forced his hand to return to his side of the bars and down to his side.

"What do you want to do?" he asked quietly while his fingers itched for her.

She shook her head, rolling it across the bar. "I don't know."

"Yes, you do. You have to."

His retort clearly caught the princess by surprise and she lifted her face to stare squarely.

"I don't say that to be cruel," Hyam continued. "I say it because it is truth. Like it or not, you are the princess. You cannot afford indecision. To be frank, since this now involves me, I cannot afford your indecision either. You must take action, and swiftly. The pieces are on the board; make your move."

To his surprise, the princess chuckled. Ruefully, to be sure, but she chuckled.

"It is a pity you are a human; you would make a wonderful Councilman. I would love to have you at my side when I am Chieftain."

Hyam forced himself to season his grin with wry. "Well, I can't be a Councilman, but I tell you, when I'm not imprisoned? I make a hell of a rebellion leader."

Her smile bloomed brightly before dying away as reality clouded over once more.

"So what will you do?" Hyam asked softly.

"What I must," the princess sighed. "I must focus on the Secondary Council. When I return to the prison, I should be seen speaking to the other eleven rebels. And I should probably avoid being seen at your door, at least for the time being."

"Okay," Hyam agreed quietly. "See? That wasn't so hard."

She choked out a laugh. "Saying it isn't difficult, no." Her eyes sought and found his. "It's in the doing that the difficulty lies."

If he counted measured seconds, Hyam could keep breathing and not forfeit all credibility. He waited, counted, breathing in, out; in, out.

The Weight of Stars and Suns
Dawn Christine Jonckowski

"It is what I must do, not what I *want* to do," the princess finished, words so soft they were nearly lost under the sound of breaths and heartbeats. Hyam could hear heartbreak. But for what? For him? It seemed impossible.

Impossible.

Yet here they were.

"And what do you want to do?" Hyam finally asked, his voice low and graveled.

This time it was her arm that reached through bars, that broke the barrier between royalty and rebel. Her burning violet skin that ignited his as her hand brushed his shoulder, settled on the back of his neck. Vivid purple fingers against warm olive flesh. She pulled his face near the iron gridwork, tilted hers, and ever so tentatively, pressed her warm lips to his.

It was the space of a breath.

It was the duration of eternity.

A star broke open, a far planet was born. Elements danced in a patterned round and the cosmos froze for a heartbeat.

"That," she whispered, her forehead melded to his. Then she was gone.

And for the first time since he was imprisoned, Hyam felt truly, truly alone.

✧ ✧ ✧ ✧ ✧

If she lay perfectly still in her perfectly dark sleep chamber and took perfectly slow and measured breaths, Dameia could fool herself into thinking her heart was finally slowing once more to a normal pace.

But then of their own volition, her hands came to her mouth, fingertips resting on lips she imagined were still warm from the touch of Hyam's.

It had really happened.

She had kissed him.

A human.

A slave.

No.

He was more than that, more than the labels made him to be. He had a name.

She had kissed Hyam.

"Gods," she groaned under her breath, even as her belly curled in forbidden pleasure. It had taken every strength to pull her mouth from his and slip out the cell door. An artful dodge past the few second cycle guards who were fervently fighting sleep at that hour (and failing spectacularly) and Dameia was once again safely confined in the Chieftain's complex behind the thick stone walls that kept everything in, and from which she could now no longer truly get out. Walls that had protected her for twenty-two seasons—walls that had been warm friends against which she leaned, careened, scratched on with childish chalkings—these same walls now bent in toward her, leaning heavy on her shoulders.

Her heart pounded.

She had kissed Hyam.

Running silently on the balls of bare feet through corridors she'd mapped with a lifetime, Dameia had slid inside the door to her wing and collapsed against the rough grain just as the second cycle watch meandered past. She'd counted footfalls, then counted double to ensure they continued undistracted down the hallway. Hurriedly shed her dress for sleep garb and dove through the gauzed curtains of her bed, the light blanket yanked up from ankle to chin lest anyone suspect she had not been there the entirety of the second cycle.

Her heart pounded.

She had kissed Hyam.

Even as her mind battled to stay in the prison cell with her rebel and her recollections, Dameia fought back to keep it a captive to the duties at hand. She had scant hours to sleep before meeting with the Secondary Council in the morning to receive their findings. Once the findings were assembled properly, they had to present them to the Chieftain and the Council.

The Chieftain.

How would she face him, knowing what he knew, knowing what she'd done? How could she pull off such an incredibly feigned indifference so as to throw him off the scent of what he already suspected, what was already fact? She didn't know what she would do.

Yes, you do. You have to.

Hyam's words bled through. He was right.

In the morning, Hannah found her mistress awake early and ready for the day. The princess stood by the hearth fire, her eyes deep and distant. What the human companion could not see in the flames was the last smoldering scraps of the dirt-streaked dress Dameia had worn on her final visit to Hyam. Hannah saw only squared shoulders and a stubbornly-set jaw. She saw notes from the Secondary Council strewn across a desk, historical tomes on the great Chieftains of Tav's past stacked precariously on the floor with odd bits of paper sticking out at various points marking some specific virtue or conquest the princess hoped to emulate. She noticed her princess no longer content in her typically preferred daily wardrobe of a serviceable military dress, but arrayed for ceremony in cream with chains linking her shoulders, rings through her ears, and a solid metal circlet dangling from her fingers awaiting the maid's expert braiding skills to secure it to the royal's head.

For herself, Dameia blinked gritty eyes that had had little sleep and much study. Her hands ached from voluminous notes, fingers cracked and dry from sifting so much paper. Her throat was raw and her purse lighter by several scores from an early hunting of the Warden to threaten and purchase his silence. His gaze held an all too uncomfortable gleam of knowing, but he had finally, finally agreed to still his tongue on the matter of her prior visits, with just enough time for the princess to race back behind her own prison's walls and ready for the day as if nothing more extraordinary had happened outside of putting on a new dress.

Dameia had to admit: It was a fairly spectacular dress, so far as ceremonial garb went.

Not until her human companion urged the princess to sit so she could do her hair did Dameia allow herself to breathe as if hell itself wasn't licking at her door. As the human's fingers parted and wove dark tresses into braids in and around the polished circlet, Dameia allowed herself to believe that her plans were going to work, allowed herself to believe that no one—Tavarian, human, or otherwise—would suffer any more than they already had. That she could deliver on her promises. On *all* of her promises.

At Hannah's prompting, Damiea turned to look at her finished hair in the mirror. Looking back at her was someone Damiea didn't readily recognize. For meeting her gaze was not an untried princess who leaned too heavily on the mightiness of her father, but a determined royal primed to make her own unique and indelible mark on the world she was poised to inherit.

Her heart stilled.

The pieces were on the board; it was time to make her move.

✧ ✧ ✧ ✧ ✧

"Princess."

Arganon's greeting as Damiea swept into the meeting room and took her place at the head of the Secondary Council was just as much salutation as it was shock as he took in her garb. She didn't break stride, didn't let him see her cold pleasure at his surprise and resulting deference. To his credit, Arganon had always shown her due respect, but this. This was a new level. This was recognition of her power, admiration for her role, and resolution to her rule all rolled into one.

The princess sat, inclined her head in recognition of Arganon's address.

It was another sixteen-sun day, an especially auspicious day for the Secondary Council to be presenting their findings to their princess. Blessedly, it had—at least thus far—stayed a sixteen-sun day. Dameia didn't know how she would have handled the chaos if the day had crowned with fifteen or even fourteen suns.

Maybe to everyone else she seemed to have a firm grasp on her control, but the truth was she was clinging by fingertips.

As long as no one could tell how close she was to the edge.

The Secondary Council shifted restlessly in her prolonged silence, probed by protocol to remain standing until she at last addressed the group.

"I hope you bring me good news, Arganon," Damiea finally spoke. On a relieved sigh, the entirety of the congregate save Arganon sat. For his part, Arganon offered a half smile.

"Good and better news. Though that, I suppose, depends entirely on how one chooses to view the situation."

"I prefer to be realistic, sir, as does my father. He will not be pleased at sweetened words, and neither am I." Dameia arched an eyebrow, pleased to finally be the one on the giving end. "Tell it to me true, Councilman, and let me be the final judge of good and bad."

"Very good, your Highness," Arganon agreed. "First, the members of the Secondary Council all agree that our suns are burning out, which at least poses no immediate threat to our planet. Although the suns will continue to burn out—the rate at which we have yet to determine—it is this Council's belief that despite the recent evidence, the extinguishing will occur at a slow enough rate so as to enable us to prepare for Tav to become more like a single-sun planet with dark and light and rotating seasons. In fact, we should retain up to fifty percent of our suns permanently."

Dameia shook her head in shock. "Councilman, this is . . . this is excellent news! With the collective gathered here today, we can

The Weight of Stars and Suns
Dawn Christine Jonckowski

begin to plan for changes in agriculture and engineering. If there be no immediate threat, we are well able to educate ourselves on the reality of changing climate and pass that knowledge along to the citizens. We are not in so dire a place as we once imagined." Hope sparked a small fire.

Arganon looked down at his notes, steepled his fingers as if to build a tiny sanctuary for the news Dameia pronounced as excellent.

News he was about to deflate with a very pointy knife.

"*Neqeba*," his calm cracked on the reverential address. "*Neqeba*, unfortunately, on the heels of that good news, there is some looming bad news."

Dameia stilled.

"How bad?"

"Potentially catastrophic."

"Tell me," she demanded in a low voice that feigned calm. The Councilman's chest rose and fell with a deep and preparatory breath.

"We, uh, we do not know the precise timing, *neqeba*, but based on the star observations made and concurred by several of our best astronomers, we believe that a few of our suns are set not to burn out, but actually supernova instead within a generation. Maybe two." Arganon let his eyes drop closed for a moment, collecting his own calm. "When the suns supernova, the force of the burn will scorch everything within reach, which includes the entirety of Tav. Whatever is not become ash from the enlarged burn will be utterly flattened by the debris emitted with the explosion." The councilman's gaze locked onto Dameia's. "No matter what we do to protect our way of life now, eventually, *neqeba*, Tav will burn, and all of our intentions with her."

Dameia gripped the arms of her chair as her vision blurred and narrowed and her mind sang the high whine of an impending faint. Of all days to take rein as the impending ruler, to grab hold of her destiny. To choose to make her rule her own. The very same day she learned that she would be Chieftain of a doomed race.

She could not imagine Tav unmade. The solitary sun-ringed planet had stood for millennia. And of course—*of course*—on the edge of her term, it should be found sentenced to death.

Death by a fiery weapon aimed straight at its heart.

The room was silent, eerily still, as if each believed that one move could topple the entire now-endangered structure of their world. Dameia looked at each scientist and astronomer in turn. All these brilliant minds, and none would make a difference. None could. Her world now bore an expiration date.

"I promised my father a solution," she began softly. "I promised him a solution, and I am not in the habit of breaking my promises to him." Well, at least she hadn't been until lately, but she let that thought run by without capture or rumination.

Arganon's mouth worked to form a response he couldn't quite manage. Mercifully, an astronomer rose to his feet, and Arganon sank gratefully into his chair, deflated and defeated.

"*Neqeba*," the astronomer began with the customary inclination of his grizzled head. "I'm afraid there is no solution in this case. Nothing that will reverse the progression of nature and save our world. Perhaps what is best is for us to enjoy the time we have left."

The Weight of Stars and Suns
Dawn Christine Jonckowski

"I doubt that is an answer the Chieftain will find palatable, but if it is what we have, well," Dameia met each individual pair of eyes in the room.

"It is time we tell my father."

✧ ✧ ✧ ✧ ✧

All things considered, Dameia thought that her father took the news rather well.

He didn't even throw things until after the Secondary Council had departed.

He received the news of his planet's death sentence with eerie calm, thoughtfully raising the right questions at the right time and dutifully pondering the responses given. And when he learned that the Secondary Council's best solution was to adapt farming for the extinguishing suns while simply enjoying the time left to the planet, the Chieftain paused only long enough to shoot a glareful of daggers at his daughter before turning back to the Secondary Council and offering an alternative.

The Chieftain wanted to take Tav underground.

He theorized that while the surface of Tav would be turned to ash and dust, if they could build a network of communities below every city, Tav's citizens could essentially hunker down under the blitz and survive, then later emerge under the remaining suns and rebuild on a planet that effectively been reset by fire. Not one scientist or astronomer could adequately refute the Chieftain's recommendation, largely because no one had yet to survive the supernova of a star so close to a planet but mainly because the solution had come straight from the Chieftain.

One did not traditionally disagree with the Chieftain if one preferred one's head to remain firmly attached to one's body.

The Secondary Council was officially thanked for their contributions, bound to silence until an official royal decree could be issued, discharged to return to their separate corners of the planet, and summarily dismissed. Arganon shot the princess a glimpse of equal parts thanks and pity, as if he knew that the Chieftain's response to her behind closed doors would be less than the respectful and royal sagacity that the Secondary Council had received.

It took both too long and too short of a time for the room to empty of the Secondary Council. The door shut behind the final astronomer. Dameia felt suddenly small, dwarfed by the soaring mosaicked ceilings, the high arched windows that pulled cross breezes down and through. A page of notes rippled on wind that whispered like a roar in the silent hall. The Chieftain turned to face his daughter from his seat high on the dais. Pressure leaned on her eardrums and her heartbeat echoed loudly within while she fought to maintain her composition. She could hardly figure what he was angered by, what part of this could possibly be her fault or personal shortcoming.

She was about to find out.

"All that time," the Chieftain began, the very picture of calm.

Dameia waited.

"All that time, all that study, all those brilliant minds," the Chieftain's voice built a crescendo with each word, "and the best solution you could come up with was to 'enjoy the time we have left'?!" He snatched up his goblet, started to drink, thought better of it, and hurled it against the far wall. Pottery shards rained.

"Might I remind you that you are Tav's future ruler, Dameia," he continued now at a deadly calm. "The interests of this planet come before your own, the love of this planet comes before your own, the lives of this planet come before your own."

"I know," Dameia's voice came out high and small.

"I am not sure you do." The Chieftain sat back in his chair. "You should have been working more in concert with the Secondary Council. You should have questioned everything that I did. You, Dameia, should have been the one presenting alternative solutions for preserving life on our planet, despite what the scientists initially said about its sustainability. Not me. Instead, you have been flitting about a prison cell speaking solely and at great length to one particular prisoner under the guise of learning the secrets to this most recent human rebellion. And I would hazard a rather educated guess that you have none of that information—nor an adequate solution—either."

Dameia had no response. How could she? He was absolutely and irrevocably right. And there was nothing she could now do to rectify the situation.

"You disappoint me, Dameia." His pronouncement was quiet. Cold.

She winced. More than the anger, more than the accusations (which were unfortunately accurate), it was his disappointment that ached most. She had let her Chieftain down, but more than that, she had failed her subjects. Oh, they would never know, and her father would never implicate her failure when decreeing that work begin to move Tav underground.

But she would know.

She would always know.

There was nothing to say. Nothing to do except pledge to herself to right her course and set her own life on the backburner in favor of the lives of Tav. After all, she was their future Chieftain, and setting all personal life aside was what Chieftains did. She pressed her lips firmly as hot tears rolled down her cheeks, streaking them with evidence of her failure.

On a sigh, the Chieftain rose to his feet and strode toward the door. He didn't stop to look at his daughter, not to judge, not to pity, not to care. When his footsteps began to crunch on the shattered remnants of his goblet that littered the stone flooring by the door, he paused, hand on the knob.

"You should know," he began, not turning his face from the door, "I have begun clearing the prisons. There is too much refuse and long past time it was taken out. Now that the Secondary Council is dismissed, my next priority is the swift and decisive trials of the twelve human rebels. Court begins first thing tomorrow. While I cannot promise any particular outcome from the Courts, any of these rebels would be considered fools to hope for *my* explicit grace."

He turned the knob, dragged the door open on the protest of tight hinges.

"I expect to put them to death. Every last one."

The Chieftain left the room, vacuuming all hope along behind him.

The Weight of Stars and Suns
Dawn Christine Jonckowski

Dameia waited just long enough to be certain that her father was behind the doors of the Main Council chambers.

And then without thought or hope, she dropped to her knees and wept.

✧ ✧ ✧ ✧ ✧

Once again, Hyam was awoken in the dead of second cycle—as much as he could pretend it was the dead of an Earth night when weak sunlight still filtered through the ceiling—only this time, it wasn't the princess at his door. Not that he expressly expected her based on their last and supposedly final encounter, but disappointment still twinged through him when it was the Warden's mealy face that appeared at the bars.

"Get up, you worthless bag of bones," the Warden growled wetly.

"Is it time to leave for the ball already? And here I am not even dressed yet," Hyam drawled. He knew better. The residual ache in the bridge of his nose reminded him that he knew better. He was a human, and this Tavarian held more cards on Hyam's life than his intelligence probably warranted. But the firm press of prison dirt on the backs of Hyam's legs also reminded him. Reminded him of why he was here: He was a rebel.

Knowing better and doing the opposite was kind of his thing.

After all, look how it had worked out with the princess.

Not that he should think of her now. Or ever, really. But there it was. She was indelibly etched in his brain. And there was nothing he cared to do about it. Or rather, there was plenty he cared to do about it, but nothing that he would be allowed to do, nothing he would *actually* do.

For now it was enough to pledge never to scrub her from his mind.

Or his heart.

But that was another matter entirely. And not one he imagined the Warden would care much to hear about.

"Fancy duds won't help where you're going, rebel."

"You only say that because you haven't seen my dress," Hyam winked but remained firmly rooted in his recline on the floor. The Warden shoved a key into the door and for the first time in days, the metal grate to Hyam's cage ground open with the squealed protest of disuse, much like he imagined his knees would as soon as he was forced to his feet.

Which was exactly what happened next. The Warden grabbed for the front of Hyam's tunic and hauled the rebel to his feet. Hyam's knees did creak with protest, not that the Warden stopped to notice. He was too busy yanking the young man around and roping his wrists thickly behind his back to notice something as trivial as the sound of knee joints objecting.

"Now, I'm not really sure these ropes will go with my gown," Hyam continued pleasantly. "Do you have something in a blue?"

|| The Weight of Stars and Suns ||
Dawn Christine Jonckowski

The Warden growled low in his throat in response as he spun the prisoner back to face him. Pulled him in close so they were nearly nose to nose, so the rebel tasted his spittle as he spoke.

"Look here, rebel. I've had about enough of your tongue. So if you plan to keep it—which I imagine you might, given the fact that you're up for trial tomorrow and can use all the fancy words in defense that you can manage—I suggest you shut it down for a time and just listen for once in your worthless life."

Hyam credited himself greatly for not flinching as he was showered—quite literally—with the Warden's warning. The stench of his breath alone could have peeled back the prison walls. The wetness of his words just added insult to injury.

The Warden took his momentary silence as assent. "Good, then," he grumbled. "You're being transferred to the Court prison. All twelve of you worthless rebels are being tried in the morning. If you have any living left in you that you plan on doing, I suggest you remember your place in this world and stay in it. Might not get you out whole, but might stop you from getting out dead."

Hyam blinked. "Well, thank you for that surprisingly sincere warning, sir."

The Warden's eyes narrowed in response. "And there you go again with that mouth." He grunted out his displeasure before shoving Hyam forward out of the cell, then across the second threshold to the corridor.

Where the princess awaited.

Rebel and captor stopped short, both somewhat dumbfounded.

"Princess," the Warden gruffed, bowing his head and shoving Hyam down onto his knees.

"Warden," the princess acknowledged in return, her voice a strange lullaby in response to the Warden's snarled speech. She stepped forward to meet the pair. "I require a moment with your prisoner," she commanded.

"I'm sure you do," the Warden leered. The sharp look that passed between them was not lost on Hyam, nearly sliced the tips of his ears with its ferocity. Immediately, Hyam could feel the tension on his ropes release as the Warden stepped back. "You have five minutes." And he disappeared.

The princess dropped to her knees, right there in the prison dirt, right in front of Hyam. She brought soft, cool, lavender hands to his face and lifted it so his eyes met hers. The shine of regret beamed out at him.

Shock built upon shock.

"What are you doing here?" he finally managed.

"They are putting you to trial tomorrow," she started slowly.

"Yeah, I'd figured that one out for myself."

Her look sharpened. "Hyam."

Oh, his name on her lips.

"Say it again," he said softly.

"What?"

"My name. Not 'rebel' or 'prisoner' or 'scum,' or even 'human' like it's a dirty word."

"For the record, I've never called you 'scum,'" the princess replied, affronted. Hyam chuckled softly.

"No, you haven't," he agreed. And waited.

The Weight of Stars and Suns
Dawn Christine Jonckowski

She relented. "Hyam," she said again. His eyes slid shut and he smiled. "They're putting you on trial, but I have it on good authority that they don't intend for you to live." Her voice caught. Hyam's eyes opened.

"Well that certainly puts a damper on my plans, now, doesn't it?"

To her credit, the princess offered a laugh, however weak, before sobering again almost instantly. She leaned her forehead to his. "I don't think there is anything I can do to save you."

And there it was. Her kernel of love, his hopes for a new world, this budding . . . *thing* between them. All the new possibilities they now both wanted to explore, despite not yet admitting to each other. All of it toppling down under a system hell-bent on keeping them firmly in their predetermined places. A system ferociously adverse to change.

His hands bound, Hyam reached out to caress her with his words. "It is enough that you want to."

They heard the Warden's approaching footsteps, and were suddenly frozen with all the words they could not—would not—say.

"Dameia," the princess finally said. "My name is Dameia." She smiled sadly, rising to her feet. "In case you cared," she finished, echoing his own words.

"I do," Hyam replied. "I always have."

And for the second time in so many days, she was gone.

As the Warden marched his prisoner down to join the eleven others in the Court prison, Hyam reflected on his life. Since it was going to shortly come to an end, it seemed a good time to do so. By and large, he thought it had been a decent life for a human on Tav.

Wholly unremarkable until he joined the rebellion. Even more remarkable since he'd been captured.

All of that, all of his failed rebellion plans, all of the life he would never get to live, and Hyam could only come up with a single regret:

He had not kissed Dameia one last time.

ACT II
DARKER

6

What did one wear to a trial?

Hours before Hyam was to take the stand, hours even before most Tavarians would even consider it a semi-decent hour to be out of bed, Dameia stood in front of her closet fretting over vestments.

Which seemed ridiculous.

Her one true friend in the world was headed for certain death, and she was concerned about what shoes to wear to hear his guilty verdict.

But it wasn't really that, was it? Dameia stood unseeing before the rainbow of clothing not because of vanity, but because she was frozen into inaction. She had paid off the Warden before, which earned her those final precious minutes with Hyam, and in the end, what would it matter? His life would be snuffed out like so many humans before him without thought or care from the Tavarian Courts. After all, just order another human to climb aboard his assigned mate and they'd have another slave to fill Hyam's place in the ledgers soon enough.

The cold detachment of it all shivered the princess.

Hyam had been different. Where others sowed hatred with their rebellion, he brought easy camaraderie. He had not sought to reverse the roles to lord over Dameia while she groveled in the dirt. Instead, he aimed to simply be an equal. To be valued for who he was, regardless of the color of his skin.

Dameia had knelt in the dirt of her own accord. She had valued him as equal.

By the end.

And wasn't this indeed the end.

She tucked the fragile bloom of his memory—his smile, his wry wit, his skin, his lips—in a deep and secret pocket of her heart, and finally covered it with standard ceremonial garb.

But before she left her dressing room, Dameia reached into her jewelry box for one last thing, a fraying ribbon that she wound and tied around her right arm just above the elbow. As her agitated hands finally fell silent and slack at her sides, the sleeves of the cream-colored tunic dropped down to her wrists and covered the ribbon.

It was bright and blood red.

The traditional Tavarian color of mourning.

☼ ☼ ☼ ☼ ☼

Her first glimpse of Hyam was him as a link in the chain of twelve humans being brought from the Court prison into the Court proper. They marched down the paved open air corridor with steps minced by heavy shackles. The suns striped their faces as they passed the many columns bracing the roof above the walkway. Twelve souls were yanked through the open doors to the high-ceilinged Courtroom; who knew how many would come back out.

Any.

None.

Dameia's breath caught. She tried to turn it into a convincing cough for those milling around her. Reached up to toy with the silken red ribbon twined under her sleeve.

A blink and a breath, and the next glimpse was full of his steady eyes holding hers as the heavy carved doors to the Courtroom swung shut, severing their connection and holding the rebels hostage in silence until the Tavarians outside the doors sorted themselves rabble from justice and the guards could reopen the doors and finally allow the room to fill with those other than the convicted.

For her part, Dameia stood watch over the crowd, occasionally offering a nod or a noncommittal noise in response to a question about the day's goings-on. To the casual observer, she appeared blasé at best, as if formality was the only thread that tugged her in.

But she knew better. Now, anyway.

Tav's courts were full of observers who were anything but casual.

A short trumpet blast announcing the Chieftain's arrival briefly interrupted the din surrounding the Courtroom. Dameia's father presented in full regalia: formal tunic, the creamed sash of royalty cutting across his chest while bright metal bands circled wrists and forehead. Heavy chains connected shoulder to shoulder, a neat counterbalance to the heavy indigo cape that rippled down to his calves. She had never once attended a trial before this day, but somehow she knew this show wasn't standard fare, wasn't to intimidate the rebels.

It was for her.

She lifted her chin higher.

The Courtroom doors opened, and the violet masses poured in.

The prisoners were arranged in two straight rows, chained wrist and ankle to stout metal bars in front of them. Hyam stood second from the left in the front, shoulders square, head up, eyes forward and burning. From her assigned seat in the royal box, Dameia could see a single ear or the muscled line of his shoulder, sometimes his full profile if the rebel next to him shifted just so.

Her heart was a useless mess in the cage of her chest.

Then everyone was rising to their feet as the Chieftain and the Court—made up primarily of members of the Council—paraded down the center aisle to take their places. One split off from the Court, his robe a deep indigo and almost as wrinkled as his face, and ascended to the podium at the center.

The Judge.

With three quick raps of his gavel, the room came to instant order.

"Slaves," the Judge began in a strong voice that belied his aged frame. "You are brought before this court today and charged with conspiring against the Tavarian government to overthrow the rule and gain power for yourselves. Do you deny this?"

The rebels stood tall, proud, and silent as precious time slipped by.

|| The Weight of Stars and Suns ||
Dawn Christine Jonckowski

"Very well," grunted the Judge. "Let it be known that your consent of these charges is indicated by your silence." He shuffled through several papers, scanning what evidence had been found. Dameia wondered how much of it hadn't been found so much as created.

"You should know," the Judge continued, pausing to meet the gaze of each rebel in turn, "that the Chieftain has advised that the penalty for your crimes be death by beheading. A penalty, I imagine, that will put quite the kink in your plans," he added with mocking amusement. "However. As per the rules of this Court, I will entertain other recommendations from the Council before making my final decision."

The Judge turned to the collection of Council members. "*Zakar?*"

Silence. Cursed silence.

And then.

One single hand slid up.

Dameia slowly released the breath she didn't know she'd been holding. There could still be hope.

Gesturing toward the owner of the hand, the Judge said, "The Court recognizes Councilman . . . I'm sorry, who are you?"

"Arganon, sir."

Dameia gasped as the scientist who had headed the Secondary Council rose to his feet and emerged above the crowd of Council members. She wasn't the only one flummoxed at his sudden appearance on the Council.

"Who?" the Judge repeated, confusion increasing the wrinkles of his forehead.

Arganon smiled indulgently. "Forgive me, sir. Until yesterday afternoon, I was a member of the Secondary Council formed by the Chieftain to investigate the issue of Tav's dying suns. As our commitment came to a close, the Chieftain invited me to remain in the Capitol as a member of the Council to help plan and prepare the planet for the outcomes we predicted based on our study. A thousand apologies if I inadvertently trample on some protocol. This is my first event as a Council member; sir, I'm even at this moment wearing borrowed robes so that I may participate today."

The Judge swung his gaze over to the Chieftain, whose brief nod gave assent to everything Arganon had said. "Very well," the Judge sighed. "Let us hear what sentence you would determine for this refuse."

"My Chieftain. Princess Dameia. Judge. Esteemed members of the Council. I come before you today in full knowledge of the price these slaves ought to pay for their actions, but also as a representative of a dying planet. Those of us in this room are privy to the findings of the Secondary Council as well as the preparedness plan we are even now developing in the Council with the Chieftain's wise guidance.

"If we are to, in the space of up to two generations, be a fully functioning underground species able to survive the solar holocaust that surely comes our way, then I believe we must have every available hand at this project. Rebel or no."

The room began to heat with mutters and suggestions on the legitimacy of Arganon's birth.

"No."

| | The Weight of Stars and Suns | |
Dawn Christine Jonckowski

The Chieftain's single word rang sharp and cut through the rising noise, breaking it into silence. Dameia watched the muscles in his jaw work. Yes, his subjects saw him as wise and benevolent, but that did not mean that he was not above demanding his way.

Or sulking when he did not get it.

And the Chieftain not getting his way?

Well that was certainly rare.

Those around him tended to prefer living with their heads still attached.

Arganon raised his hands in supplication. "My Chieftain, surely I understand the traditional punishment for these crimes, and on any day would argue exactly as you have: for their deaths. But still I maintain that ending these twelve lives denies us twenty-four hands that could be laboring toward Tav's subterranean glory.

"I propose to the Court that we sentence these twelve men to hard labor for the remainder of their days, or until such time as they are no longer needed to perform these duties, at which point they shall be executed. They will reside in a secluded sector of the human colony and allowed no interaction save for themselves and the foremen who work them. If they do not perfectly conform to the rules set out for them, their lives will be forfeit. If they become too ill, too injured, or too old to continue their work, their lives will be forfeit. If they commit another infraction, their lives are forfeit.

"Either way, Sire," Arganon's gaze locked with the Chieftain's. "Tav benefits from their labor, while you still get what you desire: death in exchange for their crimes. Perhaps just not along the specific timeline you imagined."

Time stopped, Dameia's heart stopped, everything stopped while the whole of the Court held eyes on the Chieftain and awaited his response. It made sense, of course. Work them until the end of their usefulness. Then—and only then—kill them. Tav was, after all, living now on borrowed time. All hands, even rebel ones, would be needed.

Dameia allowed hope.

The Chieftain's hard stare released muscle by muscle. It was all the consent the Judge needed. His gavel cracked hard across the desk.

"So let it be written: Rebels, you are found guilty of high treason via conspiracy to overthrow the Tavarian government. You are hereby sentenced to hard labor until the end of your days, be that due to illness, injury, infraction, or age. You are additionally to be removed from the Colony proper and placed in seclusion under controlled guard. This sentence sustains no terms for renegotiation based on behavior or tenure and will be carried out unto completion for every individual thusly charged.

"Warden, please remove the prisoners to the Court prison until the segregated living arrangements are completed. We will set a team of slaves from construction aside to complete this within two days. Once the rebels are rehoused, the Council will send the foremen to oversee their labor duties."

As soon as the proceedings had begun, they were over. Dameia wobbled between relief and tears. Hyam would live . . . for now. But at what cost? A back broken by work, a spirit crushed by seclusion, a wit silenced by time. What life was that?

Perhaps he would have been better off dead.

The Weight of Stars and Suns
Dawn Christine Jonckowski

As if her thoughts had telegraphed directly to him, Hyam managed to turn his head imperceptibly so and meet her gaze. Once he had it, he nodded his head ever so slightly. And she knew.

He did not intend to stay imprisoned forever.

And he did not intend to escape via death.

If Hyam planned to live, Dameia would help him do it.

His chains jangled loudly through the bars and the dozen rebels were unceremoniously marched away surrounded by a retinue of prison guards.

Once the human sideshow was gone, the Tavarians lost interest and began filtering out as well. Part protocol and mostly emotion rooted Dameia to her place until a voice at her ear made her jump.

"Well at least he's not dead. Yet."

It was the Warden. She did not turn to look at him, but felt his slimy knowing smirk. Dameia fought for calm, dug for aloofness.

"And as long as he stays that way, our agreement stands and you will receive the scores we agreed upon," she murmured just loud enough for his ears. She felt the air between them contract as he leaned in closer and she fought the urge to cringe, to run, to turn and fight. All of the above.

"You wouldn't be the first, you know." His half-whisper huffed on her ear, sent shivers all the way down one leg.

"The first what?"

"To take a human lover." She heard his lips pull into a wet salacious leer. "We're not so different, humans and Tavarians, down there."

At that, she did turn on him, slowly and with deliberate deadly calm. "You would do well to keep a still tongue in your head, Warden. To suggest such things is near treason, and Tavarians have hung for less."

His eyes narrowed into a suggestive grin. "You would know that, too, now, wouldn't you? Tell me, how does it feel to call for the execution of one of your own citizens while paying to keep a slave alive?"

Dameia's fists clenched repeatedly at her sides. There was nothing to say. He spoke truth. Clear, cutting, treacherous truth. He knew it, too. The Warden's face slid into a slow, slick smile.

"Don't worry, you've paid me well to keep your secrets, Princess, and I'll keep them locked up as tight as your rebel. You just let me know when you decide you want the key. Give him a little taste of Tavarian royalty, eh?"

If they hadn't still been in the midst of a crowd, if her father wasn't still keeping a rather obtrusive eye on his daughter, if the Council wasn't still regarding her with wary uncertainty of her preparedness to be the next Chieftain. If, if, if . . .

. . . she would have cracked him a good one, right across that open-mouth saliva-stringed grin.

Instead, much as it pained her, she let both the Warden and his sneer stand there untouched until he finally broke the standoff by sinking into a feigned respectful but mostly mocking bow. "*Neqeba*," he offered, then backed out of her presence and exited the Court.

The princess remained, eyes shut, mind focused on mastering her breathing and finding her calm. She felt eyes on her. Knew that if her father suspected of her friendship with Hyam, other

The Weight of Stars and Suns
Dawn Christine Jonckowski

Council members couldn't be too far behind in concluding the same based on palace scuttlebutt. The odds had been stacked against her from the beginning, and if she did not control rumors, they would lean even farther from her favor.

The wisest thing she could do—for both of them—was to forget Hyam.

She knew that she would continue to be a fool.

✧ ✧ ✧ ✧ ✧

A Royal Address from the Chieftain

Loyal Citizens:

For the past many days, we have lived under the rotating light of thirty-three out of our traditional thirty-six suns. The darkened suns have caused great concern for you, as well as for myself and the other officials of our esteemed government.

In order to address this deep concern, I created—under the direction of Princess Dameia—a Secondary Council of the greatest scientific minds across the entire planet. This Secondary Council has studied the extinguished suns, presented their findings, and together we have devised the best way to move our great planet forward.

Over the course of the next several years, we may experience additional burnout of our suns. Do not be afraid. The Secondary Council is certain that the suns will not extinguish at a rapid rate, providing us with ample time to update planting cycles and adapt our way of life to be closer to that of a single-sunned planet. We will also experience global cooling. Additional information on predicted future weather patterns and how you can prepare yourselves and your families will be forthcoming.

The Secondary Council also believes there could be a possibility of a solar flare from several of our suns. These flares will be enough to damage life on the surface of Tav. Therefore, as a precautionary measure, over the next several decades you will see construction of secondary cities underneath our existing surface structures. As these underground cities mature and become habitable, we will further instruct you on how quarters will be assigned and how to proceed with your relocation in preparation for these possible solar flares.

Above all, citizens, I urge you not to panic. Each cycle on Tav continues to burn brightly. I hold your souls in highest estate and will not rest until I am certain that you will be protected from every possible future natural disaster. Take comfort in the foresight and charity of your government. You will not be forsaken.

As we have always done, Tav endures.

☼ ☼ ☼ ☼ ☼

The royal announcement was met with the expected level of pandemonium. It wasn't so much the science of the extinguishing suns that worried them as it was the change. Global cooling? Weather patterns? Updated planting cycles?

Not to mention the possibility of underground living. How would a race so used to a plethora of suns manage to survive underground in actual darkness? How and when would these living arrangements be assigned?

The Weight of Stars and Suns
Dawn Christine Jonckowski

And what of the humans? Tav had reached a point where it could not survive without its slaves, and yet not a single Tavarian wanted a human actually living with them. The chattel must remain outside. They hoped for the same segregated setup below as they had above.

Overwhelmingly, what they failed to grasp was the gravity of the situation. Mainly because the Chieftain—ever the politician—had insisted on downplaying the coming apocalypse so as to minimize panic. He loved his citizens. Of course he did not want to subject them to the doom of the planet's surface. But he understood that while individuals could be smart, the masses were traditionally stupid and the smallest comment could bloom into the largest terror. If the Tavarians truly understood the seriousness of the natural disaster facing their planet, he would lose every modicum of control over them. Riots in the cities, protests on the Capitol steps, or worse: begging the humans for information on the space vehicle that brought them here in hopes of using it to take the Tavarians away from their gasping planet.

Not that the humans now had any passing knowledge of how that ship worked or where the remains even lived.

But still.

Order above all.

So the Chieftain lied.

Although he preferred to think of it instead as a creative interpretation of the truth for the protection of his citizens. Certainly his daughter and several Councilmen had disagreed with him, and vehemently. Councilmen who were older than the Chieftain, whose

The Weight of Stars and Suns
Dawn Christine Jonckowski

limbs bore significantly more tattoos chronicling far greater military achievements than the Chieftain might hope for in his own lifetime.

And yet.

He was the Chieftain. Not them.

His word became law.

And would eventually doom them all.

✧ ✧ ✧ ✧ ✧

Hyam had never crossed the veranda outside the palace ballroom. If he had, he certainly never would have stopped in his traversing to ruminate on the weight of each slab of paving stone that created the oversized terrace. He would have perhaps marveled at its size, been surprised to learn that once Tavarians filled it in their formalwear, the skirts of the ladies alone—depending on the styles at the time—could make the vast space suddenly incommodious.

But never, never would he have thought about the weight of the stones.

Now, he thought about them every first cycle.

And cursed them every second.

The twelve rebels' first task was to dig up the veranda and then begin digging the entrance to what would eventually be the underground version of the Chieftain's complex.

Every first cycle of the day, he swung a heavy hammer to break up the stone, often needing dozens of the weighted hits to make the first crack. Once the stone began to break into manageable enough pieces, he filled a basket and then toted the load to a hastily

The Weight of Stars and Suns
Dawn Christine Jonckowski

constructed storage quarry from which they would eventually reuse the stones in the underground complex.

Swing, crack, gather, tote.

Swing, crack, gather, tote.

Swing, crack, gather, tote.

This rhythm now drove his days, with only the alternate crack of a whip to interrupt. Move too slowly, whip crack, sting. Break the stone into too-small pieces, whip crack, sting. Make a sound or say a word, whip crack, sting. Hyam's throat felt full of the dust of disuse. He wasn't sure anything would come out even if he tried to speak.

It had been ten days of this labor life so far. Already a few whispers around the solitary bunk at second cycle hinted that death would have been kinder.

Hyam lay on his hard bunk and silently disagreed.

As long as he was alive, there was hope.

Although, admittedly, right now swinging his hammer and toting heavy rough stone with torn up hands under the heat of the multiple suns, that hope was a little more difficult to come by.

That's when he saw her.

Dameia walked with three older Tavarian *zakar* along the covered walkway that bordered the veranda and served as one of many spokes connecting the various wings of the Chieftain's complex. No longer wearing the drab colors of the short military dress she had favored any time she visited the prison, now she strode along in more traditional royal garb of a light and spotless cream. Not a thing that could have withstood the dirt of his cell floor, that was certain. Her hair no longer flowed in loose curls over her freckled shoulders, but spiraled instead atop her head in intricate braids that roped a single metal circlet to her brow.

She didn't glance away from her companions, not even once to let her eyes land briefly on Hyam. And why should she? When the Judge had given sentence, he caught her attention and nodded ever so slightly. With that nod, he conveyed his acceptance. Whether the Court had ordered his immediate death or this long drawn-out process of killing his spirit by degrees each day, he would endure. He released her of any responsibility she felt toward him. He would not be what held her back from becoming the great Chieftain she was destined to be. He would accept the small part he had played to inspire her, then he would work and die in silence and not think of her again.

Only he wasn't doing so well with the not thinking about her part.

Instead, he thought of her every cycle of every day. When he closed his eyes exhausted at the end of a long first cycle, it was her soft smile that he saw on the backs of his eyelids. When he dreamed, it was her lips he felt. When he awoke, she was his first thought. When he labored, she was his reason.

Definitely not doing well with not thinking about her.

She, on the other hand, appeared to be flourishing just fine without him. Which Hyam accepted, or at least he told himself that he did. To look at her in her royal element, every inch the princess, and then to look at himself: barefoot and bare-chested in breeches with a grimy strip of cloth tied around his forehead to keep the sweat from stinging his eyes, every inch of exposed skin—and even every inch unexposed—streaked with dirt. He looked less and less human

The Weight of Stars and Suns
Dawn Christine Jonckowski

every day, feeling more like the animal that Tavarians dubbed humanity to be than an actual person.

No, he had played his brief part in her life.

Now it was time for her to press on and move forward without him.

He would accept this.

And maybe tonight he would finally, finally stop dreaming of her.

Swing, crack, gather, tote.

Repeat.

✧ ✧ ✧ ✧ ✧

Except . . . she *had* noticed.

In fact, after avoiding the construction site for ten days, Dameia could stand it no longer and purposefully directed her meandering conversation with Arganon and two other advisors to wander down the walkway that bordered closest to where the rebels were working. As they passed the dozen slaves swinging their hammers under the relentless heat of the suns, it appeared to all—even her ambling companions—that she gave no particular notice to the noise and goings-on of the construction.

But as she stared hard at Arganon, giving all pretense of attempting to focus on his words over the noise of breaking stone, in the periphery of her vision stood Hyam. The corded muscles of his arms bunched and stretched as he swung his hammer, his chest shone slick with sweat.

He looked at her.

She knew he did.

But to return his gaze was a treachery she could not give in to at that moment, despite the burn of every muscle in the hollow of her chest. She crossed her arms across her torso to hide the fact that her fingers itched and flexed to reach out and touch the rebel slave.

Princess Dameia walked on.

Away from the rocks, away from the dirt, away from the rebel, away from the treason it was to feel anything but contempt for him.

✿ ✿ ✿ ✿ ✿

She passed him the next day.

And the next.

And the next.

And the next one after that.

And that second cycle, she came for him.

✿ ✿ ✿ ✿ ✿

So long as the rebels made no noise, the compound guards didn't care if they slept or not. The rebels could mill about the small grounds all second cycle for all the guards cared. After all, if a rebel keeled over from exhaustion, he signed his death certificate with his fall. One less rebel to worry about.

The Weight of Stars and Suns
Dawn Christine Jonckowski

Hyam did his best to sleep whenever he could. A sleeping Hyam was a silent Hyam, and a silent Hyam could give the guards no reason to whip him. He already had great history of digging graves with his tongue.

But the wee hours of this particular second cycle found Hyam at the compound well. "Well" was a generous term, really, for the trickle of water that came out of a slim pipe in the thick wall that separated the rebel prisoners' compound from the rest of the colony. The prisoners themselves had used their newfound construction skills to take smaller rocks from around the compound and floor a basin at the foot of the wall to collect the water for drinking and the occasional attempt at bathing.

For himself, Hyam had awoken with palms throbbing. Dirt had worked its way indelibly into the cuts in his hands and several were raised and angry red from the excess irritation. Hyam rinsed and scrubbed his hands as best he could with a cup of water and was wrapping them in damp strips of cloth torn from his bedsheet in an attempt to draw some of the heat out when the alarm sounded.

The prisoners were already conditioned to that sound. Wherever they were in the compound, whatever they were doing, it was all dropped as they scrambled to assemble in two straight lines in the dirt courtyard in front of their barracks. The alarm served as their daily wake-up call, but this was a particularly odd hour of the second cycle to assemble for that. Hyam hastily tied off the strips around his palms and sprinted to join the assembly.

An inspection.

All twelve stood ramrod straight despite the exhaustion that read clearly in their eyes. The Tavarian guards who paced along their line-up had no care to look humans in the eye, however, especially not these particular humans, and so while their exhaustion was not noted, it was also not mocked. When one already had nothing, small blessings were certainly inventoried.

Then the heavy wood gate opened on a dismal creak and in walked the Tavarian General.

Followed by the Chieftain.

Followed by a handful of Councilmen.

Followed by the princess.

Hyam drew himself up a little taller, kept his eyes trained forward. He would not look at her. Not in this crowd. Not under these conditions. And not because of pride, either (though of course he would have preferred she see him in nearly any state but this), but rather a healthy sense of self-preservation. For them both.

The Tavarian procession threaded through the two lines of prisoners. Hyam felt Ithai stiffen next to him as the entourage stopped to study the young rebel. The General looked at posture. The Chieftain merely glared at their individual existence. No doubt he had hoped that at least one or two of them would have misstepped enough by now to warrant execution, and no doubt he had hoped that Hyam would be counted among those.

The handful of Councilmen, at least, seemed to have some care for the individuals. A younger *zakar*—not a Councilman, as evidenced by the tattoos that wrapped his wrists, but a physician— took his time to examine each prisoner as best he could and relay some notes to his neighboring Councilmen. After all, a dead human was a non-working human, and if this Council intended to survive the solar holocaust by hiding underground, they needed as much labor as possible to build the subsurface cities. For his part, Hyam would receive some salve to clear up the budding infections in his hands.

Small blessings.

At the end of the line was the princess. Who stood largely silent, observing each prisoner equally as she waited for the line to move on.

And then the line halted, leaving her facing Hyam.

Without breaking frame, he inhaled and let her clean, fresh scent clear some of the prison dirt from his sinuses.

Small blessings.

"How are you?" she murmured through lips that barely moved.

Hyam continued to stare straight ahead, pretending that her proximity did nothing to him, pretending that he wasn't fighting everything inside of him just to keep his breathing at an even tempo.

"I'm fine. Considering."

She fought a smirk at his blithe response, turned her head to feign disinterest as she studied the line of Councilmen ahead of her. "You're a terrible liar, Hyam," she said, amusement coloring her quiet words despite the stately turn of her head. "I'm going to find a way to get you out."

Hyam let her defiant proclamation wash pleasure over him, but he had to refute. "You can't, Dameia. If I escape, I die. If they find you helped me, *you* die. My death? I can handle. Yours? No. So don't ask me."

At this, the princess turned her head back ever so slowly and arched a single brow. "Then I'll put you back when we're done."

"Done?"

"Hyam, I can't do this without you."

She filled his gaze. She filled his senses.

She filled his heart.

It was already treason to befriend her; it would be worse to love her.

"Yes, you can," he said softly. "Besides, if we're not careful, you'll have to."

The Councilmen began to move on. It would be too obvious for Dameia to remain in front of him much longer. He wanted her to move as much as he wanted her to stay.

An impasse.

From the beginning, they were doomed to always be at an impasse.

"Then we'll be careful," she promised quietly. "Wait for me, Hyam." And she walked on.

Wait for her. He would wait for her. He'd been waiting for her, ever since that first encounter in the prison cell not long after his capture. Perhaps even before that. Hyam had been waiting. For her.

Even if he hadn't known it.

He might be her doom; she would certainly be his.

But he would wait for her. He really didn't have much other choice.

With a deep breath, Hyam re-squared his shoulders and raised his chin a notch. Watched out of the corner of his eye as the Tavarian parade finished the first row of prisoners. Sensed them as they passed slowly, slowly along the line behind him. Felt the barest brush of soft fingers against the hands he had clasped behind his back. Translated her promise to return for him.

Knew the emptiness as soon as the retinue exited the compound.

At the bark of the guards, the rebels marched silently back to the barracks and climbed wearily into hard bunks.

"Hyam," Ithai whisper-shouted from the bunk above.

"What?"

"Was the princess *talking* to you?"

Hyam's heart stopped. "No."

"Eh, I heard some murmurs too, Hyam. Don't lie." Oren rolled onto his shoulder to face Hyam.

"She didn't say anything," Hyam insisted. These men were his friends, most of them close enough to be brothers. They were comrades. All they wanted was the same thing he did: equal rights for humans. He'd had no secrets from them for the entirety of his life.

Until now, that is.

It was for their own safety, he told himself.

"Shut it, all of you, and get some sleep," Yair grouched from the far corner of the room. "He said she didn't say a thing, so she didn't say a thing. Besides, what would the likes of her have to say to a dirty rebel like him?" The older man yanked his threadbare sheet up and wadded it under his head as a pillow. "Now sleep. They'll sound that alarm sooner than you'll like in the morning, and if you want the smallest chance of getting out, you'll need to be alive to do it."

"Do you think we'll ever get out, Hyam?" Ithai asked quietly. Hyam could hear his friend's heartbreak, as much as Ithai tried to hide that tender heart under thick layers of bravado. He thought of

Dameia. If she was going to get him out, he was going to make sure that she got them *all* out. He might keep secrets from them, but he would not abandon them to die alone while he lived.

    "I don't know for certain, Ithai, but we're alive. And while we're alive, there is still hope."

7

Meditation was worthless.

That's what Dameia had determined.

She didn't consider herself religious by Tavarian standards. Shortly after her mother's death, the tiny princess had decided that the multitude of gods who supposedly held the good of the Tavarian race in the palms of their many hands were essentially useless. If they would have nothing to do with saving her mother despite the loud and relentless prayers offered by both royal family and citizens, then she would have nothing more to do with them.

And that was that.

Except.

Except she was royalty. Her whole life was ultimately designed to be a paragon example to her citizens. Which meant pantomiming religion to suit the masses and appease her father (who, by the way, had stopped believing in the gods himself at a rather young age).

Ergo, the morning found Dameia sitting cross-legged in the Meditation Garden, hands on her knees, eyes shut, feigning meditation but mostly fighting sleep. Once in a great while, simply having the time set aside to focus and ruminate uninterrupted had allowed her to solve a problem or make an important decision, and for that reason, she generally didn't mind this portion of her religious rigmarole. It was also entirely possible that she had learned how to maintain her meditative posture while napping, but that was a secret she would never tell. She could only hope that today's mindfulness would present some sort of miraculous solution for getting Hyam.

She should be so lucky.

Her first—and only—religious mentor had suggested that during meditation, she picture her problem as a tangled ball of string, and imagine slowly unthreading the ball motion by motion, pull by pull, until it was a single long line of unknotted thread.

So Dameia had pulled on every string. Ends, beginnings, middles; any part she found, she tugged. But that morning's meditation had done nothing to unwind the mess. If anything, it was a further frayed knot simply snugged tighter by her mental ministrations.

Meditation was worthless.

But appearances, those were everything.

The princess picked up the small mallet and rang the singing bowl to signify the end of her meditation period. She would have rather thrown the bowl against the stone wall that bordered the garden. It wouldn't have solved her problems, though she liked to think the aggression would help a little. Her father certainly seemed to be practicing the aerialization of objects as of late. But, appearances. So she maintained her calm and smiled beatifically while the temple attendant floated silently along the circling gravel walkway. The attendant—no doubt practicing her best version of piety in hopes of one day becoming a priestess—bowed her shorn head as she performed the cold tea service and then retreated to leave the princess with her supposedly now-zen thoughts.

She sipped the tea.

That's when she heard the voices.

Not the kind most hoped to hear post-meditation whilst sipping the cold tea. *Real* voices. Real voices of guards who lacked either knowledge or respect for the fact that their conversation was occurring right outside of sacred temple walls where silence—or at least *sotto voce*—should have been maintained. Dameia was just salty enough over her unproductive false meditation to consider vaulting up the wall to give them what small piece of her mind was untangled. Her feet were halfway under her already.

Until she heard what they were saying.

"You know, when I signed up to help guard those rebels, I thought I might finally be in for a bit of fun," the first voice huffed.

"Fun?" his companion scoffed. "Since when was second cycle guard duty ever 'fun?'"

"Well, they're rebels. I figured they'd have some spice to them. Some fights, some plotting, some escape attempts, *something*. What with how keen the Chieftain is for them to die, I thought we'd have had at least three executions by now. Except . . . these rebels? They don't *do* anything! Least not outside of what they're supposed to. What kind of rebels are they, anyway?

"And that's not even the richest part," the guard maintained, a clear eye-roll in his voice. Their feet crunched to a stop on the gravel path. Dameia breathed silently and slowly, straining to hear every word, every movement.

"Riddle this, then," he continued. "Did you know that the bars surrounding them aren't all standard?"

"What do you mean?"

The guard's voice dropped a level. The gravel shifted as if he were pausing to look left, right, behind to ensure no one else retrieved his gossip. Dameia leaned in, an unbeknownst mirror to the guard's companion on the other side of the wall.

"I mean that there's a gap in the bars wide enough for a man to fit through. And it was made that way on purpose. All the guards know about it."

"Come off it, no one would do that," his companion chuffed.

"Truth of the gods, it is," swore the guard. "I think the Chieftain wants them to escape so he can justify killing them. He has a powerful need to see this lot dead, though the 'why' is beyond me, what with all the underground buildings and all."

"Eh, you really think we're going to have to live underground?"

"Pfft, how should I know? Besides, they're saying it's a time off anyhow. When it happens—if it even happens—I plan to have been a pile of bones for a great while. It's not going to change anything for us, so I say why waste a good day wondering."

The Weight of Stars and Suns
Dawn Christine Jonckowski

"That's the truth of it. Say, how long til you're on duty again? Can I tempt you with an hour or so at the brewery for some orangetail beer?"

"That slop? Eh, fine, but you're buying . . ." The gravel gave percussion to their unregimented steps past the Meditation Garden and on to the center of the Capitol Plex. Whereas on the other side of the wall, Dameia's tangled thoughts knotted further over this new revelation.

There was a clear escape route from the rebels' compound. It might be heavily guarded on the outside so that the instant a rebel tried to take advantage of the false freedom, they fell under fire. Or perhaps that false freedom went even further, and they would be allowed to make a more complete escape, only hunted once it was finally discovered that they were missing, giving the Chieftain excuse to execute additional rebels and any other human found to be aiding and abetting the escapee.

There was no denying it. The Chieftain was brilliant. Cold, calculating, damning, and brilliant.

She would just have to be smarter.

Tossing back the rest of her cold tea (so as not to offend the temple attendant who served it to her; after all, appearances), Dameia bounded to her feet. While she had a lot yet to learn about this gap in the gating, she was absolutely sure about two things:

Her father really, *really* wanted the rebels dead.

And she was going to get Hyam out.

It seemed that meditation wasn't quite so worthless after all.

The Weight of Stars and Suns
Dawn Christine Jonckowski

✧ ✧ ✧ ✧ ✧

Four days straight, the princess passed by the construction site.

Each of those four days, Hyam watched out of his periphery for her to leave something, anything. A clue: a head shake, a nod, a note, anything. And for four days, nothing.

Hyam was a man of action. This relentless inaction was starting to itch somewhere deep in his chest, a pent-up quake whose aftershocks twitched his muscles deep into the second cycle.

Heaven help him if this persisted a fifth day.

Which, of course, it did. Five days and nothing.

So far, she hadn't even passed the site.

Hyam channeled his energy into hammering the rock. Relentless strikes on an equally relentless stone. It too mocked him. Reaching deep, he pulled on his aggression, summoned the rage against all he faced: the captivity, the waiting, the utter inability to *do* anything. And with a guttural cry, he brought his hammer down on the rock with the force of his impotence.

The rock shattered.

The hammer shattered.

Hyam's emotions nearly shattered. Almost, but not quite. He stood with a death grip on the wooden handle, staring unseeing at the crumbles of hammerhead that remained, willing himself to breathe—in, out, in, out—until he could gather his calm again.

"Hyam, you okay?" Ithai said quietly out of the side of his mouth as he passed, an overlarge load of rock on his narrow

The Weight of Stars and Suns
Dawn Christine Jonckowski

shoulders. Hyam responded with a terse nod, silently begging Ithai to keep walking lest he draw the attention of a guard. The Chieftain wanted them all dead, Hyam most of all. He wasn't about to give the Chieftain reason to act on that desire. Not if he could help it, anyway.

Ithai walked on.

But a guard approached in his wake.

"What's this, rebel? Breaking the tools we give you to work with?"

Hyam added steel to his spine, forced himself to stand straight and look the guard in the eye. "Apologies, sir. The stone would not relent, and I must have struck an odd corner with the hammer. It was not intentional." The fact that he groveled gnawed at Hyam. But for the greater good of staying alive, he would have gladly given the guard a demonstration of what he would have preferred to do with the hammer. Which would not be practiced in such a way that the guard would be conscious to see the results.

The guard snatched the handle of the ruined hammer from Hyam's grip. Examined it end over end. Grunted. Tossed it back at Hyam, lifting his eyebrows in surprise at the rebel's quick reflexes. "You'll need to pay for that, rebel. What you lack in scores, we'll take from your flesh. Unless you have the currency, you'll spend the second cycle on the pole forgoing both food and water."

Hyam's eyes slid shut in frustrated defeat. Everyone knew that humans were forbidden to carry a balance of scores. The mockery of the guard's comments stung deeper than the humiliation of the punishment. And the pole was nothing to laugh at itself.

"Well. Since I don't see you reaching for coin, rebel, then flesh it is." He grabbed Hyam by the arm, purple fingers digging between muscles in a firm grip designed to injure if a prisoner tried to wrench away. "Come on, then. Let the others finish for the cycle and return to see what similar disrespect could earn them."

Hyam was dragged off the construction site.

Shortly after, a royal procession passed the site for a progress report.

Only Ithai noticed the princess' frantic searching gaze as she counted the rebels and only came up with eleven.

✧ ✧ ✧ ✧ ✧

Eleven. There had only been eleven.

And she hadn't seen Hyam.

Tucked into a corner of a corridor where her heart was least likely to echo its pounding beat, Dameia forced herself to find calm. He could have just been out of sight range. Perhaps that moment was his turn at the trench latrines. Maybe she had miscounted. Except she knew she hadn't. She had numbered them all. Twice.

Just because Hyam wasn't in that number didn't mean he was dead.

She hoped.

She hoped hard.

She hoped until it was on the brink of a prayer to the gods she had discounted long ago.

And then she made herself breathe. Brushed hands down her rumpled tunic to smooth away the evidence made by worried fists. No doubt that her father would glee over Hyam's death at dinner if it had indeed occurred. After a few deep breaths and then more, Dameia stepped out and continued down the corridor to meet the Chieftain for the evening meal.

Unless an execution had indeed occurred, which would undoubtedly lift her father's spirits, the meal would pass again in cold, polite silence. Dameia was at a loss. She had thrown herself headlong into the underground accommodations project, meeting daily with Arganon and the Capitol's best engineers to develop plans for the city that would live entirely under the streets of the Capitol Plex. She had begun to regularly attend Council meetings, even going so far as to offer constructive and actionable feedback that had more than once been voted into practice by all members, including the Chieftain.

And yet his chill remained.

Dameia entered the dining room and sat at her usual place, waiting on edge for her father to arrive.

The doors swung open and the Chieftain strode in.

Dameia's heart pounded to a halt: There were blood spatters on the hem of his tunic.

And he was smiling.

"Daughter," he greeted her pleasantly.

Dameia inclined her head. Dug deep to find words and coax them past the stutter-stop of her throat. She hated to ask. Had to know. "Father. I take it your day treated you well."

The Chieftain sat with a loud and contented sigh, reclining briefly before sitting forward and lustily digging into the platter of glazed wild grouse. "Ah, a near perfect day. As you witnessed, we are making progress in the Council with our taxation program. Soon our slaves will breed enough that we may offer humans to the other provinces around the planet, which will also bring revenue to the Capitol. It was such a productive cycle that I was able to spend some overdue time in the combat ring with our General." Here he paused to wash down the grouse with fizzed bloodwine. "Bastard nearly beat me, but at the final moment, I prevailed. Even drew blood from the old beast!" The Chieftain laughed—how long had it been since his daughter had heard that sound?—and gestured down at the spatters painting his hem.

    The Chieftain laughed and Dameia nearly sagged against her chair in relief, allowing her face to break into a wide smile.

    There hadn't been an execution after all.

    So then where was Hyam?

    The meal finally dwindled to bones and scraps. Just as Dameia was about to excuse herself, the door swung open and the Chieftain's personal attendant announced the arrival of the Warden. Dameia watched his entrance with surprise. Never had someone of such rank been admitted to the royal dining room unless there were extenuating circumstances. She focused her breathing. Would not let herself imagine what the Warden's presence here could mean set against Hyam's absence at the construction site.

    "Ah, Warden," the Chieftain greeted, pushing back his chair so that the other *zakar* could kneel and kiss his hand. Dameia winced inwardly at the thought of those slimy lips on her own skin someday. She would find a new Warden. One who wasn't quite so . . . wet.

    "My Chieftain, a thousand apologies for missing our meeting this afternoon. I trust you received word that it was an unavoidable situation in the rebel camp."

The Weight of Stars and Suns
Dawn Christine Jonckowski

The Chieftain raised his goblet to the Warden. "Yes, I did, and for that, you are excused with no need for pardon. There also is no need, is there, to remind you that those rebels are your priority above all else."

She knew they avoided speaking plainly because of her proximity. She knew that despite his good mood, her father still baited her. Just to see. Just in case. Dameia refused to succumb. She lifted her goblet and sipped disinterestedly.

Let them talk.

"Then let us retire to another room to discuss your reports. It has been a long cycle for all, and I do not see the need to additionally burden my daughter with these banalities." The Chieftain rose to his feet, indicated for the Warden to do the same. "Dameia, on the morrow," he said, inclining his head in the traditional parting. Dameia inclined her own head in return.

"On the morrow, Father."

When the Warden made no initial move, the Chieftain raised an eyebrow in his direction. Forgetting himself for a moment, the Warden blinked and knelt on an apology to kiss the princess' hand. Dameia was almost too distracted by the smear of his lips on the back of her fingers to feel the scrap of paper he pressed into her palm. Her fingers closed at the last second, tucking the paper firmly into her fist as the Warden met her eyes with a sly grin. She forced her chin up, kept her mask of indifference firmly in place. He rose to his feet and followed the Chieftain out of the room.

Dameia stood rooted in place until the door swung shut behind the departing figures. Counted heartbeats until she was sure that her calm prevailed. With the scrap of paper clutched tightly, she left the dining room and walked as fast as she dared to her chambers where Hannah awaited to help her turn down for the second cycle.

"Good evening, *neqeba*. Can I interest you in some reading or some music? We have—"

"Out." Dameia's abrupt command cut off her human companion. Hannah's face briefly blanched, then recovered quickly.

"O-of course, *neqeba*. Is there anything you require befo—"

"Just go."

Dameia instantly regretted her curtness as soon as Hannah bustled out of her chambers to return to her own family in the human Colony. The older woman had forever been someone Dameia could rely on, and here she was sending her away in a cold fit not unlike those of her father. She would have to make it up to Hannah tomorrow.

For now, there was the Warden's note:

Hyam is on the pole
The guard changes at fourth watch.

✧ ✧ ✧ ✧ ✧

Hyam couldn't remember what his fingertips felt like.

He stood—if standing was what one could call it—arms pulled taut over his head, wrists bound around to the back side of the thick wooden pole that had spit more than a few slivers into his spine by now. To relieve his aching shoulders, he could arch his back. To relieve his aching back, he had to let his weight sag back to his shoulders. No position was comfortable. Which he supposed was entirely the point of being on the pole in the first place.

Not to mention the lack of blood and resulting absence of feeling in his fingertips.

As punishments went, this had to be one of the worst that didn't involve splitting open his skin. And Hyam had plenty of experience with many sorts. After all, there was a reason he'd joined the rebels and ultimately ended up becoming one of their leaders.

Truth be told, he was still somewhat amazed that the guards hadn't just slaughtered him on the spot, what with how keen the Chieftain had been to have the rebels' heads. Make that *his* head. Hyam wasn't a fool. He had read the leader's face at the farce they had the audacity to call a trial. Knew that the ruler suspected much but had proof for little, and thus his solution was to simply rid himself of the problem. That "problem" essentially being Hyam.

The other eleven were just a bonus.

Extra heads for the spikes to even out the display.

The Chieftain did "grisly display" to the hilt.

So for someone whose life was absolutely and precariously balanced on the edge of losing it, hanging from a pole was actually a pretty good day. Except of course for his back. And his shoulders. And those fingertips too. Those were pretty important; they were going to sting with the points of a thousand needles when the guards finally untied him in the morning. Swinging that hammer was going to be quite the feat.

But one thing he remained grateful for was that Dameia would not see him like this. Of course, she would understand the prejudices of the guards against humans, and especially these rebels, and likely know that the punishment did in no way befit the crime.

Still.

Trussed up like a plucked bird for roasting was not exactly how he preferred to be seen.

A man had his pride.

Hyam arched his back to alleviate the pull on his shoulders, wiggled his fingertips, or at least his brain told them to move. Whether or not they actually did was anyone's guess. The numbness had now passed beyond his fingertips and over his wrists. From mid-forearm up, his extremities simply felt like dead weights pulling on his bones.

He had no idea how long he'd been hanging there. The other rebels had filed past in silence when they returned from the construction site. They may have been forced to look at his humiliation, but none could be made to further it. Waves of compassion rippled off each rebel as he passed Hyam, and their young leader took strength from their solidarity even as the derision of the guards hammered against his resolution.

That had all been some time ago. Now the constant thrumming ache in his body overrode his normally keen sense of time and he hung in the lowered light that spilled over the few buildings in the rebel compound.

Somewhere a guard called the passing of the fourth watch. A quick flurry of guards keen to leave their posts and turn in to soft beds and perhaps softer arms, then silence. An unusual lull that should have been filled with the bustle of the new watch setting up along the perimeters, eyes everywhere.

The Weight of Stars and Suns
Dawn Christine Jonckowski

Instead, unnerving silence.

Then the rustle of approach. Hyam closed his eyes against the impending insults from the new guard about the prisoner on the pole. Just a little longer, and it would be counted morning and he could be cut down. Give his bloodless hands a hammer and let him go.

But when no abuse came, when all he heard was stillness briefly punctuated by a soft intake of breath, Hyam dared to open his eyes.

And found himself looking straight into the stricken eyes of the princess.

☼ ☼ ☼ ☼ ☼

Dameia knew what it meant to be on the pole, in theory if not in actual practice. She knew it had been designed to wrench the shoulders, to seize the back, to drain blood from the hands so that even when the offender was cut down, his punishment doubled with the sting of blood flowing back and awakening the deadened nerves.

But actually seeing it.

Not only that, but seeing it when the one who hung there was someone who mattered to her.

That brought it all too close.

In the space of her first look at Hyam hanging, eyes closed, face drawn, arms stretched, a thousand regrets welled up. First for the man in front of her, whom she never expected to hold so dear as she did. Then for the others who had hung there before whom she had not mourned, whom she had not seen. For her own race who found this an acceptable way to treat another life. The creatures who were raised specifically for slaughter and devouring at the dinner table were offered more respect than this.

Why should the color of the humans' skin and the planet of their origin be the qualities on which they were judged?

Hyam's eyes opened and instantly stormed over. Surprise, regret, anger, pain. It was all there, too fast for Dameia to sort and assign. All she cared about was that he was alive.

"You shouldn't be here." His words came out dry and broken from a throat cracked by disuse.

"Shut up."

Hyam's gaze widened. "I'm sorry, what?"

Quickly, Dameia closed the gap between them. "I said, shut up," she repeated softly. Angst filled her, spilled up and over her cheekbones. She rested one cool palm against his burning face, and as she had before in the prison, rested her forehead against his. "I don't care where I should be or where I shouldn't. I don't care. All I care about is the fact that you're alive, Hyam. I counted only eleven on the construction site today, and my father came to dinner with blood on him, and I thought . . . I thought you were lost."

Hyam sagged farther into his shoulders, heavy with the weight of her worry, the equal pull of her relief. "I'm here," he finally whispered.

A beat, and Dameia finally found her tongue.

"But you can't stay here."

"On this pole? No, that wouldn't be ideal. At some point I'd like the use and feel of my hands again. I find them fairly useful." His

The Weight of Stars and Suns
Dawn Christine Jonckowski

wit in the midst of the dark moment shouldn't have surprised her. He seemed unable to focus on the gravity of a situation for long, always able to make light, to make her smile at the most inappropriate times. It was one of the things she'd begun to love about him. She leaned away to look him full in the face.

"I mean in this death sentence of a punishment." Dameia paused to quickly scan the compound. "I don't know how much time I have until the next watch, but Hyam," her other hand raised to capture his face fully, "on my mother's grave, I swear to you that you will not die here. Meet me behind the barracks in two days at fourth watch." Her hands slid from his face to rest on his bare chest. Her palms burned on contact, her fingers splayed to feel as much of him as she could.

Hyam shook his head, grimacing as the movement wrenched his screaming shoulders. "I will not let you put yourself in danger for me."

Mirroring his own cocky tendencies, Dameia quirked a brow and said lightly, "Too late." She felt his sigh blow gently across her face.

"Fine. Two days. But please, be careful," he begged.

"I will." Her pulse pounded with need, her hands trembled and ached against his skin. Giving in, she wrapped long arms around his torso, gathering him close, lifting him up to both ease the pressure on his joints from the pole and for the short luxury of having him warm and solid against her.

"You will be free," she whispered her promise close into his ear.

Too quickly, she forced herself to release him. The bonds pulled again at his shoulders, the air rushed in between them, suddenly cool to the heat of their bodies and raising gooseflesh along her arms. Dameia stepped back.

"Two days," she said.

"Two days," he repeated.

On a nod, the princess spun quickly on her heel and raced soundlessly through the small complex, disappearing behind the few short buildings and out through the unattended guard's entrance. She barely broke stride to drop a small clinking purse into the outstretched and waiting hand of the Warden, didn't pause to acknowledge him or thank him, didn't see his calculating grin that followed her as she fled.

8

Two days.

Two days of watching and waiting. Watching her pass by the construction site time and again. Waiting for the guards to somehow find him out. Watching how the other rebels regarded him, how they wondered. Waiting for them to ask what else had transpired outside of the torture, for surely such a punishment could not result in this level of calm.

When Hyam had been cut down from the pole, Ithai had been there to catch him, Oren to shove a piece of rough tree bark between his teeth where he could grind out his pain as the other rebels briskly massaged the blood back into his arms and helped him stumble back to the construction site. Hyam counted it a small miracle that he had even been able to close his fingers around the handle of his new hammer, much less swing it down on rock with any effectiveness.

The more macabre of the rebels had begged that second cycle to know what it was like to hang on the pole. While surprised at their dark obsession with knowing, Hyam could almost understand. If there was a possibility that they too could ever end up on the pole, it would serve better to know what they were about to get into. Although the greater witness to the experience was less his description and more the number of slivers they helped pull from his spine, the jellied way his shoulders responded every time he swung the hammer that next morning, the strain around his eyes as he forced his hands to flex around broken stones. The other rebels helped wherever they could, but the punishment had been Hyam's. No one was keen to share it and so quickly.

Overall though, they marveled at his calm. He had hung on the pole unjustly. Had been fed nothing, allowed no sleep, and after all that had been expected to perform at optimum levels the following cycle.

And yet.

And yet Hyam worked without complaint. Not even a single utterance once they were back in the barracks for second cycle. He had taken a short moment to describe as best he could the hell of the hanging, and then with brief but heartfelt thanks for their assistance since his release, had turned his face to the wall and gone promptly and deeply to sleep.

The following day after that, well. He had worked expectantly. The rebels murmured amongst themselves as Hyam thundered his hammer on the rocks, gathered and toted them with a vigor that wasn't natural for someone who could barely lift a spoon at the previous cycle's meal.

Two days.

| | The Weight of Stars and Suns | |
Dawn Christine Jonckowski

He held the secret close. They wouldn't understand. He wouldn't ask them to.

He just had to make it two days.

At the end of the second day, Hyam calmly left the construction site with the rest of the rebels. He ate his gruel with unidentifiable stringy meat. He retreated to the barracks in silence. Feigned sleep as one by one, his eleven comrades fell into their own dreamless slumber. Marked the watches on his fingers as they were called.

Finally.

Two days.

Fourth watch.

He slipped off his bunk, out the door, and behind the barracks.

And there she was.

She motioned to him silently. So he followed. Along the fence. To the corner where it collided with the colony wall. Through a man-wide gap, and into the dense trees that bordered the southern edge and flowed briefly up a small mountain.

He was free.

✧ ✧ ✧ ✧ ✧

It was inevitable. A matter of time only. It was the silent shared knowledge that this was the first time either had been fully understood, the first time either could be fully themselves. It was the quiet desperation of two souls who knew they should not be together, and yet knew—they *knew*—that together was the only way to be.

It was the beauty of olive hands on lavender skin. The breathlessness of first touch. Eyes meeting, and suddenly, they weren't human or Tavarian, they were just Hyam and Dameia.

It was the music of a first hello not strained through by bars or held back with chains and rope. Whispers turned words turned lips onto each other.

It was a kiss that could be unhurried, that could linger, tasting hopes and the flavor of dared dreams. Limbs that could freely tangle and cling. Breaths that could be exchanged and sent sweetly back again.

It was the magic of beginning.

It was forbidden.

It was perfect.

It was everything.

Everything.

☼ ☼ ☼ ☼ ☼

She leaned against him.

"I know almost nothing about Earth. Tell me your stories. I want to know."

He shifted against her. "Then you'll need to offer up a fair share of your own, Princess. Perhaps tomorrow you can share some of Tavarian lore."

She smiled.

The Weight of Stars and Suns
Dawn Christine Jonckowski

"Tomorrow. Tomorrow sounds lovely."

And so it began.

☼ ☼ ☼ ☼ ☼

Once I told you of the moon.

Yes, I remember that.

Lighting the night is not all she does.

Oh, is she a goddess?

Some worshiped her in the beginning, yes, but no, that is not this story. Hush and let me tell.

First we need to talk about the waters. Whereas Tav is watered largely by the underground springs due to water's rapid evaporation under the suns, Earth is nearly three-quarters covered by water. The largest bodies are oceans and seas, followed by lakes, rivers, and streams. Our oceans and seas, and some lakes, are salt water.

Salt water?

The water tastes much like tears. It is life-giving to some, but perilous to others. The moon, her cycle around Earth actually affects the way gravity pulls on the water, and we have tides and currents, forces that swirl the water across the globe, that pull the water up on the shores where land meets sea and rolls waves across the sand.

Men build vehicles called boats and ships to travel on top of the water. These vessels are powered by wind or mechanics, and do everything from transporting humans and trade goods across the world to catching fish for food.

These fish and other creatures that live in these waters, some are the most beautiful things you have ever seen, the way they leap and play in the water, or the colors they display beneath the waves. Others hide in darker crevices and if you were ever to meet one, you'd know why. They come in all shapes and sizes, some as small as a speck, others as large as the palace itself. Some the size of a man.

In the days of old, there was legend of a creature called a "mermaid," a woman who was fish from the waist down. These mermaids were said to be lovely beyond compare. But they were a nasty lot, and tales were told of how these beautiful mermaids would sing with their exquisite voices and transfix sailors upon the seas, luring them to their deaths by shipwreck upon giant rocks.

Half woman and half fish? Your world has some strange creatures indeed.

This coming from the lady with purple skin.

Carry on.

Rivers are narrow bodies that carry water from one place to another. Sometimes they originate in lakes, others from mountains or even underground springs that have broken through. Most eventually empty into another lake, sea, or ocean. The land around them is fertile with plant and animal life.

But being in the water . . . I have heard that being in the water is a fantastic and humbling moment. To wade into the sea and feel the vastness all around you. To realize just how small you are in the cosmos. To float and swim and dive and feel the water close above you. To hear its power as it thunders on the shores, to know its strength as over time, its flow carves caves and splits solid rock. To feel its gentle rock as your boat rests upon its surface.

Someday I hope to feel the ocean.

✧ ✧ ✧ ✧ ✧

The Weight of Stars and Suns
Dawn Christine Jonckowski

You've lived on Tav all your life, haven't you?

Born a slave, yes, but don't plan to die one.

Of course not. But what can I tell you of Tav that you don't already know?

Tell me about the origin of the Tavarian gods. That is one I don't know. No one has been exceptionally keen on letting the dirty humans worship the holy Tavarian deities.

Oh gods, the gods.

You say it like it's a bad thing.

I will tell you the lore, but know now that I don't believe a bit of it. The gods—if they even exist—gave up on me long ago. I waste what time I do with them purely for royal show.

Fair enough. To quote you, carry on.

Why thank you.

The Tavarian gods. In the beginning was a star, Hapshid. This star was discontent to remain stationary in the heavens where it had been born and so traveled across time and space seeking a finer resting place. Hapshid continued to roam until she discovered a comet, Dryan. The comet was as lonely and restless as she. Hapshid found in Dryan a kindred spirit, and she fell in love with him.

But Dryan was bound by nature to travel far and wide in a predestined course in ways that Hapshid was neither designed nor content to follow. Though she loved him with all that she was, he would not stray from his path for her. Hapshid finally rested in one place where she would wait for a thousand and a half years for the briefest of encounters with Dryan. He would fly past, pausing just long enough to caress her before he continued on his way.

Hapshid grew lonelier.

Finally, she could stand it no longer. As Dryan approached for the final time, Hapshid stood directly in his path. He begged her to move, but she would not. Dryan collided into Hapshid with the force of a thousand thousand years. The impact cracked the comet, and he left a dark, burnt-out piece of himself behind. For herself, Hapshid was left bruised and broken. Her tears wore the broken piece of comet round and smooth. The seven star gods watched her mourn and acknowledged her sorrow. Five seasons later, she gave birth to thirty-six children.

Though she loved her children, Hapshid could no longer stay in a sky without Dryan and chose to follow her lover. She gathered her children around the dark piece of the comet and charged them with keeping it safe, warm, and full of light until she could return with their father. Three of the star gods— Moammut and his sisters Lehigh and Peyhah—pledged to watch over the children in Hapshid's absence. The children circled around the dark piece and set their own path to rotate around it and continually warm its surface. As a gift to keep the children occupied, Moammut caused the suns' light to permeate the dark piece and evolve it to a planet, Tav. Lehigh set forth vegetation and animals, while Peyhah created the waters below to sustain all living things. For his final gift, Moammut dipped his fingers in the stars and shook the drops onto the surface of Tav to become the first generation.

You came from star droppings off a god's fingertips, and you say Earth legends are strange?

I have yet to say I believe it to be the truth.

Point taken. So tell me how Tavarians worship these gods.

Tavarians worship the trio of star gods, with Moammut as our creator and Lehigh and Peyhah as our sustainers. Priests offer morning chants to Moammut for his gift of life for another day. Temple volunteers present sacrifices of fine oils and rich meats to Lehigh and Peyhah for their sustenance. Worshippers may make personal sacrifices and prayers at any of the three altars dependent upon need, and some choose a patron god to worship based on personal

The Weight of Stars and Suns
Dawn Christine Jonckowski

preference or experience. The highest form of worship, however, is temple meditation, which must be practiced once a week, whereupon one prostrates oneself before each altar and then spends a span of time in the garden meditating and communing with the gods. At the close of the meditation, the worshipper participates in a cold tea ceremony in remembrance of the gods' acts of creation that brought Tav forth from cold darkness into warmth and light.

My mother was a fervent believer, and raised me to be such as well. Some of my earliest memories of her are in the temple of Peyhah, whose waters also represent fertility, on her knees begging for another child. It never occurred to me to be hurt that I was not enough, or to wonder why she prayed so fervently for a prince over a second princess. I was simply thrilled at the prospect of a playmate.

Finally, she became with child, and we celebrated with a rousing parade in Peyhah's honor, bringing her likeness through the streets with swirling dance and flowing drink. We brought fresh roasted sand hen to her altar every first cycle, and poured fragrant oil out to Moammut and Lehigh every second.

When her time came and my mother fought to bring her new child into the world, I prayed with all that I was that the gods would look on her with mercy and spare my mother. We had done all they asked and more. I could see no reason why they would not show her favor and save her.

But they let her die. In their cold impotence, they let her die. Likenesses of all three watched over her childbearing bed, and they turned a blind eye to her struggle. They let her die.

Or . . . or they were nothing but pieces of carved rock to begin with, ineffectual to create or sustain life because they neither lived nor breathed themselves.

And so I stopped believing. I buried the gods with my mother and I stopped believing.

So if the gods did not bring me to you, what did?

Destiny.

And maybe a spaceship.

That too.

        ✧   ✧   ✧   ✧   ✧

Unlike Tav, Earth does not exist within the same temperature range day in and day out. Because the planet orbits around a singular sun, it has what we call "seasons," or times of the year—or, how long it takes to orbit the sun once—where the weather is different. Seasons range from mild to extreme depending on where you are on Earth, but typically cycle through winter, spring, summer, and autumn.

The part of the world where one of the Origin Generation was from experienced some of the most definitive seasons. The height of summer wasn't much different than every single day here on Tav; he said this often drove acute homesickness in the early years of his time here. On the hottest days, however, he said he most missed winter back on Earth.

Winter is the coldest season. The world is frozen. Snow falls from the sky.

It falls from the sky? Does it hurt?

Not a bit. Snow is made of tiny frozen water crystals. When water gets cold enough, it freezes and becomes solid. The lakes and rivers can freeze and the tops of them will be covered in ice, cold and shining like glass. But the water in the atmosphere isn't gathered in reservoirs like lakes. Instead, it collects in the air and in the warmer seasons falls in drops from the sky called rain. And in the colder months, snow.

|| The Weight of Stars and Suns ||
Dawn Christine Jonckowski

I cannot imagine a world where water falls from the sky. How do the people survive?

It is not painful, and is in fact quite ordinary if you live there, much like how seeing a ring of suns across your sky is ordinary to you, but was fairly fantastic to the Origin Generation when they landed on Tav.

I suppose this is truthful.

The snow when it falls and collects is a cold, white blanket on the ground. While it can be difficult to travel in it depending on how deeply it falls, much play and sport occurs when it snows. Children make small balls from the snow and throw them at each other in snowball fights, harmless play battles that at worst send melted snow down your back under your clothes. Some people sit on large pieces of polished wood or metal called sleds and ride the snow down a hill or embankment for the thrill of the speed. Others will strap thinner pieces of wood called skies to their feet and use those to ride down a mountain while standing up.

But my favorite story was always when the Origin Generation would speak of snow angels. On Earth, many religions believe in angels, heavenly beings that watch over us and help do the bidding of their God. Most angels look much like humans, except with large wings growing from their backs.

Well that sounds terrifying. I think I prefer the half-fish women.

Oh no, angels are not scary, at least they're not supposed to be. Though I would suppose that would depend entirely upon whether you believed your God was pleased with you or not.

At any rate, when it snows, humans will lie on their backs in the snow and fan out their arms and legs. When they stand, the impression they leave in the snow looks like a creature in a robe with large wings. Snow angels. If we can find a sandy area, I will make an angel for you there.

The Weight of Stars and Suns
Dawn Christine Jonckowski

But someday . . . someday I should like to feel the shiver of cold and make a snow angel.

Someday I would like to make a real snow angel for you.

✧ ✧ ✧ ✧ ✧

What else shall I tell you?

Your tattoos. What do they mean?

Everything. These markings are both sacred to the individual and serve to tell an immediate story to all we meet. These here, starting at the wrists, document my bloodline. This one tells you that I am of the royal family, this indicates that I am first-born. The half-finished design of this ring here denotes that I am unmarried; the design is completed as part of the Tavarian marriage ceremony, where the new husband completes the design on his wife's left arm, and she completes the design on his.

Once I am coronated, I will receive the royal crest spiraled across the mantle of my shoulders, like you see on my father. I will be the first female to bear those marks of Chieftain, and not just simply queen. This will likely spark great debate in the Council as to how they will modify the queen markings to be more masculine for whomever I marry. There is already hot discussion on the title he will bear. Ridiculous, really, considering there is no Tavarian to whom I wish to be joined until death.

Is that so?

Mmm, indeed. I find myself to have more peculiar and exotic tastes.

Lucky me.

Indeed.

|| The Weight of Stars and Suns ||
Dawn Christine Jonckowski

As my reign continues, other diplomatic successes will be documented on my skin, starting along my back and running down to my legs. The designs you may see on my father's thighs speak largely to his work supplanting human rebellions.

I choose to refrain from comment.

You can be sure I will bear no such marks. If at all possible, I should like to bear markings of improved relations between Tavarians and humans.

We could improve some relations right now, you know.

That we could. That we could indeed.

☼ ☼ ☼ ☼ ☼

And so it went. For cycle and days and cycles. Story after story. Lost sleep was a cost of nothing for the time to be lost in each other. Even running on borrowed fuel, each managed to outperform every single day, as if shared words made them stronger. As if stolen touches and tastes were an elixir of life.

If only they had noticed.

If only their time had not been so borrowed.

If only.

☼ ☼ ☼ ☼ ☼

"There are so many things you wish to do on Earth before you die," Dameia murmured, her words a soft hush against Hyam's chest. Never in his life would he have imagined this scenario, stealing every second cycle in a dense grove of trees with the princess of his captors. She curled warm under his arm. His skin pricked with pleasure.

"Truth. Once they realized that no one on Earth was returning for them and what that meant for the folly of their negotiations with the natives, the Origin Generation determined that any humans born here on Tav be filled with the tales of Earth. Their hopes were that eventually we might find our way home, so to prepare us to know of Earth and perhaps how to survive there when all we know is Tav." Hyam ran a hand down Dameia's silky unbound hair. Marveled that she would care to lean her whole self against the dirt and sweat of him.

She sighed. "I almost wish you hadn't told me the truth of your arrival from Earth. It was much easier to believe the Tavarian stories."

Hyam's brow furrowed. "You should always seek to know the truth, or the best version thereof based on every facet. As a ruler, it will be your responsibility to uncover the truth in all moments. You can be sure that many will try to feed you versions and leave out vital specifics, especially those that might make them look bad."

"I know. I said it was easier. Not that it was right."

They leaned together in silence. Too much silence. His mind circled. They could continue like this, but for how long? Every cycle he sneaked out, he risked death. Even if by some miracle the rebels were pardoned for their supposed sins, still to love her like this courted fairly extreme mutilation and subsequent execution if discovered. He could hang his hope on her somehow attaining Chieftainship within the next few years and convince her to establish human equality. An interracial marriage to a human leader—such as,

The Weight of Stars and Suns
Dawn Christine Jonckowski

say, a dashing young rebellion leader—at that point could then be seen more as a political statement than a scandal. But even that timeline stretched years beyond the point of being realistic.

Not to mention the whole Tav getting roasted by its suns part.

If only he could freeze these moments.

If only he was Tavarian.

If only she was human.

If only.

But he couldn't live only on stolen cycles without hope of a proper future. Nor could he ask her to. She deserved more. More than secrecy. More than the love of a slave who would never be free. More than a man who could give her nothing but the shame of being loved by someone "less than."

He would not be that man.

Hyam had always been a man of action. A man who courted death, not princesses.

It was time to take action again.

"You asked me once in the prison cell to tell you my plans for the rebellion."

The violet fingers that had been tracing whorls along his abdomen stilled, tightened.

"I did."

Hyam cleared his throat, cleared his mind.

"I think it's time you knew."

☼ ☼ ☼ ☼ ☼

Dameia didn't want to know. Early on, knowing was what had brought her to Hyam. It had seemed chance that his was the first—and ultimately only—cell she entered under that call for knowledge of the rebel plans. The rebel mind.

And instead, she learned a rebel's heart.

Now that she had him, now that he was here with her, and in this moment they were safe, what could knowledge gain her? It could do nothing but puncture this perfect bubble of sanctuary that existed every second cycle during the span of the fourth watch.

Except.

Except what kind of life was this? Could she be content only with stolen moments, hidden passions? Would she eventually resent that they would never walk down the Capitol Plex with fingers intertwined for all to see? Dameia wanted to believe she was above that need, that they could both live in these confines forever.

She knew better. Refused to admit it, but knew better. She peeked up at Hyam's face. He felt the shift and tilted his head down so his gaze met hers. And there she saw a swirling war between what he felt for her and duty toward his race. He was a storm of action, held at bay, building, building, building to being nearly uncontainable. The dammed force would only be safe for so long.

Dameia sighed ever so quietly.

"Then you ought to tell me," she said finally, her reluctance lost in his relief.

"We want to leave Tav."

His blunt announcement punched the air out of her lungs.

|| The Weight of Stars and Suns ||
Dawn Christine Jonckowski

"What?" Dameia sat up, desperately sucking air and fighting the staccato tattoo of an instantly quick and pounding heartbeat. The air rushed in between them, suddenly cool despite Tav's constant warmth. Dameia shivered, half from the chill and half from Hyam's preamble-less pronouncement. "Why?" Her heart broke on her question.

Hyam held up his hands. "Dameia, look at us. We are nearly identical to Tavarians in biology and anatomy. We spoke a similar enough language so as to be able to easily communicate mere hours after landing on this planet. We know how to build and create, sing, dance, cook, bear and raise young, protect families and structure hierarchical leaderships, most of which we also do for the Tavarians. The differences between Tavarians and humans are so negligible. If we are to be truly honest, it's a difference of skin color and the fact that Tavarians are native to this planet.

"If that is all that separates us, why shouldn't humans fight for equality? When we could easily live alongside Tavarians. We've already adopted many of your ways simply to survive on Tav. With equality enforced, we could own land, build trades, bond to a mate of our choice, be that human or Tavarian.

"But time and again we have fought for that equality and time and again had it denied us, had promises broken and trust destroyed. And so it was recommended that instead of fighting another losing battle for equality, we return to our home planet and rebuild our identities there."

The monologue blanked Dameia's mind. The humans wanted to leave Tav. Might even already have a plan to execute just that.

How could she lose him when she had just found him?

Hyam took her silence as encouragement to continue. "That was where the planning ultimately stalled. Something about being raided by soldiers and thrown into individual prison cells where I would end up having the most fascinating conversations with the princess of this god-forsaken over-sunned rock."

"And end up falling in love with her."

"Love?" The word escaped Dameia's lips on a disbelieving chuckle. "Well that's hardly the explanation I expected."

Hyam jolted back, clearly wounded. "Dameia, truly? You think all of this has just been a lark? That cycle after cycle I risk my life, sharing body and soul with you simply because it's *fun*? You can't possibly expect me to believe that you don't feel it too. That you don't feel the heat and pull of this connection. That you don't spend every second imagining ways to pass by the construction site so we can share the briefest of glances to sustain us until the second cycle."

Heat boiled up from Dameia's core, burning away any sense of reason. "And you can't expect me to hear that you want to leave Tav, leave *me*, and simply accept that as if it has no bearing on my life." She pushed to her feet, propelled into a pace with her fervor. "And if you think you can bandage over that pronouncement with a declaration of love, then you are sadly mistaken."

Hyam leapt to his feet, planted himself in her path, reached hands out to capture her shoulders and make her look at him. "I assure you, my declaration—as you call it—was not without sincerity, and it was certainly not a bandage. This plan to leave Tav has no legs right now. We had not even officially decided that's what we were going to do. It was a mere suggestion on a table, because

The Weight of Stars and Suns
Dawn Christine Jonckowski

nothing else is working. Nothing is working, Dameia! We beg for equality, for better lives, for lives befitting the creatures that we are, and all we are given are falsehoods and placations. Promises no one intends to keep. And nothing ever changes, nothing ever improves."

"So what, you decide to make a princess love you so that you can use her for your betterment?" Dameia couldn't stop the bitterness that welled forth. Hyam's hands dropped from her arms; his eyes frosted.

"Oh yes, because being imprisoned in a hard labor camp with the knowledge that everyone from the guards to the Chieftain himself is over-eager to relieve me of my head is 'betterment.' Please. Tell me more about how loving you is improving my situation." He crossed arms over his chest as if to cage the quiet and deadly rage that threatened his words.

She met him with equal silence and rage. It was all too much. Too much in her head, too much in her heart. Too much reality invading this perfect sanctuary she had created with him, and she didn't want to let it in. Didn't want to admit that anything he said was truth to be dealt with. Couldn't think beyond the thought of losing him due to his own choosing.

Then bleak reality: She would lose him either way.

Hyam's chill released, his face sagging with grief. "I'm sorry, Dameia. I shouldn't have . . . I didn't mean . . . I'm just . . . I'm sorry."

She stared at his beloved face. The arms that wrapped her in safety, the hands that cupped her in wonderment and reverence. The strong chest that caged in a stronger heart.

"I am too," Dameia whispered.

|| The Weight of Stars and Suns ||
Dawn Christine Jonckowski

✧ ✧ ✧ ✧ ✧

    He watched her walk away, trailing her confusion and grief and anger behind her like broken ropes. She walked away and he had no idea if she would ever return.

    She didn't come back.

    For five days, he waited.

    And she didn't come back.

9

The first day, it was anger. Dameia snapped twelve times at Hannah for the most innocuous of things. Threw and shattered a plate in an action that was entirely too alike to her father's rage for her comfort.

How dare he. How dare that rebel have the audacity to throw the word "love" around and expect no consequence. He couldn't expect that that pronouncement would be some wondrous miracle balm that would instantly relieve the fact that he had been—was still?—planning to leave Tav. Leave her. Never mind that he hadn't known her when first he made those plans.

Logic was in short supply during the mad.

She didn't want it anyway.

Stewing. Stewing was good.

Because if she was angry, it didn't hurt.

That came on the third day, the hurt. Claiming a vicious headache, Dameia gave in to cowardice and hid in her bed where no one could see the tears running relentless rivers down her cheeks. Hannah, now newly timid in approaching her mistress, asked quietly after her, ducking her head like a frightened bog mouse in case anything should fly at it. She received no answer, but beyond the door could still make out the quiet sobs that escaped around fist or muffling pillow.

When Dameia emerged later, she found a cool plate of dinner and beside it, a single wildflower that she knew to grow nearly exclusively within the human colony. Tavarians saw it only as a weed; it had taken the humans' arrival for anyone to find beauty in the stems. Even so, most Tavarians still turned up noses when they saw the pinky-white starburst blooms tucked in the hairdos or hands of the slaves, despite the flower's scintillating fragrance.

This was a peace offering, a silent acknowledgement from slave to mistress of the pain suffered.

On the fourth day, Dameia was pale silence.

Finally, the fifth day. The princess sat unseeing on her veranda, sipping blackflower juice, flipping mindlessly through the latest report from the astronomers.

"You're in love, aren't you?"

Dameia gagged on her drink at her human companion's forthright and unfortunately astute scrutiny. As the princess fumbled, Hannah reached across the table to take the cup from her mistress and blot the drops of blackflower juice from the eighth page of the report.

"I'm sorry," Dameia managed through a roughened throat. "*What?*"

Hannah merely blinked matter-of-factly at her. "Pardon my forwardness, *neqeba*, but in the absence of a mother, I thought it might help if another older woman made the observation that you

The Weight of Stars and Suns
Dawn Christine Jonckowski

seem so unwilling to make yourself. There is no denying that you have not exactly been yourself as of late, worse than when you were strongest at odds with your father the Chieftain." The older woman sat back with a far more familiar pose than most humans would dare in the presence of a Tavarian.

Most humans except Hyam.

The thought made Dameia's core ache hollow.

"And what, pray tell, has you coming to the conclusion that I am then in love?"

Hannah returned with an even gaze, began ticking off on her fingers. "You're constantly exhausted. I see dirt tracks in your chambers early in the morning that weren't there when I left for the day, which could indicate that you're sneaking out to meet someone. And yet despite the lack of sleep and exhaustion, you are far happier than I believe I have ever seen you."

Dameia's chest emptied out as her companion spoke. If Hannah suspected that she was sneaking out, who else did?

"And finally," the human woman continued, "in the space of but a few days, you have swung rapidly from rage to sorrow to silence. In all the world, here or otherwise, there's only one thing I know of that can do that," she leaned forward with a soft smile and an audacious yet gentle hand atop Dameia's. "And that's love."

Breaths came in short, shallow gulps. Twin ghosts of relief and fear hovered at Dameia's shoulders. She didn't love Hyam . . . did she? And even if she did—which *fine*, yes, she did—how could she forgive him? She couldn't live with him. Laws and lifetimes were rather firm on that.

And yet.

And yet she couldn't live without him.

"Don't be ashamed to love. It is not a weakness," Hannah advised gently, mistaking Dameia's panic. "Love is a strength, *neqeba*. It is a choice. The best decision you will make in a lifetime. And shared love can only make you both stronger, no matter what you face in life." The older woman ran her hand over Dameia's hair, the first maternal touch the princess had experienced in years. Tears welled up.

"Does he love you?" The soft question punched straight through.

Dameia's heart cracked open.

"Yes," she whispered, her voice catching on so much emotion. Then stronger, gaze turning to meet her companion's. "Yes, he does."

A smiled warmed across the human's face and the edges of her eyes crinkled with age and wisdom and joy. "Then he is a lucky one indeed to have the deep love of such as yourself."

It was obvious the companion assumed that Dameia's love interest was Tavarian. And why shouldn't she? Relations between humans and Tavarians were strictly forbidden. They were courting an impossible love, an impossible future. There was nowhere they could live freely, nowhere they could love without persecution. For that reason, though humans were occasionally used by some of the more cruel Tavarian masters for pleasures, it was usually short-lived, brief enough to be dismissed as rumor and conjecture. Never once investigated for truth. The vast majority of Tavarians found the very idea of humans repulsive for no other reason than that was what they had always been taught about them.

The Weight of Stars and Suns
Dawn Christine Jonckowski

And yet Dameia studied the older woman across the table from her. Hannah had served her faithfully since the princess' early teen years. She had walked the young princess through the physical changes as she grew, taught her secrets for styling her hair, assembling her wardrobe, and the finer points of which of the twelve knives to use first at a formal dinner. Yes, she did it partly out of duty. But the warmth and care she had shown Dameia for all this time. Even when Dameia proved in moments to be unlovely. If that too wasn't a form of love, then what was?

And how dare Dameia assume that she was the only one so conflicted over this wonderful and audacious decision to love? Of course Hyam felt the same way, from the love to the conflict to the need to the terror. They both stood to lose everything if they were discovered, and she had treated him as if his feelings were a mere convenience instead of truly life and death.

She was a monster.

She had to go to him.

Assuming he would take her back.

And then there was the additional matter of making sure that Hannah continued thinking that she loved a Tavarian, making sure that no one else drew similar conclusions that led them too close to the truth. She could only pay off so many for silence before someone decided that it was more profitable to talk.

"Please don't tell anyone," she implored quietly, desperately, with the seasoning of a single tear.

Hannah smiled gently at the princess, a mother's warmth even for someone whose ombré purple skin was worlds different than her own. "Your secret is safe with me. But say," she leaned in conspiratorially, "try to leave more of the dirt of your second cycle trysts outside, eh?" Dameia's skin purpled deeper with her blush, ears afire with what she knew Hannah imagined, and how close to the truth she was.

Minus, of course, the one small detail of Hyam being a human.

With a chuckle, Hannah rose to her feet and collected the breakfast dishes. A brief bow, formality returned, and the day's activities lined up to address like soldiers for inspection. With a sigh, Dameia sucked the final dribbles of blackflower juice from her cup and headed to a meeting with Arganon. If she worked her path correctly, she would have just enough time to pass by the construction site. Hope against hope that Hyam would see her, that the cadence of her steps could somehow tap out a message of confession and yearning.

Need propelled her down hallways and covered walks with far more insistence than the strongest brew of blackflower juice. So fast that she nearly ran over her father and his retinue at a cross. Her sandals caught on stone, pitching her toward a sprawl, rescued by the strong arms of the Chieftain as he grasped her shoulders and countered her back to her feet.

"Dameia! It's as if the gods themselves pursued you. What has you rushing so purposefully this morning?"

She blinked up at her father, her mind suddenly blank. "Hyam . . ." she choked on a winded throat.

The Chieftain's face screwed, perplexed. "What?"

The Weight of Stars and Suns
Dawn Christine Jonckowski

Dameia straightened, cleared her throat and her thoughts. "I am," she corrected, continued, "going to be late for a meeting with Arganon."

"Ah, that fool can wait," the Chieftain scoffed. "Walk with me a bit, daughter. The windbag cannot rail at you on punctuality if you are with the Chieftain. Besides. I feel that as of late, we have both been so caught up with the politics and finer points of running a planet that we have lost touch as a father and daughter." He linked his arm through hers and propelled her down the walkway.

"Well, unfortunately, there isn't much to tell beyond the politics and planet-running, as that is the majority of my days right now." Dameia willed a light tone and a slow heartbeat into her speech patterns. "And what isn't taken up by that or further study is me stuffing as many moments of sleep in as I can."

The Chieftain laughed. A foreign sound for the tension that had surrounded the pair for so long. Dameia allowed that ray of joy to crack one small part of the wall between them. She smiled.

"An important skill to learn, as once you become full ruler and wife and mother, you do find yourself sleeping at the oddest times and in the oddest places hoping that collectively it will be enough to sustain you a full day." The Chieftain smiled back at his daughter, but her brain snagged on his deliberate addition of the words "wife" and "mother" to the litany.

The pair paused in their meandering.

Stopped right in front of the construction site, where the rebel slaves had progressed to the stones closest to the walkways. A slave was bent at the waist, back to the entourage, fighting to pry a stubborn wedge of rock from the ground, close enough that she could smell his sweat under the relentless burn of the suns.

The Chieftain turned to face Dameia. "Have you given any thought to your marriage?"

At that moment, the rock gave way. The slave straightened and turned to add it to his piled load. Lifted his eyes so that over her father's shoulder, Dameia could see the man's face.

Hyam. Two, maybe three arm lengths away.

Hyam.

Her smile faltered, froze.

Hyam slowly, deliberately placed the stone piece atop his towering pile. His eyes never left her face, but this time, they were blank. No warmth. No love. Worse, no *life*. She twined her hands behind her back to stop herself from reaching out. She stood on smooth, polished stone, he on dry clouding dirt that worked its way into nose, mouth, lungs, food, everything. Mere reaches apart, but worlds away. Dameia willed her heart to pulse its desire toward him, to fill his ears with the echo of its beat as clearly as if his head lay quietly on her chest. His face remained a carved mask. She wondered not for the first time if she had already lost him.

"M-marriage?" she finally managed to reply, sliding her eyes directly into her father's gaze. His face crinkled with unbridled mirth.

"Yes, marriage. You can assume the throne singularly, but to truly secure it, you must produce an heir. It works further in your favor if you have an heir even before you have a throne." The Chieftain settled into an easy stance, as if that alone could calm his own suddenly panicked heir. "Naturally, for someone of your station, there are certain criteria in a mate that must be met. Should you have

The Weight of Stars and Suns
Dawn Christine Jonckowski

such an individual in mind, the Council would be happy to consider him. If not, we have been amassing a list of suitable candidates ever since you came of age, and would be happy to recommend the most successful match. It may sound archaic, but your mother and I were arranged, as were my parents before us, and my father's parents before them, and each union was dutifully fruitful and reasonably satisfied with the pairing. I see no reason why you wouldn't benefit from the same." The Chieftain's gaze bored deeper into hers.

"Unless of course there is someone you wish us to consider."

"No," Dameia forced the word out. "There is no one."

"Splendid!" He clapped his hands in an uncharacteristic moment of glee. "Then it is decided. The Council will have a match for you by season's end." His hand fell heavy on her shoulder, his smile a blinding glint that blotted all thoughts of the future. And his eyes actually twinkled. Which until this moment, Dameia had always thought more a pretty turn of descriptive phrase than a real physical possibility.

The Chieftain turned to his entourage. "We may have a wedding at the High Temple Holidays after all!" The group broke into cheers and well wishes for the future bride, pledges to love and serve her husband and children as they did the Chieftain and his daughter. For his part, the Chieftain enveloped his daughter in an embrace, then parted with a laugh to either plan or destroy her future, depending entirely upon which point the plans were viewed from.

Dameia remained, staring dumbfounded at the space of walkway flooring her father had just vacated, rooted to the spot where any remaining hopes were shattered.

The Weight of Stars and Suns
Dawn Christine Jonckowski

She looked up. Straight into Hyam's gaze. He too had been frozen, but the brush of her eyes on his sight snapped him back. Quick flashing colors of rage and pain flared in his eyes, and then, the empty blankness. He picked up his tote of stones. With neither grunt nor strain, he hefted it onto his shoulders, and fueled, she was sure, by the strong fumes of betrayal, turned and powered across to the quarry.

He did not look back.

Dameia waited for him, for the chance to whisper a brief apology, to beg him to come back to her. She waited until even with the excuse and pardon due her station, she was rudely and unforgivably late to meet Arganon.

Hyam never returned.

○   ○   ○   ○   ○

Marriage. Of course she would marry, and a son of some high order of something Tavarian.

Not Hyam.

Not a human.

Humans weren't even allowed to marry. After an extensive, intrusive, and occasionally uncomfortably public examination by Tavarian medics, human mates were assigned each other based on the best likelihood of producing strong offspring. Romance abounded in the colony, just not generally between assigned mates, though it wasn't entirely unlikely for some attachment and affection to blossom after the birth of a child. Or the loss of one. But those

The Weight of Stars and Suns
Dawn Christine Jonckowski

were the exceptions. And when (not if) romances developed outside of an assignment, every mate involved turned a blind eye. All in the name of survival.

Survival. Every other human on Tav was focused on survival, and here he was, pounding his frustration onto a rock over the news that the Tavarian princess was naturally going to be betrothed to a Tavarian male.

After he'd heard the news, he hefted his load of rock with a vigor fueled by rage, then like a coward, quickly offered to switch stations with Ithai. The younger man had been pounding at the same stone for the better part of the cycle trying in vain to make a single chip. Not only was Hyam reasonably certain that this rage would fuel some progress on the station, it was also conveniently out of all sightlines of the complex's walkways. Even if Dameia waited for him—though by now he despaired to hope—she would not see him. Ithai gratefully took Hyam's station, none the wiser, and by the time they were wrangled for their final bowl of gruel, Hyam's fury had cleared the stubborn stone.

The next day, they would start digging.

As the rebels were chained for the long trudge back to the small compound, Hyam's frenzy finally began to dissipate. He was weary. Unendingly weary.

This was not the life he had wanted for himself, for his people. None of it.

So he would forget Dameia. Too long had he been distracted by her, buoyed by her care and concern, by what he thought was genuine and mutual affection. He had been willing to do anything for her, risking death every second cycle just for moments of her time.

Nearly ready to settle his whole existence under the mask of obedient prisoner slave just for the privilege of breathing her time after time.

No more.

His people needed him. Needed their freedom. And while he couldn't promise much from behind bars, he could pledge every last drop of his life to making sure they were free, even if he never was.

The rebels filed into the compound, were unchained with bowls of thin gruel thrust unceremoniously into their cracked and bleeding hands. As the men slurped greedily, Hyam sidled over to Ithai and murmured around his bowl.

"Spread the word. We will not give up our dreams. Tonight at fourth watch, we assemble. I know how we can escape."

✧ ✧ ✧ ✧ ✧

As it drew near to fourth watch, Dameia exchanged her sleep shift for a simple brown military tunic. In the false dark of her sleep chamber, she dressed, fingers nimbly lacing, tying. Her feet were shod in sturdy, silent sandals; her arms were bare of ornamentation, and her hair was loose and soft around her face. An outfit tailored for a secret rendezvous, yes, but more importantly, the same look from the first time she had encountered Hyam in prison, when he was but a nameless rebel who had no real estate yet in her life. She hoped the significance of her choice would not be lost on him.

She hoped her plea for forgiveness would not be lost on him, either.

The Weight of Stars and Suns
Dawn Christine Jonckowski

As a last resort, she plucked Hannah's wildflower from its cup of water in her sitting room and tucked it carefully, lovingly behind her ear. Finally, she slipped out the door, following the path her feet had come to know so well, out of the complex, back sliding carefully along walls, gates, and buildings, dodging the sweeping gazes of the guards, out far past where most Tavarians deigned to be seen, and through the brush of trees to the back of the rebel complex.

Would he be there?

If he wasn't, how could she find him without alerting the entire compound?

It turned out that none of that would matter.

Because as soon as Dameia ducked through the gap in the bars, she raised her head and looked straight into Hyam's eyes. And the dumbfounded faces of eleven other rebels.

✧ ✧ ✧ ✧ ✧

As soon as the trees rustled, all twelve rebels froze. An animal? Worse, a guard? Was this the moment it all ended? Hyam's brain twisted and whirled hoping to find some plausible explanation as to why all twelve were skulking at the back of the camp looking not more than a little panicked and guilty.

Then Dameia stepped through the brush and the bars, and all of his fluttering thoughts dropped dead to the ground.

"*Benzona*," Oren muttered the curse under his breath. "Is that the *princess*? What is she doing here?"

Yair merely continued to choke on his own air.

Ithai cocked his head to the side like a sand hen and said simply and with wonderment, "Is that one of our wildflowers in her hair?"

The rest of the rebels uttered a similar cacophony in whispers and fear.

Hyam stared at Dameia until the rebels fell into uncomfortable silence. He wasn't any more sure than his companions as to why she was actually there. To condemn him? To use him? To rescue him? Though the final thought seemed preposterous after their last face-to-face interlude, and more so in light of the conversation he had overheard just that day.

For the first time since she'd opened the door to his prison cell, Hyam did not know what to say to her. Both tender words and biting wit were inappropriate, for various and sundry reasons. Not to mention that any trace of familiarity at all would raise even more questions with the rebels surrounding him.

And then she solved the problem for him.

"Hyam. Please," she pleaded. "I'm sorry."

Eleven mouths fell open in shock, only to be filled seconds later with whispered exchanges and oaths. *"How does she know his name?" "I knew she talked to him that day at the inspection!" "What is she sorry for?" "Do you think she's here to kill us?" "She's not helping us escape, is she?"*

Hyam held up a single hand and they all fell silent.

"This is hardly the time or place for that, Dameia."

Across from him, her feet planted, hands fisted on hips.

"This is the only time we get, Hyam. This is the only time we have. What, am I to convey my regrets to you while you're in the

The Weight of Stars and Suns
Dawn Christine Jonckowski

middle of the site, in front of the Chieftain and the Councilmen and a dozen others who would happily see you dead before a single word could escape? Even if I'd wanted to, today you disappeared the moment you heard my father." A single tear rolled down that regal face. His heart cracked ever so slightly.

Beside him, Ithai shot Hyam a long and loaded single-browed glance. Hyam fought to keep his breathing steady, his eyes forward, his hands at his sides, even if clenched to the point of drawing blood from the bite of ragged fingernails.

"Right now, Dameia, this cannot be about us," he answered softly, firmly, a voice of velvet-wrapped metal. The air around him contracted with the shock of eleven humans who were beginning to fit pieces into place. A rebel who had means to escape. A princess in dusky, dirt-streaked military dress who slipped through prison bars. Words like "sorry" and "us" and first-person addresses.

He wasn't sure if the wave of emotion they sent crashing over him was more pity, anger, or incredulity. Perhaps a good overflowing mixture of all three. He mirrored her pose, hands on hips, lifted his chin a notch. He didn't expect her to fold. Not this princess. Not after all he'd experienced. She was the strongest individual he knew. And he loved her for it. All her foibles and stubbornness and beauty and glory. He loved her for all of it. All of it.

And now she stood before him. Before all twelve of the condemned rebels. Their secret laid bare. Her heart a plain display before them all. His true feelings given away by the clench in his jaw, the bunch of his muscles as he fought the urge to reach out to her and instead crossed arms over chest, as much to hold in his heart as to keep hers out.

He loved her.

He loved her.

And it was the absolute worse timing in all the universe for all of it. All of it.

"It has to be about us," the princess finally replied, pressing on with fervor. "It's about us because it's about *you*, and you are part of the 'us.' I love you. I love *us*. And without you, there is no 'us.' So it has to be about us. It *has* to be." She paused, froze, as if suddenly aware of the eleven additional sets of eyeballs trained on her, intently drinking in every word.

Yair finally found his voice. "Oy, Hyam. Did that purple princess just say she loved you?"

Hyam broke gaze with Dameia just long enough to shoot the older rebel a deadly and silencing glare. "Not now, Yair," he muttered through clenched teeth. This cycle, this entire rebellion, nothing was going as he'd planned.

For better or for worse, it was all because of her.

She loved him.

"*Charah*," he swore softly.

"Hyam," Dameia spoke his name, and it was once again the most pleasurable sound he'd heard. His syllables on her tongue a sweet refrain only she knew, a song only she could sing. Her eyes implored. They were running out of time. With a nod, he finally consented her to continue.

"You can't escape just yet, or you'll all be killed before any one of you can do any good," she began.

"Yeah, likely because you'll tell on us," Yair challenged hotly.

Hyam whirled. "Yair." He barked the single sound, a harsh, sharp warning. "Enough."

The princess took a single step, closed the gap between them just that much more. Hyam drew a breath, desperate for her scent even in the midst of all this. He could almost feel her heat, almost taste her kiss. Forced himself to focus on the fact that this time there were eleven additional witnesses, and reined his thoughts back.

"When you hung on the pole, I promised you wouldn't die here, and I'm going to keep that promise. Even if it means losing you." He saw her eyes fill and threaten to spill over. Willed her to be strong in front of the doubters and dissenters.

"We don't have much time," Hyam stated quietly. Not enough time in that break between watches. Not enough time with her. Never enough time with her. He had to be strong for those around him. Everything from their trust in his leadership to their very lives hung in the balance because of who stood before them. Because of the color of her skin and the lilt of her speech.

It just wasn't fair.

Then again, it never had been. Not now, not before, not ever.

And it was proving impossible to remake the world.

So they had to leave it. Leave her.

He couldn't leave her.

He had to.

"Choose one or two others to accompany you and meet me back here in two days." Her voice broke in to his musings. Dameia widened her gaze, broadened her address to the entire dozen. "If you can find it within yourselves to trust me, I will get you out of here. Out of the compound, out of slavery, out of Tav. I swear it." And then it was time, and she had to go. "Two days," she reminded. Then her focus narrowed back to him, and she said a single word, filled with every weight of love the word could hold.

His name.

Just his name.

"Hyam."

And his heart broke wide, wide open.

"I know," he managed. And he did. And then she did too.

And then she was gone.

The rebels tramped quickly and silently back to the barracks. Piled in, hastily tucked themselves back into various bunks and blankets.

Whereupon all hell broke loose. Again.

But this time it was all them. No Tavarians. No pandemonium, no mayhem of soldiers and blunt trauma with spear handles and meaty purple fists. No rough ropes wrangled around shoulders and wrists to bundle a dozen rebels out of a cave and away to prison cells. It was all hushed human voices full of equal parts wonder and repugnance.

Then again, parts perhaps not so equal.

Yair was the most insistent, calling for quiet and bringing the rebels down to silence before breaking it with his own voice. "Hyam," he half-whispered, a deadly hiss in the stillness. "A Tavarian? You disgust me." He spat on the ground, punctuating his distaste.

The Weight of Stars and Suns
Dawn Christine Jonckowski

"Eh, at least it's the princess!" A voice called from the back corner of the barracks, dripping with false respect.

Yair glared in the general direction before turning back to Hyam. "You would betray us? Your brothers? Your race? For *her*?" The question hung, dangled midair with no twisting breeze of response.

Hyam built his face of stone.

"We can't trust her, Hyam," Yair continued. "How many times have we trusted the Tavarians to hold to their pretty purple words, and how many times have we been left to the dust? Every time, Hyam. *Every time*. Her promises are worth no more than the millions we've been made since the *Genesis*. And where have all those oaths led? To the exact same ends the Origin Generation foolishly agreed to in the beginning." He crossed reedy arms over his chest. "If we follow her in two days, we die," Yair pronounced, meeting each set of rebel eyes in turn before landing back on Hyam. "Better to die here years down the road than to put foolish trust in her and find our heads on spikes in two days' time."

"I don't know," Oren broke in, musing. "It would seem she has at least passing interest keeping Hyam alive. If like all Tavarians, her fancies pass quickly, perhaps it would behoove us instead to capitalize on them now and use her adoration to free us. We could then be long gone by the time she realizes that her 'love' for a human was no more than a now-waning curiosity." He shrugged. Murmurs rippled through the barracks.

Ithai was the only one to stand next to Hyam in every sense. Wrapping his arm around his friend's shoulders, he scanned the other rebels, his near innocence daring them. "Who are any of you to judge their love? Who are any of you to say whether or not it is true or real? More, who are any of you to give any care for who Hyam loves? You who love many women to whom you are not mated. You who know the histories of race and skin color and the dissention it caused long ago on Earth. You who are descended from a varied palette of those who came on *Genesis*."

Yair grunted. "At least they were all human and not purple freaks."

"We're not all that different, you know," another rebel shot back.

"And how would you know?" Yet another voice from the many. "Are you a Tav lover too?"

Chaos birthed. Voices rose, volume threatened to reach the sharp ears of guards and put a quick end to any discussions, pro or con.

"Are you all quite finished, then?" Hyam's question sliced with deadly calm.

They fell absurdly and surprisingly silent.

Hyam rose to his feet, shrugging off Ithai's arm. Pacing, stalking between the rows of hard bunks and harder men. "Think what you will of us. Love her, hate her, love me, hate me, I don't care. What I do care about is the goal of our rebellion and every rebellion prior: Freedom. She has offered us a far better opportunity than we are like to get with anyone else behind these walls. And I will hear her out in two days' time.

"If you choose to join me, be ready at fourth watch and I will select two to accompany me for this initial meeting. If you choose to stand apart, I will respect that. I will do nothing to save

The Weight of Stars and Suns
Dawn Christine Jonckowski

you, if that is indeed your choice. In return, I ask that you do nothing to hasten my death or the deaths of those who join me. For I assure you, if we die, you die too."

He stopped tall in the middle of the room, feet planted, arms fisted on hips. "We get out of this the same way we always have. Together.

"Whether we are alive or dead when we do so, well. I leave that entirely up to you." Hyam slid back into his bunk, bunched the thin blanket under his head. "Now I'm going to sleep, and I suggest you do the same. Princess or no, the work will still be there in the morning, and tomorrow is not the day I plan on dying." He closed his eyes to shut out the eleven faces before him.

In the morning, Ithai and Oren stood by his bunk. "We are with you, friend," Ithai pledged quietly. Oren nodded his assent, though with somewhat less enthusiasm.

Yair and eight other rebels stood across the room, bunched with arms crossed and faces pinched. Hyam simply nodded at them. All of them. Accepting their decisions, no matter which side. And when the alarm rang, he fell into place beside all his rebel brethren and marched silently through the gates and to the construction site.

There was work to be done.

☼ ☼ ☼ ☼ ☼

The Warden saw all twelve men heading for the gap in the bars that second cycle. He saw the princess slip through. Felt the weight of her bag of scores hanging from his belt, which she assumed would fund his silence.

It would.

Until it wouldn't.

He drank in as the prisoners puzzled out what had been happening between the dirt-crusted rebel leader and the Tavarian princess. He'd known for some time. He'd known before she had even figured it out. He was the Warden.

He knew things.

He saw the line between them stretch tight, threaten to break, then ease, likely with some pretty twist of phrase from one to the other. He didn't care that the mismatched pair hadn't imploded. In fact, it was better for him if they didn't. The longer they lasted, the richer his reward.

The Chieftain paid him handsomely to do his job, and the princess nearly as handsomely to look the other way, but in truth, the Warden worked for no one but himself.

And soon—very, very soon—it was going to pay off in a very big way.

He chuckled to himself and whistled all the way home.

10

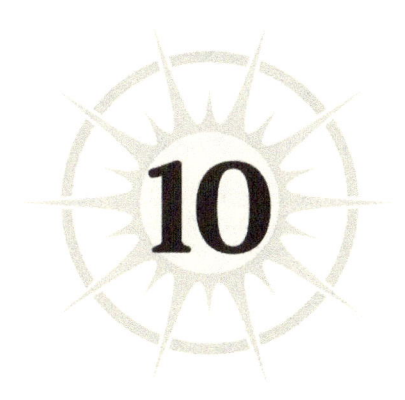

Once upon a time, the humans had arrived on Tav in a mechanical behemoth they called a "space ship." The word as foreign on a Tavarian tongue as the humans were to their eyes, the natives managed to eventually work their lips around the word "ship," but not their brains. Lights that flashed without the aid of fire. Pieces that whirred and spun and smoked without pulleys or heat.

The fact that these forty creatures had just fallen straight out of the sky.

What kind of shiny creation dropped from the heavens and belched out fully-formed man? Small wonder humans had been greeted with fear and apprehension and forced into slavery before their buzzing, smoking metal wonder could erupt further and threaten to rule them all.

After the humans had been trundled off with what they thought to be a grand fanfare of hospitality (little did they know), Tavarian soldiers stood guard until the Chieftain of the age made his way toward the wreckage they did not know was wreckage. The elder Tavarian had walked slowly around the heap, cautiously examining, jumping back as the creation burped a third or fourth or twelfth plume of thick black smoke. By the end of his circling, the metal monster the humans titled by that strange and curious foreign word "ship" was deemed a most serious threat. After a short plea to the gods for their safety, the soldiers battled the beast until the smoke cleared and victory declared.

That was where the fireside tales ended.

As a child, Dameia had been content for them to end there. Her people had prevailed and the humans had become their willing slaves. What else was there to know? What else should she care about?

Until now, when she cared about—more than cared about, *loved*—a human. When she pledged to help him escape. When she knew that "escape" had to mean more than just the barred complex he existed in now.

It meant Tav itself.

And that meant finding the ship.

Which meant talking to someone who could help her find it.

The historians.

A lowly government position, historians had the distinct pleasure of spending hours hunched over books and bound notes learning the ins and outs of Tavarian history, of knowing the laws inside out and backward, of having a finger on the pulse of every Council meeting to ensure the resulting decisions were law-abiding and legal. Historians could eventually emerge from the stacks to be promoted to other positions within the Tavarian government. More than one especially driven historian had eventually landed himself on the Council, though that was more the exception than the rule.

The Weight of Stars and Suns
Dawn Christine Jonckowski

Others were so bookish and socially awkward so as to relish the fact that their roles essentially demanded solitude and endless study, with the occasional break to discuss a finer part of the law or an especially odd addendum with their equally bookish and awkward colleagues.

Historians weren't much invited to the Chieftain's social events.

Especially not after one upstart historian had the unfortunate audacity to question the appropriate usage of budget on food and drink at the previous Chieftain's golden birthday celebration.

It wasn't much of a boon to one's social rank to admit friendship or relation to a historian.

At least Dameia knew that they'd keep their mouths shut. If for no other reason than no one generally cared to listen to them.

Even the historians' world did nothing to invite company. The Archives were nearly as stuffy and dull as the historians themselves. From the outside, the large stone building was wholly unremarkable, its innards almost as much so. Not a single window broke the pattern of the thick walls, leaving the echoing chamber inside to marinate in its utter stillness. Visitors—rare though they were—claimed the atmosphere within was twice as hard to breathe due to the weight of centuries of dust, paper, and ink. Dameia could scarcely believe she was going to willingly spend any span of time there.

Surprisingly, though she wiped sleep from her eyes after that morning's particularly dredging Council meeting—whether that was because of the general aspect of these meetings or the princess' mounting lack of sleep was anyone's guess—when she told her father that she planned to spend the remainder of the morning with the historians in the stacks of the Archive to learn more about her planet's history and rulings, the Chieftain smiled proudly and wrapped an arm around her shoulders.

"You've got the makings of a great Chieftain yet, Damiea," he praised.

She doubted he would have said that if he knew her true intent.

To the thick silence of the Archives, the heavy groan of the yawning maw of a door should have come as at least a small surprise. It wasn't as if visitors to the Archive were often or prolific. But to Dameia's own surprise, only one head was there, nose in paper. Only one head tipped up from its bent posture at a long, heavy table. He was young for a historian, a career that few her own age were eager to get into. His eyes were bright, warm, inviting, his angular-yet-kind face a far cry from the odd conglomerate of features that generally arranged themselves on historians.

Whether the looks made the historians or the historians made the looks, Dameia had never quite been able to puzzle.

But this one. In the windowless chasm of the Archive lit only by protected sconces and torches to safeguard the volumes, he was his own light. Broad of shoulder and narrow of hip, he was built far more like one refined for combat. The gaze he lifted to hers was clear, the smile warm and welcoming.

"My Princess," he greeted, dipping his head into a respectful salute to her station. "To what do we owe the honor of your presence in the Archives today?" He closed the tome he'd been studying, his long sleeves falling back as he lifted the book back to its stack and revealing several tattoos banding his forearms. Curious for a

The Weight of Stars and Suns
Dawn Christine Jonckowski

historian, those who would sooner use ink to preserve history than mark their own limbs.

"I . . ." Dameia's voice failed in the dust. The historian quickly rounded the long table to bring her a cup of blackflower juice that had been heating over a small fire stove. The heat of the beverage soothed her throat and strangely warmed her in the stuffy room.

"Even the best among us often find our sounds coated in the dust of ages here." He smiled kindly, a brilliant, even crescent that lit his face. "You are among friends here, Princess." His head bent in another bow. "My name is Matime. How may I be of service?"

Dameia gathered her calm, arranged her royalty. "I need your assistance in seeking some information, but you must pledge me your utmost discretion in this matter. No one must know what I am researching until such time as it shall be revealed." Which of course, she hoped was never. But a pretty and monarchist turn of phrase never hurt.

"Of course, Princess. You have my word. What is it that you seek?"

She drew up tall, commanding. Just to make sure.

"Bring me everything you have on the humans' ship."

✧ ✧ ✧ ✧ ✧

By the close of the next day, Dameia had spent more time in the Archives than all of the previous Chieftains. Combined.

The Weight of Stars and Suns
Dawn Christine Jonckowski

And yet she was still no closer to finding where the remains had been hidden. She knew it had been observed and documented to whatever end the Tavarian understanding of the metal beast could describe. Which she figured was still lacking, even as she understood that no one on the planet would likely have any knowledge of how to wake the ship.

Therein lay the second problem. The Tavarians certainly knew next to nothing about the ship. What could the humans possibly know? Several generations removed them from that crash, and one had to assume that without ability to practice, any knowledge they'd had was most likely lost to time. She heaved another book closed and dropped head into hands. How in any way was Hyam planning to get the ship into a state to carry the humans back to Earth?

A soft rustle of fabric against wood brought her head up and swiveled it to see Matime settling himself into the chair next to hers, the soft clink of stoneware and welcome tang in her nostrils alerting her to the fresh cup of blackflower juice he had come to deliver. He seemed another thing yet to puzzle out, but Dameia simply didn't have the energy for one more mystery, one more secret.

There wasn't much need to figure him out, anyway.

Although, when Hyam left—no. To even think it seemed disloyal, to her own heart, to the heart he entrusted to her.

Besides. It wasn't as if progress at this point was entirely forward-moving.

One wouldn't think it would be so difficult to find a massive ship.

The Weight of Stars and Suns
Dawn Christine Jonckowski

"Dear Princess," Matime's polite timbre broke into her jumbled thoughts. "You seem distressed. Is there a way I can ease your burden? Be of any further assistance aside from fetching books and blackflower juice and reassuring my silence? Which of course, you still own."

Dameia stared back into his kindly eyes. She had so few she could trust anymore. Perhaps he was one deserving. Historians traditionally had few acquaintances anyway; who was he like to tell? She would trust him with nuggets only, half- and quarter-truths that could pave a road in the right direction without necessarily giving him a full map.

But first.

"Why did you become a historian, Matime? You, well, rather don't seem the particular breed."

The young Tavarian chuckled an effortless laugh as he reclined into a more casual repose. "It's my shoulders, no? I'm a bit broader than the average historian; they constantly complain about having to specially make my robes to accommodate. It comes from my mother's side. Probably looks better on me than her, too."

Dameia was too chagrined to offer a smile at his easy self-deprecation. "I simply meant—"

Matime held up a hand as the aforementioned shoulders shook with continued laughter. "My Princess, please. I apologize for my off-brand humor. Yet another disappointing family trait, though this one from my father's side." A smile slashed his face. "While it would have pleased my father more to have me become a soldier—indeed he put me through many ages and paces of training, even going so far as to inscribe certain ceremonial tattoos on me himself as

I progressed, albeit awkwardly, through the levels—it was my mother's quiet and constant dedication to increasing her knowledge that lit in me a fire for learning. I would train with my father every first cycle to earn his pleasure, but spend the second cycle curled in the one corner of the sleep chamber where the suns' light crept through, reading until my eyes were bloodshot and dry." Those elegant shoulders rose and fell in a shrug somehow both practiced and casual. "Eventually my thirst for knowledge beat out my poor swordsmanship. And when my father died and shortly after, the Chieftain posted the need for a new generation of historians, no one could deny this was my destiny. My uncle sold my armor and weapons to buy my apprentice robes. To this day, he remains puffed proud over my station, though even if you yourself pressed, he would never admit it."

"That explains the ink," Dameia murmured.

The historian arched a practiced brow. "You noticed?"

Her face heated. "Well, when I arrived yesterday, your sleeves shifted as you picked up—yes, I noticed," she backtracked.

He laughed again, an unhurried and delighted sound quickly soaked up by the surrounding volumes. "As well you should be observant, seeing as you are our future Chieftain." Lifting his own mug to lips, Matime inhaled a long pull of the fragrant beverage before setting it carefully back on the table. "To be fully transparent, I do hope someday to emerge from the stacks and become a member of the Council. Perhaps even the Judge? It would be quite the honor to my family to rise to bigger success and use this knowledge for the betterment of my planet. Though," he shrugged again, "should I remain here all of my days, I can hardly find reason to complain."

The Weight of Stars and Suns
Dawn Christine Jonckowski

"So you would aspire to someday sit on *my* Council?" the princess asked.

"Well, whoever the next Chieftain is, which I suppose would be you. So, yes." Matime smiled again, easily and plainly. "But tell me, Princess. You are not here to inquire about my unlikely aspirations of Councilhood. How else may I serve my future Chieftain?"

Dameia sighed. Glanced around. Once. Twice.

They were alone.

He seemed innocent enough, despite his casual political aspirations.

She would grant him trust and truth.

But only in part.

If he chose to dissect, it would be his own folly to decipher what was truth and what was not. And if she played politics as well as her father had taught her in both practice and observation, she could make it so that any question asked may result in rapid loss of life by the Chieftain's own troublesome temper.

It would at least make the historian think twice if he planned to betray her.

Not that his guileless smile transmitted that he would.

But Dameia had been raised in the heart of politicking. She knew well enough that when it came to Tavarian government and aspirations thereof, few things were precisely as they seemed.

After all, look at her.

Princess. Future Chieftain.

Human-lover.

Her thoughts snapped back. Hyam would be waiting for her at second cycle. With two additional rebels. (Assuming they hadn't all mutinied on him by now; she'd seen the looks, heard the comments. He had as long a road as she.) Dameia needed to bring them answers, hope. Even if in the beginning, it was only small snatches.

    She looked into Matime's waiting and expectant face.

    "I had been hoping to commission a sculpture to celebrate my father's incredible prowess with regards to subduing human rebellions, and I wished to use parts from the human ship. While I hoped to find clues on my own so that this surprise might remain between myself and the sculptor, I find I am unable to locate the original ship." Dameia paused, breathed deeply. Forced her voice to remain in its usual octave and not jump up with nerves. "I don't suppose you know where it is?"

    Matime's grin broadened to nearly overtaking his face. "My Princess! Had you only asked this from the beginning, I could have spared you all this time of searching within the Archives, though I would have been greatly deprived of your excellent company. Of course I know where the ship is.

    "It is where it has always been: at the original crash site."

☼   ☼   ☼   ☼   ☼

    "You're saying my daughter, the princess, has been spending the past two days in the company of a *historian*?" The Chieftain's incredulity was so tangible it nearly had color.

    The Lead Historian was secure enough in his own career to dare looking affronted. "You did say not long ago that you wished she would spend more time with those her own age."

The Weight of Stars and Suns
Dawn Christine Jonckowski

The Chieftain merely grunted.

"And," the Lead Historian quickly added, "he is not just any historian. His name is Matime, a fine young *zakar* from a military family. His father attempted to bring him into soldiering, but Matime has more a head for histories and laws. He is well-built with a strong, sensible mind. And has mentioned not more than a few times that his aspirations are for the Council."

His interest suddenly piqued, the Chieftain sat forward in his chair. He had been enjoying spiced tea hour with the Warden, catching up on the progress of the rebel contingent on the underground building project, when the Lead Historian passed through the Court Veranda and mentioned having seen Dameia alongside a young historian for the last several days. The Chieftain was already pleased that she was, of her own accord, spending time in the Archive ostensibly learning her government's laws and histories.

Now he learned she was possibly there less for the knowledge and more for the scenery, in the form of an apparently visually pleasing and driven young Tavarian male.

He wasn't sure which possibility pleased him more. Both were rather favorable, all things considered. Especially as he had just been musing in passing to the Warden who he might offer up to his daughter for her marriage arrangement. Which the Warden had been oddly tickled to help conjecture.

"A military background and an ambition for the Council, you say?" mused the Chieftain. "Along with my daughter finding pleasure of some sort in his company." His lips curved into a slow, plotting smile. He turned to the Warden.

"I believe we should invite him to dinner tomorrow."

For his part, the Warden smiled his own slippery grin into his cup of spiced tea. It would seem the game was getting thicker, and he was all too happy to encourage the players when it ended at his advantage. "An excellent plan, indeed," he agreed.

"It is settled!" the Chieftain exulted, punctuating his pleasure with the resounding smack of his palm against the polished arm of his chair. "See to it that Matime is invited to dine with us tomorrow," he ordered the Lead Historian. "And do make sure he understands that this is not entirely a request."

The Lead Historian bowed deeply, his face a mask behind which he fumed at Matime's quick stardom and calculated how he might use it to his gain. If Matime indeed ended up marrying Princess Dameia, well. Then the Archives should at least merit a significant increase in scores for their budget. The future husband of the Chieftain could not forget from whence he came, those lowly, dusty stacks. The Lead Historian would make sure of it.

"Of course, Chieftain. It shall be done as you request." And he was gone in a flurry of robes, leaving plumes of dust in his wake.

The Chieftain's wide smile faced once again in the Warden's direction. "It appears we may have a solution to our marriage problem more rapidly than anticipated." He sat back, sipped the dregs of his spiced tea. "A historian. Not quite who I would have pictured," he admitted.

"Children rarely fancy who their parents would have expected, do they?" The Warden's words were heavy with meaning that as yet had no relevance to the Chieftain. Yet. But they would. And soon.

|| The Weight of Stars and Suns ||
Dawn Christine Jonckowski

"I do imagine that this will not be the least of the surprises she may hold," the Warden finished. He set his teacup down with a smack of glistening lips. Sat back and smiled.

They had no idea.

The Chieftain, Dameia, the historian, those filthy rebels.

Not a one of them.

It was all so much better than he could have ever planned.

☼ ☼ ☼ ☼ ☼

Meanwhile, somewhere in the wilderness beyond the Capitol Plex, Damiea crunched through forest and underbrush behind Matime as the pair made their way to the crash site. Never would she have imagined that the ship would be left where it had landed, though if the legends of its size were anywhere near truth, moving such a monster from that particular location would be near impossible. Forests on Tav—especially one of this size—were such a rarity that the thought of devoiding it of a path of trees to drag the metal beast out was more than most could stomach.

And thus, lost to all but a few through creative misinterpretation of fact, the ship remained.

Dameia kept half a gaze on the broad shoulders in front of her while watching the forest floor for roots or snags or any assorted ill-liked critters that might try to impede her progress. (She truly could not stand the dozimids; nothing that creeped along tree trunks on twelve legs that suspended a bristled abdomen plated in small body armor should really be acceptable on any planet.) For the heat and the nature of their quest, Matime had shed his voluminous historian's robes, revealing a simple sleeveless military tunic that closely mimicked those Dameia favored for her late trysts. The forest trek afforded her ample time to study his arms, corded with very un-historian-like muscle. The tattoos banding them outlined an impressive military lineage, documenting some of his own training achievements, though when he first doffed the robe and caught her interpreting, Matime laughed and assured her that the achievements lay more in his father's imagination than any actual skill of his own doing.

    Which still didn't explain the enduring military silhouette he carved against the light. One would have thought that by now his bulk would have disintegrated into the same reedy-limbed look that every other historian bore.

    It was almost as if he continued to labor at training. Surely lifting stacks of books—weighty as she now well knew them to be—could not cut such a figure. He was as carved as Hyam, though broader for access to full nutrition, and not marked with the scars of rebellion and general humanity.

    Hyam.

    She warmed at his name tumbling through her thoughts. Allowed herself the brief pleasure of dwelling within the shape of its sound, even if it echoed in her head alone. Slammed and bolted the door against the persistent reminder that Hyam did not want to stay, could not stay, that she was even now doing all she could to help him escape.

    To help him leave Tav.

    To help him leave *her*.

The Weight of Stars and Suns
Dawn Christine Jonckowski

Her feet moved of their own accord even as her mind wandered a different path, and suddenly, she slammed straight into the solid wall of the historian in front of her.

"Here, Princess. Behold, the metal monster that birthed Tav's slave race."

Dameia lifted her eyes. It was everything and nothing like she expected. The crusted hull jutted from under vines that over generations had crept around and chained the ship to Tav. A jagged split broke from spine to belly where the force of the impact had arched the frame beyond its capability. The underside still bore several layers of char from its entry into the atmosphere, though time had flaked much of the brittle skin, and rust grew in cancerous lesions.

It was hideous and breathtaking all at once.

She circled the breached structure, breathing the tang of oxidized metal, trailing purple fingers along seams and panels and plates that hands like Hyam's had constructed generations and galaxies away from this moment.

"I suppose you'll want to return with the sculptor so that appropriate inventory can be made of the parts and plans drawn up for the work." Matime's smooth baritone broke across her observations.

"Yes," Dameia murmured distractedly.

"I thought as much, and thus I hope it does not appear too forward that I have plotted this map for you so that you may find your way back," Matime admitted, handing a folded paper to the princess with a nod of deference. She took it, both surprised and pleased at his foresight and how much easier he was inadvertently making her treachery.

"No, this is . . . thank you, Matime," Dameia said, honesty combing through each word.

He answered with a broad smile, perhaps a shade too bright for how his rank lined up to hers. "I am confident that after several visits, you and your sculptor will be able to bring about a thing of meaning and beauty to gift your father the Chieftain. Truly, you are a wonderful daughter to him. He should be so honored."

"Indeed," mused the princess. She ached to go inside, to poke and prod at the metal beast's innards and see if after all these years dormant, it could be awoken. But she could wait for second cycle, for Hyam. To give him the sacred moment of stepping over the threshold into the center of what had carried his ancestors in its metal womb across planets and stars. That moment did not belong to her, nor to her race.

She could wait.

Right now it was time to return, time to brave her way back through the palace as if her heart did not pound with the knowledge that they were one step closer to his freedom, one step closer to her loss. She would sup with her father as if she wasn't already stained treasonous, prepare for the cycle's repose with her human companion as if she wasn't going to truncate it to slip out again to compound and forest with a small rebel entourage.

"Shall we?" Dameia asked. Matime nodded, offered his hand to help her over some debris. Against her better judgement, she took it. His fingers tightened against the bones of her own, rubbing knuckles against each other with strange ache and friction. The wide, disconcerting grin retreated behind the mask of perfect respect, and Dameia wondered if she'd imagined the whole thing. If he wasn't just the straightforward and helpful—albeit unconventional—young historian trying to make his way through palace politics on good looks and earnest labor to succeed.

The pair picked their way wordlessly back through the forest, emerging a bit mussed and leafy, but otherwise no worse for wear. Matime respectfully plucked a piece of wayward greenery from Dameia's hair before bowing and making his way back to the Archive.

She did not see him tuck the leaf into the belt of his tunic.

Nor did she witness the quick change in direction that moved his steps from a straight line to the Archive and instead pointed them directly to the Warden's office.

✧ ✧ ✧ ✧ ✧

This time when the princess broke through the barred fencing, Hyam expected her. As did the two rebels who followed them both between the bars and into the finger of forest that came around the mountain base. Though her news certainly took him by surprise.

"I found the ship," she stated without preamble.

Hyam blinked in shocked response. It had only been two days. He expected a plan, probably nothing more concrete than a sketched outline of how they might approach this whole escape. But the ship itself? It had only been two days. He had barely managed to contain a mutiny and she had found a ship that if history was to be believed, had been lost to humans—or at the very least, quite hidden—since shortly after its original crash.

Oren broke the silence first. "You found the human ship? Where is it?"

"Follow me; we don't have much time." The quad slunk away under cover of tree and brush.

Two days. Four cycles. How had she managed such a feat in two days? Hyam puzzled it in his mind. He had prayed for a miracle, but such a quick return was more than he'd dared to hope.

He wondered—feared—who she'd had to involve in order to find it. Trust was a luxury he'd not been able to much afford outside his own race, and even within it, depending. For her as royalty, what was that thin line between trust and fear? Who might tell her anything for fear of her station? And at the same time, who might then report her doings to another for their own gain?

It was not a lecture to have now. Ithai and Oren needed to believe her trustworthy. She *was* trustworthy. Or at least always had been to Hyam. But for him to question that now, to voice warnings that might imply that he discounted her, it would be the worst move he could make.

Well, maybe not the worst. He'd certainly stuck his foot in it much deeper before.

But at least a very, very bad move.

They crunched through the underbrush until stopped by Dameia's upheld hand. She turned to the rebels. "Are you ready?" she asked simply. Hyam nodded. They pushed through the final veil of branches, and there she was.

The Weight of Stars and Suns
Dawn Christine Jonckowski

The *Genesis*, the once-gleaming mother who had spawned the humans' beginning on Tav. All three men regarded her in reverent silence.

Ithai was first to approach the ship. He laid a flat hand against her sun-warmed side, as if translating the years of her people's sorrow into her bones. He circled the ship, muttering to himself all the while of her disrepair and the grandeur she must have had in her prime. To see the vessel brought so low, her children enslaved on a foreign world, it wrenched at Hyam's core as he watched the younger man pay his respects. Oren stood in awestruck silence. It was a reaction Hyam well knew.

"I'm sorry, we don't have much time," Dameia apologized in hushed tones. "We will return, and soon, and I will make arrangements to observe your safety while we are here longer to investigate the ship. But for now . . ." she trailed off.

Hyam curled his fingers gently around her arm, drawing her gaze from the ship to his. "I just need a moment," he said. She nodded, knowing.

Within five paces, he was poised to step over the threshold and enter the belly of the ship. As he crossed in, all else fell away. There was no Tav, no Dameia, no rebels, no slavery, just this moment: Hyam and the ship that had carried his ancestors and their dreams through constellations only to fail them at the last.

He was here for her redemption.

In the muted heavy air, dust hung suspended in shafts of light that pierced through age-eaten holes in her husk. Knobs and buttons and flat, dark panels that despite the murk of age reflected back his awestruck face. Chairs that looked like thrones, though the cushions had cracked in the heat and were bleeding plumes of yellowed stuffing. Pads of paper half-eaten away by critter and age that bore symbols and combinations in the language he knew, but whose strings meant nothing to him. Tucked into one work station, a worn image of a lovely woman, dark eyes in a darker face with a round and smiling infant balanced on her hip. He plucked it up, turned it over. Fading ink scribbled its way across the back: *So we may be with you wherever you go. Return to us. Return to me. All my love, Yvette.*

What had become of Yvette and her apple-cheeked child back on Earth? What had she believed about the fate of her beloved? What had been his fate? Aside, of course, from slavery. With whom had he mated? What had he done for his primary tasks? Did he die with the name of his Earth bride on his lips, or by then had relations and offspring here on Tav taken greater real estate in his soul?

So many questions.

Would he ever know the answers?

He bowed his head for the dead. Not for the Origin Generation itself who had foolishly and too quickly agreed to the contract that enslaved Hyam so many multitudes of years later. But for the *Genesis*. For those left behind on Earth to wonder.

Except.

Except there was still some chance they could do something to rebirth *Genesis*. Bound as she was by vines and age, derelict even in her grandeur, Hyam felt her pulse. Felt her purpose. Knew that beyond what his eyes could see, there was still life buried deep within the ship.

He just had to find it.

|| The Weight of Stars and Suns ||
Dawn Christine Jonckowski

But for now, it was enough to have stood in this hallowed womb, to feel the long stretched connection that threaded him and every human on Tav to the planet that was truly home.

Hyam stepped out of the ship reborn with purpose. Ithai and Oren could sense it, stood taller in its light.

"We must return," Dameia warned the trio softly.

Hyam nodded. "Yes," he agreed. "We have much work to do."

11

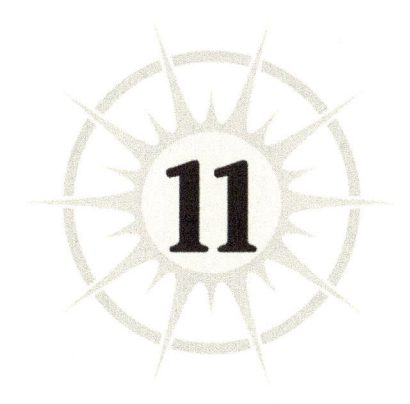

"Princess," the Warden slurped, his greedy gaze lingering on certain features a little too long for comfort before swinging back to the sword he was polishing with long lazy strokes. Her appearance in his office at this hour was hardly a surprise. In fact, he had been waiting with purpose. He knew she would be coming, and soon.

The Warden was about to become a much, much richer man.

"To what do I owe the pleasure of your company? Have you tired of your human already? Does he need a good stringing up before your next visit?" His lips twisted in a wet, suggestive smile.

Dameia forced herself to keep a steady and weighty eye on the Warden. To do otherwise would only encourage more of his salacious suggestions. Or at least, more than the "more" that was already going to be volleyed her way.

The *zakar* was incorrigible.

"I have come to bargain for more time, and more men. I want a blind eye to up to three men leaving the compound for the entirety of fourth watch, not just the lengthy guard change. You have my word that they will be returned by fifth watch, and that while they are with me, no Tavarians will be harmed, nor will they interact with other humans."

"More men?" The Warden arched bushy brows. "My, my," he tisked with a slight gurgle. "I never thought you to be so . . . adventurous. Though I suppose if one wants all one's bases covered . . ." he trailed off.

Dameia's look hardened, but she refused to give him any measure of satisfaction. "Just tell me if you will do it or not."

"Ohhhh, Princess," he purred, saliva stitching zigzags across his mouth. "Surely you understand that this, like all politics, must be negotiated."

A heavy bag of scores clanked down on his desk in response. The Warden took his time setting aside the polishing cloth, folding it in precise creases before tucking it away in his pocket, then slowly sliding the sword back into its sheath. Not once in the process did he break his gaze with Dameia. Without opening it, he picked up the bag of scores and weighed it in one hand.

"A pretty cost," he wagered. "Your humans must know some obscenely pleasurable tricks. Tell me," he leaned in, volume dropping low. "What is the price of a scream these days?"

She wanted to demand he stop. Wanted to take the heavy bag of scores and put a sizable dent in the side of his oily face rather than in her pile of savings. But the longer he continued to believe that her interest in the humans was purely for physical satisfaction, the safer they all were.

The Weight of Stars and Suns
Dawn Christine Jonckowski

"Either you accept my offer or you do not. There is no need for your commentary," she replied evenly.

The Warden chuckled, a sound more like a burbling wet cough than a laugh. "Princess, you realize exactly how at my mercy you stand? Each of those rebels exists within three breaths of death. Many on the Council are keen to see them relieved of their heads, and so see us relieved of their burden. That includes your father as well, whom I imagine has no inkling of his daughter's predilection toward human flesh. Though," he mused, cocking his head to one side, "you're not the first. Not even the first royal."

She would not rise to the bait.

He dangled it, and then he dropped it.

"You, like others, believe our esteemed Chieftain to have practiced utmost celibacy since the passing of your dear mother." He streaked the spittle from his lower lip with the back of his hand as he waited for his words to sink in. "Perhaps you should ask him about *her* someday, the human he took for his longest and darkest seasons. It has been a very, very long time, and even a Chieftain has needs, Princess. As I'm sure you have readily found."

Dameia stood a silent stone. She would not let him darken the beauty she had found with Hyam, regardless of what he or any other Tavarian thought of it. Even her father had found good and comfort in a human, if what the Warden said was to be taken as any form of truth. And assuming that her father had treated the woman with at least some modicum of respect.

She hoped.

Oh, she hoped.

Else the humans would have another reason to rebel and hate him.

She loved her father. And she loved Hyam.

She did not want to be forced to choose between them.

"Again, I ask you Warden: Do we have a deal?"

He leaned back in his chair, knees wide, gaze hooded and dark. Weighed the bag from hand to hand. "This will buy you two rebels at a time. Any two, it doesn't matter to me. They're all the same. But no more than two," he warned. "If after a few cycles, your tastes still absolutely demand three, we might come to a . . . new agreement." His slick smile implied in ways that had Dameia's stomach somersaulting.

Oh that her father could see her politicking now, masking her emotions and playing to get precisely what she wanted, despite what the other party thought they were conning out of her.

"Agreed," the princess pronounced, sticking her hand out to the Warden. "We have a deal." Dameia refused to shudder when his clammy, meaty palm closed around hers, held on longer than most found polite.

"Indeed," the Warden consented, dropping her hand finally and dipping his head. "Your expanded access begins tomorrow at second cycle," he said, shaking the bag of scores accompanied by a suggestive little eyebrow dance.

Dameia nodded once, turned to leave.

"Oh, and Princess?" his voice snaked over her shoulder. She glanced behind. His lips spread in a glassy smear of a smile.

"Do enjoy," he sneered.

|| The Weight of Stars and Suns ||
Dawn Christine Jonckowski

☼ ☼ ☼ ☼ ☼

Matime was asleep on a stack of books, face pressed to pages he'd been squinting over not long before, breath heavy and deep while saliva threatened to drip from his open mouth and pool in the spine of the manuscript when the Warden's message arrived. The runner dropped the envelope next to Matime's nose and hightailed back out of the musty room as fast as he could, ostensibly back to his own bed and dreams.

Rubbing sleep from the corners of his eyes, Matime picked up the envelope, slit the seal, and pulled out the folded paper.

She is breaking two out starting tomorrow. Watch the ship and report back. If all goes as planned, we will have them in the palms of our hands in no time. You will triumph. All Hail.

Matime blew a weighty breath. He had grown up the only child of a widower military man. It had been his father's dream to see him a soldier, but his uncle's twisted mind warped that dream until his father too began to believe that they should overthrow the Chieftain and train up Matime to take the throne.

For himself, Matime had been given no choice in the matter. And as a young boy, sure, ruling a planet sounded like quite the adventure.

But as the years passed, he proved to have neither head nor heart for rule. His military prowess was adequate at best, his strategy for war abysmal. And that was the nicest that could be said of it all. Every moment he was in the training ring, he yearned to be buried in his stacks of books, drinking in knowledge as if his whole life up until then had been a drought. Matime absently rubbed at his tattoos, remembering the sting both of receiving them and of knowing he didn't truly deserve them.

Then his father had died, and while part of Matime's heart died with the old man, secretly he rejoiced for the unfettering. He went to the Archives that very day and pledged his life as a historian where his knowledge could be used for the good of his people *and* his ruler. His desire to progress to the Council was true, but ended there. Nothing in his heart drove him for more, and certainly nothing propelled him toward the throne.

Aside, of course, from his uncle.

When his father's death revealed a multitude of debt that Matime could never hope to repay, his uncle stepped in. Profitable from both job and bribes, his uncle poured out scores to cancel every debt and generously fund Matime's training in the Archives.

Matime was once again—and always would be—tied to the purse and puppet strings of his uncle, the Warden.

And he hated every moment of the dance he was commanded day in and day out to perform.

For his uncle still held aspirations of putting Matime on the throne, if not through military force, then at least through marriage. He had created in his nephew the perfect specimen for the only child of the Chieftain. Broad of both shoulder and mind, Matime would satisfy the carnal feminine desires of a daughter and the militaristic specificities of a royal father.

After that, it would be a matter of ceremony and poison to plant him solidly on Tav's throne.

|| The Weight of Stars and Suns ||
Dawn Christine Jonckowski

Not that the puppetry would end there, of course.

But he did at least hold some hope that as Chieftain, he could make small commands here and there that would snip at least a few of the strings.

Vain hopes at best, but it was all he had to cling to.

That and a true admiration for the princess. No matter, since she apparently had an inclination for some dirt-faced human rebel.

For now.

He did honestly enjoy Dameia, for her wit and intelligence as well as her beauty.

Besides.

It did seem as if, one way or another, her human would soon not be of this world, and Matime would have Dameia all to himself.

And then perhaps if they played the game just right, together they could rid Tav of the political plague known as the Warden.

He could be happy as the husband of a Chieftain.

He could be happy.

As long as he was finally freed of his uncle, he could be happy.

And so the game played on.

✧ ✧ ✧ ✧ ✧

In the same dead hour of the second cycle, in that oh-so-brief time between their foray into the forest with the princess and the moment the alarm would sound to rudely call them to another cycle of slaving and torture, the three rebels sat in a tight triad in the far corner of the barracks by turns marveling and lamenting over what they had seen.

"I always knew the *Genesis* existed, but I suppose I never really expected to see her in person," mused Ithai. "What must it have been like to witness her construction on Earth? To board her and fly through sky and space?" His young face bloomed in wonderment, lit for the first time since long before they had been imprisoned after the raid.

Oren was significantly less rapt. As in, not at all. "But did you see? The ship's full of holes and rust. That junk heap couldn't hope to break atmosphere, much less make it all the way back to Earth." He turned to Hyam. "What are we doing, really? What can we do with a pile of scrap metal and a bunch of rebels who know more about brick-making than flying?"

"We have the Origin Generation texts," Ithai began.

"Books be damned, Ithai," Oren snarled his interruption.

Hyam sighed. He didn't have any more answers than either of them, but by virtue of having been nominated a leader of this latest rebellion, they expected plans. They expected strategy.

They expected miracles.

Except this time, he was fresh out.

"I don't kno—" he began, and then saw the light in Ithai begin to dim. It wasn't just the light of hope that was dimming, it was Ithai himself. Hyam looked—*really* looked—at his best friend. Always a thinner, lanky frame, Ithai was now dwindling to bone draped in skin. His eyes were pits in his face, clavicles jutting out of a sunken-in chest. He didn't have the same fortitude that Hyam did; he could not exist on the gruel and hard labor. Ithai was meant for poetry and courting soft women to softer beds, for spending days in the sunlight penning the deep thoughts of his generation for posterity, for planting flowers and bringing pretty little bouquets to widows who would call him "darling."

Not for this.

Never for this.

None of them were made for this, it was true.

But some were less made for it than others.

And it was up to him to ensure that they all survived, body, soul, and spirit.

"I don't know ... much about spaceships," Hyam finally redirected. "But we know that the Origin Generation had knowledge that they recorded and saved. Once they realized that no one from Earth was coming to their rescue, don't you think they would have begun plotting their escape? And that couldn't have happened without the aid of a ship." Hyam's voice intensified as his conviction built. "If we cannot fly her as she is, what if we can scavenge pieces from *Genesis* and through the guidance of the texts, create a new ship?"

Oren fixed him with a straight stare. "You're mad."

"No, no," Hyam held up a hand. "Hear me out: We probably can't build a very big ship, but what if we could manage a smaller pod of some sort? Maybe it can't get all the way back to Earth, but we could find a neighboring planet that would allow us asylum and facilitate hailing Earth. If they were to find out that after all this time, we are alive? Don't you imagine they would send an immediate rescue mission?"

"Oh, like they did after *Genesis* crashed?" Oren's sarcasm dripped thick as syrup. "You've got a better chance of solving this rebellion by marrying your purple princess."

Ithai shot Oren a brief but surprisingly deadly glare. "I agree with Hyam."

"Of course you do," Oren muttered. Ithai treated him to another steely look.

"We have to get off Tav, Oren. And if anyone can get us out, Hyam can. I know where the Origin Generation hid their texts. Their manuals, their maps, everything. If Princess Dameia can find someone who will agree to pass the texts through her, I can begin studying them for information on construction. Then you and Hyam can harvest the appropriate parts from *Genesis* and we can build a new, smaller ship."

"And who is going to pilot this thing? Unless you suppose that will be in your precious texts as well."

Ithai lifted his chin a notch. "I imagine it could be. And before you insinuate that I am also crazy for believing I could fly a ship too, let me remind you of all the construction we have accomplished in the colony to better our human living conditions after just reading and studying the Origin Generation texts on architecture and city planning." He crossed his arms over his chest. "How much different could it be to learn to fly based on their words?"

Oren only grunted, his displeasure and skepticism already much accounted for.

The Weight of Stars and Suns
Dawn Christine Jonckowski

For himself, Hyam was buoyed by Ithai's renewed optimism. If they were going to attempt this admittedly crazy and improbable plan, at least one of them needed to remain positive.

And they needed to involve another human.

Not his first choice of approaches, but these were certainly desperate times.

"Who do we know who is trustworthy and can bridge the gap between the colony, the princess, and ourselves?" Hyam's eyes met each of the other two in turn.

"My Aunt Hannah is the princess' human companion," offered Ithai. "We don't have to tell the princess yet that we are involving her. I could just ask her to pass a note for me, mentioning that I've always been especially close to my aunt and I just want her to know that I'm all right. My note will speak to the princess' trustworthiness. If Hannah is willing and able to help—as I am certain she will be—I will have her locate the texts and pass them to us through the princess."

"Her name is Dameia," Hyam responded before he could stop himself.

Oren barked a short laugh, leaning back from his seat on the floor to recline against the foot of a bunk. "Well that may be, but not all of us have quite the same familiarity as you do, Hyam. Not all of us are privileged so as to be on a first-name no-title basis. Visited in prison and rescued by royalty. My, my, what must you have done to earn such distinction." The rhetorical question hung heavy.

Hyam steeled himself against Oren's distaste and insinuations. "Oren, I've never asked you to understand or even approve of any of my interactions with the princess, up to and including this quest we are setting upon now. I refuse to explain anything about my relationship with her, whatever you think it may or should be. It is between us and us only." He stood to pace, stopped to plant himself in front of Oren.

"But for this, for my brothers? Today you are coming first. Today I put everything—and every*one*—I may long for on Tav aside and put the safety and well-being of my people first. It does not matter what I lose here, be it individual or even my own life, if it means that our human brethren may have the chance to return home and live free."

"Pretty words," mused Oren, picking disinterestedly at dirt and rust lodged under his fingernails. "One can almost see how you got to be a rebellion leader." He looked up at Hyam, gaze unreadable. Sighed. Lifted lazily to his feet. "But seeing as the only other option I have right now is to die in a labor camp, lower than a slave, on this God-forsaken rock of suns, then count me in on this ridiculous, harebrained scheme of yours." He walked slowly to his bunk.

"Just don't blame me when it doesn't work." He sat on the hard wood they all called a bed, tucked his feet and rolled to put his back to the pair.

"I think Yair's enduringly positive mood is rubbing off on him," Ithai offered under his breath, amused.

Hyam couldn't help but smile at the jest. "Imprisonment is bound to make one crotchety from time to time. But he's a good man, he'll come around. When he sees what we have accomplished, he'll come around."

This plan, it was going to work.

It had to. It simply had to.

| | The Weight of Stars and Suns | |
Dawn Christine Jonckowski

☼   ☼   ☼   ☼   ☼

By the next morning, the Chieftain's step nearly had a bounce to it; would have if he was the sort to bounce. But as he was the strictly militaristic type, and after all, the Chieftain, he settled for a purposeful stride instead as he crossed the complex heading toward his daily Council meeting.

Construction on the underground cities was beginning across the planet. Not a single human toe—rebel or otherwise—had stepped out of line since the sentencing so long ago. Which he counted as a bit of a pity; it would have been immensely satisfying to rid himself of the dozen troublemakers. Nothing incited obedience quite like a display of severed heads. Though he had to admit that Arganon had been right: It had been better to round up the rebels and put them to harder forced labor than lose the opportunity to glean whatever work from them they could until such time as they expired, by accident or design.

He was still bidding for design. These rebels, for reasons he could not explain, left a far more sour taste in his mouth than had any before them. And there had been many.

He refused to believe that it had anything to do with the insinuations the Warden had made about Dameia's prison visits.

Not that he could cast the first stone should she have brief proclivity toward a human male.

But did it have to be *that* one?

The Chieftain's steps slowed to a stop in front of the construction site where the twelve rebels labored under the unrelenting suns. Stripped to the waist and pouring sweat rivers through the layers of dirt that coated them, they all looked the same to the Chieftain. Weak animals who had dared to rise above their station in life and now served the cost of that decision.

He watched as they dug into the ground, hauled away barrels of dirt, as several would disappear below with wooden beams and large slates of stone. They worked in silence punctuated only by the crunch of their sandals on rock shards, or the occasional grunt as they hefted a load.

To think this race supposedly ruled their own planet far and away.

No wonder they'd made such a mess of it that they needed to find other worlds on which to live. Laughable. They were utterly and entirely laughable.

Shaking himself from his musings, the Chieftain purposed his way across the covered walk and into the corridor that branched off with a plethora of meeting rooms. With the sound of a gong and a quick announcement by the Council Guard, he swept into the Council chamber.

This. This was his haven, his home and heartbeat. This was where he protected his planet, governed his people, directed the fate of those who dared oppose his laws.

This was where he ruled.

This was also where he occasionally got very, very bored. As the Council members read long reports in a monotonous drone, he felt his head tip forward in the beginnings of sleep and snapped

The Weight of Stars and Suns
Dawn Christine Jonckowski

himself back to the present. A quick glance to his left revealed that his daughter too struggled to contain her focus, and instead had taken to sketching winding vines up the sides of her notes. So intent was she on the shapes of the leaves and buds that she jumped when her father's whisper hit her ear.

"I've invited a guest for dinner," the Chieftain pronounced. It wasn't anything particularly out of the ordinary on most days.

This wasn't going to be most days.

He nearly laughed with glee.

Nearly. He was the Chieftain. After all.

"Oh?" She lifted neither eye nor pen.

"I believe you know him," he teased out the reveal, hoping for a flash of pleasure that would give away her feelings when he said the name.

Her face stayed. "I know many 'hims' that you might invite to dinner. Which one in particular is this?" Her pen began tracing different shapes.

"Someone I believe you have gotten to know much better than usual as of late," the Chieftain hinted. "A historian."

At this, Dameia's head finally turned. "Matime?" she asked, one fine brow arched in slight surprise.

The Chieftain sat back, partially deflated. He'd been assured they spent much time together over the past several days, this well-proportioned historian and his daughter, that he had even accompanied her on a long walk through the forest. Not an act traditionally done without some underlying reason, usually of the romantic bent.

He had definitely been aiming for a more pleased reaction.

"Yes, I did recently make his acquaintance in the Archives, and he was quite helpful in my research, too," Dameia finally allowed, sliding her focus back to her doodling. "He's a fine enough individual."

At that, a slow smile grew across the Chieftain's face. There it was. She was his daughter and a fine politician to the end, giving away little and less with every interaction. Learning to conceal her emotions so they could not later be used against her. She would indeed make a fine successor when the time came.

And after dinner, he would have a good idea on the one who would spend the rest of his life ruling at her side.

Letting the subject drop, the Chieftain pulled himself tall on his chair and recommitted his attention to the goings on of the Council. But not before his eyes caught note of the emerging details on his daughter's illustrations.

Breaking forth clearly from the vines and aimed to stars she'd penned in the upper margin was a vehicle that was unequivocally and undeniably the human spaceship.

☼ ☼ ☼ ☼ ☼

Dameia hid in an abandoned watch deck that miraculously managed to be both concealed from outside view and afford a clear sightline to the rebels' construction site. Curled against the sun-warmed stucco-coated stone, she watched Hyam in the brief moments he emerged from underground, her face clearly painted with a look of love that tipped solidly into misery.

The Weight of Stars and Suns
Dawn Christine Jonckowski

She wasn't a fool. She could put her father's equation together.

They'd spoken—well, *he'd* spoken and to his point of view, she'd agreed with her shocked silence—of an arranged marriage. Now the Chieftain had heard rumors of growing camaraderie between his daughter and a historian with an impressive military lineage and aspirations for Councilship. What other conclusions should he draw but that this would be a natural pairing?

And so Matime would come to dinner, and Dameia would be expected to entertain him as if he were a suitor. As if her heart had any form of yearning for him.

The half-ring of suns, and the two dark pits where the burnt-out husks of former suns still hung, began to sink toward the horizon while the balance prepared to rise on the opposite side.

Twelve dirt-crusted rebels emerged from underground and at the bark of a Tavarian foreman, fell into two straight lines of six. They were quickly cuffed and chained, banded together. Brothers. Prisoners. Humans. Animals. Herded off the site and back toward their compound where she knew bowls full more of liquid than any verifiable nutrition awaited them. They were beginning to exhibit signs of their wear.

She hoped Hyam had a plan. The ship was a gorgeous monster. But in severe disrepair even to her unpracticed eye.

If they could fix her broken spine and shredded skin.

If they could figure out how to breathe life back into her frame.

If they could manage to steer her off Tav and back home to Earth.

If, if, if.

There were a lot of if's involved. Far more than Dameia was altogether comfortable with, but maybe Hyam saw something she didn't. Maybe the rebels knew more than they let on.

Gods, she hoped they did.

Unfolding her legs, the princess sighed and made her resigned way down to her chambers. If she was to be put to auction for Matime's tastes, she might as well look the part. The farther down this road she could send her father sniffing, the less likely he would be to uncover the actual truth. She hoped.

Hope. That fragile, shimmering thread that bound all things together. Tied up her world and for now kept it all from leaking out where it shouldn't.

She let her feet carry her to her chambers where Hannah was already tittering.

"I see my father has kept you informed," Dameia said dryly.

"Don't worry, *neqeba*, everything is set for bathing, and I have had one of your best dresses cleaned and readied for dinner. You will be radiant." Hannah beamed as she swirled around Dameia, relieving her arms of the basic ceremonial metal bands and bracelets, diving fingers in hair to unpin the tight braids. Tresses fell in waved clumps and Dameia felt the glorious release of letting her hair down.

"You must be absolutely beside yourself," Hannah continued as she herded Dameia into her bathing chamber where a steaming fragrant tub awaited. "To have this wonderful suitor meet with your father at last." She helped Dameia into the tub and all but pushed her under the water to rinse off the day's dirt.

|| The Weight of Stars and Suns ||
Dawn Christine Jonckowski

Submerged under the ripples and floating flower petals, the pieces fell into place. Hannah assumed that the dinner guest was also the subject of Dameia's recent romantic woes. And why shouldn't she? The whole palace was an intricate network of gossip chains and spies. Just as Hannah had observed the evidence of Dameia's second cycle trysts, so the staff had likely seen Dameia's repeated trips to the Archive and at least their retreating backs as they set on their forest adventure. Followed quickly by the Chieftain's sudden inclusion of the young muscled historian in their dinner plans, what other conclusion was there to draw but that romance was brewing between this strapping *zakar* and the royal daughter?

She had to play along.

Dameia emerged from the bathwater with a different face. "I'm nervous for this dinner," she confessed, and despite the game, it wasn't at all a lie.

Hannah switched from overexcited companion to motherly in an instant. "My darling girl, to recall your face from just a few days ago as you wrestled with your feelings and disclosed your beliefs of his, I have no doubts of the strength of your beloved's desire for you. That he would bravely attend your father when both have full knowledge of this desire, well. That is no easy feat for a suitor. Least of all the suitor of a princess." Hannah sluiced the suds and petals from the princess' skin and hair and wrapped her in a soft towel as she stepped out of the bath.

"Besides," the older woman continued. "Your father's invitation is a positive sign. I have a feeling that he would not be opposed to a quick beheading of any suitor he deemed an ill fit for his daughter," she said with a teasing twinkle.

Dameia blanched. Hannah had no idea how close she danced to the truth. The Chieftain was already keen on snipping the thread of Hyam's life with only the slightest provocation. If he were ever to learn that his daughter loved a human slave, especially a rebel human slave, Hyam's head would be on a spike so fast that his corpse would have whiplash. Dameia forced the bile down and turned what she hoped was a close facsimile of a smile toward Hannah.

"Yes, well," she trailed off. Hannah chuckled and gently nudged her down onto a stool so she could comb through her damp hair. Dameia closed her eyes and tried to let her worries slough off with each pull of the comb. She felt Hannah's fingers deftly separating, twisting, twining. Brushes slipped across her face, liquids painted her lids and lips. She was draped in soft fabrics that swished against her legs and left her arms bare, arms that were then decked with etched and hammered bands set with dazzling stones. And when she finally looked at her reflection, a princess stared back.

She was a feast heading to a dinner hoping not to be devoured.

It was going to be a very long meal.

✧ ✧ ✧ ✧ ✧

It all started well. General pleasantries and the associated awkwardness of a dinner guest who knows he's being inspected from every angle. And by the ruler of his entire planet, no less. But by the time the dinner plates heaped before them with steaming sand hen and assorted vegetables, it seemed that everyone had run out of things to say. Dameia's gaze fell somewhere in her lap. The Chieftain's face cragged stonier by the moment as he undoubtedly puzzled over whether he'd misunderstood the pairing. Matime for all of his mild-mannered historian-ness proved to be a lusty eater, digging in with abandon to the point that Dameia wondered if he even noticed the fact that not three words had been exchanged since the main course was served.

If this was her convincing her father that she was in love, she was a poor actress indeed.

And then Matime—gods bless him—came to her rescue.

He looked up abashedly and chuckled the easy laugh she'd come to expect. "My deepest apologies to you both," he began, setting aside the roasted leg of sand hen and wiping greasy fingers on the cloth to his left. "Historians aren't much accustomed to such fare, and for a moment my mouth won out and I forgot myself in your company."

The tension released like a breath.

Her father chuckled, a rare sound of late. "Is that a gracious political hint that I need to speak with my Council about the historians' pay?"

Matime offered a laugh in return. "Oh no, sir, it's not that at all. It is simply that we often become so enamored with our texts that we forget to perform basic tasks such as eating or drinking. In fact," he offered, amusement blooming, "there is a tale of a historian so engrossed in his research that he neglected to sleep or even bathe for twenty-eight days complete. It is said that once his colleagues braved the stench enough to drag him out and douse him in water, it took an additional three days for his scent to also take its leave of the

Archives." The bright smile slashed its way across his face. "Or at least that's the story they tell to all new historians when warning of the siren's song of allure these volumes can often sing."

"And you?" the Chieftain queried. "Have you ever offended your fellow historians in a similar way?"

"Certainly not to that degree!" Matime replied with a wink in Dameia's direction. She stretched what she hoped was the approximation of an indulgent smile across her face. It was more difficult than she'd anticipated to appear convincing. "They like to make claim that I once abandoned a carafe of blackflower juice in a back corner so long that upon its discovery, there was enough growing inside to populate another planet. But I maintain that tale grows taller with each retelling, as I distinctly remember retrieving that carafe only one day after forgetting it. And nothing grew inside." He laughed easily at himself, pushing his sleeves up and over muscled arms, revealing his tattoos as he stretched to snatch another leg of sand hen from the platter in the center of the table. Dameia forced herself not to stare. Though at least her blush could be genuine.

"Tell me more of your family, Matime," the Chieftain switched course. He gestured to the bands inked up and down Matime's forearms. "How does one with such a military lineage find himself content in the airless chambers of the Archives?"

"Ah, that's only a bit of a tale, sir," Matime answered. It escaped no one's notice that he dropped his hands to his sides as if to straighten his robes, allowing the voluminous sleeves to slide back down over the ink that branded him. "My father—gods rest him—like all fathers, wished to see his only son follow in his rather daunting footsteps, and to that end pushed me in and through his military trainings likely far too early for anyone's tastes. Least of all mine. Not for lack of trying, as any dutiful son who loves his father wishes to please him, but I was a failure by every definition. Only through breeding have I managed at all to look like a soldier—it's a whole family affair—but I assure that is where the prowess drops off. I should much prefer a book and pen in my hand to any sword any day. My passion is for the law, as much of an oddity as that makes me in my family. I'd rather interpret and govern the law than wield it in the form of a weapon."

Dameia watched the interaction, guarded. If she were any sort of normal Tavarian female, she would be a blithering mess over Matime's attentions. Or more of one. She cringed inwardly, recalling her earlier ogling. His speech was precise, his gestures contained and elegant. And he was built like a god; his shoulders alone should have inspired poetry. He was precisely the particularities any father would wish for his daughter: strong, polite, handsome, smart. Digging back to her childhood fantasies of princes and love and happily-ever-afters, Matime was exactly the proportions to fill that hazy silhouette from her young imaginations.

And yet, none of that mattered, because the Tavarian princess had grown instead into surprising tastes: She loved a human.

"I imagine your family must be proud of you, Matime." The Chieftain's voice broke into her musings. "A fine scholar with a direct line to Councilship. My roster is full, but I imagine that someday you will progress to a fine Councilman who can offer firm and lawful guidance to his Chieftain." Here he turned loaded gaze on his daughter, smiled heavy with meaning.

Dameia shook her focus into the conversation. "Yes, proud family, I'm sure. Especially your uncle."

"Uncle?" The Chieftain's eyebrow arched in a practiced lift. With a skidding whine, he pushed his chair back from the table, settled in for what he surely hoped to be a long and engaging after dinner conversation. Barely lifting his finger, he tapped the rim of his goblet. Slaves scurried from places unseen to top off the fizzed bloodwine and clear plates, all in quick and practiced silence that put them on the edge of invisibility.

Matime sipped from his newly refilled goblet. "Ah, yes. After my father passed, it was my uncle who took me under his wing and funded my apprenticeship in the Archives."

"Another military *zakar* like your father, I presume? Since you said it runs in the family."

"Yes," Matime confirmed. "In fact, you likely know him well."

"Oh?" The royal eyebrow arched further, just shy of folding itself in half.

Matime smiled, all fondness, all genuine, all teeth. It made Dameia's spine itch.

"Indeed. If you recall the Bloodless Uprising many a year ago when a captain in your military who was nearing the end of his service on the lines successfully managed to capture and contain the entire rebellious revolution without bloodshed, you rewarded him with one of the most prestigious roles a retired soldier could hope for in the Capitol.

"My uncle is your Warden."

12

His uncle was the Warden.

The refrain echoed in every corner of Dameia's mind as she slid through the now-regular ritual of evading detection while sneaking to the rebel compound.

Of course.

Of course Matime's uncle was the Warden. Because nothing else would have better suited this fantastic tangled mess that all Dameia's plans had become.

After the historian had made his somewhat graceless announcement, Dameia had nearly choked on her fizzed bloodwine, coughing rather indelicately into the crook of her arm and waving away the concerns of her dinner companions as best her flailing could. More concerned were they with her health than the peculiar timing of her fit; she could only hope no connection had been made.

Her hope, that fragile thread, was becoming significantly more frayed, the fuzzy ends tickling the temptations of disaster in ways that did not make her altogether comfortable.

Because here she was, sneaking to a prison compound to conjure two rebels who had little and less knowledge than she did about the ship that had inelegantly deposited their ancestors upon this rock, holding to some baseless belief that between the three of them, they could figure out how to get some or all of the humans home to Earth.

Absurd didn't even begin to describe the plan.

Hyam and Ithai awaited her, with Oren standing watch at the barracks, and with a swift and silent exchange of nods, the two rebels followed her back through the bars and out into the forest.

Dameia shifted silent feet through the tangled vines carpeting the forest floor. Here, the light filtered through heavy oval leaves the size of her hand, sending dappled diamonds of light arrowing onto faces, shoulders, limbs. Silently, Hyam stretched a hand to help her over a swatch of thickly rocked terrain. Her pride and her thoughts kept her blind; Hyam's light shrug betrayed the scratch on his own ego. Ithai reached over to grip Hyam's bicep with narrow fingers, his own toes unsure and scrabbling for purchase. They continued through the trees.

The air between the trio hung thick and heavy with all the unanswered. They drove forward fueled by healthy determination or unhealthy foolishness, which depended entirely upon the precise moment you asked any of them. Three steps, determination, two more and some thought stew, foolishness. A glimpse of the ship through the regrowth of the forest, equal parts. Ithai charged straight inside the behemoth to begin studying her intricate inner workings, flicking switches and toggles and pressing buttons, all determination.

The Weight of Stars and Suns
Dawn Christine Jonckowski

Dameia hung back, Hyam beside her, both paused under the weight of their foolhardy.

"What are we doing?"

Hyam turned at the sound of her heavy question.

"At the moment, we're standing here like fools staring at the skeleton of a ship that none of us knows how to repair, much less fly, believing we can work miracles to make her or some smaller facsimile thereof airborne again just long enough to deposit a few of us on a neighboring planet that can contact Earth and bring us home."

Tavarian fixed human with a stare.

"Or did you mean more existentially?" Hyam continued unfazed, leaning a hard muscled shoulder against one of the newer tree trunks. Its youngness creaked in protest, but held fast against the human's recline. "Because if you're looking for a deeper meaning to why we are all here in this moment, why our lives have converged just so, how the cosmos aligned that two individuals of wildly different origins and species could find each other in the whole mess of stars and suns and manage not hate, but love?

"Well, then I have no idea." Cheeky grin.

Dameia loved him a little bit more in that moment. His fingers laid on the strings of her soul and knew just which ones to pluck so that the music resonated in her heart. It was just one of the many, many things she loved best about him.

"But," his voice broke into her warm musings, his leg crooking back to rest a foot against the tree behind him, "to validly respond to the more serious question to which you still seek answer, it's early, Dameia. We are only now beginning to discover what we don't know that we don't know."

"It's already a long list," Dameia sighed.

"Granted," Hyam allowed. "But once we identify, then we can begin to systematically solve. It's not that much different than running a government."

"Sure, a government that is asked to solve the impossible based solely on conjecture and what may be recalled from half-senile minds in a community that neither of us—might I remind you—is allowed to visit."

Hyam studied his fingernails, unconcerned. "So, kind of like that whole burned out suns problem, eh?"

His nonchalant response froze her, reply half-formed on her tongue.

"I know," Hyam chuckled. "You hate it when I'm right."

☼ ☼ ☼ ☼ ☼

Inside, Ithai was insulated from the banter, from the forest noise, even from the circumstances that colored every day of his life as a human on Tav. Here he stood amidst the trappings of the home world he had never known. In a section of living space not flattened by the crash, he could see bunks turned into small havens with photos and knick knacks brittled by heat and age. He resisted the siren song of curiosity, knowing full well how quickly he would drown in the little time he had. Turned, closed the door on the history of his people, and made his way to the bridge.

Light as he had physically become through work and weary, his steps still echoed in the ovened chambers of the beast's heart. A

The Weight of Stars and Suns
Dawn Christine Jonckowski

solitary cell wending through veins. His fingers trailed along panels made of substance he had no vocabulary for, warm to the touch but not the screeching hot of a metal. The floor was both resistant and grippy beneath the cakes of dirt on his feet. His steps stayed sure despite the dust.

Finally, he emerged at the hub of all her direction. Buttons, toggles, and switches everywhere. Shiny surfaces that reflected his face even as they drank in his image. Odd rectangular slots that appeared designed to receive a particularly shaped something. Most were empty. One had frozen mid-gulp; Ithai could not dislodge the piece.

But he could push it.

It slid in with little resistance.

Clicked.

Silence.

✧ ✧ ✧ ✧ ✧

"We have texts that Ithai believes will help us rebuild the ship and learn to fly it." Hyam changed the course of conversation. "He had them stashed in the colony. Ithai promises he has a loyal aunt in the palace who can be trusted to pass the texts to you so that we may study them and learn." He lifted an eye from the study of his fingers to meet his princess' face. She was shooting a practiced eyebrow arch right back.

"Is it truly wise to involve another human, Hyam? More and more people seem to be finding out about this; how can we be sure that everyone involved will stay silent when necessary?"

"They are all loyal to me, Dameia, I promise."

"To you, yes! But not to me. Evidenced enough by the fact that out of twelve rebels, three remain to assist with your plan. *Three*. To carry out a plan to save them all." The princess' tattooed arms folded across her chest, in defiance or to protect her weary soul, Hyam could not tell. "That says much of you three. Little of the remaining nine that you will still yet save if we can manage to push this broken mother back into the sky." She began to pace a dry crunchy cadence in the undergrowth.

"I trust Ithai with my life, as I trust you, Dameia. And I would never knowingly put you in harm's way; Ithai likewise with me. We are brothers, in name if not in some small part by blood. We did not grow up with luxury, with gifts and other ways to show affection. All we have is our trust. All we have *ever* had is that trust. As my brother loves me, he would not put me or someone I love in danger." Hyam pushed off the tree with one foot, and in three long strides was at Dameia's side, silencing her crackling pace, turning her to face him.

"Trust me, Dameia."

She offered only distressed silence.

"*Trust* me, Dameia."

Anguish, on both sides. For how could either claim love if trust was not unfurled as well? Hyam leaned his forehead to hers, his hands framing her beautifully strong and fragile face, the light freckles of her lavender skin peeking between his splayed fingers.

"Trust *me*, Dameia."

|| The Weight of Stars and Suns ||
Dawn Christine Jonckowski

A sigh. Of assent. Of defeat?

"I will. I do."

One breath. Two. A shared release.

"Ithai's aunt is your companion, Hannah."

✧   ✧   ✧   ✧   ✧

From his perch in a dense tree high above the scene, Matime witnessed the princess being pulled into embrace by the rebel human. Heard murmured conversation, but not enough to decipher plans. Saw the human place a tender kiss on the forehead and then the lips of the Tavarian who stood to rule the planet. She would inherit this world, and yet in that moment, Matime was convinced her entire world stood before her in the form of a dirty human rebel.

Something stirred deep in his gut. Jealousy? Hate? How could he feel either when like him, she had only ever been a pawn in a larger plot? The only difference was that Matime knew the plot, knew the characters, knew the end. Dameia did not.

He could not hate her.

He could not even hate the human, much disappointed as his uncle would be should he learn that.

He could hate this situation, hate how he was drawn in to the middle of all the politicking and secrecy, hate how he was a pawn in a plan to utterly destroy this princess' life, be that physically or metaphorically.

But he could not hate her, could not hate them. Even as he played the princess and her father like temple flutes.

The game played on.

He watched the lovers.

So closely that he did not see the slight shiver of the ship. Did not hear the strange chirrup it emitted, followed by a thump deep within the hull, before falling silent once more. When he saw the lovers startle apart, he took it as a reaction to the hour, to the realization that they had moments only to get the prisoners back to the compound before their deal with his uncle wore out for the cycle.

It was the only part of the interaction he would not report to the Warden.

✧ ✧ ✧ ✧ ✧

The piece slid into the slot and disappeared and Ithai didn't give it another thought. None of the buttons seemed to do much. Which wasn't surprising, as whatever power source gave the ship life had clearly drained from either time or impact (or both). So that was yet another item on the already long list of what all they had to figure out to make this plan work.

And yet, for all the intricacies and impossibilities, Ithai still had faith.

They would leave Tav.

Every sign pointed toward it, from the inconvenience of the raid and being imprisoned, to the sentencing and work camp, to the oddly wonderful lilt of love between Hyam and the Princess Dameia. Ithai smiled as his fingers continued to dance over buttons and switches.

The Weight of Stars and Suns
Dawn Christine Jonckowski

Hyam and a Tavarian. And not just any Tavarian. The princess, for goodness sakes.

It defied all logic, flew against everything they had been raised to believe about the Tavarians, everything that their everyday lives even seemed to corroborate about the purpled and inked race that enslaved them. (Though arguably, the Origin Generation had enslaved themselves, but that was a topic for another day, a blame that would never correctly be assigned so long as humans lived as slaves on Tav.)

And yet.

There was something so enduringly lovely about the way the princess looked at his best friend, not like he was an animal to be broken and controlled. More as if he himself had hung the necklace of suns around the planet. As if he was her entire world, despite the fact that she stood to inherit the very world they all stood upon.

His fingers danced onto a button encased under a clear bubble. The bubble flipped up, so he pushed the button.

Nothing happened.

Or did it?

Had the ship shimmied ever so slightly under his feet? Or was that just the aftereffects of a hard cycle's work followed by truncated sleep? His wasting frame didn't stand up to as much as it used to. His head often pounded, a heavy beat that nearly drowned the rumble of his shrinkingly empty stomach. He probably needed a break from the pressing heat of dank air within the ship. His vision was beginning to fuzz and narrow, his ears echoing with a faint burble of chirps.

Not the ship.

It couldn't be.

Couldn't be. She wasn't alive.

Alive.

Was he?

Weight pressed hard on his skull. A beat while his hands scrambled to grab support.

Then his head filled and he fainted dead away.

☼ ☼ ☼ ☼ ☼

It wasn't Hyam's revelation that Ithai's aunt was Dameia's own human companion that startled her half as much as the quick drumbeat thump that resonated from deep within the ship. The lovers broke apart, both wary.

"You heard it too," Dameia whispered.

"I did."

Without further words, both charged into the belly of the beast, following as best they could the memory of where the single heartbeat thud emanated from within the monster. The main hallway fed a broad vein straight to the bridge where they found Ithai, a crumpled pile of bones on the floor. Instantly, Hyam was on his knees beside his friend.

"Ithai, Ithai," he called gently, urgently. "Come back, brother." He looked up at Dameia.

"We need to get him out of here."

As one creature, human and Tavarian gingerly unfolded the fallen man enough for Hyam to scoop him up in his arms and lead

The Weight of Stars and Suns
Dawn Christine Jonckowski

the charge back into the sunlight. In their rush, neither saw the silhouette that descended from a high branch. Their feet on the underbrush drowned out the sound of another's landing. Their focus on the ashen face framed by the forest floor debris of dried and fallen leaves kept them from noticing the purple face that peered briefly through shoots and stalks before vanishing into the wood.

Hyam leaned in close over Ithai.

"Brother, Ithai, come back. Come back, now." He gently patted his friend's face with one roughened hand while the other pulsed on the fallen man's chest, coaxing a heart to pump better, faster. Hyam pressed down the panic rising in his own heart. He would not lose Ithai like this, to the suck of an airless room as the younger man delved into its secrets praying for a revelation that could lead them home.

Home.

Could they call it home if not one human left in the colony had even seen it? Maybe Tav had never quite felt like home to Hyam because he'd been fed on the idea of rebellion from an early age. It couldn't be a home until he could serve as a master.

Although lately . . . lately he'd felt more at home. More at home in a stark prison cell and a starker rebel compound than in the relative comfort of the colony.

All because of Dameia.

Perhaps home was less a place than it was a person.

Well, a Tavarian. Whatever. Someone you loved and who loved you in return. Maybe that was what made any place home. No matter where in the cosmos you landed.

Ithai's eyelids fluttered.

"Is hotter than *tachat* in there," he mumbled, grappling for focus. Hyam laughed with relief.

"Yes, brother, it certainly is. Welcome back." He grinned widely, anxiety retreating.

"I was . . . pressing buttons. Couldn't get anything to do nothing. I think . . . went in but didn't come back out. And there was a bubble? Not sure . . . Gonna need to read up." Ithai struggled to pull his feet under him.

"Slow down, Ithai, you were out cold for a long bit," Hyam spoke to the younger man in soothing, hushed tones. "Let us help you, brother. We'll get back to the compound and you can rest for a while."

Ithai's eyes sharpened quickly on Hyam's face. "What if I can't work? Don't let them kill me, Hyam. I can't—I'm not ready." Panic shot through his voice.

"Look at me, Ithai: No one is dying today. No one is dying tomorrow, either. You are going to live a long life. Long enough to bore everyone on Earth with your tales of adventure about growing up on Tav. No one is dying today. Least of all you."

Ithai stared at Hyam for a beat, and then nodded. "Okay. Okay. Let's go home."

Hyam draped his friend's arm over his shoulders; Dameia did the same, and together they lifted Ithai to his feet.

"We're working on it, brother. We're working on it."

They set off into the forest.

And the skeleton behind them let out a single soft pinging chime.

13

At three twenty-six a.m. Central Standard Time, in a small room off a tight hallway in a windowless section of a building in Alabama, a screen that had lain dormant for more years than anyone could count suddenly whined to life. In the middle of a black field floated a single grey-blue dialogue box.

Incoming distress signal from Genesis. *Please respond.*

14

"I daresay that young *zakar* would make a fine addition to your Council someday, Dameia," the Chieftain mused as he poured himself a generous carafe of blackflower juice the next morning. He sat out on her patio, regally arranged as ever in the morning light. The princess had emerged feeling bedraggled from the previous cycle—if impeccably dressed due to Hannah's silent ministrations—to find both her breakfast and her father delivered to her. And stifled a groan.

The last thing she wanted to be in the morning (especially before a single drop of blackflower juice) was cordial. The last thing she wanted to do was continue to play this game, where the stakes were everything and the prize . . . well, she hardly knew. Was the prize Hyam? And in what form?

Slave?

Equal?

Husband?

She could scarcely dare to hope. Maybe the citizens expected her to be young and radical; gods knew her father had been when held up to the light of his father before him. But to free and then brazenly marry a human. A human who would not just be the legitimate and recognized mate of a Tavarian, but the mate of their Chieftain.

That might be a tad more radicalism than anyone's blood pressure could rightly handle.

Besides.

She was supposed to be sending Hyam home to Earth. Many a Tavarian soldier had maintained a briefly long-distance relationship with his lover or his wife (or both, depending on his morals) while on assignment across the planet. But across worlds?

Foolishness.

She would never survive.

Besides.

He would return to Earth and be reunited with more of his kind than the colony could ever offer him. When faced with such a feast, how could she blame him for disremembering the meager portions of his birthplace?

She may as well consider Matime. He was a good match, and not only because his skin fell within the acceptable color scheme. Though at the end of the day, that was still the primary reason.

Dameia sat carefully, leaving the entirety of the metal latticework table between her father and herself. "He certainly has his attributes," she finally allowed evasively, pouring a generous carafe of blackflower juice and gulping half of the scalding drink in three immediate swallows. She gasped in the heat of it, feeling the punch as the blackflower's effects slammed through her system, yanking her dragging synapses from their slumber.

The Weight of Stars and Suns
Dawn Christine Jonckowski

The Chieftain's laughter boomed across the tiled patio. "Attributes? Is that what you call them these days?" He swirled dredges around the bottom of his carafe, reached over to snatch a favorite pastry and take a careless bite. Dameia watched his casual confidence. Of course he should feel this world and everything—every*one*?—was his for the taking.

Because it was.

They were.

All of it.

"How did you know the right mate, Father? Was my mother truly the only one you ever loved?" Dameia's questions shocked even her, and she dropped her eyes as soon as the words escaped. She had never asked her father about her mother, not a shred about her likes and dislikes and what she was like as a young queen, much less the more revealing and intimate sides of their relationship. Like love.

Assuming he'd felt it. If the relationship had been arranged or not.

She hoped he'd felt it, for her mother's sake, at least.

Dameia lifted a tentative gaze to gauge the Chieftain's silence. A shadow fell behind his eyes, a darkness he seemed unwilling to cross himself and determined to keep others from fording. It had been a long, long time since they'd spoken of the Queen. The Chieftain's lips worked to form a reply, molding and remolding syllables and still not finding any that were to taste.

Finally: "I loved your mother. Until I die, she will be the only Tavarian I have so loved."

Dameia's own heart unclenched, even as her inquiry fixated on the qualifier.

The only *Tavarian* he had loved.

So it was possible.

(Anything was possible, but her father in love with a human, however briefly? It was too big a dare; her thinning string of hope couldn't manage to wrap all the way around.)

The question danced on her tongue, too tantalizing. She couldn't just leave it there.

She should.

She couldn't.

Trailing a finger around the lip of her own emptied carafe, she spoke the words. "There's an old rumor that you sought comfort from a human after my mother passed." Her throat could barely release the words, so stuck with hesitancy they were.

The Chieftain's retort had no such problem. "Cursed race, can't keep a still tongue in their heads." Heat flared off his sharp gaze, crescendoed along with his speech, and dropped to frigid just as fast. He turned a flat, empty stare out across the patio. "I suppose it's fair that you know: Yes, I did keep a slave for . . . *comfort* after your mother died. And I have regretted every single thing that ever came of it."

Silence reigned in the aftermath of his admission. The chill of the Chieftain's delivery left Dameia both shocked and unsurprised. Had she expected him to somehow admit to loving a human?

She was a fool.

A fool in love with a man who was counting on her to help him escape the very one who sat across from her on the suns-bright patio.

The Weight of Stars and Suns
Dawn Christine Jonckowski

"Do yourself a favor, Dameia," the Chieftain's voice broke in. She looked; his face, always lined by suns and rule and worry, was now etched with a deeper weight. "Do not become entangled with a human—*any* human—for any reason. It can only go badly for you."

He had no idea.

Neither of them did.

No idea.

15

"Abrams, this had damn well better be good for you to be interrupting me. Do you know that was the Prime Minister of the Global Alliance on the vidcon? Do you know how long I've been trying to get this meeting on her schedule, and you interrupt me with 'something I'm gonna wanna see?' Aphrodite herself had better be descending on that hippy colony on Venus or something. The Prime Minister! And I was interrupted by an *intern*!"

Winnie Abrams drew herself up to every inch of her four-foot ten frame. Which included all four inches added by her vintage stack-heeled Mary Janes.

"You need to see this," she commanded. "Sir," the afterthought addition to include some shade of deference, however sardonic.

Director James S. Bergman, the man who oversaw the entirety of the U.S. arm of the Global Alliance colonization program, following a pocket-sized intern like a dog at the promise of a biscuit.

He really needed a raise.

The Weight of Stars and Suns
Dawn Christine Jonckowski

The Lilliputian in front of him charged through the complex network of hallways faster than legs that short really should have been able to. He lengthened his stride to keep up. Noticed the eight pencils sticking out of her frizzy bun at haphazard angles. (The IT team had a daily pool for how many pencils Winnie would have stabbed into her hair by day's end. At the moment, the record currently stood at thirteen, but the Director wouldn't be surprised if that tally was overturned before her internship concluded. And one of these days he really had to remember to ask how he could get in on that bet.)

What was her function? Ah right, she specialized in "vintage hardware" (her words), which meant she was buried in a tiny room with prehistoric computers and crap systems (his words) that had been used to monitor some of the original colonization missions, tasked with mining the old dinosaurs for any last vestiges of helpful—or amusing or interesting or even, God forbid, illegal—data before the systems were wiped and recycled. So much as a system that was well over 100 years old could be recycled. The Director was gobsmacked that any of them even started. A testament to Winnie's loving and peculiar ministrations, most likely.

She probably deserved a raise.

Winnie opened the door and the pair stepped into the oppressively dusty room.

Scratch that, the Director thought to himself. She *definitely* deserved a raise.

Still.

"Okay, you got me here. What is it that I need to see? And God help you if it's some vintage video game that's been archived

The Weight of Stars and Suns
Dawn Christine Jonckowski

and buried under federal data. I can't apologize to the Prime Minister by saying I was interrupted to witness an original remake of Pong."

"No, no, trust me, it's much bigger than that, sir. Much bigger." Winnie swept piles of disks and drives off a stained office chair that had seen decidedly better days. The Director chose not to dwell too long on the many possible origins of that particular stain, and managed to sit with minimal gritting of teeth when she gestured the invitation. This suit was due for a visit to the dry cleaner anyway.

The tiny intern buzzed about the various stations she had set up and hooked into the miniscule monitor wall she had constructed on her first week with an electric screwdriver, little assistance, and none of the necessary permission. A few twists and plugs later, the display from a tiny monitor in the corner was fuzzing to life on a larger monitor in the center.

Which bore the grey-blue dialog box.

Incoming distress signal from Genesis. *Please respond.*

Yes, yes he definitely did want to see that.

Well, he did, and he didn't. The Director felt his blood congeal around his heart as the plethora of implications soaked in, even while that same organ plummeted into his stomach and bounced back up into his lungs with daring, skeptical hope.

"It's been—"

"One hundred twenty years, sir," Winnie broke in, bouncing herself close to airborne on the balls of her feet. "*Genesis* dropped comms one hundred twenty years ago. Give or take a few months. So why is she just now reaching out? And what in heaven's name have they been doing out there since then?"

The Director reached for his cell phone, dialed his administrative assistant. "Yeah, Gillian? Can you let the Prime Minister know that I am going to have to call her back?"

✧ ✧ ✧ ✧ ✧

Just one cycle after supping with royalty in the light, Matime was hidden in the deep recesses of the artificial darkness of the Warden's house, eating a less palatable meal with even more unsavory company.

The Warden had truly deplorable table manners.

It was true that his uncle had paid for his training, true that he was proud of Matime's accomplishments. But only so far as they served the Warden. Matime was under no illusion that should he fail to produce the desired results, he would be unceremoniously cut off and a new branch grafted onto the misshapen family tree. There were plenty of soldiers with fewer scruples who would gladly come alongside the Warden for a chance to overthrow the Chieftain and bed the princess. Though he couldn't rightly tell which reward some would count the better one.

As he watched the older *zakar* slurp and dribble his way through the meal, he wished even more fervently to be released from this particular binding travesty. But he was indebted in so many ways to his uncle. And nothing—*nothing*—ever came without its price.

"So tell me what you've seen," the Warden managed around a wet lump of half-chewed bread. Matime fought his gag reflex, moved his focus down to the napkin in his lap, picked it up and creased it thrice before he could speak.

"Not much. The princess and the rebel continue to display great affection for each other. The third one—the bony one—goes into the ship and to what best I can tell, pokes at the innards with little success. There is no life left in the ship, so I do not see what he hopes to accomplish." Matime chose his words carefully. Though he was bound to his uncle to spy and report, that didn't mean he had to completely incriminate Dameia. After all, if the Warden was successful in making Matime her husband, he would need to be able to look his new wife in the eye once in a while. It was getting more and more difficult to do so even now, knowing what he knew.

Slathering his napkin across his lips without much success, the Warden harrumphed and pushed his chair back from the heavy table.

"We need more," he pronounced.

"More?"

The Warden eyed his nephew as if he were slow. "Yes, Matime: more. We need to figure out how to catch them in the act of something. Something other than just breaking out." He steepled his fingers. "Any rebel toe even slightly out of line will cost them their lives. But that's not enough." His grin slid wide and menacing. "We need to catch them in a more . . . *uncompromising* position."

Matime blanched. "Why? Isn't killing the human enough? Surely I can best win her favor by comforting a broken heart. Less is possible if she too is implicated."

"Dear boy," the Warden sighed, a longsuffering noise full of pointedly waning patience. "I don't want to just break her heart. I want to destroy her.

"Because if I destroy her, I destroy her father. And that, nephew, is the bigger win."

It was then, *finally*, that Matime felt the metal stiffen within his spine. No grudge, no mutiny was worth the absolute destruction of an individual when the only grievance against her was her connection to the ruler. (Which, of course, was hardly her fault. As if anyone could control to whom they were born. There was a whole colony of slaves who would have much preferred being born to parents on Earth to corroborate that truth.) Yes, Tavarians held deep disdain for any of their race who copulated with a human. And if the emotionless sex was frowned upon (though not *technically* illegal), so much worse would be some declaration of true love.

But even he—even he—could not see the logic in punishing her love with this level of destruction. To saddle her with the guilt of knowing that if not for her, her beloved would still live. (Though he had to assume that that logic had entered her mind at least once or twice before being overruled by a wayward heart.)

So he stood to his feet. Calmly. Placed his napkin atop his mopped up plate. Calmly. Brushed the crumbs from his robe. Calmly.

And said to his uncle: "Then I want no part of this any longer."

And before the Warden could part his spit-glistened lips to reply, Matime turned on his heel and left the dining room, the house, the grounds. Calmly.

And once he reached the main road, he ran like hell.

The Weight of Stars and Suns
Dawn Christine Jonckowski

✧ ✧ ✧ ✧ ✧

The Warden didn't need to stand at a window to know that his nephew ran.

He knew.

Matime wasn't done. Far from it. He was far too entangled in the Warden's web. His gallant—however misguided—proclamation and theatrical exit were not enough to release its grasp.

The Warden would simply have to be a little more creative about how he used Matime. And Dameia. And the Chieftain.

He would be their master. He would own them.

He would win.

The game played on.

✧ ✧ ✧ ✧ ✧

Director Bergman had a headache.

No.

That was too simple a statement for how he felt.

He had three world powers fighting an all-out nuclear war inside of his skull.

With fireworks. (Because somehow those made a nuclear war worse?)

Definitely lots of fireworks.

Outside of his skull, he had three major powers of the U.S. Colonization Program arguing at top volume over what it could possibly mean to have received a distress call from a ship everyone assumed disintegrated—along with all of its cargo and passengers—over a century ago.

They hadn't even gotten to the part where they had to tell the commanding officers of the Global Alliance.

Maybe he would call in sick that day.

"All I'm saying is that if there's a chance that someone is out there, we are morally obligated to return to the planet and find the state of things."

"And who do you suppose is going to fund this 'moral obligation' of yours? Look at how much it cost to fund that mission the first time around."

"A hundred and twenty years ago! Come on, Alan. Our travel and technology has improved so much, it would be hardly more than the cost to take your family on a European cruise. And I know that you know how much *that* costs."

"It may not even be a thing, or a person. Whatever. It's old software, old hardware. It could be a virus or a hack, an elaborate hoax by some zit-faced teen in his mom's basement who happened upon an old internet article about Tav and thought it might be funny to make some Global Alliance employees run amok searching for life that isn't there. It could be some final disintegration of the ship, or a signal that for whatever reason—maybe the same mysterious reason the ship crashed in the first place—took a hundred and twenty years to get here. Come on, folks. Use your heads. It's been over a century. *Nobody is there*, and I'm not shelling out millions of dollars just to find out I'm right."

|| The Weight of Stars and Suns ||
Dawn Christine Jonckowski

"Here's a wild idea," a pixie voice piped in from the corner where everyone had forgotten she sat taking notes. Everyone turned to stare at Winnie. The intern, after all, had been the one to receive the distress signal. It only seemed fair to include her in some capacity. Even if it was just to let her take her own notes.

She stood. (Not that anyone could tell much of a difference.) Tucked a thick lock of dark, curled hair that had escaped its pencil-stabbed bun back behind her ear. "If our technology is so advanced, shouldn't we have some sort of something—I don't know, say a satellite or probe?—that can give us ground images so we can see if there's anyone there? Call me crazy, but that sounds like a much more cost-effective option than sending a fully-crewed ship out only to find that a century of decay short-circuited a random wire. And *if* there are people there, well. Then we have proof to back up our funding request. Because if there are folks there, something tells me that the Global Alliance will want to know their stories."

The executives stared at her, dumbfounded.

"Now why didn't we think of that."

Winnie shrugged at the financial executive's revelation. "You're thinking too high-level, caught up too much in the shock of this new reality where *Genesis* survived the crash and possibly left humans behind. Or at least survived enough that we could go study her to figure out what went wrong, maybe try again, better this time." She blinked once, completely unconcerned by the fact that the question had been entirely rhetorical.

The financial executive narrowed her eyes at Winnie, quizzically. "Who are you, again?"

"Winnifred Abrams," she chirped, offering a hand that still bore her note-taking pencil. Seeing the pencil, she quickly retracted long enough to stab the pencil into her hair (bringing the day's total close to eleven, and giving her the look of some long-ago crowned goddess), before holding her palm out a second time. "Technological engineering, specializing in vintage software and hardware. Intern." The executive grasped her hand in a dutiful shake, still somewhat bewildered by this tiny ball of energy and logic in front of her.

"Vintage software, eh?" The executive shook her head, still puzzling. "Well then, friends," she turned, dazed, to the rest of the group. "Let's go see what Satellite Observation can cook up for us." And out they went, followed—at the encouraging nod of Director Bergman—by the miniscule intern.

For his part, the director reached into his pocket for the travel-size vial of painkillers. Whereupon he promptly downed four pills, chased by a sizable gulp of water.

An intern.

She really did deserve a raise.

Or at the very least, a job offer.

✧ ✧ ✧ ✧ ✧

SatOps was perhaps a bit perplexed by the diminutive intern and the energy that vibrated off her with little effort, and again by her direction to point the space eyeballs at a planet no one had even bothered to look at since the latest and furthest placement of perimeter satellites and probes afforded them decent view (with the

The Weight of Stars and Suns
Dawn Christine Jonckowski

little help of some massive magnification software) twenty years prior.

But when said intern was accompanied by three rather important executives who seemed bound by the gravitational pull of her excitement, one tended to do whatever one was told, no matter who gave the order.

This pleased Winnie.

She could get used to being in charge.

It would take time to send probes out that way; as noted, no one had given Tav even a cursory look since *Genesis*—and the investments of all who funded the mission—crashed. But they promised to route a team of satellites and contact all of them, including the adorably ferocious intern, as soon as they had sightlines. Satisfied (for the most part; Winnie had been hoping for decidedly more immediate results), all returned to offices and desks, attempting to push aside all the what-ifs of Tav and *Genesis* to focus on everything else they were supposed to be doing to earn their paychecks.

The following Tuesday, the team was pinged and came running.

SatOps had found Tav.

It had proven more difficult than imagined, due in part to old, neglected data, and the fact that the planet now only boasted thirty-three in its necklace of suns.

Nonetheless, cameras had located the crash.

And then they found . . . *people*.

Bergman was on his phone instantly. "Gillian, contact the Global Alliance HQ and cite a Protocol 113. I need them on vidcon in an hour. I need scientists, I need a ship, I need a crew, I need funding, and I need it *now*." He hung up and they all continued to stare at the screens, at the grainy, bustling lives they saw through the remote pupils of a satellite that bucked every few seconds as it fought the planet's peculiar gravitational pull.

Because there *were* people there.

And not all of them were human.

✧ ✧ ✧ ✧ ✧

Hyam breathed the soapy sweet smell of Dameia's hair as she leaned against him, her head tucked and snuggled beneath his chin. They'd left Ithai to a full cycle's sleep hoping to bolster his failing body after the previous cycle. Oren had no desire to poke around the ship (and truth be told, Hyam had no desire to let him), so Hyam had been rewarded with a now rare night of solace with his beloved.

No agenda.

No plan.

No goals to accomplish.

Just her in his arms and him feeling like as long as she was there by his side, he could conquer the world. Which world didn't matter. This one. Another one. Who cared.

She was his.

For now.

The thought came unbidden into his head. If they were successful in this admittedly harebrained scheme to get the ship off

The Weight of Stars and Suns
Dawn Christine Jonckowski

Tav and onto a nearby planet, it would mean leaving her behind. And not just for a time. For *all* time. Forever.

She would move on. She would have to. A Chieftain's daughter would not be alone for long, not this close to ascending the throne. Not when—as she'd finally admitted—her father all but had her married off to some Tavarian historian already.

Hyam had watched her speak of this Matime, his heart curling in on itself with every word. He knew. He knew this was a possibility. An inevitability, even. But to be so blatantly faced with it. With the thought of another man—*Tavarian*, whatever—holding her, wiping her tears, sharing her joys, driving her ecstasy.

It was more than a man should be asked to face.

And yet.

He'd brought it on himself, hadn't he? This harebrained scheme was *his* harebrained scheme. (So originally it had been Ithai's, but Hyam wasn't in the mood to split said hairs.)

It was ostensibly his decision to leave her.

Just as it had been his decision to love her.

Despite their difference.

Despite the price on his life.

Despite what she would face if discovered.

Despite, despite, despite.

He loved her.

If love was for fools, then he was the most foolish of them all.

A single tear rolled down his face and into the thick nest of braids on his princess' head. Disappeared unnoticed into the twines and pins that anchored the elaborate mess against their earlier pleasure. Dameia felt his subtle shift and tipped her head back to smile straight into his soul.

How could he leave her?

His gaze shifted from hers to the contrast of olive skin on purple. Thought of Ithai tossing in fevered sleep. Of the ten remaining rebels waiting—expectantly, bitterly, both—in the barracks. Of his people, resting weary bones on rickety cots or the unforgiving floor of an equally unforgiving master.

How could he stay?

✧ ✧ ✧ ✧ ✧

Deep in the royal complex, the Chieftain sat ensconced in artificial dark, lit only by a single candle, his fingers steepled over books and ledgers and notes. But it wasn't grain production or construction progress or Council elections keeping him awake far into the second cycle.

It was his daughter.

Or more importantly, the individual who would stand beside her as her husband.

She was subtle about her affections for Matime. Subtle almost to the point of disinterest. Which would have worried the Chieftain if his daughter was anyone else but the future Chieftain. Rather than feel concern, he chose to see the advantageous side of her thickly veiled emotions and how it would benefit her in future politicking.

The Weight of Stars and Suns
Dawn Christine Jonckowski

It wouldn't occur to him to be worried until it was too late. Much too late.

Perhaps rather than waiting for her to exhibit some wild—and admittedly uncharacteristic—display of affection for the militaristic historian, he should make her make a move. It was well within his rights as father and ruler. He knew the game (didn't he?), knew the players (didn't he?), knew the moves and how to trap and corner. If she would not move on her own, he would move her himself.

Three days. The Chieftain would give his daughter three days to do something. Say something. Anything. Anything to give him indication, however subtle, of her final decision of affection for Matime. And if she did not, he would simply announce a betrothal for her.

She would thank him.

She would.

Yes. Three days. A decisive nod, and the Chieftain finally abandoned his desk. He always slept best when all the pieces and players in his life were in their rightful spots.

(Didn't he?)

✿ ✿ ✿ ✿ ✿

Bergman had a headache.

Again.

Still?

Maybe always.

He'd managed to get funding. Which was always a joy and a half to squeeze out of the Global Alliance. Fortunately—at least from his point of view; certainly not from the Global Alliance's point of view, because it then meant they had to fund the mission, whether they wanted to or not (damn politics)—someone had unobtrusively filmed the moment when the heads of the Global Alliance learned via vidcon that *Genesis* had managed to survive enough to produce offspring who were, at least from SatOps' grainy view, coexisting peacefully with another race nearly a century later.

And then that film had been released on the internet, going madly viral in a matter of seconds.

(He strongly suspected Winnie. Her myriad of skills was becoming frighteningly apparent.)

The public reacted in a fantastic smorgasbord of intrigue, horror, excitement, and fear. They all but demanded that the Global Alliance send a crew, if not necessarily to rescue the stranded humans, then to at least learn the truth about *Genesis* and meet the non-humans who seemed to have adopted the Earthlings. Practically overnight, some descendants of the original crew gathered in New York City and held a silent vigil complete with candles and poster boards bearing photos of their long ago lost ones. Whom none of them had ever known. Not that that seemed to matter to anyone in the least. They stood by a fat oak tree that—unbeknownst to most aside from them, at least until that moment—bore a small plaque that denoted the tree a memorial of those lost to the flames of the *Genesis* as she fell.

The public ate it up. Every bite. And slurped around for more.

|| The Weight of Stars and Suns ||
Dawn Christine Jonckowski

Thus, the Global Alliance had no choice. Bergman's phone had rung at three a.m. Central Standard Time, and he learned through the haze of interrupted (and badly-needed) sleep that his funding had come through.

Glory be.

But of course, that was only one problem solved. And naturally, the mission approval caused many more. Every country wanted to contribute to the mission. Which was both wonderful and maddening. Japan insisted on providing the ship, but Houston argued that it was their ship that went down the first time, and who was going to trust them this second time? Oddly enough, one of the descendants of the original crew was herself an experienced and space-traveled bioengineer from France who had facilitated several other colonies for the Global Alliance. (The fact that France now had a space program still somewhat boggled Bergman's mind.) She proclaimed loudly and with great passion—which Bergman felt was rather on the feigned side—that she should be one of the crew to go meet and potentially rescue her distant (*really* distant) relatives. Broadcast news got a hold of that gem and dug in with all its teeth. Within days, the bioengineer was the world's darling, and Bergman had no choice but to guarantee her a spot on the crew.

Her track record was stellar, but still.

Bergman hated being coerced.

But he had a finalized crew. Which was something, at least.

Now it was several hours past any sort of acceptable quitting time for the day. Although normal hours had become a joke just as soon as Tav had been rediscovered, both by the small SatOps team and then by the adoring fans worldwide. (Some celebrity had designed a tshirt splashed with the tagline "Peace-Love-Tav" and sold it for an outrageous amount, promising that fifty percent of all proceeds would go to some mysterious charity of the same name to aid in the "rescue mission." On any given day, Bergman couldn't turn around without seeing at least three people wearing the shirt, but had yet to learn where the funds from those stupid things were even going. It certainly wasn't to his department.)

His wife wanted to know if he had an ETA on arriving home. Dinner was long past, but his four-year-old daughter Madeline was lately demanding that only Daddy read her bedtime story. And the resulting tantrum if he didn't wasn't something he would ever wish on anyone. Least of all his saintly patient wife who had barely seen him (awake, anyway) since the whole Tav mess started.

Flowers would probably be a good idea at some point in the near future. She wasn't one to layer on guilt, but he felt it nonetheless.

Definitely flowers.

Perhaps accompanied by a babysitter and a night out.

He sighed. Pushed glasses up off his nose and into the thinning hair atop his head. He had the crew set and finalized. The ship—Houston-built with some specialized rockets from Japan and christened *Genesis II*, a happy compromise for everyone—would be in Cape Canaveral in the morning. They would start running the tests on both ship and crew by early afternoon. And if the planets aligned just so and Bergman's luck held, they would launch by the end of the following week.

It was accelerated far more than he was comfortable with, especially considering the fate of the first *Genesis*. But those were the

The Weight of Stars and Suns
Dawn Christine Jonckowski

deadlines and caveats given him. And by God, he was going to make it work.

So he could probably finally go home for the night. He could make it back for story time, if he could be all right with speeding.

He was not going to miss story time.

His thumbs were halfway through a text to his wife when a work-worn and wild-eyed astrophysicist careened around his doorjamb.

"Director. Sir." The younger man's tongue tripped over an accent all his own and a language that was very much not.

The headache's steady drumbeat thrummed.

"Yes?"

"I'm sorry to disturb, but the planet. Tav? She has thirty-six suns, no? And we see only thirty-three when we found her, yes?" The astrophysicist's fingers fluttered delicately in the air, tracing rings and counting by threes.

In another life, Bergman mused those fingers would have danced on a piano or swept across a canvas.

His own stout fingers pinched the bridge of his nose. "Right, thirty-three."

"Now she has thirty, sir. And there are five—*five!*—that are supernova in a matter of weeks."

Bergman blinked up at the young man. "What?"

"Sir," the astrophysicist choked the words out around his terror. "If you launch next week, by the time you arrive to Tav, it will be too late. It will happen while *Genesis II* is landed. Tav will be gone, and take everything—people, ship, crew, everything—with her as she dies."

He was going to miss story time.

The Director stared at his half-finished text. Hit delete. Looked up at the younger man. "Get everyone and anyone you can from your team into the main conference room in one hour. I don't care who you have to wake up or call back. I need *everyone*.

"We are not letting that crew down a second time." Bergman tipped his wrist to check his watch. "As of twenty-one hundred hours, *Genesis II* has officially become a Global Alliance humanitarian rescue mission."

As the young man raced back down the hallway, Bergman picked up his phone. Dialed a number he'd hoped never to have to call.

The Prime Minister's private line.

For emergencies only.

"Prime Minister, Director Bergman. Sorry to disturb. There's been a change of plans. I need the crew ready to go by morning. In order to rescue the humans from Tav, we need to leave now."

As he talked and assembled files, folders, notes, and a seventh—twelfth? He'd lost count—cup of coffee, he tapped out a new text to his wife.

I'm going to miss story time. I am SO sorry. Explain when I get home. Probably sometime tomorrow night? Love you.

His phone buzzed back a reply.

Madeline says you owe her a pony. Good luck. XOXO

Forget one night with a babysitter. If he ever got this ship into space and back home again, he was taking his whole family on a cruise. For a year.

|| The Weight of Stars and Suns ||
Dawn Christine Jonckowski

✧ ✧ ✧ ✧ ✧

In the dead of the second cycle—such as it could ever truly be dead of any cycle on Tav—a figure crept through the rebel compound. Sneaked around the back of the barracks, following in the same footsteps the princess did nearly every fourth watch. The same steps she'd taken there and back just a little while earlier.

Slipped unnoticed into the barracks, and moments later, emerged with a deadened figure draped over one shoulder. (He still smelled of her.) Then disappeared.

At the morning call, the rebels awoke to find Hyam's sandals still on the floor, his bunk empty.

And they knew.

Nothing came without a price.

And Hyam's price had just come for him.

16

This was not how Dameia ever pictured it.

Not that she was the sort who had spent overmuch of her childhood dreaming of a dashing warrior charging through the palace to sweep her off her feet. She knew she would marry, but figured it would be an arranged match like her parents had, one with a solid mate whom she would grow to love, and he her. Like her parents.

She had always believed herself far too practical to be romantic.

That was, until Hyam. When suddenly all of her sense turned to mush and flowers.

Then.

Then she began picturing Hyam standing up from the crowd at her father's voice. Hyam walking up the center aisle to claim his right to her hand. Hyam's smile brimming up to Hyam's eyes, and Hyam's lips sealing the betrothal vow.

It was ludicrous.

But when had dreams ever needed to make sense?

When did love contain any amount of logic?

But no. Today she stood beside the Chieftain, draped in the cream cloth and linked chains of ceremonial garb, and it would not be Hyam's name that he would call. Not Hyam's hand that would fold over hers. Not Hyam's kiss.

It would be Matime's.

Oh, she'd done an excellent job of convincing the Chieftain of the match. It was the plan. Maybe sooner than she'd hoped, but she calmed her breathing by chanting over and over inside her head that betrothal was not marriage. Betrothal was not marriage. Betrothal was not marriage.

Betrothals could be broken.

If necessary.

After all, they were nowhere near figuring out how to push the human's ship back into the sky. Perhaps it would be necessary to fall onto a backup plan that could involve equality. And then she could be the primary example of acceptance by marrying a human herself. Likely shocking the entirety of the Council into early graves, but she'd want to replace them with her own choices anyway. This way would just happen to make the funeral pyre builder a very rich individual in a very short amount of time. Something she didn't think he'd entirely mind.

The sound of horns brought her out of the graves and back to the living. They were gathered along the formal walkway to the Capitol. Large sheeted stones paved the lane under the multitude's feet, heating toes through the thick soles of sandals as they jostled to keep the route clear for the intended. Thirty-six smooth columns

The Weight of Stars and Suns
Dawn Christine Jonckowski

erupted from the sandy dirt edges along either side of the walk, heavy monuments to Hapshid's children that strained through the crowds who gathered. Purple shoulders wedged politely into each other, vying to be even a breath closer to the Chieftain and his radiant daughter. Weighted suns beat straight down on dark heads, letting off the perfume of tightly-packed bodies.

Dameia looked down at the crowds from atop the dais crowning the seven sacred stairs that led to the Royal Gate. They couldn't wait.

She could.

But it was time.

The Chieftain stepped forward.

"Great citizens of Tav," he began, his voice booming across the assembly. The crowd stood silent under the burning suns.

"Today, we celebrate one of the most enduring traditions of Tav. Today I stand before you with my successor, Princess Dameia, to humbly ask for your loyalty as we expand this family tree."

The crowd applauded. For what did they know of the inner workings of politics? A royal wedding was a treat to behold, and they imagined that whichever strapping specimen stepped forward at the Chieftain's invitation was of course the Princess' delight.

"My citizens, there is one among you who is a solid branch to graft onto this lineage. A loyal subject who has served his Chieftain well and will serve his mate even better. May he earn the same respect of you as you project onto us. May he stand beside his mate as a full member of the royal family with all dues and rights that pertain thereunto. May his seed increase our numbers, and may his strength of spirit and of flesh enable his mate, his future Chieftain, to lead Tav with wisdom and integrity.

"Matime, come forth!"

The command rang across the square, and for one breathless moment, no one moved.

And then, from the rear of the assembly, feet shuffled and shoulders swayed as a tall, muscled Tavarian draped in luxurious robes that only vaguely resembled his chosen craft of historian stepped from the masses and stood a single lonely character on the walkway.

Silence shattered by titters of *neqeba* young and old. Awe at his build, his elegance, his gait, his face. Everyone who saw him wanted him, or wanted to be him.

Everyone except one.

Dameia's throat became a desert as Matime's feet carried him forward.

This was wrong.

Wrong, wrong, *wrong*.

But what could she do to stop it?

He was up the stairs now, his hand emerging from the soft folds of his sleeves, expecting hers to be reaching back. An eyebrow winged up at her hesitancy. Then slowly as an old machine with grinding gears, she raised her hand from her side. Felt his solid warm fingers close around hers. He stepped up, beside her, in front of the Chieftain. His free palm cupped her cheek and on a breath, he leaned in.

Just as his lips began to brush hers, a cry went up from the crowd.

| | The Weight of Stars and Suns | |
Dawn Christine Jonckowski

Not of exultation, but of pure revulsion.

Dameia jerked her head back from Matime's startled face, wheeled around to see . . .

Hyam.

Bound, dirty, bloodied, and shoved to his knees before the Warden. Nearly unrecognizable, but she would know his shape anywhere.

Dread wound its way up Dameia's spine, curled up around her heart, and squeezed.

"What is the meaning of this, Warden?" The Chieftain's voice boomed out over the crowd, full-bodied with his anger. "How dare you interrupt this sacred betrothal ceremony with the filth of a prisoner."

In that moment, Dameia sensed rather than saw Matime then turn to face the scene, felt his whole body tighten, his lungs balloon with the quick intake of breath. She could not tear her eyes from Hyam's bent and beaten form.

"A thousand apologies, my Chieftain," the Warden's voice cut smooth as glistening glass, his head bowed low in deference. "But as this ceremony involves my beloved nephew," he tipped his head up from the bow without yet straightening his spine, "I could not keep silent on my grievance." At this, he rose to his full height, shoulders strong and broad even with age, his fingers pushing Hyam's head down while appearing loath to touch such a creature.

"Explain yourself," the Chieftain commanded. "Who is this slave and what has he to do with this ceremony and your nephew?"

A wide, salacious grin slit across the Warden's face. "He is no mere slave, my lord, but the imprisoned rebel leader." With that, his fingers tightened in Hyam's hair and jerked his head up to reveal his face to the onlookers. The crowd gasped, drew back as one whole. Blood crusted beneath the prisoner's nose, his eyes puffed and blackened. His lower lip glistened and swelled, clearly split down the middle. Stripped to the waist, bruises bloomed across his chest and stomach, nearly indecipherable from the smears of dirt and blood.

The shock robbed Dameia of voice. She stood, a royal statue, staring at her lover, unable to move or think or breathe beyond the single word that filled her head and threatened to scream out.

Hyam.

"Not only has this slave already rebelled against you, Chieftain, he has rebelled against the laws of nature. He has dared too high. He has sullied the throne of your great reign. He has taken what rightfully belongs to my nephew." The Warden's eyes shone feverously, his voice rising in intensity with every statement until he was nearly shouting. "He has ruined our great Tavarian ruling line! And what's worse: He has been *allowed*."

The Chieftain's brow furrowed, confused. "Speak clearly, Warden. I command it!"

The Warden's eyes locked on Dameia's. Plainly telegraphed. His wet lips parted and on a shower of spit and betrayal, he damned them both.

"This rebel prisoner is your daughter Princess Dameia's lover," he spat.

A roar erupted from the crowd, disbelief and disgust as loud as the Chieftain was silent.

The Weight of Stars and Suns
Dawn Christine Jonckowski

In the melee, Hyam's eyes locked on Dameia's. She translated every broken hope, every string of anguish, every volume of love. Every sorrow for what they both knew—maybe had always known—was coming.

The Warden may as well have just brought Hyam's head and left the rest of him to rot. He was as good as dead. And there was no telling what consequences her father would enact on her.

"What proof?"

The Chieftain's voice cut through, cool metal.

The Warden's chin snapped down. "Matime himself suspected the Princess' proclivities and followed her. He has witnessed their . . . *affections* for each other." He leered at Dameia; her entire being flamed with the knowledge that Matime had seen them—he had *seen* them—and had reported everything to his slime of an uncle.

His uncle who already had suspicions because of her black payments.

Who already knew.

Who had set them up.

And she who should have known much, much better, walked blindly in. And what's worse, trailed her beloved behind her in the blind ecstasy of want. She had wanted. Oh, she had *wanted*.

That want would be the end of everything.

Everything.

And it was all her fault.

Beside her, Matime stood, ramrod straight. Her gaze cut swiftly to him. Fists balled within his sleeves and tension drew lines out from eyes she once thought kind. He would not meet her focus. Murmured, "I am sorry, Dameia. Truly."

"You and your apology are nothing to me," she hissed. Turned back to look at Hyam's bent frame. "You will pay for this, Matime. You and your uncle. I swear it."

The Chieftain whirled on her swiftly. His ears missed nothing. "So it's true," he breathed.

She refused to cower. Bore herself up tall. And with a loud voice, proclaimed, "Yes, it is true. All of it. I love this man. He owns my heart and I, his.

"I am not ashamed."

"*You should be.*" The growl emanated deep from within the Chieftain's core. "Take him away!" He roared out across the multitude. The Warden's face split with pleasure as guards erupted from the crowd. One on each side, they wrenched Hyam to his feet. His piercing gaze never left Dameia's face, even as his weakened limbs struggled to bear his weight, to stand, to walk.

He said only one word. One. Said. Did not shout. Did not scream. Yet his voice arrowed through the crowd, laden with all his lips and hands and touch could not do.

One word.

"Dameia."

Anguish, courage, belief, trust.

Love.

The guards turned as one and dragged Hyam out of the shocked silent crowd.

"Hyam!" Dameia screamed for all she was worth and more, for all that was stretched to breaking as he was carried away.

"Hyam!" Tears chased free and heavy down her face.

"*Hyam!*"

A flick of the Chieftain's finger, and guards surrounded her, too. Thick arms encasing her, holding her back, counteracting her struggle. She was powerless. Turned her streaked and stricken face to her father.

"Please," was all she said. But his face was set, hard immovable stone.

He addressed only the guards. Commanded for all to hear. "Place the princess under house arrest. Remove her companion. Post guards. She is to interact with no one other than myself or any Councilman I shall deem fit. Three days hence, both of the accused shall be sentenced for their crimes. There will be no trial." The Chieftain paused, chest heaving, radiating anger and betrayal. His next words were for Dameia alone. "I am judge and jury," his words poured out, hard and edged. "I will rule. I will reign."

The Chieftain nodded once, and the guards began to move. Dameia's feet faltered, her steps unwilling to walk her away from the final place she was sure to see Hyam alive.

"Father," she pleaded.

He was heat and fire. An unyielding force.

"You disappoint me, Dameia."

And he turned away.

The princess was eventually picked up completely and carried, sobbing and struggling, back to her quarters where only silence and solitude awaited.

The next morning broke with three fewer suns, as if the whole planet felt the lovers' broken darkness and mourned with them.

✧ ✧ ✧ ✧ ✧

Hyam decided that the universe had some sort of dark humor to have him end up in the same prison cell where it all began. He even reclined in the same spot, arranged the same way. Though accomplishing the arrangement hadn't been without considerable wincing. The Warden had been particularly gleeful about roughing him up before hauling him to the ceremony for everyone's displeasure.

He dragged a hand across the crusted blood beneath his nose.

So here he was.

It would finish where it started. He held no illusions. The Chieftain had been ready to execute him at a moment's notice when he was only a rebel prisoner. Now that he was a rebel prisoner who had also had the audacity to love a Tavarian princess, well. He supposed the only reason he wasn't dead already was because the Chieftain was plotting exactly how to make a perfect example of him. To terrify the humans against ever following in his footsteps in even the slightest manner. To exact total control over his daughter and make her watch or hear or feel every single thing they did to him.

Wasn't this a pleasant train of thought.

| | The Weight of Stars and Suns | |
Dawn Christine Jonckowski

He turned his mind instead to Dameia, to the way her face broke open and her voice clawed from her throat, screaming his name like a desperate prayer. He pictured the way she would look up at him with her heart in her eyes. Cataloged every curve of her in his memory; memorized the feel of that lavender skin on his.

They could take much. Life and limb and a few things in between.

But they could not take his dreams. They could not take his memories.

They could not take the fact that it had happened: he loved her and she loved him. That? That was done long ago. Not a soul on the planet could undo it.

He hoped the Chieftain was kind to his daughter, in the end. She was still his blood, his heir. As long as she lived, Hyam could die happy. As long as she lived, there was hope. After all, her hard heart had been changed; where hers had gone, others could surely follow. His death might even serve as catalyst to rebirth Dameia as the Tavarian leader of the human rebellion.

But he still wanted to be around to see it happen.

He wanted to stand beside her.

He wanted to invite a revolution with her.

He wanted to stay and love her.

He *wanted*.

And that want had been their undoing.

Hyam pulled himself to his feet on a creak of protesting joints and unhappily swollen muscles. Paced corner to corner to loosen the tightened sinews. At the end of it all, he would not regret a moment. He would not change a single decision. Not to rebel, not to befriend Dameia, not to love her. He would walk to his death with his head high, his heart beating and bursting for her for all to see. He would carve the feeling of her warmth on his soul and die with her name on his lips.

As if the heavens had heard his thoughts, the outer door heaved open on a long, low whine. (Had it already been three days?) The Warden posed, a silhouette in the door frame flanked by two guards who were one and a half more than was truly necessary to subdue Hyam in his weakened state.

"You," the Warden sneered. "I recall once warning you to remember your place in this world. It seems you decided—most unwisely, I might add—to ignore my caution. And here we stand, me with your life in my hands. You with nothing." His thick tongue snaked out to lick already spit-glistened lips. Three steps forward, and he grabbed bars in one hand and reached through to grab Hyam's arm with the other. Yanked the prisoner forward, making his forehead a dull mallet to ring against the metal grate.

"I suppose I should thank you," his voice dropped down to just Hyam's broken and boxed ears. "After all, it's not your blood I thirst for most. And it is not the Princess' nectar, either, sweet though it may have been before *you* seasoned it. Your descendants will curse your name for eternity for the hell I intend to rain down on them because of your mighty deeds." A cold grin cut across his face, his words flicking saliva and running tiny rivulets through the caked dirt on Hyam's face. His fingers dug fresh bruises onto Hyam's arms.

"But lest you think you are anything of importance, let me assure you: You are not. You were only the means to an end.

The Weight of Stars and Suns
Dawn Christine Jonckowski

"And what a pleasant end it shall be when I destroy the Chieftain and rule the planet."

His words snaked ice and needling chills down Hyam's spine. The Warden thrust him backward in the cell, stepped away from the bars and sniffed as if the very thought of Hyam was an unpleasant odor.

"It is time," he said, low and even. "Guards, escort the prisoner to the Arena."

✿ ✿ ✿ ✿ ✿

Dameia sat in silence and solitude, watching the day's worth of suns crest over the wall of her garden, her prison. It was the third day.

It was the third day and even though she'd known this was coming—not just for three days, but from the moment she first saw Hyam as *more*—she could not believe, could not face the reality that today was most likely Hyam's final cycle of life. She'd seen her fair share of public trials. Especially when a human was involved. The blade of judgement fell smooth and swift. He would not live to see these suns set.

She would.

Most likely.

The cycle before, a scritching at the servant's exit from her bathing chamber roused her from her sightless staring stupor. On the other side of the wood, Hannah had sneaked herself through the network of backstage corridors designed to continue the illusion that the slaves moved about invisibly, and had managed to arrive unobserved at Dameia's door. (More than likely, the guards knew nothing of this particular door and passageway. Why should they? Why should they stoop to know the goings-on of the slave network? As long as food appeared and hot baths were drawn, they were content in their ignorance.)

"Dameia," the older woman's kindly voice had spoken—for the first time—her royal charge's first name without preamble or title. "Dameia, are you there? It's Hannah; I wanted . . . I wanted to check on you, to bring you some hope."

The princess hadn't answered, too choked by the simple care of a woman who had been all but forced to raise a headstrong teenager not her own and had managed to love her anyway.

Hannah had seemed to feel Dameia's storm of emotion through the paneling. A soft slide of flesh on wood as she had placed her hand on the other side of the door.

"Dameia. Daughter. You have been as much mine as any child I have borne. I know you. I know your features and your fears, your hopes and your hurts. I know your face and the feelings it betrays in ways no one else could ever read.

"Child, for this crime your father assigns you, I do not condemn you. I do not hate you. Even though it will lead to the death of one of our own, I still cannot hate you. Not only because of the love I bear for you, but for the love I see clearly in you for Hyam."

At the sound of her former companion speaking the name of her beloved on tones of warmth and compassion, the princess had choked back a sob. Hannah had crooned softly on the other side of the door.

"Oh my darling girl. None of us fault you. For you have seen us as we truly are: as ones worthy of love, of esteem, of devotion, of equality. How could any of us despise you for granting what we have so longed for? That you would stand up before the Chieftain and the Council and your betrothed, stand up for Hyam and the deep love you share?

"It is the greatest honor and witness we could ever ask of our future ruler."

Dameia had shoved a fist in her mouth to stifle her sobs. "I'm sorry," she had finally whispered around her knuckles, her lips close to the jamb.

"No, no," Hannah had soothed in return. "You have nothing to be sorry for, Dameia. *You loved.* Where is your sin? His death is not on your head, but on those who practice this intolerance, this prejudice. They will answer for their crime against Hyam's life.

"But for you? For you, Dameia, we ask that you live. That you come into your ruling years bearing witness to the man you love, bearing witness to Hyam's life. The man whose very *name* means life. Carry him with you, Dameia. Carry him with you for the future of this planet. Do not let his life—not his death, his *life*—be in vain.

"And in this, Hyam will live forever."

They were the final words Hannah was likely to ever say to Dameia. At that moment, a guard had shifted outside the main door, and Dameia had felt the pull and vacuum as Hannah had scurried back through the network of corridors, back to the stifling washing assignment deep in the heart of the sweltering kitchen that had been her own punishment for Dameia's crimes. The princess had stayed curled by the door at length, just in case, but eventually had dried her tears, tucked Hannah's words and hopes into her soul, and sat out in the changing light to await the third day.

"I had hoped never to face a moment like this."

The sudden sound of her father's voice behind her made her innards jump. But Dameia forced her outer shell to remain motionless. There was no reason for him to be here. Not when he hadn't made an appearance any of the other two days. Not when there was a battalion of guards at his beck and call to transfer his wayward daughter wherever she needed to be.

Not when she bathed in enough guilt of her own making and hardly needed his to rinse with.

The weight of his sigh breezed past her ear. His proximity filled her senses. His bones creaked as he sat beside her.

She was a statue.

"You were right," he said softly.

This. This finally drew her focus. She turned her head, while willing her face to betray nothing.

The Chieftain spread his hands out over his lap, smoothing away invisible wrinkles from his royal garb. The royal cream sash rippled under his worrying fingers, settling with a bare quiver against the rich brown and gold of his clean military tunic. A thick cape tugged at his shoulders; it seemed today he felt its weight more than ever. Another deep sigh. His chin lifted and he stared out, over the wall, past the town, regions unseen.

"I loved a human, once. After your mother." The admission caught in his throat, tripped out of his lips. "Her name was Abigail.

The Weight of Stars and Suns
Dawn Christine Jonckowski

"Some would call it grief, some madness, but I fell in love with her. She was there with me, after. After the ceremonies were through and the ashes scattered. After the mandated mourning periods, when everyone else can go on again with life and you . . . you're just stuck there wondering how you can get up and face another cycle. How the suns dare to shine when your heart is only darkness."

A woman hazed in Dameia's memory. Light of laugh and spirit, with kindness for eyes and a dance for her gait. Cool hands that had once brushed Dameia's small child forehead before being frowned away by the foreboding presence of the Chieftain. A teasing lilt to her speech so vastly different from the warm, dusky laugh of the late Queen.

This had been the woman her father loved last.

She waited.

"I loved her . . . and then I killed her."

Metal grew up Dameia's spine. She would not do this. She would not give him this. She refused to *feel*. "If you are trying to offer comfort, this is of small solace," she squeezed each word through tight lips.

The Chieftain sighed, pushed to his feet. Paced a short path into the stone. "The Council began to suspect. Doubly so when I subtly began backing a push to allow Tavarians to breed with humans in order to expand the slave pool." His eyes lifted, tortured. Dameia stared hard glass straight back. He resumed his pacing.

"It wasn't what I wanted for Abigail. I wanted more. For her. For us. For our family."

Fingers curled into tight fists at Dameia's sides. "How dare you," she growled. "How dare you talk about the good of your *family*, the good of your *human*, when you hold Hyam beaten and broken in a cage."

"For *your* good, Dameia," the Chieftain's voice rose. His daughter's eyebrows rose at the same rate as his volume, pure skepticism. "And yes, for the rebel's too! The Council suspected Abigail and would have publically tortured her far beyond what you have yet seen endured by one. Because she was different. Because she dared to rise above herself and consider herself worthy of their Chieftain.

"When it was I who was not worthy of her."

Time ticked. Dameia's silence ballooned. She knew he craved a reaction. To his love, to his passion, to his crime.

No, not a reaction. An absolution. He wanted to prove they were the same, she and he. That their hearts and their love were of the same ilk simply because they were for the same species, and not their own. He wanted this hidden history of his to somehow assuage every human life snuffed out under his decree. And there were many. The banded ceremonial tattoos that ringed his arms and spiraled down torso and legs wrote witness to that.

Which line of ink was hers, Dameia wondered. Which needled whorl stood for the innocent human woman who had had the misfortune of being loved by the Chieftain?

"I loved her, and I killed her," the Chieftain finally repeated into the growing silence. "To protect her from the Council. And I have fought every day to ensure that no other human suffers the same fate she did. Only to have a daughter whose heart fell similarly to her father's."

"I am nothing like you," spat Dameia.

The Chieftain shook his head sadly, continued. "For this reason, today I will order the rebel's death," he declared quietly, each syllable a weight. "Not because I bear him ill, but to protect you. To protect your reign." His shoulders squared, face resigned, voice final and firm.

"Because I love you, I will break your heart."

His words fell on the ground between them, scattered thorns that neither would step on. A gulf neither would cross. A divide. A finish line over which there were no winners.

As he turned to go, Dameia repeated: "I am nothing like you."

"No," her father agreed softly, pausing to lay a single hand on her stiff shoulder. "You are far, *far* better." He lingered a moment, hoping for a relent, a crack, a window. Anything.

Nothing.

So he left.

And as he exited, called the guards to collect her to the Arena.

☼ ☼ ☼ ☼ ☼

In an open desert plain outside the main streets and throughways of the Capitol Plex, the Arena burrowed itself deep into wide sand, a half-natural and half slave-dug amphitheater that had played host to every range of occurrence. From coronations to condemnations. The greatest highs to the deepest lows. Sand packed behind thick stone slabs that drove stairs and seats into the walls of the Arena's bowl. Along one shallow end, a wide, treacherous balcony shoved its way over the crowd, thin-lipped and open to the long fall of the Arena floor below. Were it a wedding, brightly braided fabric with metal bells would suspend off the edge. Whereas a political prisoner of the Tavarian sort might find himself suspended off the same edge. Slaves were pushed into the pit from a grated tunnel at the base. Assuming they lived even that long.

Not everything warranted the Arena, of course. Most death-sentence slaves barely saw the outside of the jail long enough to remember what it looked like in the afterlife. A quick beheading in the courtyard as soon as they passed over the threshold, and it was life as usual for everyone else who was still whole from the neck up. Perhaps a rebel might be hung outside the colony, but he was generally dead long before being strung up.

The Tavarians liked to think they had a little dignity in the way they treated their dead slaves.

Unless, of course, that slave happened to be a rebel *and* a traitor.

Hyam would be deemed a traitor of the worst sort. And if the Chieftain's tales were anything to be believed, his death at the hands of both Chieftain and Council would be exceedingly more torturous than any seen in recent memory.

For this, the crowd hungered. Packed in deep and tight since the early hours (one must, after all, have a good seat and a clear view of the action), their restlessness grew in direct correlation to their thirst for blood.

This human, this slave, this rebel, had sullied their divine princess.

And she, too. She had stood before her subjects, in the midst of being betrothed to one of their own, only to turn and freely claim love for the filthy creature. Mayhap they did not wish her death. But they could wish a different sort of torture. They surely could wish a long, painful death for her lover, and she forced to watch every last bead of life drip out from his body.

The lust for blood and revenge ran deep.

Finally—*finally!*—the horns sounded and the Council members filed into their seats. Food vendors scurried to sell a final roast sand hen wing or cup of fizzed bloodwine before the Chieftain arrived and sales were cut off. (Because what went better with death than snacks and wine?)

The observant few noticed a new face among the Council, a young face they had seen not much earlier.

Matime.

Exchanged historian robes for Council robes.

The few began to applaud. Within a breath space, the whole surged to their feet, the thunder of hands drowning out food sellers and individual thought.

Fine-built historian.

Spurned lover.

Hero.

At least ten Tavarian maidens swooned and had to be carried from the Arena to be revived.

The Weight of Stars and Suns
Dawn Christine Jonckowski

The crowd pressed in.

Then came the Chieftain, and cheers pulled easily from their throats.

Then came the princess, and the cheers emptied to silence. Conflicted, they stared as she mounted not the dais but a barred-in pedestal reserved for the accused. She was not chained like most who regularly occupied that space.

But she certainly wasn't free.

Their hunger gnawed.

And then.

Then the rebel prisoner arrived.

The rebel prisoner arrived and the crowd roared. Screamed for the spectacle of his death. Screamed to the point of hysteria as he was dragged between two guards to the Arena floor below the Chieftain and the stoically broken princess. Draped and chained on a thick beam freshly anchored into the ground. On his knees only because his legs were a mess of bruises and blood, beaten just to the point of breaking. But through the dirt and crust, his eyes cracked open in the blazing sunlight, sought and found his beloved.

The heat of the suns was ice next to the fire of his soul for hers.

His body may have been failing, but his heart: that was steadfast.

His name ripped from her chest, the only outward consent to the torture within.

The masses only screamed louder, burying her singular voice.

It was chaos and two single heartbeats that pounded as one.

The Weight of Stars and Suns
Dawn Christine Jonckowski

But as the Chieftain lifted a hand to silence the maddening crowd, another roar burst forth to drown them all.

A great fire bloomed in the sky, tearing a hole in the canopy of their air. It melted through the atmosphere, pushing its way uninvited to the surface, where the great beast heaved to a rest on flame and propulsion at the desert edge of the Arena.

Silence.

Princess and rebel forgotten—a fairly impressive feat, all things considered—the crowd pivoted to stare at the metal monster perched on their planet. It wasn't something that lived in their thought catalog. They had no point of reference.

Well, a few on the Council—Matime, Arganon—and the Chieftain and the Warden and oh gods, the princess and the rebel, too.

They knew.

On a clunk and a hiss, the mouth of the ship yawned wide and she gave forth her cargo.

Twenty-five figures exited in formation.

Twenty-five *humans*.

From Earth.

And they did not look happy.

ACT III
DARKEST

17

"Ma'am, I think you're going to want to see this. It appears we will be interrupting an execution with our arrival."

The words of her First Mate, Brandon Behr, echoed in Captain Katherine Woolsey's mind as the crew marched behind the Tavarian guards to the Capitol. Ostensibly, they were not prisoners, but that was a little difficult to prove by the armed battalion surrounding them at the moment. She tugged at the neck of her silvered flight suit, feeling sweat trickle from under the sensible brunette bun at her nape. Behr's own dark hair spiked with damp as he pushed it back off his face in a vain attempt to cool.

She had leaned over the screens and surely enough, the natives were arranged in a bowl clearly jeering at the human being half dragged, half carried into the center before flopped on a post and chained there like chattel.

"It's like the damn Coliseum down there," Woolsey had muttered. "I hope this is as unjust as it seems, or we are going to look like idiots when we charge in and rescue him."

The Weight of Stars and Suns
Dawn Christine Jonckowski

They hadn't looked like idiots. Or at least they didn't think they had. Perhaps the thousands of purple faces staring back at them had had a different take on the experience. But from what Woolsey had gleaned of the situation—including the tear-streaked face of the lavender woman in the half-cage—it was a pretty unjust situation that required some serious heroics be interjected.

Behr had initially talked her out of charging in with phase blasters whining and ready to tear holes in purple heads. But only just. Her trigger finger sure did itch right about now.

They had been surrounded almost immediately by armored spear-bearing guards, rounded up like cattle and driven from the sunken desert amphitheater into the heart of the city whose walls brushed against the deep pit.

The battalion led the crew of *Genesis II* through several intersecting covered walkways and finally deposited them in a large space that resembled a courtroom. "The Chieftain will attend you shortly," the leader of the pack barked. Heavy doors swung shut behind him, and the crew was alone.

"I'm getting the sense that humans haven't been entirely welcomed here," Behr observed.

"Whatever gave you that splendid idea?" Woolsey shot back dryly. The rest of the crew stared at her with a mixture of shock and confusion and a twinge of space travel sickness. (She'd told the botanist to take the anti-nausea pills. It was hardly her fault that he never listened. And why in the world had they needed a botanist anyway? Who assembled this crew?)

But before she could address their nerves—and thank God, before the botanist could puke on anyone's shoes—the doors swung

The Weight of Stars and Suns
Dawn Christine Jonckowski

open on a protesting creak, revealing the Tavarian ruler (Woolsey assumed, anyway, based on the unnatural amount of glittering metal adorning him and the way the others lined up behind him like proud ducklings) and a litany of his various government friends. They marched without preamble straight down the center of the room, forcing the small crew of *Genesis II* to part like the Red Sea and allow them pathway. Under great and silent pomp and circumstance, the leader arranged himself on a throne-like chair, the retinue of assorted governors (or whatever they were) assembling in lesser decorative chairs along narrow tables lining the front of the room.

Woolsey felt Behr twitch beside her, imagined he was seriously rethinking his suggestion of coming out unarmed.

Because she was certainly regretting listening to him.

"Humans of Earth," the royal boomed, a powerful voice built for ruling, that took for granted being obeyed, was unused to being ignored. She might have to change that. Doubted he'd be overly fond of the idea.

"Welcome."

Wait, what?

✧ ✧ ✧ ✧ ✧

The Chieftain sat facing the small group of humans. He could smell their wariness. The female who identified herself as their captain constantly fought a hand that spasmed to grab for the weapon holstered at her side.

He knew why she was here.

Regretted the display they'd interrupted. For various reasons, not one of least was ridding himself of that rebel in order to save his daughter, but also for the bloodthirsty monsters it made the Tavarians look to be.

He was, of course. A bloodthirsty monster, that is. At least when it came to these rebels. And his humans. *His* humans! He knew this crew saw them differently, saw them as long-lost brothers and sisters that needed to be rescued from this alien race. Especially after the death display they had so rudely interrupted with their arrival. But his humans had been contracted by the folly of that original group of refugees. They had been born here, on Tav. They were his. They belonged to him. To Tav.

Not to Earth.

And certainly not to her. Not to this Earth human with the audacity to land on his planet with the express design of making demands on him.

Not that she'd made any demands. Or even spoken to him, really. Yet.

But he knew.

He knew.

If she thought she was going to out-maneuver or out-politic him, she was sadly mistaken. He was a master at this game, a master at dealing with humans who got in his way. And this woman? She had never met a Tavarian before. And she'd never dealt with their Chieftain.

She thought she knew what was coming.

She didn't.

The Weight of Stars and Suns
Dawn Christine Jonckowski

"Humans of Earth," the Chieftain began in a tone that arrested immediate awe from the lesser among the human crew. "Welcome."

He saw the split of confusion across the captain's face, a quick flit that was gone nearly as fast as it appeared. She clearly expected anything but congeniality.

"I *am* the Chieftain of this great planet, of *all* who live and breathe under her suns," he stressed subtly. "We welcome your diplomatic mission from Earth and beg to understand how we may be of service during your brief stay."

The captain snorted. "I am Captain Woolsey, I have a gun, and I'm fairly certain you're not stupid enough to think this is actually a diplomatic mission."

The Chieftain arched a single brow. She took it as an invitation.

"You may rule this rock, Chieftain, but under Global Alliance directives, that only gives you purview over your own natural citizens: the natives of Tav. Which means that all *humans* who inhabit Tav are still subject to the government and laws of Earth, or more accurately, the Global Alliance. So you can use your big words and scare tactics on your purple folk as much as you'd like, makes no difference to me. But even if that human down there killed one of your citizens, he still falls under Global Alliance rule and has a right to a Global Alliance trial for his crimes."

"He did not kill one of ours," the Warden sprayed an interjection from his spot just behind the Chieftain's throne. "He did far worse, and he will be executed for his crimes! You have no jurisdiction here!"

"Oh, but you'll find I do," Woolsey replied smoothly, turning to her interrupter.

Stoked as his own fire was, the Chieftain sensed the spark igniting between the human and his Warden and chose first to douse that before dealing with the rest.

"I'm afraid my Warden is right, Captain. You see, in our Archives, we house a contract bearing the signatures of all forty of the original humans whereby they indentured themselves and any of their offspring to us unto eternity. And whether your world or ours, I do believe that we all find signed contracts to generally be legally binding, do we not?"

Woolsey's face blanched before flooding with red fury. "You cannot sign anyone—regardless of race or species—into slavery! It is against every law in the galaxy! It was ratified by the Global Alliance and every off-world representative."

"Ah yes," the Chieftain sat back in his chair. Paused to nonchalantly pick some sand from the Arena out from under a fingernail. Flicked the bothersome grain over the arm of the throne. "But you see, Tav was not consulted in this decision, was it? Tav is not a member of your 'Global Alliance.' Therefore, you cannot hold us to rules and regulations to which we did not agree," he turned a gleaming eye back to the captain. "Can you?"

Woolsey's lips tightened to a thin line, all but disappearing from her face. He watched that finger twitch again as if already seated against her strange weapon. The Chieftain was indeed needling her. He wanted her to blow. Because if she did, then he had every right—Global Alliance or no—to fight back under the banner of protecting his citizens. If she attacked any single individual in the Courtroom

The Weight of Stars and Suns
Dawn Christine Jonckowski

(and while he had a few unfavorites he'd hope were her first targets, he wouldn't be overly picky about who he lost if it meant achieving his goal), his guards would be on top of her in an instant. There were twenty-five of hers, all concentrated, and over fifty of his, between the visibles surrounding and those tucked back in secret corners and crevices for added protection.

The humans didn't stand a chance.

"With all due respect, Chieftain," a younger woman with a noticeable accent from Woolsey stepped forward. "Undoubtedly you have noticed your suns burning out. And while I'm sure that in your wisdom, you and your government have accounted for how to adapt to this changed ecosystem, I have to wonder if you are also aware that five of the suns still burning are on the verge of a supernova. And when they go, they will utterly destroy the face of Tav and all who live here."

Arganon slid to his feet, smiling graciously. "While we appreciate your concern, yes, we are already aware of this issue and have survival plans in place. Even now, we are constructing sub-surface dwellings where our citizens will remain safe from the destruction above. In fact, your human brothers and sisters are aiding in the development of these new housings and will reap the same protective benefit when the time comes." He finished with a small bow, dipped his head toward his Chieftain, and sat down as smoothly as he'd risen, clearly believing the issue handled.

"And when will those dwellings be complete?" the woman countered.

Arganon stuttered a bit from his chair. "Well, we don't have a specific end date yet, aside from 'as soon as possible,' though the main structure of the Capitol prototype has just recently been completed. But our wise *zakar* assure us that we have plenty of time. These suns will burn for at least another generation, maybe two, giving us plenty of time to finesse development and quarter assignment."

Woolsey was agape. "You don't have a generation! Those suns are going to supernova in a matter of weeks! And a sub-surface dwelling is hardly going to save you, even if you were able to pack every last one of you underground." She started toward the throne. Every guard tensed in on her; the Chieftain rose a finger and they breathed back a pace, however wary of this fiery human.

"If you refuse to release these humans to me, you sentence them all to death. You and all your own race also stand to die; the stars will not differentiate based on the color of your skin. Your entire planet hangs under an imminent death sentence, Chieftain.

"The question now is: What are you willing to do to save your people . . . and mine?"

☼ ☼ ☼ ☼ ☼

For all the madness and mayhem of the morning, it was silent in the royal dining room.

Once the Earthlings had arrived all but demanding that every human be rounded up and brought with them to return home immediately, well, everyone had forgotten about Dameia. Maybe not Hyam, who just happened to be one of the Tav-born humans in question that these new arrivals were championing.

The Weight of Stars and Suns
Dawn Christine Jonckowski

But they all surely forgot about the princess.

Which suited her just fine. There had been entirely too much attention focused on her lately anyway.

The guards had deposited her rather unceremoniously back in the complex, not bothering to confine her to her quarters before rushing back to the melee at hand.

Three things she knew:

One, somehow the humans of Earth had found them.

Two, despite his supposed private affinity for humans, her father was not pleased. Less so when their demands included giving up his slave population.

Three, the interruption meant that Hyam was still alive.

For now.

Wouldn't it be just like her father to make some bloody sacrifice of Hyam. Not just to finally finish what he'd wanted to do at the original trial, had been salivating to do since the Warden's calculating reveal. But to use Hyam's death as a power play against the humans from Earth. To prove to them that he could do what he wanted to whom he wanted when he wanted, completely regardless of what they said and how fiercely they shook their fists with those odd weapons in them.

Dameia sat staring out over the table into the small patio beyond. She had been so prepared for Hyam's death that she couldn't figure out how to process his life. Her heart swirled a mix of incredulity and hope and love and joy all frosted with a heavy, heavy layer of dark despair. Hyam's life was a bone her father was not like to let go of any time soon.

His execution was stayed, not revoked.

Hope was a dangerous morsel to taste.

"Dameia, is that you?" Hannah's figure had initially scurried past the door, only to do an about-face as soon as she glimpsed the princess' defeated hunch at the table. The older woman rushed in and threw her arms around the Tavarian princess in a familiar way that was just not done.

Or at least not done until now.

It seemed protocol and stations had all but been erased over just a few days. And Dameia was just fine with that, thank you.

Because she really needed a hug.

Hannah pulled back, searched Dameia's face from arm's length, her eyes flitting, probing.

"He's alive," she finally breathed. "He's alive and you must go to him."

Dameia's eyes filled. "Oh Hannah, I don't know if I can." She dropped her chin; salty tears splashed into her lap.

"What? Why not?"

The princess drew a deep breath, raised her face to meet her companion's. "You know my father."

Hannah's face screwed. "Ugh, what has he to do with any of this?"

"Because," Dameia sighed. "Because he will see Hyam dead. If not this morning as he desired, then at another greater and more theatrical opportunity. He will not waste his powerful vendetta, his citizens' ire. Nor will he pass on the occasion to use Hyam as an object lesson for the visitors."

Her voice trembled to a whisper. "And I just don't know if I'm strong enough to say goodbye to him again."

The Weight of Stars and Suns
Dawn Christine Jonckowski

Hannah's face widened. "Again?" she parroted in disbelief. "Dameia, you never said goodbye to him the *first* time. After all he has endured for you, this is how you thank him? This is what his love and his sacrifice are worth to you?"

"*How dare you.*"

Dameia could only blink in shock until her tongue finally loosened. "I . . . I didn't think—"

"No, you didn't," Hannah interrupted her agreement. She pulled a ring of keys from under her belt. Smiled tenderly at her poor beleaguered princess. Leaned in, placed a cool hand on the royal's cheek. "You know where he will be. Go to him, Dameia. He deserves to see the woman he loves."

Neither stopped to acknowledge that "woman" was a purely human term. That Hannah had in that moment effectively claimed Dameia as one of her own. That Dameia had welcomed the distinction. The princess rose to her feet, wrapped her companion tight in her arms. Held on for dear life.

"Thank you," Dameia whispered, her heart cracking. She felt her companion smile, knew she was forgiven.

"Go," Hannah urged again.

And so Dameia went.

☼ ☼ ☼ ☼ ☼

If they were going to keep putting him in the same cell, Hyam thought that they could at least let him move in a few creature comforts. A blanket? Maybe at least a pillow. A clean tunic without three days' worth of dried blood dyeing it would be nice.

Or a plaque. A nice plaque with his name engraved on it. He could be okay with that.

At least that way someone would know he had been here.

Someone would know he had lived.

His head dropped back against the wall on a sigh. Humans were technically forbidden any sort of death and burial rituals. Most humans were carted away by the guards as soon as they became a corpse, if not scant moments prior. Once a month, two unlucky slaves would be selected and with rags tied tight across their noses and mouths, would open the mass grave not far from the colony to add in the past month's casualties. The bodies were allowed no preparation or preservation, became pungent and bloated piled in the suns.

Hyam had been selected for the task once. He had retched for three days after.

Their lives were lived with no recognition, no record, no allowance for remembrance. Death was more a fact of life than living was.

And yet.

He *really* didn't want to die.

He'd stood (if one could have called it "standing") calmly and faced the impending order of his death with a stoicism wildly mistaken for courage. But under the stalwart resignation, his very fibers trembled, vital muscles threatening to quit and embarrass him in front of the masses. Not that he imagined his death would be allowed to contain much dignity—quite the contrary, if rumors were

The Weight of Stars and Suns
Dawn Christine Jonckowski

to be believed—but at least he wanted to approach it as unsoiled as possible.

Fortunately, his weakening sphincters were rescued by the arrival of the ship and the interruption her hot-tempered cargo had posed.

And so, much to the frustration of the Chieftain (who just really, *really* wanted Hyam dead) and the intense disappointment of a crowd hyped for a good old-fashioned torture and execution, Hyam was still alive.

For now, anyway.

He held no illusions that this brief respite was anything but that. The Chieftain was going to find a way to rid Tav of Hyam. He was just now operating on a slightly delayed schedule.

Just then, the door creaked open. Hyam closed his eyes once again against the inevitability of his death.

If only he'd had a chance to see Dameia one last time. (Maybe while he was cleaner, too. Come to think of it, had she ever seen him not coated in at least one layer of grime?)

When he didn't hear an immediate bark about getting to his feet followed with a string of various and sundry insults about his intelligence, lineage, and the marital status of his mother prior to his birth, Hyam dared to open one eye and roll his head to face the sudden guest.

His princess.

His Dameia.

"Either you are one masterful escape artist, or I've taken one too many blows to the head and you're really the Warden," he managed around a dry throat and swollen larynx.

A choked laugh answered him. "It really is me," Dameia's voice replied, quavering ever so slightly with stuffed emotion and put-on bravery. "But it's still entirely possible that you've had too many hits to the head."

Hyam's laugh started a quiet huff through his nose, built to a gentle scoff through cracked lips, and then bloomed a full chortle that bounced across the cell walls. "I would certainly agree that since I've made your acquaintance, Princess, I've garnered more than my fair share of blunt trauma." Through the horrible truth of his statement, Hyam still turned a dazzling, honest smile.

"It's a pity that after all of it, your sense of humor remains unimproved," she volleyed back with a ghost of her old smile. The smile that knew life and love and laughter and not house arrest and death orders and torture. Then her mouth dropped, the light cheer gone. Her fingers twisted in each other, she bit her lips, staring anywhere but at him.

"Dameia," he spoke only her name. Rose to his feet, however stiffly.

"I'm sorry," she blurted, tears welling up and spilling down her face.

Hyam shook his head, genuinely confused. "For what? What have you done that warrants an apology to me?"

He watched her, witnessed the war inside her, the war between her feelings and her station and everything she'd thought was right and wrong before she met him. Loved her more for the fact that whatever she would come up with to answer him was surely not an offense in the least, loved her for thinking this mantle was hers alone to wear. Finally her fingers unwound and her arms fell listless

The Weight of Stars and Suns
Dawn Christine Jonckowski

to her sides. She raised haunted eyes to him and shrugged heavy with the weight of her ascribed sin.

"I wanted you."

Hyam cocked his head ever so slightly, inviting her to continue despite the building flood in his throat of reasons why none of this was her fault.

To her credit, she stood tall and regal, despite the tears, despite whatever pain that coursed through. "I wanted you," she repeated, stronger now. "I wanted you and I didn't think beyond that. I didn't think of the consequences, what they would do to us—what they would do to *you*—if they found out. *When* they found out. I didn't *want* to think about it, so I didn't. Instead I chose to live in the moment and drag you down with me. And then worse, I claimed to love you all while drawing you nearer and nearer to death with my selfish want."

A quick knife iced through Hyam's heart, and he gripped the cell bars to keep from falling. "Wait, *claimed* to love me?"

Her tears coursed harder, faster. "How can I say I love you," her voice cracked, dropped to a whisper, "when this is what I have done to you? How is that love?"

Hyam nearly laughed with relief. "Dameia," he said, and finally—finally!—she stepped to the bars. Her hands fisted over his, clinging for dear life. He curved into a warm smile, inviting her. She dropped her forehead to the grating, allowed him to reach a hand through and cup the back of her neck. Breathe the scent of her.

"You have loved me more and better than anyone else in my lifetime," his voice came soft against her hair. "You never saw me as human, as 'other.' You never saw me as competition, even. You saw me as a complete and sovereign being. You saw me as a heart and soul starved for something I'd never tasted, and you poured into me again and again, making me stronger, making me want to be the man you saw when you looked at me.

"Even more than that, you trusted me. You invited me in to those dark, secret places that no one else knows. You freely gave of yourself, even to the point of helping me find a way to leave Tav, to leave *you*. And yet you still returned for me every second cycle.

"You would help me leave this planet never to see you again. Not because it was what you wanted, but because it would keep me safe. Because you thought of me above all else, including yourself.

"*That*, Dameia, that is love in its purest and rarest form."

She sniffled, hiccupped, but did not argue. Did not speak.

"And this little setback we're experiencing right now? Is not your fault. The Warden has been planning for ages to overthrow your father. We are merely pieces in his chess game."

A soft laugh broke through her tears. "Only you would call a death sentence a 'little setback.' And I have no idea what chess is."

"But see, you forget," Hyam smiled, bringing his hand to her chin to tip her gaze to his. "The sentence was never decreed. No verdict was spoken. Technically, I remain a free man." He took in his surroundings as if for the first time. "Well, free-*ish*."

"Wait," Dameia's head snapped up from the bars. "Say that part about the Warden again."

Hyam blinked. He figured the bragging hadn't been limited to him. Then again, of the two, he was the only one who would take the secret to his grave, and imminently at that.

The Weight of Stars and Suns
Dawn Christine Jonckowski

"The Warden has been planning for ages to overthrow the Chieftain."

"How do you know this?" she demanded. "Are you sure? Do you have proof?"

"Well, he bragged to me himself just before they dragged me to the Arena. It's about as sure as one can be, hearing it from the source. Though I regret that I don't have solid proof beyond my word, which is worth little to most, and less to the Chieftain." Hyam shrugged. "I'm sorry I don't have more details."

"You may not," Damiea released her grip on his hands, the bars, began pacing the small space, reenergized. "But you know who will?"

Hyam had a sneaking suspicion, and a not-so-sneaking suspicion that he wouldn't necessarily be thrilled with the answer.

"Matime," she dropped the name like a gavel, loud, fast, and final. Her feet stopped, her eyes bright and glittering with dark purpose, her lips twisted into a bitter sneer.

"Perhaps it's time I paid a visit to my 'betrothed.'"

☼ ☼ ☼ ☼ ☼

Matime, for his part, was doing his own thoughtful march, pacing the length of his new chambers, chambers that befit a member of the Council. A junior member, but still. Even a junior member had better accommodations than an accomplished historian of the Archives.

Naturally, it wasn't anything that matched what he would have had as the princess' official betrothed, but it was more than enough already. He'd spent the past three second cycles sleeping on the floor, finding the bed too soft for his liking. He doubted that the princess would have found favor in him abandoning her to sleep on the floor.

Not that she had found much favor in him to begin with. Beyond his usefulness in locating the ship, anyway. And keeping her father off the rebel's scent. Then again, one could argue that he'd been using her just as much. Or his uncle had, through him. It all tended to get a little convoluted and tangled in his head if he thought about it too much.

He resolved that by not thinking about it.

Or trying not to.

Her face, though. The pure longing and naked pain when the rebel was brought forth for death. That deep love. Now that he had been audience to it, he didn't know if he could have settled for anything less, from her or anyone else. His uncle could hang, for all he cared. For all his uncle had cared about him. Him, Matime. Not what the Warden could get from him, not how he could be used for the Warden's advancement and advantage. But for himself. For all he was and all he thought and all he felt. He'd said it before, but he meant it this time: He was done being a pawn in his uncle's games.

So when there was a knock on his door at dead of second cycle, he was only marginally surprised to see Dameia on the other side of it, and not his uncle.

"Princess," he inclined his head, but did not step aside to let her in.

|| The Weight of Stars and Suns ||
Dawn Christine Jonckowski

It didn't stop her. She shoved the heel of her hand into his breastbone and propelled him back into the room, shutting the door firmly behind her.

"Your uncle is plotting to overthrow my father. If you cooperate, I may choose to let you live. So tell me everything, and tell me right now." Her tone brokered no space for argument. She let her hand drop, nodded toward a chair, stood judge and jury in front of him with arms crossed tightly across her chest.

So he sat.

And he told her. Everything.

18

"We're running out of time."

Woolsey made a face at her first mate. "Thank you, Behr. I'm well aware of this fact."

After the face-off with the Chieftain, the crew had been escorted back to their ship while the Chieftain presumably decided what to do with their news of imminent doom. They were surrounded by a ring of purple Tavarian guards and scowled at mightily if anyone so much as peeked out of the door.

But they were alive. And free. (Well, free-*ish*.)

For now.

She'd take it.

But Behr was right: They were running out of time.

Even if the Chieftain had an incredible—and unlikely—change of heart within the few days' time he'd promised, getting the humans not only ready to leave but onto *Genesis II* itself was going to be a tremendous undertaking. And they only had two weeks.

However long that actually ended up measuring on Tav.

She sat with Behr in the ship's canteen, her feet up on a table, chair leaned back on two legs. Behr assumed a far more dignified pose. The rest of the crew was presumably asleep, or doing other things that people left in too close quarters for too long were wont to do. Woolsey half wished she could put aside her thoughts and responsibilities so easily.

"I've already got Boaden and Rennemeyer working on the logistics of getting everyone aboard, since this is going to be a far different undertaking than it would be on Earth," Behr remarked into the silence of Woolsey's deep thought. "But we have one more problem."

Woolsey's head dropped back on a groan. "I'm afraid to even ask." She closed her eyes, dug fingers into her temples and rubbed. "Hit me."

"The Tavarians."

The captain's head tipped to the side and she opened one eye to peer at Behr. "And how, pray tell, were these purple people-beaters *not* already a problem?"

Behr fixed her with a loaded stare. "We're humanitarians, Kate. Under the law of the Global Alliance, we must do our utmost to rescue *all* beings in danger."

Woolsey harrumphed. (She'd always wanted to do that.) "Humanitarians, Brandon. Not Tavarinarians, or whatever those bloodthirsty backward heathens call themselves. Besides, we don't have enough room for everyone."

"*All* beings, Kate. That means the Tavarians too. We can take some. And we can call another ship."

The Weight of Stars and Suns
Dawn Christine Jonckowski

She could hear him fold his arms over his chest. Feel the judgement roll off him in waves. Sighed long and loud to signal her disgust, disagreement, and resignation (in case he couldn't already tell).

"Fine," she said, the way only a woman indicating everything is most certainly *not* "fine" can say. "If that bloody Chieftain agrees to let us have the humans, we will offer sanctuary to any of his kind who want it." She sat forward, tipping her chair back onto all four legs with a violent thump. "But don't expect me to be happy about it." And walked off.

Behr shook his head. "I wouldn't dream of it," he replied after her retreating form.

✧ ✧ ✧ ✧ ✧

If the Warden was surprised to see Dameia fall into step with him the next morning on his way to the temple for morning worship (which she had as yet never attended, but there was always a first time for everything), he managed not to show it.

"Good morning, Warden," she greeted him pleasantly enough.

His hesitation was slight. "Good morning," he eventually replied, his customary wet sneer spreading across his face.

He must have figured there wasn't much more could be done by her, considering the events of the past few days.

He was about to find out exactly how wrong he was.

"I hear that negotiations are proceeding with the Earth humans," Dameia broached easily. The Warden grunted in return, staring hard at his sandals. They reached the temple, passed through the doors flanked by kowtowing temple workers and shorn priestesses. Continued off the main thoroughfare down a small side hallway that led to the royal dais in the heart of the temple where prayers would soon begin.

"Pity they interrupted your well-oiled plan to kill a rebel, humiliate a princess, and ruin a chieftain."

The Warden's head snapped up, his feet stopped. Turned toward the princess. "Be careful what you accuse there, little *neqeba*," he growled close to her face, saliva bubbling at the corners of his mouth.

"Oh," she feigned surprise, delicately tipping fingers against her mouth. "Did I mishear? That palace gossip surely gets the best of me sometimes," she simpered. He huffed decaying breath and a fine spray of spittle square in her face. Dameia refused to flinch. Outwardly, anyway.

"You think you know so much?" His tone dropped menacingly, his fist bunched in the front of her tunic, backing her up and holding her captive against a hard pillar. "You think just because you got on your back for a human that makes you so special? As if you're the first one who has ever done that? As if somehow you should be revered for your whorish act?" His words stung her heart nearly as much as his spitting stung her eyes.

"Let me tell you something, Princess," he dropped the title mockingly. "Maybe you weren't my ultimate goal, but you and that filthy rebel will make pretty additions to my trophy collection.

Perhaps the head that's on his neck isn't the only one of his I'll be displaying. Perhaps that will make others think twice about which animal they choose to ride in the future."

Dameia's stomach turned at his gruesome and explicit descriptions. Saliva strung between his lips as he bared his teeth in a grin of cold victory.

"Do not for one moment dare to imagine that the arrival of those pathetic Earthlings in their big shiny ship has changed anything. Your rebel will still die. Not only will he die, he will beg for it by the time I'm done with him. And you? You will, too. Maybe your father is too soft for it, but I will see you pay for what you have done."

The princess refused to struggle in his grasp, instead squaring her shoulders and standing tall as best she could against his tight and uncomfortable grip. "You have no jurisdiction over me, Warden."

The Warden sighed happily. "Ohhhh, but I have your coin. All those scores you paid me for my silence. All that proof to your treachery."

"I signed no contract, have nothing but my word against yours."

"Ah, but see, I've already proven that your word is no good."

"Perhaps," Dameia agreed. It was time to play her cards. "But I think you'll find that most will rule more in the favor of love than of treason."

One bushy eyebrow crept up the Warden's face. "And since you did both—or so one might presume that you loved that creature—you figure one cancels the other? One outweighs the other? Believe me when I say that folk will more remember you leaving my nephew at the altar for a dirty slave than they will romanticize the idea that you and that cretin loved each other."

Dameia chuckled. "You have such a lovely way with words, Warden. And I did not leave Matime at the altar, as a betrothal is hardly a marriage ceremony. He will manage just fine, I should think."

The Warden grunted. "With a few shoves in the right direction," he agreed offhandedly. "Boy couldn't have found which way to point his stick without me telling him, much less get himself a throne."

"I should think you wouldn't want him anywhere near me as my betrothed now," Dameia inserted quizzically. "After all," her tone turned dangerously warm, "you've made no secret of your belief that I am now—how did you so eloquently put it?—ruined."

On narrowed eye, he leaned in, lips close to her ear, rank breath steaming against her neck and sending unpleasant chills down her side. His voice as dark and deep as his treacherous soul.

"And who says I need *you* in order to put Matime on the throne? Who says I even need my idiot nephew?

"Maybe I'll just put myself on the throne the way I'd always planned."

He wanted her to be horrified at best. Indignant, at worst. After threatening the life and limb of her lover and herself, and her father on top of it all, Dameia knew that the last thing he expected from her was a smile.

Which just made her lips curve all the wider.

| | The Weight of Stars and Suns | |
Dawn Christine Jonckowski

"Would you care to repeat that last sentence to my face, Warden? And I'll thank you to kindly remove your filthy hands from my daughter."

The Chieftain. Right on time, just as he always was for morning worship. Dameia silently thanked the gods for his consistent punctuality. Regardless of her prior unbelief, she'd give them that one.

While the Warden's mouth stringed open and shut on repeat as he worked to fabricate some reply, the princess ceremoniously removed his hand from its clench on her tunic. Stepped aside, her brow arched delicately against his treason. No sooner was she out of his grasp than the Chieftain twitched a finger and the Warden found himself surrounded and anchored by the royal guard.

"Get him out of my sight," the Chieftain growled darkly. "And the next time I set eyes on him, his head had better not be attached to the rest of his body."

"Yes, sir!" The guards snapped to attention, ready to march the doomed Warden from the temple. As they passed her, Dameia leaned in to mark her own hot, dark words on the Warden's skin and make it crawl.

"You are lucky that the head atop your neck is the only head of yours that may be displayed, Warden. I've heard it said that the—ahem—*smallest zakar* often have the biggest aspirations. And since your aspirations were the largest of them all, *well*."

The last thing he saw before the guards pulled a hood over his face was the princess' deep-cut smirk.

He would not see another face again in the short remainder of his life.

The guards half-marched, half-dragged the shocked and struggling prisoner back through the temple and out toward his doom. Sucked of the contingency, the room seemed to suddenly loom larger around the two remaining occupants.

Dameia watched her father, wary. He had aged suddenly. Whether that was due to the events of the past several moments, or if it had been steadily occurring for a season and she just refused to see it until now, she couldn't tell. But it abruptly and surprisingly rather broke her heart.

Underneath everything, he was simply a father trying his best to protect the daughter he loved.

The Chieftain blew out a longsuffering sigh. Broke the thick silence. "I owe you thanks," he finally said. His head shook, disbelieving. "Clearly, I had no idea. Otherwise I never would have trusted the Warden as I did. Never would have promoted such a match with his nephew."

"Matime is innocent," Dameia stepped forward, breaking into both her father's sightlines and his rhetoric. "When I learned of the plot against you, I confronted him and he told me everything. He is—somewhat unbelievably—just as much a victim as you and I. A puppet of his uncle's, tied to purse strings and jerked about as the Warden demanded."

The Chieftain emitted a noncommittal noise, crossed his arms over a broad chest. Paced a step or two one way, back the other, as if his footfalls could puzzle out the goings-on of the morning.

"And what of this plot? How did you learn of it to begin with?"

The Weight of Stars and Suns
Dawn Christine Jonckowski

Here, Dameia could offer nothing but truth, however distasteful he would find it. "Hyam," she said simply.

The Chieftain looked up. "Who?"

"The rebel you have been so intent to kill since first you saw him. Before he was taken to the Arena, the Warden bragged his plan to Hyam, figuring that Hyam would take it to his very imminent grave." She planted herself in front of her father, a clear roadblock to his pace, an immovable that forced him to stop and meet her gaze. To undoubtedly absorb the truth she spoke.

"When the Earth humans arrived, I returned to Hyam's cell, intending to say goodbye. Instead he gave me your salvation. Father," Dameia paused, knowing what had to be said, uncertain of the response she would receive to this truth. Knowing she had no other choice but to speak it. "He is your hero. He is the champion of this battle.

"Like it as not, you owe your life and your kingdom to him."

The Chieftain's eyes slid shut, his face a mask of tolerated pain as the truth needled through him and penetrated his defenses, his lifelong prejudices, his core beliefs about the human people and how they fit into his world. Without opening his eyes, he spoke.

"You know that I will offer you anything you desire as a reward for this, for saving my life and my kingdom." He opened his eyes, bottomless black eyes staring into hers. "I suppose you will want the rebel."

"No."

Her soft answer hit him sideways.

"No . . . ?"

She sighed, heavy, resigned. The sigh of a born leader, of one whose own life and love and joy have been trained to fall to the background in favor of what is best for the collective. The Chieftain could not guess her answer, wouldn't have wanted to. Only knew that it would make him proud even as it would indubitably break his heart.

"I want you to let the humans go."

Father and daughter each bore fissures in their hearts.

Both hearts cracked open, raw and runny.

Maybe they broke over different specifics.

But they broke at once all the same.

"You know that if I do this, your human will return to Earth and you will never see him again."

"I know," her voice, a shattered whisper.

The Chieftain's chest rose and fell on a deep sigh. "Very well," he agreed, yielding. "I shall inform the Earth humans that any Tavarian human slave who wishes to return to Earth will be freed to do so. All the rebel prisoners shall be released back to the colony. And any human who chooses to remain shall be given equal rights as a Tavarian citizen." He unfolded his arms, rested a hand on his daughter's rigid shoulder.

"I am proud of you, daughter," he said softly. His hand dropped. He left.

Dameia was alone.

Very, *very* alone.

A single tear wended slowly down her face.

It was done.

She squared her shoulders and walked out.

The Weight of Stars and Suns
Dawn Christine Jonckowski

☼ ☼ ☼ ☼ ☼

"You're joking."

Whatever the Chieftain thought the Earth captain's reaction to his emancipation proclamation would be, this was clearly not it. The Chieftain understood that his announcement might come as a bit of a surprise. But this was a little much.

"I beg your pardon, Captain?"

Woolsey stood in the Court, surrounded by her contingency, fists planted firmly on hips as if prepared for a verbal—and possibly physical as well—show-down. They had been summoned shortly after the Chieftain exited the temple, just as fast as he could get a scribe to pen the official proclamation. The Chieftain, his Council, and the Earth humans were gathered nearly before the ink of his signature was dry and the wax of his seal had hardened. His Council had barely been briefed, and were still steaming at the ears over his executive order.

"I said, you're joking," Woolsey repeated, her stance not shifting by even a twitch. "When we landed just a few days ago, you were ready to tear a human limb from entrails for looking at a native cross-eyed, and now you want me to believe I can just *have* them? All of them? Just like that?" She crossed her arms tight against her chest, defensive. "Nothing is ever that easy. I don't buy it."

Wordlessly, reluctantly, a senior Councilman seated in the front row slid a document across the table for her to read. "We would prefer not to 'buy it' either, madam," he sighed, "and yet here it is now law."

The Chieftain leaned back against his throne. Steepled his fingers and tapped them impatiently against his mouth as he watched Captain Woolsey's eyes track across the document, her first mate peering not so subtly over her shoulder to scan along.

Finally, she matched her gaze back to his.

"Then it is done."

The Chieftain nodded. "It is done. You have my authority to assemble and train them for the journey as you will. I have requested that a certain percentage continue to work—this time as paid laborers—so that we may transition away from being dependent upon their labor in order to sustain our ways of living. But they may be excused for reasonable training sessions.

"I ask only that you inform me of your departure date and supply my Council with a complete list of all humans who will depart from Tav."

Woolsey shook her head, trying to shake the contents, make room for this surprising new state of things. She could take them home. All of them. (If they wanted; fear of the unknown could often outweigh in the mind the benefits of change.) It was more than she'd dared to hope. Especially considering the gruesome display they'd interrupted with their arrival.

"Thank you, sir," she finally replied. "As I understand how both the emancipation and the exodus of your former slaves will impact your economy based on my own country's history, I commend you for this brave act."

The Weight of Stars and Suns
Dawn Christine Jonckowski

And then Behr poked her in the spleen (or somewhere equally tender—perhaps a kidney?—where he had no business jabbing without structural knowledge) and hissed, "The Tavarians. You promised." Woolsey sighed, loud and longsuffering. Just in case he wasn't completely aware of how annoying his demands were. Even if they were technically the Global Alliance's demands.

"One . . . more thing," she offered reluctantly. The Chieftain, halfway out of his chair, looked at her in surprise, sat smoothly and bid her continue.

Woolsey pinched the bridge of her nose. Few alternative life forms had ever been found on colonized planets, and certainly none so humanoid as the Tavarians. Mostly some horrifying beasts of burden or nearly brainless balls of fluff that were brought back to Earth to be bred for farm work or domesticated pets, as the case may be. Though none had lived longer than a few years under Earth conditions. She could only imagine the media and political frenzy if she stepped off of *Genesis II* not only with the captive humans in tow (which would certainly make her a hero, and that part she could be okay with), but then also followed by a flock of tattooed purple aliens. Shock? Horror? Obsession? The reactions could be any multitude of combinations.

Not to mention if Earth proved unhospitable to their systems and her mercy act simply became a prolonging of their deaths, in an undoubtedly more drawn-out and painful way than quick supernova incineration.

There really was no winning here.

But she *had* promised.

And the Chieftain was waiting.

So Woolsey took a deep breath, tried her best not to roll her eyes, continued. "As members of the Global Alliance, we are charged with protecting all life forms under our jurisdiction to the best of our ability. While Tav is not technically a part of the Global Alliance, our presence and the presence of our ship here demands that we act and interact with you as if you were. With the impending destruction of your planet, I, Captain Katherine Woolsey, along with the entire crew of *Genesis II*, offer you and your people safe sanctuary aboard our ship. Should you choose not to remain on Tav, you will be granted safe passage with us to Earth.

"There's only one problem: Small as your planet is, *Genesis II* can't take all of you. And I may not be able to get another ship here in time to assist before the supernova. So that means of your own citizens, you'll have to choose who goes and who stays.

"Who lives . . . and who dies."

☼ ☼ ☼ ☼ ☼

When the door to his cell first opened and he was told he was free, Hyam thought it had to be a joke.

Seriously.

There was no way that a rebel who had been so marked for death was now free. He was going to walk out of the prison and suddenly be met with a sharp blade through the throat, or a spear through the core.

He couldn't be free. Just like that.

Except.

The Weight of Stars and Suns
Dawn Christine Jonckowski

He *was.*

The doors opened—first to the cage, then to the cell, then to the prison altogether—and Hyam walked out a whole and free man. Oren and Hannah stood there to greet him, and by "greet," they really caught him as he stumbled on beaten and weakened legs. Held him until he could get his feet under him again. Remained respectfully wordless as he sobbed his gratefulness into Hannah's clean air-scented shoulder.

"How? Why? I don't understand," he finally managed.

Oren disengaged from the embrace, wrapped one arm under Hyam's armpits to bear him up as they proceeded slowly to the colony. "Didn't they tell you anything when they released you?"

Hyam's head shook. "Not a thing. They only unbolted the door and told me to go, that I was free. I was so sure it was an elaborate ruse and that I would only walk free as far as my death." His relief was so profound it nearly had shape.

"We are all free," Hannah began, her words colored in wonderment. "Just yesterday evening, the proclamation went out that all humans are freed to return to Earth. Prisoners would be released. And any of us who choose to remain on Tav will gain full rights as citizens. Oren, Ithai, and the others were returned to us shortly after, and you this morning."

Hyam's head already swam, overcome.

As if sensing his overload, the trio continued the rest of the way to the colony in silence. They passed beneath the gated arch of the colony, the heavy grates for once wide open and not flanked by Tavarian guards in heavy weaponry. Hyam drank it in, feeling like he was seeing it all for the first time. This prison that had been home for his entire life, opened. No shackles—real or imagined—to ring around his freedom and set its limits.

His gaze jerked quickly and suddenly to Hannah. One word, both question and statement all at once. "Ithai."

Hannah's quiet joy extinguished. "Come with me."

The trio continued not to Ithai's singular dwelling, but to Hannah's. Inside, the heat of the enclosed space threatened to drown them. And yet, in the back, shivering under a blanket, a skeleton draped in barest flesh, bones knobbing out at every angle.

With great effort, Hyam unlocked his arms from Hannah and Oren, dropped to his own bruised knees at the bedside. The head turned at the noise, eyes vacant, sunken, and glassy staring unseeing in his direction.

"Ithai. Brother," Hyam's voice came out crushed and cracking. He laid his own dirt-crusted and bloodied hand along his best friend's face, felt every bone working in the younger man's jaw as the sounds of his voice registered in an illness-fogged brain. Without turning from his friend, Hyam asked Hannah quietly, "What happened?"

Hannah shook her head. "I wish I knew. Oren tells me he wasn't entirely the same after he collapsed in the ship you were exploring. But heat exhaustion shouldn't manifest like this," she gestured helplessly to Ithai's wasted body. "Unless it simply weakened him enough to allow something far worse to take hold.

"If only I could get a medic to assess him."

"Wait," Oren broke in. "If we have full rights of citizenry, shouldn't we finally have access to Tavarian medics as well?" Hyam too turned toward Hannah, tenuous hope stringing. The older woman shook her head.

"I tried, and it wasn't for lack of access. The Tavarians are similar enough, corporeally. But not exact. And our genetic makeup predisposes us to different diseases. There are infections that are life-threatening to Tavarians that cannot touch us. Likewise, things that attack our bodies and mysteriously leave the Tavarians alone." She wrapped her arms around her middle, as if holding herself together. "They could not identify the source of his illness, nor treat it. So they are mystified while he continues to melt away into nothing." Her voice caught and held on a sob. Hyam's hope snapped on her cry.

This planet continued to ruin his people. He could not wait to leave it behind.

"Hyam?"

It was Ithai's voice. Weakened, thin, but there.

Hyam turned to his friend, slipped his hand into Ithai's seeking fingers. "I'm here, brother." Ithai's face slid into a peaceful smile, his skin stretched paper-thin over jutting cheekbones. His grip tightened, a surprising squeeze on Hyam's palm.

"You're free," he whispered with great effort.

Hyam swallowed the tears that sprang to his throat. "Yes, brother, I am. We both are. And we're going home."

The younger man shook his head ever so slightly. "I don't think I am. Not the same way you are, leastwise." His eyes slid shut and his breathing slowed, evened, deepened. Hyam stayed beside his friend for the space of several moments, watching his bony chest rise and fall. Finally, he rose to his feet. Turned to face Oren and Hannah.

"We need to get an Earth medic to see him."

Oren scoffed. "We may have been granted freedom, Hyam, but don't think we have immediate access to those from Earth. We may not be 'nothing' anymore, but we're still hardly 'something.' They may be here to rescue us, but I doubt one sick man is going to factor high when compared to the hundreds they need to get off this planet. Unless you happen to know the Chieftain personally. And something tells me that free or no, you're not exactly high on his list of favorites."

"Probably not," Hyam agreed, grinning. "I do know someone else rather close to him, though."

Hannah clapped like a small girl, a smile beaming instantly across her features. "The Princess!"

"Indeed, the Princess," he replied. "She knows not only me, but Ithai as well. She will help us, I know she will. I only have to ask.

"But first, I'm *really* going to need a bath."

✧ ✧ ✧ ✧ ✧

Matime sat in the closed session of Council, feeling over his head and out of his element. Maybe he'd had aspirations of Councilship, but that was before he knew what it actually entailed. He'd envisioned himself whipping through texts to provide legal aid to the Chieftain, settling disputes between citizens with the golden level of the law, solving political impasses with obscure provisos and loopholes known only to someone who had spent the better part of their younger years romancing books and history instead of lovers.

The Weight of Stars and Suns
Dawn Christine Jonckowski

Instead he sat, adorned and surrounded by the trappings of his ambition, bored out of his mind listening to old *zakar* argue. At this point, he nearly prayed for the supernova to swallow them up that very afternoon.

"How can we leave Tav?" the Head Councilman was saying. "Our culture, our history, our lifeblood flows through this planet. The Earth humans have no ties here. They may simply be attempting to scare us into giving up our home world so they may take it over. Then they deposit us on Earth and enslave us the way we did their ancestors."

Arganon, ever the cool head, interjected. "While you may be prudent to doubt their altruism to a point, I think we would all agree that their technology is far advanced of ours. We know in part, but if they have the ability to see the heavens from beyond, they know in full. And while it is entirely possible that this is an elaborate ploy to hurriedly rescue their brothers and feed us a gulp of our own medicine, I am like to believe that since the captain gave us the choice not only to go, but also whom to send, she is acting on behalf of our wellbeing and truly does plan to offer safe passage and a fresh start." He spread his hands across the table in front of him, shrugged nonchalantly. "If she was planning to enslave us, something tells me she wouldn't have offered. She would have simply taken. Gods know that's what our forefathers did when the first batch of humans arrived."

Matime's head spun and he wished not for the first time to go back to the Archives.

But more than that, he *did* believe the human captain. He agreed with Arganon that she probably had a better handle on their current environmental situation than they did. For gods' sake, she'd flown a ship across the galaxy to them.

It had been over a hundred years since the original humans had crashed on Tav, and the Tavarians were still nowhere near figuring out how to fly within their own atmosphere, much less across stars and space.

Did *he* want to leave Tav?

Not particularly.

However.

That didn't mean he couldn't wish for his fellow citizens to have a chance at an adventurous life, a far longer life than they were predicted anymore to have here on Tav.

"Matime?" The Chieftain's voice broke through his musings, tone indicating it wasn't the first time his name had been uttered in demand of a response. He shook his head, trying to rattle his thoughts clear.

"Apologies, sir," Matime offered, voice small.

"Your input is requested," the Head Councilman snapped sharply. From the Warden, Matime had learned that the grizzled Head Councilman was the only one who had not voted for Matime's approval as a junior Councilman. Something about his own nephew being a better—if somehow less politically connected—choice for the seat that ultimately (and with the help of some well-placed bribes by his recently late uncle) went to Matime.

The junior Councilman took a deep breath, focusing on the slow rise and fall of his chest, aligning his thoughts before he spoke.

"We can no more promise with any certainty that our citizens will live a full life here on Tav. Or even live at all. Truly, we

The Weight of Stars and Suns
Dawn Christine Jonckowski

even lack any way of knowing whether our underground shelters will adequately protect us, and we certainly do not have enough ready to save more than a handful of our entire population.

"So let them go," he advised, weary. "Let anyone who wishes, go."

And all hell broke loose.

✧ ✧ ✧ ✧ ✧

The worst part about Hyam's freedom, Dameia decided, was that she had less access to him than ever before. She could not predict where he would be, could not order anyone to bring him to her. He could be raucously celebrating his release with dozens of his fellow humans. And how keen would they be to let him walk voluntarily into the palace of the same Chieftain who had all but ordered his torture and death to see the very Tavarian princess who created the problem in the first place.

She guessed not very.

Hannah could say all she wanted about the humans venerating her change of heart, but words and reality were far too often polar opposites.

Then again, he'd only been free since just that morning, and it was barely spiced tea hour. (Whether or not that tradition would—could?—continue without the human retinue to prepare and serve remained to be seen.) So she should just push down her panic. Not an easy task when her emotions were already in tatters after the events of the past many days.

So when the knock on her door and her dull invitation to enter resulted in Hyam standing at her threshold, she could not contain the shriek of joy as she ran to him.

Arms tangled, olive and lavender.

Lips sought and found.

Dameia buried her nose in Hyam's neck, surprised to smell not the dirt and essential maleness of him, but soap and air-dried cloth.

"You bathed," the words tumbled out covered in wonder before she could stop them. Hyam chuckled.

"I did. And so much filth washed off that it's a wonder you recognize the man beneath the layers. It is possibly years since I've been this clean." His grin split white across his tanned face. New scars latticed pink and white across his lip, an eyebrow, a cheekbone. Evidence of the brutal favor shown him by the Warden. Dameia's dusk-purple fingertips wandered over the terrain of his features, drinking him in through her touch.

She wanted.

She *craved*.

And was surprised when on a reluctant sigh, Hyam wrapped his hands around her biceps and pushed space between them.

"I'm afraid I've come only to ask a favor." His words rent deep. Dameia felt her heart drop, attempted to veil her disappointment. Hyam blew out a barely contained breath. "It's not as you think," he continued. "I . . . *yearn* for you." His fingers rippled longing down her arms, naked desire in the timbre of his voice, the depth of his eyes, the grip of his hands. "But Ithai . . . he is ill, and Tavarian medics cannot diagnose or treat him. He is dying, Dameia,"

The Weight of Stars and Suns
Dawn Christine Jonckowski

here he released her and fingers dove into his clean, neatened hair. Mussed it with frustration and impotence. "He is dying and our only hope is that the Earth humans have a medic who can help him."

Dameia was instantly chastened by her own wanton desires. "Ithai?" she repeated in disbelief. Recalled the gentle young man who had stalwartly trampled through the forests with them, fearlessly pushed through the belly of the broken ship to try to learn her secrets. Stood beside Hyam even as the other rebel brothers abandoned him. Regarded Dameia not as the enemy, but as the one his friend loved.

She reached a hand to tenderly cup her beloved's face, tip his eyes into hers, raise his countenance to hope. "Go to him," she urged. "I will ensure the human medic visits before end of day."

Hyam bent his forehead to hers. Whispered his profound gratitude on a relieved exhale. Leaned in and gently tasted her lips.

"I will return," he promised. And was gone.

She watched him go.

Realized that she was going to have to get used to watching him leave.

And her heart cracked a little bit more.

✧ ✧ ✧ ✧ ✧

"Of all the things," Woolsey muttered, half to herself, half to Behr, who trudged alongside her with their medic in tow, all sweating profusely under the Tavarian suns as they followed a Tavarian guard to the human colony. Even with her flight suit half unzipped and tied at the waist, topped with a highest quality NASA-issue moisture-wicking tank, Woolsey still overheated. How had the Tavarian humans ever managed to adapt? She braced herself every time she stepped outside of the cool belly of *Genesis II* and was still continually unprepared for the onslaught of heavy heat.

"What, your philanthropy now doesn't extend to the ill, either?" Behr poked gently as he dragged a limp bandana across his damp brow. The captain fixed him with a dark stare.

"You know that's not true," she growled as Behr fell into perfect step with her. "There is just too much to do to prepare for gathering and leaving for it to be necessary that I accompany the medic. She has the training, not me. Let her do her job, for goodness sakes, and leave me alone to do mine."

Behr arched an eyebrow. "I'm sure glad that someone talked you out of a career in public relations. Your people skills need some work, Captain."

She snarled an unintelligible response that Behr imagined was full of less than savory language. Followed it with a heavy sigh. "I'm sorry, Brandon. It's just that we're under a ridiculous deadline to accomplish this mission, and to be quite honest, I have no idea most hours how we are going to manage to pull this off. We don't have enough room. The nearest ship that can come to our aid is a three-week space jump away. If they even make it, the only thing they'll likely find is a barbequed rock that had the audacity to once be a planet inside thirty-six suns. I've got too much on my mind and I feel like I'm just losing time here."

"What did you say?" Behr replied in mock surprise.

The Weight of Stars and Suns
Dawn Christine Jonckowski

"Don't make me repeat all that again. Summary? Lots to do, not enough time. The plight of every living thing. Or so I'm told."

Behr shook his head. "No, not that. Though I agree on the 'lots to do, not enough time' thing. I meant . . . did you actually *apologize* to me?"

He grinned.

She scowled.

"Yeah, well, treasure the memory," Woolsey sniffed. "I don't intend to make a habit of it."

"Here," the guard's bark halted them in their tracks. He gestured toward the arched gateway where a middle-aged former slave anxiously shifted from foot to foot as they approached. "This slav—uh, this *human*," the guard fumbled.

"Hannah," the woman supplied graciously. The guard coughed, awkwardness palpable.

"Yes, er, Hannah will take you the rest of the way. I will wait here to escort you back to your ship when you are done."

The Earth trio followed the former slave through narrow and wending streets to a dwelling at the back of the enclosed colony. Far from being the barren space Woolsey expected, the windows were hung with colorful weavings made of everything from dried vegetation fronds to strips of cast-off Tavarian garments. Forbidden from wearing anything brighter than the earthen tones, the human slaves had instead used the bright Tavarian fabrics to bring color to their homes. Other strips had been tied to old ropes and fluttered in zig zags across main walkways. Freed from the judging eyes of the guards, a few smaller children had snagged strips and tied them in brilliant twists across foreheads, up and down limbs, and around waists. They danced to a tune blown on the wooden flute of an older gentleman, a tune that tickled Woolsey's memory, though recognition eluded her. Something old and classic, she imagined. Perhaps a Beatles song?

Not that it mattered.

Entirely.

For themselves, the emancipated humans milled around in front of homes, somewhat directionless in their new-found freedom. Some stood around open cook fires, others circled jugs of fermented drink. The sounds of previously prohibited loving echoed from the darker corners of several dwellings.

And then they arrived at Hannah's, where the heavy fog of death hung over every surface. They entered her tidy yet bare living space. Slowly approached the figure on the bed. His breath came in shallow gasps, rattling in a ribcage clearly outlined against his skin. His hair, lank and damp, fell in odd clumps across a fevered brow. Woolsey could tell where the illness had eaten away at his scalp, clearing balding patches in an odd pattern.

A living corpse.

Without a word, the medic pulled the blanket aside and began poking and prodding the young man. She opened his mouth, examined his tongue. Pressed fingers to his bony arm for a pulse, and frowned at the display that shone up from the device on her own wrist. Scanned his core with the same wrist, frown lines deepening at those results too.

Finally she stood. Gestured the anxious half circle away from her patient to discuss.

The Weight of Stars and Suns
Dawn Christine Jonckowski

"It's not good," she began. "I can't tell you what caused it, but I can tell you it's not good. Something in the Tavarian environment has caused an infection that is taking over his entire body. If I can get him back to Earth alive, we can likely find means to cure him. He just needs to live that long."

"And what's the probability of that?" Hannah implored, wringing her hands.

The medic shook her head. "Not great. I'll leave you some pills to tide him over until we can get him stronger doses back home." She reached into her bag, pulled out a small packet bumped with five capsules. "Try to get him to swallow one every morning before he eats." Hannah folded her hand over the stiff square package, revering it.

"Beyond that," the medic shrugged helplessly. "I'm sorry, I can't do any more until I get him back to our treatment facilities on Earth."

Hannah nodded, eyes bright with unshed tears. "Thank you," she whispered.

Woolsey's heart cracked ever so slightly. Her hand came up and rested on Hannah's shoulder, surprising them both. Hannah's eyes flicked from hand to face and back again.

It occurred to Woolsey that these people hadn't seen much kindness in their lifetimes.

She hoped Earth could fix that for them.

"We have a medical bay on board *Genesis II* where he will be comfortable and safe for the travel to Earth. I will personally ensure that he is boarded onto the ship before anyone else and will see to his every need throughout our journey," the captain committed.

Behr's eyebrows winged upward. He coughed indelicately to cover the scoff of surprise that escaped. Woolsey aimed a cold glare.

"Shut up," she hissed. "And yes, sometimes I *can* be personable."

He smiled. "Wonders never cease."

Hannah's smile trembled, watery and brave. "Blessings on you both," she managed, enfolding the captain in a strong hug. Burying her instinctive need to pull away, Woolsey instead stood there as Hannah clung for dear life. Then slowly, slowly raised her own arms and returned the embrace.

"You're welcome."

☼ ☼ ☼ ☼ ☼

This time, when the knock sounded at her door, Dameia expected Hyam. Swung the door wide, pulled him in close. He held tight, as if he could siphon strength. She pulled him tighter. Let him bury his face in her neck this time. Whispered by his ear. "Tell me."

And so he did.

Everything of Ithai's swift decline. The medic's unhappy prognosis. The narrow chance that he would live long enough to receive a cure.

Exhausted by the telling, he sank into the settee in the parlor of her chambers, elbows on knees, head in hands. Dameia lowered next to him, gentle. Cautious.

"I never expected it to be like this," his voice broke. Dameia sat in silence, waiting. Without lifting it, Hyam turned his head toward her. "After all these years, all these fights, I have finally been granted freedom."

"But at what cost?" He shook his head. "Ithai. *You.*"

Dameia leaned in, leaned against. Wanted to absorb his pain, his loss.

Then the door swung back open.

Startled, the pair looked up.

And straight into the eyes of the Chieftain.

Dameia felt Hyam go rigid beneath her hand. Forced herself to maintain a calm she didn't particularly feel at the moment as her father faced her very human lover. In her chambers. Under his own roof.

Emancipation was a splendid proclamation. More difficult was it, though, to change years and habits of segregation and hate.

"Good evening, Father," she greeted him pleasantly enough. The muscles of his jaw bunched and released, chewing between the response he wanted to give and the response he ought to give.

"I, ah, wasn't aware you had . . . company," the Chieftain eventually replied.

Dameia rose smoothly to her feet, subtly tugged at Hyam's elbow so that he did the same, albeit somewhat less fluidly. "You remember Hyam," she answered easily, deceptively so, playing on the social graces the Chieftain himself had so ingrained in her for political moments such as these. Little would he have dreamed that she would one day be using them back on him.

He would have been proud if he hadn't been so distracted by the sight of his daughter's hand twined with that of the very man he had been trying to kill for far too long. The very man now protected under the Chieftain's own seal and proclamation.

Not for the first time did he wish the Earth humans had stayed their arrival just a few minutes longer.

At least the rebel was still leaving. Not the way the Chieftain had ultimately wanted, but leaving just the same.

Finding his own graces, the Chieftain offered a calculated jerk of the chin, an altogether male gesture. "Yes, I do find him particularly difficult to forget."

His daughter fixed a warning glare. The Chieftain sighed and with great effort, extended a hand to the former rebel slave. "Hyam," he choked on the name as if it pained him to have it travel his throat and tongue.

For the first time either could remember, a human's hand met that of the ruler in a pose of equality.

"Sir," Hyam responded, dipping his head with a respect he did not altogether feel. The shake was barely long enough to not be considered rude.

But it was a start.

The trio stood there, the ruler, the rebel, the royal, silence stretching.

Until Dameia could take it no longer. "Did you have purpose for your visit, Father? As you can see, I am entertaining company."

The Chieftain fumbled, one hand wrapping around to rub the back of his neck, loosening the muscles. Maybe so the words could get through.

Finally:

The Weight of Stars and Suns
Dawn Christine Jonckowski

"Ah, yes. As you know, the Earth humans have revealed to us that the supernovas are a more imminent threat than previously believed. As such, they have offered to also take a select number of Tavarians with them back to Earth in order to protect our race and offer us a chance to perpetuate, should Tav be annihilated."

His words gained strength as he said them, each phrase bringing him back closer to the commanding ruler that he was.

"They cannot, however, take us all. There is not room. But the Council has decided to allow a predetermined number of Tavarians journey to Earth with the humans."

Hyam's hand twitched in Dameia's. Tightened.

Hope.

Her father continued.

"We have designated a few leaders already; the remaining opportunities will be assigned on a first come, first serve basis, with lots cast as needed to ensure that families may remain together, and that an equal number of certain trades remain here as voyage to Earth."

Forcing calm into the notes of her words, Dameia asked, "And who are these leaders?"

The Chieftain's lips tightened.

And right away, hope snapped again. She knew: Not her.

And she was right. He rattled off a short list of names, Matime's one of them.

Hers not.

"Of course, you will remain with me to perpetuate the royal line here on Tav," the Chieftain finished.

As if he believed they would survive.

As if there would be a planet left for her to rule.

Hyam's fingers tightened again on hers, this time anger.

"Of course," she echoed, biting each syllable. The words broke on her tongue, spilling bitterness down her throat.

Silence beat again at their eardrums.

Eventually: "If that is all, Father, I think you should go, so as not to force me to be rude to my honored guest."

A pause, and then the Chieftain nodded. Nodded his agreement, nodded his departure to the pair in front of him. The royal daughter. The rebel under his roof.

The Chieftain was getting used to pivoting on a heel and leaving a room in silence when it came to his daughter and that man.

What was once more?

He pivoted and left.

No sooner had the door swung shut behind the Chieftain than Dameia gripped Hyam into a desperate embrace.

"There is never enough time with you," she murmured against his shoulder.

"There will never be enough," he replied. His arms trembled with the effort to pull her closer still. She cupped his face, leaned hers in to his. Breaths and hopes and heartbeats passed back and forth, and forth and back again.

"Stay," she asked.

"I want to . . ."

"Stay with me now."

"I will."

And he did.

19

"Rewind and say that one more time, because I could have sworn, Captain, that you just said you're bringing a hundred natives back with you."

Woolsey's face in the screen screwed with a long-suffering sigh back at Director Bergman, her image flickering ever so slightly as it bounced between satellites and landed back on Earth from Tav.

"No, you heard me correctly, Director," her voice crackled over the connection. "A hundred natives. Along with the rescued humans."

It was 3 a.m. in Alabama. Bergman at least sat at his dining room table—an improvement over still being in the office at this unholy hour—his face lit by the glow of the tablet that beamed Woolsey's image to him. Hour of the night notwithstanding, when you were the Director of your country's Global Alliance Colonization Program, you answered certain calls from certain people. Around the country, the globe, or the galaxy.

Hence the obscene time difference that had his wife muttering words her mother certainly hadn't taught her when his tablet jangled with Woolsey's incoming vidcon.

But the calls were usually short, typically an issue he could have solved in his sleep (which was a good thing, considering the hours these calls usually came and his commensurate level of wakefulness).

And about colonizing off-world.

Not a reverse colonization of bringing natives to Earth.

"Look," Woolsey's voice interrupted over the tiny speakers. "You knew as well as I did when we left that Tav is a marked planet. Global Alliance law states that we are to maintain the well-being of all life possible. Which, while this is unorthodox, means that we have a responsibility to rescue as many of the natives from Tav as we can before this rock hits its expiration date."

"You seem surprisingly up-to-date on Global Alliance statutes," Bergman remarked dryly.

Worlds and galaxies away, Woolsey creaked back in her chair, folded arms across her chest. "Oh trust me, this wasn't my baby. You can blame that on Behr, whom you so graciously saddled me with."

Bergman chuckled. "C'mon, Kate. You know he's the best and you know you like flying with him. Whether you admit it or not."

"I'm going to go with 'not.'"

"Fine," Bergman waved off her surliness. It was part of a charm that somehow just *worked* for her. "But the fact remains that you're bringing one hundred of a new species here to Earth, and within the month, I have to prepare to receive them. Lodging, transition training, figuring out how to incorporate them into our society so they don't end up ogled like zoo animals."

"That would be ideal. The integration, not the ogling."

Bergman's brain stalled and stopped. Whether it was the lateness (earliness?) of the hour, or the overwhelming monstrosity this project had become ever since tiny Winnie Abrams bounded into his office and dragged him to see the *Genesis* distress signal, Bergman couldn't say. It had been months since he'd had a night of uninterrupted sleep. Even the fact that he was home in his own bed to be interrupted and not slumped comatose over his desk at work was a shocking exception to the rule of late.

"Director? I think they charge these by the minute."

"Sorry, sorry," Bergman muttered, shoving his glasses up his nose, fingers through sleep- and stress-mussed hair. "Okay, I'll . . . I'll start working on it first thing in the morning." On the screen, Woolsey's mouth opened to form a smart retort. "First thing in the *normal people business hours* morning," Bergman crabbed.

"Touchy," Woolsey teased. "I'll be waiting for your plan. You know how to reach me."

Bergman grunted.

"Oh, and Jim? Love the pj's. I never would have pegged you as a Mickey Mouse kind of guy."

"Shut up, my four-year-old daughter picked them out for me."

"Cute."

"Bite me."

"Good night, Director."

"Good riddance, Woolsey."

The Weight of Stars and Suns
Dawn Christine Jonckowski

✧ ✧ ✧ ✧ ✧

Matime stared at the list in his hand, the case on the bed, the wardrobe brimming with ceremonial clothing. Forth and back again.

He had three days to assemble everything necessary for relocation to Earth. Three days to put a lifetime into a curious metal box with a handle. Not that he necessarily had much. As a historian, he lived simply; as his debt-ridden father's son, he lived frugally.

He simply had no desire to leave Tav.

Sure, he could be roasted to a crisp by exploding suns within the week.

But all things considered, that didn't seem too bad.

He'd lived enough already. It was time to be done.

For so long, Matime had danced as a puppet on his uncle's purse strings. Before that, the failure of all his father had hoped to accomplish in the military lived out through his son. And after, the one who nearly toppled an empire. All but killed a man with his witness.

Matime reckoned that the world around him had had enough of his shenanigans.

Besides. Without the constant haranguing of his father, of his uncle, Matime found himself rather directionless. He'd achieved what he always thought he wanted—a seat on the Council—only to discover that it really wasn't what he wanted. Perhaps that dream had never even been his to begin with. Another seed planted by his uncle to direct his future?

The Weight of Stars and Suns
Dawn Christine Jonckowski

Possibly.

Matime longed for his dusty tomes and stacks of brittle paper. Long stretches with his neck cricked over a particularly troublesome passage, studying, interpreting, learning, knowing.

He'd actually hoped to one day simply fall asleep atop a book and never awaken. To die peacefully in the Archives, surrounded by his beloved histories and words.

Not bored to death in a Council meeting.

And certainly not as an oddity on display in the humans' world.

They could say what they liked about integration and how progressively accepting their kind was. But Matime knew the histories. The *real* histories. Read the records of many of the original conversations the first humans had uttered of the strange purple beings who inhabited the planet. How they universally believed that the Tavarians were savages. How after they were rescued, they hoped to return and civilize the natives.

Maybe a hundred-odd years had changed some of that.

But even so.

Even if he was welcomed as a prince from a far-off world, treated to the best Earth had to offer, even (here he shuddered) offered the best of their human maidens as a betrothed mate.

Even so.

His sins demanded atonement.

Glancing once more at the list, Matime reached into the wardrobe.

Placed the first item in the case.

The Weight of Stars and Suns
Dawn Christine Jonckowski

✧ ✧ ✧ ✧ ✧

Not for the first time in the past two days, Hyam marveled at how easily Dameia moved among the humans in the colony.

It helped, certainly, that they revered her as practical deity for the role she had played in securing their freedom. Wherever she went, she trailed a swarm of children. Boys wanted her, girls wanted to *be* her. One particularly tiny daughter had streaked her face with the juice of fresh blackflower berries, proudly proclaiming herself to be just like Dameia, much to the delight of the princess, and the slight horror of the girl's mother who spent great effort to scrub the deep purple stains off her daughter's cheeks.

Hyam had hoped for quiet acceptance, was prepared for mild apprehension. After the uncomfortable scene in the palace, the wary ways every Tavarian guard eyed him as he walked out hand in hand with the princess the next morning, Hyam had suggested they try spending the next cycle in the human colony. Maybe it wouldn't be exceedingly better, but at least the vast majority of humans hadn't wanted to be party to Dameia's death the way the Tavarian guards had Hyam's.

Reluctantly, Dameia had agreed.

Word of her had arrived before she did, and the freed slaves lined the main throughway, cheering her courage and sacrifice.

The days were winding slowly toward their departure for Earth. It seemed that as each moment ticked closer, the pair moved

The Weight of Stars and Suns
Dawn Christine Jonckowski

closer to each other. They seemed to always be touching: a hand on a back, hips and thighs pressed close when seated. Late in the evening around a fire, a head on a shoulder, torsos curved together. Secret, sacred smiles as they meandered fingers twining back to Hyam's simple hut to pass the cycles together.

If he could manage to push the journey to Earth from his mind, Hyam could almost imagine that this would be what it could be like to live out his days with her. A proper home, small lavender-tinged children gallivanting around their legs.

They could be the start of something new.

Could be.

Wouldn't be.

He tried not to dwell. But the darkness crept in behind every smile, every laugh, every moment that he knew would be the last of its kind.

It was Ithai's final cycle in the colony, as the *Genesis II* crew would arrive the next to load him specially onto the ship and get him situated with minimal stress before the mayhem of actual departure. Hyam and Dameia sat at his bedside, wrapped as much into each other as was polite in decent company. Ithai's fever bright eyes glimpsed their connection. His cracked lips formed a smile, not without effort.

"I am grateful for you, Princess Dameia," he rasped.

She reached out a hand, rested it gently on his bony shoulder. "Just Dameia, Ithai. You can just call me Dameia."

His grin stretched again. "Dameia," he repeated. "Thank you for rescuing my brother Hyam. For rescuing his heart, even more than his body. It gives me hope that he has had you beside him, no matter how long the season. I wish . . . you were coming with us."

Hyam glimpsed the Tavarian beauty beside him. Her face radiated, celestial, saintly. Sad.

"Me too, Ithai. Me too."

Next, Ithai turned his gaze to Hyam. "Brother," he intoned, one shrunken hand reaching, light and curled as a bird's. Hyam's hand swallowed it up.

"Save your strength, Ithai. Just a little longer and you will be well with us on Earth. Imagine the sky, the rain, the feeling of the sea around your toes."

Ithai smiled blissfully, his eyes unfocused, words slurred and slowing. "I should have always . . . liked to visit the sea. They tell me . . . there is nothing like the . . . scent of its salts, the roll of its . . . waves. I should like . . . to have known what . . . a fish . . . looked like. To . . . dive below as a whale. To wrestle . . . a shark."

Hyam chuckled. "I'm not sure wrestling a shark is really something you want to do. He's far likelier to win than you are. I've never met one, but I do hear they have a fair amount more teeth than we do."

Ithai hummed a wordless response, his chest rattling ominously on the inhale.

"I do not think I shall live to see Earth, Hyam."

His words, suddenly clear as a bell, struck Hyam to the core. Hyam's hand tightened reflexively against the fragile bones of Ithai's fingers.

"Ithai—"

The Weight of Stars and Suns
Dawn Christine Jonckowski

"Promise me," his voice, his gaze both penetrating. "Promise me that I will have a proper burial. Grant me that singular, final honor on Tav. Carry my ashes home to Earth. That I shall leave a freed man." Ithai's eyes sought and found Hyam's. Bored straight into his soul.

"Scatter me on the sea, Hyam. That I might finally know the waves. That I might finally know peace."

Hyam's tongue worked to shape a reply. When it couldn't—*he* couldn't—he simply nodded. Ithai's eyes slid shut, satisfied.

One rattled breath.

Two.

Inhale, exhale.

Bit by bit, his face lost its pain, spread with peace. His mouth curved ever so slightly into a contented smile.

Inhale, exhale.

Pause.

Inhale.

Exhale.

Silence.

Silence.

Silence.

And he was gone.

✧ ✧ ✧ ✧ ✧

The Weight of Stars and Suns
Dawn Christine Jonckowski

Even the Tavarians attended the first human funeral on Tav. For some, it was the grave curiosity. For others, merely a social event. A place to see and be seen.

For the humans, it was a beginning and an end. The first time they had been allowed a traditional Tavarian custom. Marking the absolute end of their slavery to the natives. Auspicious in that it fell on their final cycle on Tav.

At the request of the Tavarian princess, the temple priestesses had accepted Ithai's broken and wasted shell and prepared it for the funeral ceremony.

His heart—found a little higher and slightly less left than they expected, due to a general lack of knowledge of human anatomy—was removed. Washed. Placed in a clay vessel and buried beneath a sacred tree in the temple garden, that his life force might feed into the planet itself and bring life again in new and different ways.

Once they stitched his chest, his body was cleansed with salt and water, then rubbed with vital oils. Anointed across the brow with five drops of blood from a living relative (Hannah only flinched a little when they punctured a vein and guided her arm across Ithai's face) so that he may carry life with him into the afterworld. They dressed his body in a fine white tunic belted with new cord. In his right hand, a key said to open the gate to the afterworld; in his left, a small scroll of paper bearing a traditional prayer for safe passage (modified slightly to account for his humanity).

His body was placed on a bier and carried from the temple to the pyre by four of his closest friends. Oren stood by his left foot,

The Weight of Stars and Suns
Dawn Christine Jonckowski

Hyam by his right shoulder. Two distant cousins balanced the opposite corners.

Traditionally placed in the center of the Capitol Plex, the humans had received permission to build Ithai's pyre in the center of the human colony. Dameia had only blanched at the idea for fear that it would become a social curiosity for Tavarians to attend instead of the solemn ceremony the humans hoped and Ithai deserved.

The procession made its way slowly from the temple to the colony gates. Silent mourners lined the way, falling into step behind the bier only as it passed them. There was hardly room for everyone within the colony. Some humans climbed to their rooftops, both for a better view and for solace in their grief. The better Tavarians stepped to the back, graciously ushering their former slaves to the fore, sometimes exiting the colony altogether, somehow understanding that certain griefs needed to remain protected.

Gently, the four bearers slid Ithai's body from the bier to the pyre. Each paused to whisper a farewell. Slip a memento—however small—onto the pyre with their friend. One by one, others who knew him lined up to do the same. As he stepped down from the pyre, Hyam saw the line snaking between the dwellings, winding and curling to accommodate. So many lives touched by his sweet-souled friend. Dameia joined the queue. In her hand, he knew, a ceremonial arm band she had smithed specially for Ithai. The design, she had explained earlier, denoted him a hero and a prince among his people. Her face was the only purple one in the line.

But in the back, far back and pressed against the wall surrounded by guards attempting to appear unobtrusive, another familiar and distinctly Tavarian face.

The Chieftain.

Their eyes locked.

Slowly, silently, the Chieftain dipped his head to Hyam. Acknowledging grief. Loss. Sorrow.

Apology.

It was more than Hyam could have ever hoped. He nodded in return. It was done.

The Chieftain melted away in the crowd.

The procession continued until the pyre was heavy laden with whatever small piece of nothing the former slaves had to sacrifice for their friend. Some tied colorful strips of fabric around the pieces of wood. (Blue had always been Ithai's favorite color.) Others left tiny loaves of bread. A small wing of sand hen. A carved button. A poem painstakingly copied year upon year from generation to generation. In an ancient tradition of human mourning—or so they'd been told over the years—Hannah wrapped a braid of her hair around his wrist, her freshly chopped locks swinging freely along her jawline.

At long last, the final mourner stepped away from the pyre, and with great and silent flourish, the temple priestesses surrounded the pyre with flaming torches and as one, plunged them into the base. The pyre roared on a shower of sparks and began to burn.

As the second cycle wore on, the Tavarians were the first to retire to their homes. After all, they had things to do and no humans left to do them. Many of the humans too melted away into shadows caused by dancing flames. Tomorrow they would truly be free; not all wanted to spend their final cycle dwelling on sadness.

The Weight of Stars and Suns
Dawn Christine Jonckowski

Even Hannah, overcome by her grief, was eventually escorted home, Oren's arm the only thing keeping her from sliding directly to the ground.

But Hyam remained, eyes fixed to the flames. At some point, Dameia's hand slid into his, and he clung tightly.

The suns set and the suns rose and the fire burned until only ash remained.

In the early morning, the priestesses swept Ithai's ashes into a clay jar, sealed it with a hard wax embedded with the weed flowers cultivated within the colony. The head priestess pressed the jar into Hyam's empty hands, retreated on a bow.

And then it was just him. Just Hyam, his beloved, and his best friend in a jar.

Still, he remained, and Dameia beside him.

Slowly, the others emerged from their dwellings, carrying the strange metal belonging cases provided by the *Genesis II* crew. Most had little to begin with, and so empty spaces were filled with odd souvenirs of the only home they'd ever known: spoons and kettles from their family cook fires, disintegrating books that had somehow been saved by the original *Genesis* crew and passed down the generations, small bricks they'd scavenged away from work sites and carved later with intricate whorls and mazes.

Silently, they filed past Hyam and Dameia, somehow knowing that despite the joy of their exodus, it would be cruel to rejoice in that morning.

Nearly all the inhabitants of the colony were gone to the ship, even Hannah, when Oren finally stopped in front of the pair, a case in each hand.

| | The Weight of Stars and Suns | |
Dawn Christine Jonckowski

One he set at Hyam's feet.

Hyam glanced down on a gritty blink.

His heart nearly stopped, his stomach an empty storm.

Dameia's grip vised on his hand. He knew she was crying only when two fat drops and then more watered the dust at her feet.

"It is time."

FINALE LIGHT

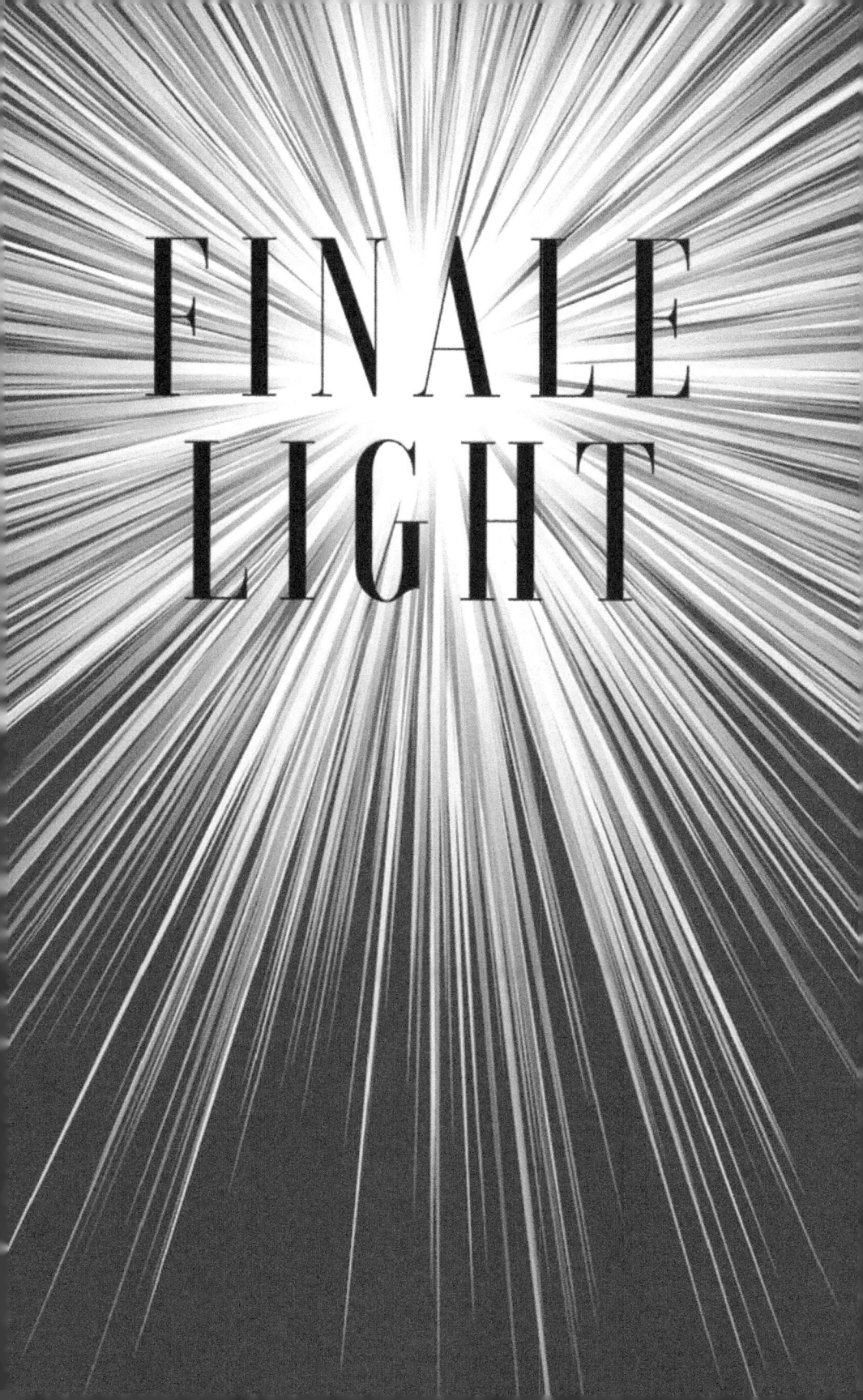

20

If Woolsey could have picked a description for the process of boarding humans and Tavarians and all their assorted belongings onto *Genesis II*, she probably would have called it "organized chaos." In fact, had quoted that very term to Behr as the new occupants acclimated to the berths they would call home for the next six weeks of space travel. She hoped they could all keep the peace for the tight quarters of the journey. Was certain to inform them that the ship had a brig, and—after explaining what a "brig" was—that she was not afraid to toss any number of them, Tavarian *or* human, into it if need be.

"We have nearly everyone," Behr said, filtering the list on his tablet to show those still missing. Woolsey peered at the roster.

"You can mark that one off," she said, poking a finger at a name in the middle of the list. "He died a few days ago, so he's not coming. Well, he *is* . . . kind of. Just in a jar in someone's case."

Behr winged an eyebrow upward, but didn't comment.

"What about these two?" His finger hovered over two other names.

"That one is one of the Tavarian leaders. He'll likely be last to board after the grand farewell from the Chieftain. You're set to film and broadcast throughout the ship so we don't have to unload everyone so they can hear him, right?" She shook her head. Royals and their formalities. "Because that gives me a migraine just thinking about it."

"All set," Behr confirmed. "And there's always painkillers in the medic's bag."

The Captain fixed him with a stare. He let it roll over him, used to her derision. He even kind of liked it. He should probably see a therapist about that once they got home.

"And this one?"

The screen flickered over the letters: *Hyam Ben-Noadiah*.

"That's the one we rescued with our arrival. The princess' inamorato." Woolsey jerked her head over to the pair, olive and purple, still and staring. Unwilling to leave, unable to stay.

"Why's her father not sending her, again?" Behr asked, his own gaze fixated on the couple, their grief so strong it was practically tangible.

"Because he's a tyrant with a stick up his rear?"

Behr grinned. "I love it when you talk dirty to me."

Woolsey swatted him with her tablet, barely suppressing the grin tugging at the corners of her own mouth. "Go do something useful," she ordered. Behr jogged away on a laugh.

To be honest, she didn't understand it either. The planet was going to burn. They knew it. The Chieftain knew it. And yet he would effectively sentence his daughter to death for the sake of his pride. For the petty need to "win" against a former rebel slave by

The Weight of Stars and Suns
Dawn Christine Jonckowski

denying the man the prize of his daughter, sole heir to a doomed rock.

Never had she been so glad to have flunked poli-sci in college and end up a pilot instead.

Pulling in a deep breath of Tavarian air, she resumed her tasks.

Politics or no, she had a ship to fly and humans to get home.

☼ ☼ ☼ ☼ ☼

In the gap of the suns, Hyam's shadow fell across Dameia's face.

On a shadow, it had all begun, and on a shadow, it would end. Her world of thirty-six suns (well, thirty now) was going to be less one star the moment that ship pulled out of Tav's gravity.

They stood, entwined, clinging. Solid as stone, unmoving and barely breathing, as if even that small act would shatter them both.

The waving, chattering crowds silenced at the sound of a horn fanfare. Her father, enthroned on a dais specially constructed for the day, glittering in his best ceremonial robes (as if he cared about the humans, as if this were some benevolent move of his to save them), rose to his feet. Began to speak, a silky spun tale of his joy at their new adventure, complete with a charge to all of bravery and steadfastness, and a written-in chuckle that the humans look after the Tavarians in the new world.

He acted as if they were friends, as if they were simply one very big, very colorful family.

As suddenly as his speech had begun, it was over.

Too soon.

It was all too soon.

She could not let go.

Would not.

"As long as I live, Dameia of Tav, I will love you," Hyam's voice breathed in her ear, deep and full of promise and pain and heart.

"And I you, though my life will be considerably shorter than yours." Dameia's rueful laugh broke on a sob. Hyam pulled back just far enough to look her full in the face.

"Don't say that. Don't even think that," he ordered. "Go to the underground dwellings. Survive. Live for me, Dameia. And as soon as they let me, I swear I will return for you."

She shook her head, tears flowing, her hand reaching to caress his face. "My sweet, fierce rebel. We both know you would only return to char and ash."

His eyes deepened, anguish and regret and rage.

"Don't," she warned, closing her own, bracing her forehead on his, exchanging breath and heartbeats. "Don't part on anger. Don't leave me with that as my final memory of you." She felt Hyam's ribs expand and contract, slow and measured beneath her arms.

"Hyam."

Not Dameia's voice, but Matime's.

The historian stood there, case in hand.

He said simply, "It is time."

The Weight of Stars and Suns
Dawn Christine Jonckowski

Dameia's heart contracted, her chest tight with the impossibility of breathing. "Let me walk with you," she pleaded, to Hyam or to Matime, she wasn't certain.

Both nodded. Hyam picked up his case with one hand, left the other tightly merged with hers.

The trio made their way slowly along the sandy desert floor to the ship's portal. Took three steps onto the metal plank that led within. A crewmember reached for Hyam's case. Began to reach for Matime's, but was sent away on a curt nod.

With both hands now unencumbered, Hyam framed Dameia's face. Brushed her hair back with nimble hands, fingers that had danced along her spine and cupped her very soul.

"Be brave," he whispered.

"You asked me once if I dreamed of more," she replied. He nodded, the memory strong across his features.

"Well, I didn't," she admitted on a watery smile. "Until I did."

"You, Hyam, were my 'more.'"

As she leaned in to taste his lips, his dreams, his hope, his love, one last time, she felt Matime's hand close over her shoulder. Pull her back. Rage burned hot and fast in her throat.

"Go," he said, thrusting his case at her. Instinctively, she yanked her hand back as if burned.

"What?"

"Go," he repeated. "Of all Tav's citizens, you most deserve the chance to live. You have a life worth saving, a hope worth perpetuating." He dipped a full formal nod toward Hyam. "A love worth protecting."

She worked to form a reply, found none, her mind blank with the sudden possibilities of his words.

"I apologize for my forwardness, but while you stayed in the colony, I took the liberty of packing many of your things for you," Matime inclined his head toward the proffered case clutched in his fist. His haunted eyes met hers. "I just couldn't stand the thought that I, who have served my purpose, should live. So, go. I beg you, Princess. Go. And *live*."

He nodded once again at the metal box in his hand. Slowly, incredulous, Dameia reached out and took hold. Their hands brushed for a moment, and she knew his bravery and sacrifice, his longing to be freed of the burdens he had carried for a lifetime.

"Thank you," she whispered, all broken hope and wonder.

Matime bowed low. Rose again and grasped Hyam's right arm in the traditional warrior's hold of respect. And with a final nod, he walked back across the sand toward the dais, where the Chieftain poised half-lifted from his chair, fingers gripping the armrests in shock.

And then his gaze locked on his daughter's.

Slowly, slowly, he sat.

Slowly, slowly, his shoulders lifted in a resigned sigh.

And slowly, slowly, he nodded.

It was enough. Her tether to Tav released.

Light with new freedom, Dameia turned to Hyam. In perfect step, they proceeded the rest of the way up the metal walk and into the belly of *Genesis II* to be reborn on Earth.

The Weight of Stars and Suns
Dawn Christine Jonckowski

"Princess," the sharp-tongued woman Dameia knew to be their captain greeted with a nod of respect as she passed. "Welcome to *Genesis II*. We are pleased to have you aboard."

"Please," Dameia replied, nodding her respect in return. "From now on, it is only 'Dameia.'"

The captain smiled, slow and genuine, a rare treat. "I'm going to like you. Now if you'll excuse me, I have a ship to fly." She walked away from the pair, barely hiding the smile that still threatened her face with each step.

Maybe true love conquered after all.

The ship gave a small shiver as the outer door banged shut, the airlock hissing tight. Together, the lovers crowded at a viewing portal, looking out onto the small sea of Tavarian faces tipped up toward the great beast of a ship. Her heart both overflowing and empty, Dameia lifted a hand. Placed it on the clear surface of the portal, her fingers—from her sight—resting just on her father's own heart. Though he loomed large in life, he seemed now shrunken under the weight of his planet's suns, head bowed over the sacrifice of his daughter. Yet he stood and offered salute to the departing ship, stood as if from so far away he could telegraph a lifetime of regrets and fierce adoration across a direct line to Dameia's soul. Telegraph his hope that she live.

She would carry pieces of him within her to Earth, and beyond, if life demanded.

"He does love you," Hyam offered softly.

Her lips curved upward, sad and sweet. "I know."

The ship roared to life, sand swirling outside her, obscuring the faces below. Still, Dameia stood, one hand in Hyam's, one on the portal, a final connection to her family, her home, her life. With the barest tremble, *Genesis II* heaved herself from the sand and ascended through the skies.

    Up far over the trees and mountains.

    Out of the white-blue of the Tavarian sky.

    Past the necklace of suns that circled the planet.

    Into the dark of the universe.

    And toward home.

Acknowledgements

This story began as a one of those strange half-dreams between waking and sleep. Getting it to the point where you could hold it in your hands took no less than a full army.

To the real life Katie Woolsey, my writing accountability partner and alpha reader who gleefully agreed to be immortalized in character (which she might regret by book two). This story exists because you guided me and encouraged me. Thanks for helping me write my way out.

To the also real life Brandon Behr, who answered a truly endless volley of texts that started with, "Hey, potentially stupid science question." Thanks for always being willing to help me figure out what Google couldn't (and even what it could, but you were more fun to talk to).

My awesome team of beta readers: Katie, Brandon, Ann Boaden, and Brandi Rennemeyer. You each graciously spent hours paging through early drafts with red pen and Post-it flags in hand. It's because of you that Tav came fully to life and I stopped using the word "night" on a planet ringed with thirty-six suns.

The #WriterBaeTribe: Mel "Grem" Carter, Haley "DB" Waring Lausier, and the Immortal Shannon Hiner. You girls kept me laughing when I wanted to cry (or when I was already crying) and managed to fall in love with a world and characters created by someone you'd had yet to meet in person. Thanks for being my writer group, my Tribe, but most importantly, my friends.

My awesome parents, who in the earliest days supplied me with endless notebooks to doodle in and blank tapes to record my stories, and in the later years tolerated me reading when I was supposed to be doing basically anything else. Thank you for supporting my dreams, even when you were fairly certain that declaring as an English major meant I was never, ever going to move out of your house. Heart, Mom and Dad.

To my own rebel leader, Nick, who told me that if anyone could write this story, it was me. You're my rock and my heart. In the vastness of space, it is my immense joy and honor to be on this planet right next to you. I love you. Always and forever.

Finally, to The One who gave me life and words with just one breath. May both reflect Your light back to the world.

TURN THE PAGE FOR

Bonus Material

A companion story to
The Weight of Stars and Suns

THE Damage OF Love AND Living

Dawn Christine Jonckowski

"I loved a human, once. I loved her... and then I killed her."

On the eve of Hyam's execution, the Chieftain makes a surprising admission to his daughter Dameia about his choices to love after his queen dies. The princess has only brief memories of the human slave the Chieftain admits to loving, and with her own human lover slated for death, even less sympathy for her father's painful recollections.

Now the Chieftain's love lives only in memory, in the haunting of his desires, and in the collateral damage of their choices . . .

. . . but for how much longer?

She'd never really seen the suns.

Not really.

Which was a pretty spectacular feat, considering she lived on a planet ringed with thirty-six of them.

It was spiced tea hour. She'd not tasted the beverage (yet?) in her short life. But she knew. From the absence of sound outside her cell, the slower quiet that blanketed whatever world existed outside her four tall walls.

She wondered if her mother had enjoyed spiced tea or merely endured it.

There was so much—so much—that she didn't know.

Too much.

And yet she still managed to know more than she should.

☼ ☼ ☼ ☼ ☼

"Your favor is showing, Abigail."

They poked at her midsection any time she visited. She turned away, feigning embarrassment at her growing girth. None of them knew. None of them had any idea what it was like to be something other than a starved skeleton caging a restless spirit.

She was perhaps the only one among them who did not yearn for a home she'd never known, did not plot to overthrow a government that saw her as refuse.

She was seen. She was known.

More than they knew.

Family that had been assigned and relations that had been chosen to very open and yet very blind eyes bustled around the scrapped-together table in the center of the dwelling. Her gift of roasted sand hen from the kitchens stuck out like a too-new patch on old rags. Shiny and rich, overshadowing the meager fare the rest had saved and scrounged to share for this feast. Not for the first time did she wish she'd simply appeared empty-handed.

Or not at all.

A few more eyes glanced off the rolls of her belly. (He told her she was beautiful, buried his face in the softness of her ample curves. Delighted in feeding her rich foods and richer drink, in watching her expand to a more pleasant roundness.) Heads shook in minute side to side patterns, expressions saying far more than voices would.

She sat at the meal, silenced not by reverence but by their displeasure. Their fear.

"It will not end well for you, Abigail."

"He is incapable of feeling. They all are."

"Come home."

But she was home. With him, she was home.

Their words gurgled a small flutter deep in her center.

☼ ☼ ☼ ☼ ☼

Every day, she paced around her room. Her cell. They called it a room so it seemed less barbaric, so they could feel better about themselves. But she'd seen the wet sneer, cataloged the vile things said about her when they thought she couldn't hear. Or couldn't understand. She knew they didn't think she was smart. Didn't think she was viable.

Twelve paces took her corner to corner across the middle, eight took her edge to edge. Fifteen to skirt around the bed, and another few to bobble over the wardrobe. When she completed her counts, she sat in the middle of the room, the heat of the suns through the grated ceiling pooling on the hard dirt floor. In her hands danced a tatty doll. Though stitched with great love of the finest material, circumstances had worn the doll down, her face dulled to reflect the exhaustion of constant containment, of living out stories that had no context for real life. Of standing in the stead of the one figure who should have been there to love through it all.

She could make the doll do many things: perform a cold tea service, kowtow through the length of morning prayer, step through the intricate High Temple Holiday dance patterns, stand tall for a betrothal ceremony.

All things she should not know.

They liked to think she knew little, felt less.

They were wrong.

☼ ☼ ☼ ☼ ☼

He blew into her chambers like a seasoned sand storm, his smile a blinding crescent across the rich pattern of his face. Heavy inked arms draped around her shoulders from behind, a weighted necklace of sinew and strength, squeezing, loving, protecting.

"My love and my light," he whispered, his words a resonant rumble that snaked gooseflesh neck to ankle. She turned expectant eyes to him and was not disappointed. His full mouth closed over hers, taking, taking, taking, and her giving willingly. His fingers danced around her sides and closed over her full belly.

"And how is our son?"

She answered with a bright laugh. "Our child," her address intentional, "grows stronger—and hungrier—every day." She reached over to pop a rare and luscious ahnav fruit between her lips. It was then that he noticed the bundle of bright cloth in her ever-shrinking lap. Curious, he rounded her body to sit beside her on the tiny veranda. A desert wasp droned aimlessly between the platter of fruit and the mismatched heads hovering near it. She swatted half-

heartedly in the bug's direction, giving him room to reach and snatch. He rolled the silken colors over in his grasp.

"A doll?" One eyebrow arched dangerously near his hairline. She treated him to an adoring and long-suffering look.

"It may yet be a daughter, you know." She plucked the half-finished toy from his palm. He gave a light harrumph in return. But he noticed her fingers twine a little tighter around the doll's skirt, worrying the fabric pattern between thumb and forefinger. He reached his own fingers over to tuck a stray piece of hair back into one of her intricate Tavarian braids. She glanced up at him, reached up to close her warm, pale hand over his, fingertips brushing the plaits she legally had no right to wear.

"What if . . . what if we're . . ." she cracked off the word, hardly able to get it out, "incompatible?" Her fear hung in the air between them, dripped slowly down. "What will this child be?"

Instantly, he slid to his knees before her, hands meeting to cup her face. Startlingly violet touch against cheeks both pinked and pale.

"It doesn't matter. This child," he intoned, eyes locking her in tight with unfettered confidence and wild adoration, "this child will be loved."

☼ ☼ ☼ ☼ ☼

Dropping the doll into her lap, she stretched her hand out before her in the shaft of sunlight. Dappled purple mixed in muddy patches along her hands. Her palms were a curious white pale. Like his, she imagined. (Not that she'd seen him in recent memory. But she knew.) Dusky lilac tinged her arms and legs. A reddish-brown birthmark stained her left thigh; she liked to imagine that to be a piece of her mother left behind, some comment on the heterogeneous mix of human and Tavarian.

She'd never seen herself in a mirror, but reflections off washing water and the face of the Warden informed her that she was not altogether tragic looking, if unconventional. The face in the water gave her some modicum of courage. She wasn't sure how the Warden's face made her feel. (Actually, she was sure. But remained curious of how she could be dampened and dirty simply from the rake of his eyes.)

They had been compatible. Anatomically, anyway.

And she was a lot of things. (Intelligent. Curious. Silent. Sad.)

But she was not loved.

☼ ☼ ☼ ☼ ☼

They'd begun to suspect. He knew it. And his not-entirely-subtle backing of interspecies breeding wasn't helping his case. Sure, what they didn't suspect was that the bill was his doing entirely, and that it had only taken weighing Saronis' purse by a good number of scores for him to be the one to introduce it. It should have bothered him how easy it was to sway the Councilman, should have given him pause how much politicking balanced on the edge of a shiny bar of coin and greed.

But his greed for her outshone it all, and so he found himself unbothered by any details aside from getting what he wanted.

Her.

Not as a slave. And while wife might not happen in this particular lifetime—much as he might wish—he could at least push for concubine. Even if the bill only provided for offspring so far as they would also be considered slaves. He would find a way to protect his coming son if he had to select the child as his own page. He could still give him a good life.

Even now, Abigail would be huffing and straining to bring him into the world. Michal had passed the news to him in a frightened whisper.

He knew the women's fears. He knew them because they were his as well. It was an entirely unprecedented event. Oh, not the act that led to this particular result. That had been going on in secret for longer than anyone would admit. Though great pains were typically taken to ensure it started and ended at that: an act, a release, a stolen advantage with no repercussions. Rumors were whispered of the monstrosity that could be born of such an unholy union, a muddy-skinned freak with three of these and two of that or none of those. A face not even a mother could love.

Yet for a child created out of such love, how could he be a monster? How could he be anything other than perfection? A lavender-tinged swirl of all their best parts.

The Head Councilman called for a vote. Voices raised. Silence answered. A gavel dropped.

He had lost.

They had lost.

Michal's face peeked around the curtain that separated the Council Room from the slave passageways and allowed the rulers to pretend for the slaves' invisibility. He was the only one who saw her; he was the only one who chose to.

She lifted her hand in a quick sign.

The child had arrived.

A girl.

✧ ✧ ✧ ✧ ✧

She didn't remember her mother outside of a few memories that were perhaps less remembrance and more dream.

They had had only the briefest of seasons together, she and her beautiful, round, laughing, human mother. It was that bright, easy laugh that stuck deepest in her subconscious, that woke her in echoes, a shadow just past the fingertips of memory.

Something deep within told her that at some point he had loved her mother. Even if he didn't love her. She could live with that. (Knew in her strange way of knowing things that she wouldn't have to live with it much longer.)

But he had loved her mother.

He had loved her.

And then he had killed her.

They all said *she* was a monster, as if it were her fault she had been born. As if she had chosen to be the mismatched offspring of two very different and yet very similar beings.

But she wasn't the monster.

He was.

✧ ✧ ✧ ✧ ✧

He wanted to ignore the small pale purple face that peered out at him from around the corner. He wanted to forget she existed, forget everything that had led to her, led to this moment.

He shouldn't have allowed it. Should have stopped it before another life was entwined. Too many were already. Even if it was just his and hers, it would have been too many.

The Council was sending a collectively very hot breath down the back of his neck. She had been his rescue after his wife's death. With a smile, she had pulled him from the sandy bottom of his hell-hole, had brought life back into his veins, and yes, love too.

Love, and now a child.

They hadn't even given her a name. Sometimes his ears pricked on Abigail calling her Ketzile. She said it meant "kitten." He didn't know what that meant, either.

Threats had begun to arrive, both veiled and unveiled. At government dinners, he would hear a Councilman recount the grisly torture inflicted upon a slave woman found compromised in a son's chambers with the same toneless bore that they would discuss crop cycles. Meanwhile, he had begun requesting his meat more well-done, the sight of even slightly red juices choking out his air as his vivid imagination placed Abigail in the Councilman's courtyard, her blood seeping between the bricks as features, limbs, assets were all carved away by a blade labeled mercy.

Mercy for whom?

And so he knew: They were coming for her. She would not be absolved of the atonement others had been forced to give for their perceived sins. For daring above their stations. For the audacity of choosing to love other.

(Had he given her a choice? Or had his pursuit and his station relegated her to an acceptance she did not altogether feel?)

Two more nubs of ango root rolled between his fingers. He dropped them into the hot mug of spiced tea. A fizz and a release, and no more evidence they'd ever been there.

Hearing his footfalls, she turned to him, all wide smile and heart in her eyes.

"I've brought your spiced tea," he managed.

"I see that," she inclined her head at the mug, patted the plush cushion next to her. He lowered slowly. "What have you done with Michal that you must bring my tea?"

She teased, he tensed.

"I have already brought her tea," he said quietly, gaze stirring deep into the cup in his hands.

The light fell behind her eyes.

"I see."

"Please," he begged, his own eyes lifting, wounded, empty. "It is the only way."

Her smile sagged. Cool fingers rested on his face, light and unworn by sand, scrubbing, or suns. She tipped his face up to level with hers. "What a world that you of all must save me by sending me to my death." Her forehead dipped against his.

"Make a better one for her," she wagered. "Promise me that you will make a better world for her, and I will go without complaint."

He couldn't say a word. She took the single tear track down his face as covenant, took the steam-curled mug, and after a brief press of her lips to his, drained it to the dregs.

The guards never heard the crash of pottery as the mug dropped out of a lifeless grasp, never heard the dull roar of anguish that was muffled by a pale and still-rounded belly. All they knew was that the Chieftain was suddenly storming out of the doors where they stood sentry, his face a mask of disgust.

"There is a dead slave in that chamber. See to it that the mess is cleaned up," he barked. They snapped salutes.

"And the child," he growled. "Take her to the Warden. He will know what to do with her."

✧ ✧ ✧ ✧ ✧

And she'd lived in this soulless cell ever since. Meals burst through a slot in the thick wooden door thrice daily.

She was required to send bowl and spoon back through each time she finished eating. One ferocious beating taught her that.

The Warden seemed to take extra delight in lashing her ash-lavender shoulders. She developed a vocabulary of silence so as not to provoke him. But sometimes the silence provoked him even more.

Season built on season. The suns rose and the suns set. (Although recently, the light in her cell shone off-kilter. Curious.) Prisoners came and prisoners went, and they never came back a second time. She knew a dozen more languished even now in lesser prisons than hers, with more bars and fewer creature comforts that assuaged guilt.

The princess, it seemed, had taken special liking to one. She heard, she knew. It would not end well for her half-sister (she almost choked to simply think the word); it would end worse for the man the fully-purpled princess had begun to favor.

But they would come for her first.

☼ ☼ ☼ ☼ ☼

He didn't hate the child. Not exactly.

It simply wrenched his heart to see Abigail's eyes in that small purple-tinged face. To know that he loved her perhaps a little too much and had doomed them all. He wished it had never happened. Surely never having was better than loving and losing.

So he tried to forget.

He locked the nameless, breedless child away and tried to forget.

Some days, he even succeeded.

But blood would out. As his own transgressor blood was outing in Dameia. Her passions threatened to run too close to the rebel slave. He could not risk her following the same path. Could not risk anyone guessing the truth about Abigail, about the child's true parentage.

And so he would do more than forget.

He would expunge.

They would all be better off that way.

Wouldn't they?

☼ ☼ ☼ ☼ ☼

It was a great and hideous irony that her first day out in the suns was also her last.

She stood, roped and alone in the center of the prison's inner courtyard. Insulated. Here, no one could hear her scream.

She lifted her face to the light. Breathed. In, out.

Feet patterned behind her. The Warden, by his gait. A temple priestess, by her swiffing glide and the light slosh of holy water in a bowl.

The Chieftain, by the ripple of his heavy cape, the clink of chain that ran shoulder to shoulder across his powerful chest. She repressed the urge to giggle that he had dressed up for the occasion, dressed up for her.

The three filled her vision.

Another set of feet, heavier. Regret and resignation. She knew she would not see this one's face.

The temple priestess approached first, dipping a finger in the holy water and drawing a straight line down her face from forehead to nose. Murmured incantations buzzed in her ears. Her face a mask, inside she marveled that the Chieftain would grant her last rites.

Would the gods accept one such as she?

Could they?

She didn't even know which god her mother had served, if he (or she?) would have welcomed the traitorous human into eternal rest or damnation.

As the Warden cinched the rope at her wrists once more (wholly unnecessary; she wasn't going to go anywhere, not physically, anyway), the temple priestess asked gently if she had any final words.

Her chin notched up, eyes seeking and latching firmly onto the Chieftain's. She held him captive there in her gaze until he began to sway awkwardly from foot to foot, and then, feeling the solid presence of the executioner at her back, she finally spoke the one word she had never been allowed to say. The one word the Chieftain would ever hear her say. Her first and last.

"Father."

Behind her head, the blade sang.

THE SAGA CONTINUES
MARCH 23, 2021

The Ashes of Hope and Hunger

The Weight of Stars and Suns
Book Two

Dawn Christine Jonckowski

A princess who sacrificed destiny for love.
A queen who surrendered dreams for duty.
And an alliance preparing to destroy it all.

© Kenneth Dillard

Dawn Christine Jonckowski is a writer / editor / dancer / musician / shoe connoisseur and lover of the Oxford comma. She is married to her very own rebel leader and they live with two adorable yet spoiled dogs in Wisconsin under an infrequently seen single sun.

Learn more at dawncjonckowski.weebly.com or by following her on Twitter: @DawnCJonckowski